Theodor Bernard Küng is a classical violinist from Switzerland. Born in Hong Kong and raised first in New York City and then in the Jura Mountains overlooking Lake Geneva, he now lives in London where he performs with English National Ballet, Welsh National Opera, the Royal Philharmonic Orchestra and other ensembles. Following modest accolades for both poetry and prose, *The Winter Wilds* is his first novel.

www.theodorkung.com
www.instagram.com/theodorkung/

GW00381857

The Winter Wilds

THEODOR KÜNG

ISBN 979 8 61 805108 8 (paperback)
Typeset in Times New Roman, Harrington, & Goudy Initalien

www.theodorkung.com
www.instagram.com/theodorkung/

To my father, who brought me to the mountains

PART ONE
SEPTEMBER

LONDON
CHAPTER ONE

RIGHT AND EARLY one mid-September morning in North London, a fox leapt from a rubbish skip and ambled down the sunny street.

The fox paused at the corner to stretch and yawn. A productive night spent screaming under bedroom windows and frolicking with lady foxes had left it feeling rather sleepy and it was looking forward to a recuperative snooze. It smelled a half-open garage door, weighing its merits as temporary accommodation.

A sleep-deprived cyclist skidded around the pavement, shattering the fox's musings. The animal leapt aside and observed with vengeful satisfaction as the alarmed commuter swerved into the very skip lately occupied by the fox, which—as the cyclist soon discovered—housed copious amounts of rotting garbage. The fox sauntered off, leaving the unfortunate man thrashing amidst yesterday's discarded avocado peels.

A chaffinch sat on the windowsill of a large, attractive house nearby. It watched as a cloud of grey-clothed pigeons rose over the heath and bore southwards towards the City.

The chaffinch ruffled its feathers, feeling rather pleased with its life choices. Unlike those dreary suits overhead, it had recognised the potential in organically sourced worms rather than processed street foods* and invested in a sound piece of window-ledge real estate complete with bird feeder before things got pricey.

Retirement suited the chaffinch. If things kept going this way it might even be able to afford that bush in Kent it'd always dreamt of. Its mood soured, however, when it noticed that the feeder was nearly empty.

---

* Most birds nowadays find the term "road-kill" somewhat off-putting.

3

It must be over a week since it was last filled, reflected the bird. Standards really were slipping . . .

The next moment the window slammed open. The startled chaffinch went one way while its breakfast went another and landed with a *splat* right in the face of the avocado-caked cyclist, who proceeded to hurtle into a row of wheelie bins.

The young man at the window inhaled enthusiastically, regarding the view with an optimism that was, frankly, sinister. Most Londoners know better than to trust the fickle promises of England's duplicitous skies and meet the prospect of good weather with feelings ranging from cool detachment to open suspicion.

But not Luther Aberfinchley; as he dressed he danced around the room with the exuberance of someone who's just come into heaps of money and doesn't care who knows it.

'Hah!' he exclaimed, for no apparent reason. Luther was in the concluding stages of his morning grooming routine. This involved such liberal amounts of hair gel and perfume that, had he not opened the window, the housekeeper would have likely lost consciousness when she came upstairs to change the sheets.

Having achieved his desired effect and with a final 'Hah!' for good measure, Luther sidled downstairs, sunlight streaming through the windows of his lavish home.

Luther rarely skipped breakfast. Most mornings found the only son of the late Lord Desmond Aberfinchley sitting opposite some young woman he'd lured home from Bobo's the night before, whose name he'd already forgotten. Luther would attempt to engage her in a conversation about how absolutely super his place was and how very clever he was to have inherited it. She'd order a cab and leave as soon as possible. He'd help himself to her bacon and eggs. The day would commence.

But not today. This was his first real day on the job. Eggs could wait.

Luther collected his keys, remarking to no one in particular that today looked like a damn fine bloody day. As he reached for his overcoat a copy of the Financial Times tumbled onto the floor.

Luther left it where it was. The housekeeper had placed it in his coat pocket out of habit, as she had for his late father. Luther was not his father and eschewed the paper, which, frankly, he considered antiquated, dull, and utterly incomprehensible. Also, he was damned if he was going to read anything with pink pages. Instead he adjusted his hair in the mirror and congratulated himself on his new position as CEO of the family company. Sod you, Pink Paper!

He swung the door shut and marched down the steps to where his maroon Bentley hummed in the driveway, like a man bound for a wedding where he's going to marry himself.

4

It was only once Luther was halfway to the office, when his phone rang and a voice at the other end enquired if he'd read the morning papers, that his mood took a sudden turn for the worse.

Luther's subsequent exclamation of 'BALLS!' caused his driver to veer sideways in surprise. This was most unfortunate for the beleaguered, refuse-anointed cyclist whom the Bentley had just overtaken. In the ensuing excitement the vehicle's occupants failed to notice the explosion of scattering pigeons, the shuddering *CLANG* of a bollard as it arrested the bicycle's wheel, and the cyclone of paper as its rider's bag emptied onto the pavement. The street sweepers would remark later that day that someone called Richard Mathern appeared to have left quite a lot of paperwork in the gutter.

The Bentley sped onwards as the sunlit skies in Luther's mind mutated into a hailstorm. The weather outside, meanwhile, remained mild and pleasant—so much so that many Londoners grew apprehensive and lowered their blinds.

*****

At No. 31 Dratford Place, Headquarters of Aberfinchley Ltd., Alistair Dawes entered the reception room of the Head office.

Powerful entities rarely work alone. Amongst the colonnaded palaces of Antiquity, if a despotic princeling wished to survive the day his progenitor kicked the bucket—the same day, incidentally, that his extended family decided out of the blue that young Prince Mul-Wattalish might not be such a loveable, legitimate, undrownable little boy after all—he needed potent friends. Every emperor has a Vizier, a right-hand man tasked with implementing his semi-divine ruler's will, administering to his domains, and thinking up gruesome ways to do away with peasants caught stealing peaches from the Imperial Orchards; a point man, in short.

As is so often the case, what is true for totalitarian bull-worshipping autocracies also applies to modern-day businesses. Behind every mogul lurks a shadowy figure who knows a lot more about the company's accounts than their boss, for legal reasons if nothing else.

At No. 31 Dratford Place, that person was Alistair Dawes.

'Good morning!' chirped Julian, the Head Office Secretary.

Dawes' eyes narrowed. 'Would you say so, Julian?' he asked, much as the ocean might ask the underside of a yacht if it was fond of sharp rocks.

'Yep,' replied the Head Office Secretary, 'it's a lovely day all round, I reckon. And may I say that your early morning commute has given your skin a wonderfully bronzed complexion.'

How Julian retained his position despite his predilection for backtalk was something of a mystery. One day he would go too far, his colleagues

5

predicted; someone high up in the chain of command would coax Mick the Security Guard off his parole, and young Julian would have to be scraped off the pavement by the cleaners. On this occasion, Dawes chose instead to leaf through the sheaf of papers he carried with him.

'I've just been on the phone with our new Chief Executive Officer,' he said eventually. 'He will be here shortly.'

'Did he sound very cross?'

'No, Julian. In fact, when I informed the UK's newest corporate magnate that the multi-billion pound empire that took his father five decades to build might go up in a heap of smoke, he giggled and offered me a raise.'

'Crikey, that's pretty level-headed of him. Do I get a raise too?'

'You haven't met young Mr Aberfinchley, have you Julian?'

'Nope. I was on leave when he visited the office after the funeral last week.'

'In that case, perhaps we might keep the witty repartee to a minimum today. I think you'll find that Mr Aberfinchley the Younger does not share his father's appreciation for banter.'

'Right-o!'

Julian removed himself to his desk. Dawes sat in one of the comfortable chairs opposite.

Ordinarily he would have repaired to his own office down the hall and waited to be summoned. But today he felt he should be on deck when the captain arrived, even if this meant tolerating the sound of Julian slamming various appointments and sundries into the online system. Dawes recalled the satisfying swish of a fountain pen on expensive stationary. How many man-hours would Aberfinchley Inc. have to sacrifice if they reversed the digitization process?

Several expensive paintings were hung around the vestibule to underscore the company's immaculate taste in art. Dawes inspected the portrait of an old Victorian gentleman sitting at a garden table, book in hand, and experienced a sudden craving for the smell of fresh grass, a glass of elderflower cordial, and Elgar.

But, he reminded himself, back to the matter at hand. Earlier that morning a large ocean-going vessel en route from the Persian Gulf had run aground rather spectacularly off the coast of Africa and was now decanting copious quantities of oil into the sea. The outcry was immediate and worldwide as governments, conservationists, and the media demanded to know who was responsible for this monumental goof.

The trouble was that the crew, ship, and cargo were all insured by different companies in an effort to dilute liability, while the ship itself belonged to someone else altogether. This resulted in a mad scramble across the City's insurance firms to ensure they were in no way connected with the affair, well before anyone thought to ask what had caused the accident in the first place.

It didn't help that the nation who claimed this particular slice of coastline was the tiny Democratic Republic of East Murumbwana, whose despotic President-for-Life claimed a God-given mandate to rule his people, the "happiest, safest, and most beautiful on Earth". He'd also denounced the environmental lobby as a Western conspiracy designed to inhibit his economy. Consequentially, there could be no oil spill—by law—and any effort to communicate with local experts was met with the resolutely cheerful reply that they knew nothing of any oil spills, everything was fine, and Praise Be to the President-for-Life (may his wisdom never wither).

Dawes' problem was sorting things out before the press got wind that Aberfinchley Ltd. not only owned the ship but had also enabled several shady arms deals with the country's government and financed a mining plant that only two months previously had come under scrutiny for toxic waste leakage.

Dawes furrowed his brow. There had also been some other matter, hadn't there? Something about hogging all the drinking water . . .

'What are those papers for?' inquired Julian.

Dawes raised a steel grey eyebrow. 'That's between me and Mr Aberfinchley.'

Julian turned down the corners of his mouth and widened his eyes, unimpressed, before returning to his work. Dawes grimaced.

'Must you type so vehemently, Julian?'

'I'm just re-arranging Mr Aberfinchley's schedule.'

'Well then, please do so quietly. Why do we have double-glazing, if not to shut out the city's cacophony and allow the brain to function in quiet and tranquillity?'

'I'll finish the schedule later.'

'Thank you.'

Dawes closed his eyes, enjoying the momentary calm.

At that moment the lift doors slid apart and out billowed Luther Aberfinchley.

'DAWES!'

The portraits on the wall eyed this new arrival apprehensively. He did not strike them as a lover of the arts.

Dawes rose to his feet. 'Good morning, sir.'

Luther's face skidded to a halt mere inches away, offering Dawes an intimate view of its expensive nose, thin lips, and eyes which one could have accurately described as "wild and deranged" from a much more comfortable distance.

'My office, Dawes. And bring coffee.'

7

The expensive shoes clomped past into the inner office. Julian watched them go before giving Dawes a look indicating extreme disapprobation.

'He seems nice.'

'Coffee, Julian,' intoned Dawes. He followed Luther through the door.

'Right away,' came the reply, followed by no action whatsoever.

Luther traversed his late father's immense office, ignoring its magnificent view of London, and threw himself into a leather chair behind a vast wooden desk. Dawes remained standing.

'It's a mess. Dawes,' Luther fumed. He'd learned of the power behind a rich man's son's anger at a very young age and could fume beautifully.

'Yes, sir.'

Dawes was well acquainted with the parameters of said mess. It was he who'd briefed Luther that morning and he knew exactly how superficial his employer's understanding of those parameters was.

The sensible part of Luther's brain knew this as well as Dawes. Unfortunately, that part spent much of its time being bullied by his brain's less sensible cerebral components, and most days couldn't make itself heard on account of being locked in one of his brain's darker basements. Luther's various cortices had already debated how to address the situation; the shortlisted candidates were, in order, Fury, Contempt, and Blame. They were to be understudied by Denial, Petulance and, if necessary, Shouting Loudly. Fury having set the groundwork, it was now time for Contempt to take over.

'Really, Dawes,' said Luther contemptuously, 'I mean, really. This is unacceptable. I'm not happy, Dawes. Not a bit. This isn't the sort of thing I tolerate in my company, least of all from you. You've been here longer than anybody. My father spoke very highly of you.'

Pity I can't say the same, thought Dawes. In the week since Lord Aberfinchley's cardiac arrest—brought on, the coroner concluded, by one or more of the curvaceous young women the billionaire octogenarian had hired that afternoon to "help him rearrange the furniture"—Luther had inherited his father's shares by deed, been duly appointed by the board, and jumped into his new position with gusto. So far his leadership involved a lot of what he termed "constructive criticism", something many in the company privately re-labelled "a load of bollocks".

Luther swivelled in his chair in what he hoped was an authoritative manner and allowed Blame to take the microphone. 'Yes Dawes, I'm afraid you've messed up rather badly. How are we even connected with this cock-up? We should never have been put in such a position. You're the most senior official here, except for me of course, and this isn't my fault, so it must be yours. Really, if you were anyone else I'd have to let you go.'

There was a ripple under Dawes' scalp.

Dawes, as Desmond Aberfinchley's closest friend and business partner, had been the power behind Aberfinchley Inc. for many years. Talking to Dawes as Luther just had would have earned more than a sacking: you'd never work again this side of Milton Keynes. Dawes remained, however, a professional. Unfortunately, loyalty to the father meant tolerating the son. He sheathed his pride—temporarily.

'I'm sorry, sir. Perhaps you might allow me to elaborate on the details, and to suggest how we might best be served in terms of response.'

Luther shook his head in that way that people who are neither sympathetic nor compassionate believe conveys sympathy and compassion.

'There's no point in trying to change the subject, Dawes. You're getting old, and old people make mistakes. On account of their being so very, very old.'

Dawes adjusted his spectacles. 'Be that as it may, sir, I think it best if we address the problem immediately. This matter has already garnered a great deal of publicity and appears to be causing quite a stir. Might I suggest—'

Julian's voice materialised from the intercom on Luther's desk.

'Hullo, chums. Front desk just called, there are some people on their way up to see Mr Aberfinchley about today's developments.'

Luther glanced at Dawes, betraying an instinctive understanding of who actually controlled the situation. Dawes hesitated just long enough to reassure him before leaning forward to press the button.

'You know we don't take unsolicited press calls, Julian. Send them away.'

Dawes could almost hear Julian stick his tongue out at the receiver. 'Would they have let them in downstairs if they were journalists? I don't think so. Apparently they're too well dressed.'

'Well then, who are they?' demanded Luther from his chair.

The only answer was a hiss from the coffee machine, which Julian had repositioned next to the intercom, accompanied by a cheery whistle.

Dawes flicked off the dial and straightened pensively.

'What, we're just letting these people in?' spluttered Luther.

'We'll make them wait and find out what they want. There's nothing to be worried about, sir.'

Luther sulked. 'Why've I got that grinning loon at the front desk anyway, instead of some nice girl? Secretaries are supposed to epitomise the sexually charged atmosphere of boardroom power. My father could've told you that.'

Dawes shifted the weight of his papers to his other arm and glanced at his watch. 'The Aberfinchley family has always had a deeper understanding of the mysteries of courtship than I, sir.'

9

'Yes, well, when you have a moment, fire that clown outside and hire someone with breasts. And why not get yourself someone young and saucy while you're at it, eh? I always wondered why my father never talked about any shared adventures in all your time together. He certainly wouldn't shut up about his own, even when Mother was around.'

'Such collaborative efforts would have been rather upsetting to Mrs Dawes, sir. You came to our wedding, as you may recall, though you were quite young.'

'Yes indeed, lovely day it was too. How is, er . . .'

'Patricia.'

'Patricia, yes. How is Patricia these days, anyway?'

'No longer with us I'm afraid, sir.'

'No! Not Pattie!'

'The accident was eight years ago, Mr Aberfinchley.'

'Tragic, tragic. Ah, finally!'

Julian came in with the coffee tray. 'The suits have arrived,' he remarked while laying out the cups. 'They said something about being environmental representatives.'

'Whining lowlifes!' barked Luther.

'Perhaps,' suggested Dawes, 'it might be judicious to meet with these people after all. We want to avoid a full-blown press conference.'

'Don't care,' said Luther. 'Throw the whingeing bastards out.'

'Okey dokey.' Julian swivelled on his heel in a way calculated to damage Luther's carpet and left them alone once more.

'How has it come to this, Dawes?'

'Well, sir, it's rather difficult these days to find staff who are both qualified and psychologically suited to the work environment. I'm afraid Julian displays a mild anarchic strain, as well as a seeming inability to wear matching socks.'

Luther rolled his eyes. 'Not Julian, you fool, this oil mess! With absolutely no notice whatsoever you call to tell me that overnight we've suffered the biggest PR cock-up in a decade. What the sodding Hell!'

'Yes, sir, and very concisely summed up too. May we begin by addressing the issue privately before dealing with the visitors outside?' Dawes adjusted his documents.

'No,' said Luther, drunk with power. 'Let them wait. First I want to discuss my expansion plans, and my proposal to streamline our staff here at Aber HQ. Did you read my email about getting rid of those compliance nerds on the fifth floor? God they're annoying.'

Dawes placed his files on the table. Very well, he thought, there were other matters to discuss. No large company ever has only one disaster to contend with.

'Incidentally sir,' he said, 'there is some concern regarding the aforementioned expansion. Your,' he cleared his throat, 'courageous proposal took our overseas investors somewhat unawares. The decision to make your announcement via social media was a particular surprise. The market doesn't like surprises.'

'Bloody Americans,' fumed Luther. 'Don't they know progress when they see it? You'd think they, of all people . . . Dammit Julian, what is it now?'

The secretary had returned, with a malicious sparkle behind his contact lenses.

'It's the environmental representatives, Mr Aberfinchley. They refuse to wait. A certain Mrs Crewe insists on seeing you.'

Dawes watched his young employer's face turn purple under its expensive tan.

'Insist? Insist!? I'm one of the wealthiest men on the bloody planet! When I tell someone to sod off, then off they bloody well sod! Who does this Crewe think she is, the bloody Secretary of State for the Environment?'

'No, Mr Aberfinchley,' said Julian with chilling nonchalance. 'She's from the Foreign Office. With her are Messrs Manyara and Tichaona from the East Murumbwanian Embassy. They've brought an inspection report for a certain seagoing vessel that apparently shows worrying oversights, one that bears the name of Aberfinchley Inc.'

In the backstage area of Luther's brain Fury, Contempt, and Blame rushed straight past Denial, Shouting Loudly and Petulance, and started banging on the door of the dressing room reserved for Panic and Bed-Wetting.

Luther gripped his chair's armrests, seeking reassurance. They failed to reassure him, but instead offered a compensatory tactile course on the gripping benefits of A-grade mahogany. Luther was not interested.

'I think, Dawes,' he said, 'that you should tell me exactly what's going on. And this time, I want you to go into great detail.'

Dawes possessed a nimble mind. Businessmen registered as taxpayers in the UK often do, enabling important details like their addresses to change from "Surrey" to "the Bahamas" at a moment's notice without any inconvenient mental strain. The neurones lining up in Dawes' mind immediately leapt aside and reformed with balletic agility.

'Well, sir,' he began, 'this is how things stand at the present time . . .'

Meanwhile, on a far less fashionable London street, a ruined bicycle parked outside a shabby office block indicated that a certain Richard Mathern had—finally—arrived at his destination.

THE SITUATION
CHAPTER TWO

N THE OFFICE of the wildlife periodical *Nature Review* a man lay draped across his chair in the attitude of a dying saint praying for martyrdom, a phone pressed to his ear. From his clothes emanated a faint aroma of avocado.

Beep.

Beep.

'Thank you for calling Research Funding UK, dedicated to championing science, engineering, and technology. My name's Ashlee, how can I help you today?'

The man leapt forward from the crumpled position in which he'd spent the last twenty minutes. 'Yes, hello, my name's Richard Mathern. I'm calling from *Nature Review* about our funding application. We received a letter today saying we're not eligible. Is there someone I could speak to?'

'Okay, do you have your thirteen-digit reference number?'

'Er . . .' Richard rifled through the papers on his desk, one of several identical desks squeezed into the tiny room. A handful of elderly, grey-faced employees squinted at their screens, typing with agonising slowness and counting the minutes before they could take their first tea break of the day.

The door of the editorial office swung open and Tom the Deputy Editor popped his head in. He motioned to Richard, who'd found the number and was reading it off to Ashlee.

' . . . Eight, six, two, two . . .' Richard waved Tom away.

'Richard,' Tom tolled from the doorway.

Richard ignored him. 'Yes,' he said down the line, 'I've just spoken to the Natural Environment Research Council and they weren't able to help either.'

Tom approached Richard's desk and leant across it.

'No,' Richard tried to drown out the sound of Tom breathing at him. 'We're beginning research next year, on the first of March. The actual fieldwork doesn't begin until the following August. Our start date falls well within the parameters set out in your guidelines.'

He placed a hand over the receiver. 'I'm really busy, Tom. I had a difficult commute this morning . . .'

'I've sent you several SqueakSpeak messages in the last half hour,' rumbled Tom. 'Have you read them?'

Richard strained to understand Ashlee's nasal whine over the phone static. 'No, we can't wait until the next round of funding applications. Is there someone I can talk to who can help me rectify this misunderstanding about dates?

'I'm afraid all of our customer service staff are currently occupied. Would you like to wait until another operative is available?'

Tom's smartphone hovered into view. 'I've flagged the messages as "Important". You should have got them by now.'

'Look,' said Richard down the line, 'I'll have to call you back.'

'Okay then. Would you like to complete our customer service survey relating to your experience with us today?'

'Sure. Do you have your eighteen-digit personal supplier ID number?'

' . . . Pardon?'

Richard dropped the phone onto the receiver and swivelled to face Tom. 'Ok, I'm all yours.'

'I've typed it all on SqueakSpeak. My phone says you've received the messages. Look, your name has a little tick next to it.'

'Sure, Tom, but since you're here in person, why not tell me yourself?'

Tom considered this. 'I went to a lot of trouble over those messages. We set up the SqueakSpeak thread to optimise communication between departments.'

Richard sighed. Six people working in two rooms hardly qualified as separate departments.

'Ok Tom, I'll read your messages. Thanks.'

'Well, as I'm here anyway, I'll just tell you,' said Tom.

Richard leant back in his chair and discovered that, unbelievably, he missed talking to Ashlee.

'Alan told me to say there's been a development,' announced Tom. 'You're to expect a call.'

'Where?' Richard asked.

Tom looked confused. 'On your phone.'

Richard sighed. 'I mean, where has the development taken place?'

Tom scratched his ear. 'Somewhere high up, Alan says. Apparently there's a big project coming in, lots of money behind it. He's very excited, says it's exactly the sort of thing we've been waiting for.'

Richard leant forward. 'Is that what the call is about?'

'What call?'

'The one I'm to expect.'

'Oh, yeah, I guess so. It says in the SqueakSpeak message.'

Richard's pulse rose. If it was enough to excite Alan, the Editor-in-chief whose gloom was second only to Tom's, it must be important.

A shimmer of pessimism in the air told him that Tom was still there.

'Something else in the message, Tom?'

'No, that was basically it. I was just wondering if I could borrow your stapler.'

Richard indicated the stapler's location. Tom took it with a nod and traversed the office like a human raincloud. The older employees waited for the *clunk* of the closing door, then ditched their work and went to put the kettle on.

*****

Luther stood looking out of the window in a manner he'd copied from TV shows about men with high-rise offices who look out the window a lot. This didn't work for him, so he resorted to pacing about the office.

Dawes entered, having verified that Mrs Crewe and her colleagues from the embassy had left the building.

'This is bad, Dawes.'

'Perhaps, sir.'

Italian suit material whispered through the air as Luther whirled about.

'What do you mean, "perhaps?" Toxic spillage rarely makes a good headline. What do you think it'll do to our numbers as they stand now? Cock, I hope they don't know about that as well.'

He sat down. 'By the way, what's this "sir" business? Seems archaic.'

'I used it when addressing your father,' Dawes replied. 'But I can dispense with it, if you prefer.'

'Nah, keep it. It's growing on me.'

Dawes adjusted his glasses and adopted a soothing tone.

'I believe,' he said, 'that matters can yet be taken in hand. What we need is some good publicity while we deal with adverse events in a discreet manner.'

At this point Julian entered and deposited a thick file on Luther's desk.

'What's this?' asked Luther, recoiling at the mere sight of it.

'These are legal documents,' said Dawes, 'and the solution to our problem.'

'How have you produced all of this so fast?' marvelled Luther.

'Julian is very able,' responded Dawes, 'and time is of the essence. We must convince our investors that we have several major on-going ventures with various environmental agencies—preferably within small, peace-loving nations that have nothing to do with petroleum or authoritarianism. These,' he tapped the pile, 'make it so. We then leak details of our altruism to the press, whilst downplaying the oil spill story.'

He leant over his young employer and slid the first documents across the table. A pen appeared in his hand.

'We've drafted a selection of worthy candidates. They range from this one,' he positioned it in front of Luther; 'funding for the BBC's upcoming documentary series, to this one; a new scholarship position at Cambridge in Natural Sciences. I've taken the liberty of making the gift out in your late father's name.'

Luther was only half listening but took the pen and began to sign. The steady flow of paper under his hands restored his confidence such that, when Julian delivered a second round of coffee, Luther pulled off a cordial sneer in his secretary's direction.

'I must say, Dawes,' he said, admiring his own signature, 'this is a rather good trick you've pulled. No wonder Daddy kept you on so far past retirement. Ha!' He jostled Dawes' arm with his free hand and smeared ink over the paper. 'Oh, cock. Have we got another copy?'

'Not to worry,' said Julian, reaching for the blotter. 'Though do take care. We've backdated these as it is. The fewer copies we print on the system the better.'

Luther looked confused, then understood. 'Hoho, I get it, boys: pretend these have been in the works for ages, unrelated to certain recent events both unmentionable and inconvenient, eh?'

He winked at Julian. Dawes massaged his temples. 'Quite, sir.'

Julian smiled and attempted to move the papers along the desk a little faster.

'Well, bugger me,' exclaimed Luther. 'You sneaky blighters! Good thing you work for me. I won't tell.' He sniggered and signed the final file.

Julian's smile soured slightly at the edges. 'I'll just send these off, shall I?'

'By all means, my good man. Carry on!' Luther grinned at Dawes. 'Close thing there, wasn't it? I dare say lesser men would've let such a mess really louse things up. But not us, eh Dawesey?'

Dawes smiled. 'No, sir.'

*****

Richard was contemplating another soul-destroying call to the research council when the unmistakeable voice of his editor-in-chief rang out from the adjoining office.

'Mathern! Get in here.'

Richard got up and crossed into the next room. Tom gave Richard a hangdog look as he entered before returning to the heady task of stapling receipts.

'Hey Alan. I hear something's up.'

Alan glared at Richard and sniffed.

It wasn't Alan's fault he resembled an angry, balding owl. A lifetime of disappointment does things to a man. In Alan's case, it had given him the air of an elderly, myopic bird facing into a strong wind. He also cultivated a virulent strain of hay fever that, somehow, lasted throughout the year. This had helped earn him a PhD in Microbiology and Germ Culture and not much else.

'Sit down, Mathern.'

Richard noted the absence of chairs. 'No thanks, I'll stand.'

Alan grunted and adjusted his glasses. Richard did his best to ignore the irregular *shtunk* noises from his borrowed stapler.

'We've been hired for a big piece, Mathern; important backers, lots of support for the *Review*, good exposure.' Alan sniffed. 'Apparently applicants were selected via an extremely rigorous process.'

'I see. Who's commissioning the work?'

Alan's eyes flitted to his computer. 'The Bühlheimer Trust,' he read, massacring the Bühlheimer name so thoroughly he had to repeat it, and massacred it again in new and horrifying ways. 'Apparently,' he continued, 'they're an affiliate of the Aberfinchley Foundation—very powerful funding body.'

'I don't remember applying to them,' said Richard.

'You must have. Anyway, they've commissioned a number of projects and we've nabbed a grant.'

'How much are they paying?'

Alan told him. Tom dropped the stapler. Their chronically underfunded publication had never known such a windfall.

'Brilliant!' exclaimed Richard. 'With that kind of backing we can fund two—no, three research projects! I've got several in the file already . . .'

'Actually, Mathern, they've requested a specific subject. No negotiating.'

'What's that?'

Alan's owl eyes blinked at the screen. 'They want us to find bears in the Alps.'

Richard considered this. 'Are there bears in the Alps?'

'Well, you'll just have to find out. They want as much publicity and regular updates as possible, in order,' Alan squinted at the screen, 'to "promote topical content and enhance the digital readership experience". Blog posts, photos, that sort of thing.'

Richard was heady with excitement. Some real work at last! 'No problem. Give me access to our online platforms and I'll have them swimming in *ursidae*.'

Alan blinked.

'It's the Linnaean name for bears.'

Alan blew his nose. 'I knew that. Anyway, we can't give you unsupervised access to our database. You'll send everything back to the office and we'll edit it before publication.'

'You can use SqueakSpeak,' said Tom from his lurch in the corner. 'They have a file-sharing system now.'

Richard stifled a groan. Submitting material for approval was a small price to pay to escape the office. 'What about my other projects?'

'Forget those. This is top priority.'

'But it's a lot of money,' insisted Richard. 'Surely there'll be something left over for ongoing threads? We could at least nominate someone to oversee them while I'm away. I've had one on the boil for ages . . .'

'The grant covers flights, lodgings, and sundries directly, so we won't see much actual money. And to be frank, Mathern,' Alan added, 'I think this might be a good thing because, honestly, I don't think much of what you're working on now. What was it . . . "Ravens and how clever they are"? Never mind. We're binning that and putting you on this instead.'

'But I'll be in charge of expenses?'

'Yes,' admitted Alan, 'pending approval from me.'

Richard rubbed his hands. 'Fine. How soon do we meet the foundation?'

'We don't,' replied Alan. 'Or at least, you don't. Not enough time. They want us to start as soon as possible.'

'Oh. What's my start date?'

'The twenty-second.'

Richard frowned. 'Of what, March, April?'

'September.'

'This Sunday?!'

'Oh, man up, Mathern,' said Alan over Richard's protests. 'You have a fantastic opportunity here. There's every reason to think this will be widely publicised, so stop being so precious. I expect you to file the requisite forms with me by tonight.'

'Where exactly am I going?' Richard asked.

'A mountain village bordering a nature reserve. Not sure where exactly, some moron's spilt ink all over the scan they sent us. Oh, and you'll need an assistant to accompany you.'

'Who am I going to find at such short notice?'

'Christ, Mathern, must I do everything? Use your brains! They needn't be an affiliate. Take anyone, as long as they're qualified. We can't spare people anyway.'

'I can go,' said Tom.

'No, you can't,' Alan and Richard replied simultaneously.

Alan sniffed. 'You must know someone who'd leap at such an opportunity.'

Richard passed a hand through his hair. 'Sorry . . . It's just a bit sudden, that's all. I wasn't expecting it.'

He was expecting redundancy, but he wasn't about to tell Alan.

'Yeah, well, seize the carpet and all that,' muttered Alan. He sounded annoyed. Then again, Alan usually did. 'Just find someone. We've sourced an advance fee to cover your equipment.'

A thought occurred to Alan. 'How's your health, Mathern?'

Once again, Richard stifled a groan. He'd been asked this question before. 'Fine,' he lied.

Alan blinked at him. 'Last month's little episode's all cleared up, then? No more seizures lurking around the corner?'

'It was just a dizzy spell,' Richard said. 'I had them as a kid, but it hasn't happened in years. They gave me some pills to make sure it doesn't recur. Which it won't because, like I said, everything's fine.'

'We wouldn't want the success of this project riding on someone who gets dizzy and falls over.'

'I won't.'

'Good. Go clear your schedule.'

Richard returned to his desk. He stared over his antiquated monitor at his fish-faced colleagues sipping their tea and pretending to work. He didn't fancy taking any of them along.

What about someone from his student days? Alan had said to pick anyone. A generous fee would surely lure some brilliant unknown from the frugality of academia.

Richard positioned the phone under one ear and opened a new tab on his computer. He remembered several people who might be interested, people he should have kept in touch with anyway. Among various scraps of personal data he unearthed the contact number for a sultry brunette who'd been his lab partner, now working for the BBC, and dialled.

A number of calls and polite refusals later Richard remembered a particular person. After a slight hesitation, he dialled the faculty.

*****

The Right Honourable Lady Leticia Crowley QC gazed down at the river Cam from her window. She'd been the Master of Brommel College for several years, but the sight of the autumn sun glinting off the water at the bottom of the garden still fascinated her. The view never failed to make her feel warm and fuzzy—something the prized prospect of the Thames from her former offices at Grabbitt, Crowley & Phist never achieved, for all its miasmic splendour.

Lady Leticia smiled benevolently down on a group of freshers ambling along the tree-lined cobbles and over the college bridge. Their faces beamed as they laughed and wondered aloud to each other whether anything in the lecture they were dodging might crop up in their exams.

Her smile withered, however, at the sight of Graham Hayle following the freshers over the bridge, the apprehension on his face contrasting with their beatific indolence.

Leticia growled softly and went to sit behind her desk in the corner of the room.

The buildings that house the masters of Cambridge are as diverse as the colleges themselves. Brommel had designated as its Master's Lodge the relatively humble north-westerly corner of its oldest court. There was nonetheless enough grandeur in the stones that Graham took a moment outside the door to brush his hair out of his face and do up an extra shirt button. He wished he'd remembered to shave; too late for that now.

Moments later he was admitted into Lady Leticia's presence. He hesitated in the doorway.

'Hallo, Hayle,' she barked.

Graham was not a timid man, quite the opposite. But, beholding the stony face of the college master, the best he could do was to whimper. 'Er, hullo, Lady Crowley.'

He waited for her to tell him not to be silly and to call her Leticia. She didn't. Instead she returned to the window, motioning for him to sit. He did so, eyeing her regal silhouette.

Lady Leticia allowed him to stew for several moments in silence. She'd perfected this treatment on paralegals in her London chambers and usually reserved it for interviewing prospective student candidates, though she occasionally unsheathed it when faced with an older college alumnus whom she wished to unsettle. Unfortunately for Graham, himself not many years past graduation, on this particular afternoon she wished to unsettle him most grievously indeed.

'So, er, how's the legal practice going?' Graham attempted to sound jovial. 'All that family law keeping you busy?'

'Oh, I hardly go in at all anymore,' answered Lady Leticia. 'I'm no longer an active partner, strictly speaking. They call me down occasionally, though, whenever they need my help with anything particularly . . . nasty.'

She returned to her desk and fixed her eyes on Graham. 'Congratulations on making Second Boat this year. Not letting rowing impede your work, I trust?'

'No, Lady Crowley.'

'I see you're working on a PhD. What's the chosen topic again?'

'Neurological Dysfunction and Erotomania in Catfish, Lady Crowley.'

'Jolly good. How's it coming along?'

'Oh, well, you know.'

'I'm afraid I don't.'

Graham squirmed. 'Well,' he said, 'it's not easy to secure funding these days and so far the results haven't been quite what I'd hoped for. But that's par for the course, really, I guess . . .'

Lady Leticia didn't blink. Graham broke into a cold sweat.

'Although,' he continued, 'the college has been very generous so far, what with the grant and access to the laboratory, so I'm enormously grateful for that.'

'It's the least we could do to support a young man of your promise.' This last comment emanated from Lady Leticia with all the merriment of a mortician who's just learned that his rent's been hiked.

'Thank you very much,' murmured Graham. He sensed this was foreplay, a cat playing with a mouse, before Leticia decided to unleash bloody destruction on him.

'I'd like to address your progress in a little more detail, if I may.'

There it was: the writing on the wall.

'You understand, Hayle, that I don't usually deal with this sort of thing myself. However, seeing as your senior tutor is off having that baby of hers, I'm obliged to address the matter personally.'

'Yes, Lady Crowley.'

'Your first reports date from November of last year, detailing your initial findings and anticipated procedure. Dr Hickinbotham deemed it satisfactory and urged you onwards, did he not?'

'Yes, Lady Crowley.'

'Good. Your subsequent monthly reports indicate that your research was going exceedingly well, showing promise beyond expectation. They detail the size, age, and health of your subjects, and your planned reproductive programme to prolong the experiments over several cycles. These reports were duly approved by Dr Hickinbotham, correct?'

'Yes, Lady Crowley.'

'But he did not personally assist you in the laboratory or request you replicate your results for him to assess?'

'No, Lady Crowley. His own research was keeping him frightfully busy.'

'Indeed,' said Lady Leticia. 'If Dr Hickinbotham were to take his research any more seriously, I fear he would be in real danger of actually publishing something; unheard-of in his long and illustrious career.'

A nervous giggle emerged from Graham's throat, but froze to death under Lady Leticia's icy grey stare.

'There is,' she said, 'the matter of your more recent reports, Hayle.'

Graham felt claws graze his body.

'About three months ago,' continued Lady Leticia, 'you wrote of financial worries and indicated that a lack of funding risked bringing your project to a premature conclusion.' She peered at Graham over her spectacles. 'You stand by this assessment?'

'Oh yes. Without the requisite funding I'd have been forced to drop it altogether.'

'And consequently lose your position here at the college.'

'Er . . .'

'And yet, despite Dr Hickinbotham's reply that additional financial aid was out of the question, your next report indicates nothing amiss. Indeed, it goes on to mention that your results took quite a positive turn.' She glanced at him again. 'A fortuitous change in circumstance, I take it?'

'Yes, Lady Crowley,' squeaked Graham.

'One that nonetheless goes unmentioned in your reports.'

'Yes, La—'

'Now, we come to the results themselves. As you are no doubt aware, we require all doctoral papers to be assessed by an independent third party.'

Graham was not aware of this and withered visibly in his chair.

'What with your thesis showing such potential, it garnered considerable attention from our external examiners. Naturally, they wished to see things for themselves.'

Graham wondered whether there was some training course in psychological torture run by ex-military goons and reserved exclusively for secret service agents, government helpline attendants, and Oxbridge professors.

'Imagine their surprise when, having roused Dr Hickinbotham from his own very important research and accompanying him to the laboratory, they discovered a roomful of empty tanks and a complete absence of erotic piscine activity.'

Graham clutched at his chair like a man strapped to a burning plane that's hurtling towards the earth. Lady Leticia removed her glasses, a sure sign that things were about to worsen.

'Oh Lady Crowley,' he pleaded, 'you've got to understand. There was so much riding on—'

'You are aware of what we in the business term "Academic Integrity," are you not, Hayle?'

'Eurgl . . .'

'And you are familiar with the college's stance on the misappropriation and misuse of funding grants, I take it?'

'Oh my God, I'm so sorry, Lady Crowley!'

'In that case,' Lady Leticia spoke with deathly calm, 'perhaps you'd be so good as to inform me at what stage in your progress you elected to abandon your research, in secret and in its entirety, and to sell your aquatic subjects to,' she consulted a pencilled note on her desk, '"Captain Cody's Frozen Fishcake Factory" in Whitstable, where I'm reliably informed the entire population—which, I might add, was the property of the college and in whom a great deal of money had been invested—was summarily minced, reshaped into fish fingers and mis-sold as "Finest Atlantic cod" while you'—her emphasis felt like the castigation of the Lord—'*you*, Mr Hayle, concealed the entire sordid affair by perpetuating a chain of bogus reports suffused with fraudulent data and imaginary results.'

Leticia caught herself leaning hungrily towards the vulnerable arteries housed in Graham's throat and sat back. 'Well, what do you have to say for yourself?'

Graham trembled, like an ant sensing a hovering boot in the unseen cosmos overhead. As Lady Leticia rose from behind her desk, she observed the blood drain from his face. Graham knew the fear of the damned.

'Poor Dr Hickinbotham has been grievously upset by the whole affair. However, in light of his long service and erudite contributions to the university, we have chosen to consider his involvement as a regretful lapse of judgement brought on by overwork. For you, however, no such excuse can be made. And, as you know, I take any stain on the reputation of my college very personally indeed.'

Lady Leticia adjusted her spectacles and turned again to gaze at the spectacle of loveliness outside. The silence of the gallows permeated the room undisturbed save for the distant laughter of carousing philosophy students and the almost imperceptible rattle of Graham's twitching retinas.

The Master's elegant hand stroked a lethal-looking paperweight on her windowsill.

'I confess,' she said at last, 'much of my disappointment stems from my own fascination with the aquatic world and my hopes for new insights into its mysteries.'

A punt full of happy undergraduates in the early stages of drunken bliss drifted over the murky water below the window. Graham's eye quivered violently.

'Tell me, Hayle,' said Leticia. 'Have you ever gazed upon this river we love so well and wondered what monstrous things might lurk at its muddy bottom, that graveyard onto which the waste of ages sinks in darkness, never to be seen again?'

She faced Graham. Her grey eyes flashed behind her spectacles.

'Would you like to find out, Mr Hayle?'

What might have happened next will forever remain a mystery, for at that moment Leticia's P.A. appeared at the door with an urgent call from the Faculty of Natural Sciences, conveying the wish of the Environmental Department that Graham be requisitioned for an important field study.

*****

Richard exited his office that evening in a state of happy bewilderment. He inspected his mangled bicycle, concluded that their relationship had come to a sorrowful end, and continued on foot.

What should he do first? His imminent departure panicked him a little, as did the seemingly endless inventory of camera-related apparatus he'd been forced to memorise that afternoon. What was the difference between a Nikon D5 and a D7500 again? Was the Spypoint Link the tripod for the Feisol CT-3342 or vice-versa? What the hell was a Pulsar Quantum LITE XQ23V? Had Alan mentioned whether the company would cover the cost of personal effects or just the technical equipment? It would be October soon. How cold would it be in the Alps? Damn, he'd forgotten to speak to Graham about transportation to the airport . . .

Richard rummaged around in his satchel looking for the files Alan had given him and discovered that rather a lot of his personal paperwork was missing.*

His roving hand came across one particular document that had survived; a note from his GP detailing his next follow-up meeting and a series of upcoming tests. In all the excitement he'd quite forgotten about it.

Richard did a quick mental calculation and shrugged; he'd be back in the UK soon enough. The tests would have to wait.

His mind full of plans, he joined the heaving multitude of homeward-bound Londoners as it flowed underground in a haze of bottled aggression and occasional verbal abuse.

A few blocks away, the lights in the high windows of Aberfinchley Ltd. were going out. They would continue to do so throughout the evening until

---

* Much of it had by this time been salvaged from the gutter by squirrels to be used as bedding and would prove a boon during the oncoming winter, but Richard didn't know that and was rather peeved.

even the most desperate interns could take no more and went home for a few hours' sleep and a change of underwear.

On the top floor Luther and Dawes laboured away across a desk littered with empty coffee cups. Dawes was attempting to conclude the oil spill business, but Luther, secure in the knowledge that things were in hand, had lost interest.

'And that, Dawes, is why we should be outsourcing our web design.'

Dawes looked up. 'Because your school friend has a start-up in Dalston?'

'An exciting business opportunity,' corrected Luther, 'offering state-of-the-art service for half the price of what our IT department costs. I'll tell you all about it tomorrow.' He stood up in a way that hinted at his imminent departure.

Dawes adjusted his spectacles wearily. 'May I suggest, sir, that we return to the earlier matter? It's late afternoon in New York, I've arranged a call with—'

'Don't be ridiculous, Dawes!' interrupted Luther, already at the door. 'I've got a table at Bobo's tonight. We'll continue tomorrow. Be here at ten. Hang on,' he pulled on his coat. 'I nearly forgot. There's a party theme tonight, "Champs and Tramps". Best make it the afternoon. Tell Julian to book you in at two.'

Dawes rose and collected his papers from the desk. 'Very good, sir.'

Luther oozed off. Dawes removed his spectacles and massaged his eyes.

Julian poked his head through the door. 'Need help with those papers? I've taken care of the other files, those are the last.'

Dawes shook his head. 'I'll do it myself. Send the documents to Alice, I'll finish in my own office.'

An hour or two later Dawes emerged onto a street thick with noise. Resolutely constructed in exactly the same places as their medieval predecessors, the glass-fronted buildings leaned companionably toward each over, making traffic a nightmare. Though paved and perpetually awash with light, the roads in the City still followed the old mule trails down to the river's edge. Their twisting narrowness was maddening even when there weren't four hundred thousand people all trying to get home at once.

Dawes suppressed a shudder as he was jostled by the flow of bodies. Mere days had passed since Des' funeral. Luther had hardly mentioned his father all day.

A woman and her child were struggling against the flow. The toddler had mastered that particular kind of aimless wandering that children enjoy, which usually results in them head-butting strangers in the genitals. Dawes stepped off the kerb to allow her to pass and managed a half-smile to the grateful mother.

A tall, elegant old man in a grey suit followed Dawes through the crowd. Nobody took much notice of him. Rather than jostling or pushing, they would turn aside at the last second, allowing him to pass. Their eyes never met his, but slid off his face as if not registering him at all. The exasperated mother squeezed against a wall to make space for him. Her son, however, eschewed such formalities and surged forward, forehead foremost. The child stopped abruptly after a few steps to find that he had—rather unexpectedly—passed straight through the man in the grey suit.

The confused boy turned to look at the retreating figure. The man in grey turned also, and winked.

At this the child set off such a horrific din that his mother decided to cancel her evening yoga session and instead caught the next cab home, resolving to spend the evening alone with a bottle of wine watching well-spoken men in leather boots and tight uniforms dash about on television instead.

The grey man turned away, unheeded and unnoticed, absorbed by the river of people. He soon veered off and joined those making for the pubs and bars. The rest of the crowd proceeded towards the station where the trains waited, ready to remove them from the heaving, seething city.

THE HOTEL
CHAPTER THREE

WITZERLAND ENJOYS A history of attracting visitors. And for good reason: it's gorgeous. Those who use the world's natural beauty as evidence for divine creation inevitably invoke Switzerland as a prime underpinning of their argument. However, before staring at scenery became a bankable activity, the region went through some tough times. A nice view is, after all, poor consolation to a peasant trying to grow enough potatoes to feed a family of twelve and struggling to find a piece of ground that's even remotely flat in which to do so. European history being the anthology of wanton bloodshed that it is, Switzerland's neighbours have more than once elected to march through it on their way to kill each other and usually treated any chance encounter with the inhabitants as an opportunity to practice their murder skills. Consequentially, the nation's founding fathers were forced to take up arms simply to ensure enough peace and quiet to allow them to continue starving to death without interruption.

Even then, the region's biggest selling point was that nothing much ever happened there, land-locked neutrality being synonymous with boredom in the minds of most would-be industrial entrepreneurs, war heroes, and maritime explorers. But by the eighteenth century quite a lot of people had had more than enough excitement in their lives and fancied trying boredom as an alternative. These included some of the finest artisans in Europe as well as a number of dispossessed aristocrats, a few prudent merchant bankers, and a decent helping of honest nobodies who liked the idea of running an inn without seeing it burned down by marauders every fortnight. Together they helped make Switzerland a haven of quality watch-making and obliging financiers, blessed with a selection of attractive eateries and a political system so stable you could keep horses in it. This winning combination of pleasure, permanence, and productivity continues to thrive, and you can hardly throw a stone without hitting some kind of hostelry—unless a bank stands in the way.

Be that as it may, you'd have to lob your stone with considerable force to bounce it off the Gasthaus Meierhof. A comely establishment offering the best in comfort and cleanliness, it unfortunately stands some way off the beaten track in a country suffering no shortage of tracks to beat. This goes some way towards explaining its name's deplorable absence among the more renowned Swiss boutique hotels.

Frau Meierhofer herself had long ago gone to the great conciergerie in the sky and ownership of the hotel had passed from hand to hand before reaching the current proprietors, Mr and Mrs Indergand, who ran it with modest success. It was no secret in the village that Frau Indergand did most of the actual running, while her husband oversaw what he called "The Atmosphere". His duties consisted mostly of pottering about humming to himself and inspecting the many decorative curiosities dotted around the rooms, fruits of his travels as a younger man. On busy days he might move an item from one shelf to another for the purpose of effect, but otherwise the feng shui of his private museum remained largely undisturbed. In the erudite places of this world Meinrad Indergand's collection would have been highly regarded, for housed in the Gasthaus Meierhof were many treasures with origins as far-flung as Greece, Rwanda, and Japan. It did not enjoy the same popularity at home, where his wife was starting to seriously consider binning the lot and putting up some nice pictures instead.

On the night we meet this estimable couple Josephine Indergand had retired to bed early, understandably fatigued by a hard day's dusting of tribal masks and ceremonial tortoise statuary, leaving her husband to welcome the guests. Herr Indergand was happy to oblige; as it happens he was already halfway through an exciting volume featuring an athletic young protagonist, a saucy young temptress, a wise old mentor figure that reminded him rather pleasantly of himself, and a host of menacing Muscovites in the background. He made himself comfortable by the fire, brandy within easy reach, his bare feet resting comfortably on the dog's stomach, and settled down for a quiet evening.

*****

Somewhere in the gathering darkness a small red car wound its way up the mountain road. It was having great difficulty in doing so and communicated its displeasure by periodically coughing at its occupants through the dashboard.

'I wish you'd read the fine print at the rental office,' said Richard over the unhappy drone of the engine.

Graham gripped the steering wheel as though sheer willpower would breathe new life into the struggling gears. 'This vehicle is perfectly adequate. It's the bloody mountain that's too steep.'

'Well, if you hadn't been so busy eyeing up the girl behind the desk we might've got something with more oomph.'

Graham shook his head. 'Criticism, so soon into our partnership . . . and to think you were so pleased to see me at the airport.'

'I was pleased to see you,' retorted Richard. 'But you've got to admit, it's been a trying day. I can't believe they lost our bag.'

'I'm amazed they only lost one! There's so much luggage in the boot you'd think we were going on a surveillance mission.'

'We are.'

'Like spies I mean. There's nothing like a hasty getaway to Switzerland to arouse the espionage instinct. This bear story is tosh, isn't it? You're secretly here because you've killed a man and you need to lie low for a bit. I can tell. I have a scientist's eye for observation.'

'This explains why you were so needlessly cryptic at customs when they asked about our destination.'

'Actually, I'd forgotten the name of the village. Also, the bloke who interviewed us was very rude.'

'Great start to the trip. In my first article I'll describe the inside of a Swiss airport interrogation cell.'

'You sound annoyed.'

'Really? Unbelievable.'

'Never mind, young Richard. Here we are! Two intrepid adventurers, bound for glory. I was quite chuffed to receive your call, actually. Lucky for you that my busy schedule allowed for me to take part in this little project of yours. Onwards!'

Graham pressed down on the pedal. The car groaned and its engine began to shudder so violently that he eased off. His spirits undimmed, he reached into his pocket and produced a little green plastic bag. 'Mint?'

Richard sighed and turned away. It was hard to stay angry with Graham for long.

They hadn't been out of sight of the mountains since they landed. As they journeyed on, the landscape had slowly closed in on them. The plain had become a valley, then a dale, finally narrowing to little more than a defile winding upwards towards a faraway col. The road was squeezed between the rocks on one side and a sharp escarpment on the other. A rushing torrent could be heard far below, though the bottom of the ravine was already hidden in darkness. The car's feeble headlights illuminated the road as it twisted through a seemingly endless wood of dark pine and glanced off the posts mounted every few dozen yards along the roadside, their reflective spots flashing in the dark like the eyes of so many hidden creatures amongst the trees.

'Well,' sighed Richard, 'unless we find a better vehicle we'll have to carry the equipment ourselves. Incidentally, I'd like to go through our schedule for the next few days. Tomorrow we need to gauge the lay of the land so we can pick the best spots.'

He produced a handful of notes from his bag. Graham frowned.

'Tonight? Don't think so mate. The only things we're doing once we get to the hotel are, in order, eating a huge dinner, quaffing some restorative pints, and going straight to bed.'

Richard brandished the papers in protest. 'But I've mapped everything out. It took me ages! We need to start as soon as possible and there are things we need to do early tomorrow, like collect the permits from the mayor's office. You need to know what's going on!'

'You can tell me over breakfast.'

'Here, I'll put them in your bag for you to read later.'

'Shan't.'

'Look, Graham, this project is really important to me. If I get this right it could mean a big break and more interesting things to follow. I need everything to go as smoothly as possible.' Richard winced as the car lurched around a bend, axles throbbing.

'Don't care,' replied Graham. 'My stomach is beginning to digest itself. Food first, work later.'

Darkness had fallen with incredible swiftness and Richard struggled to make out the landscape pressing in around them. Putting his face up against the window he could just about see the diminishing ribbon of grey light above them, partially eclipsed by the perimeter of the brooding Alps.

The towering curve of the mountainside swept up into the sky like a solid wave of black earth. The lights of small homesteads in the wooded valleys below twinkled through the gaps between the passing trees. Soon both the forest and the darkness thickened so that the lights faded altogether.

'We're going to be late,' Richard grumbled. 'We're supposed to be there now. They'll be wondering if we're not dead.'

'Don't be daft,' dismissed Graham. 'It's early yet; I bet they're up to their ears in drinks orders. They've probably forgotten about us altogether.'

*****

Herr Indergand looked up from his book. He was under the distinct impression that there had been some kind of noise, but he couldn't identify the source.

The fire had collapsed into embers. Beneath his feet he could feel the gastric rumbles of Suzy, the dog, for whom the athletic days of puppyhood were over and who enjoyed the hearth in equal measure to her owner.

The hotelier shrugged and returned to the page. He'd been in the middle of a riveting scene in which the hero was on the verge of discovering the villain's identity in a blood-curdling face-off atop the Empire State Building. He took a sip of brandy before proceeding.

Egad! The kindly old mentor with whom Herr Indergand had so readily identified was behind the kidnapping the entire time! This was not to be believed. He must read on, discover the villain's loathsome motive, and rejoice at the scoundrel's inevitable defeat at the hands of the handsome young operative.

It was not to be. Through the comfortable fog of alcohol and couch cushions the same curious interruption sounded once again.

Herr Indergand looked up in annoyance. A moment's careful consideration led him to conclude that it was the front doorbell. It took him a few more moments to remember that he ran a hotel and that they were expecting guests.

Whatever his faults, Meinrad Indergand remained a consummate professional. The realisation that travellers stood on his establishment's threshold craving hospitality demanded of him nothing less than the most fulminating alacrity he could muster. He lost no time in placing his book on the side table—having ensured that it was safely bookmarked for later—swigged the last of his drink to fuel his imminent rush for the front door, and adjusted his collar button so as to look presentable when he got there. He noticed that in his relaxation he'd loosened his cufflinks. Frowning at his own negligent attitude, he fastened them again with the patient zeal of a dedicated hotelier.

'Well, old girl,' Meinrad addressed the sleeping Suzy, 'it would appear the day's toils are not yet done.' Suzy snored loudly in response.

Then, pausing only for one final anticipatory sigh, he reached for his shoes.

He emerged from the sitting room into the hallway as the doorbell rang for the third time. The old wooden desk gleamed with polish and the large mirrors on either side of the glass-faced door radiated warmth from the soft lighting.

Atop the desk sat a wicker basket intended to exhibit floral items to charm the guests. Presently it contained a large cat, who'd recognised in the basket a prime real estate opportunity. As Herr Indergand approached he trod on a number of assorted leaves, branches and pinecones, which lay where the cat had flung them.

The cat opened one eye. Recognising the source of an easy scratch, it lolled over the rim of the basket and exposed its fuzzy tummy.

Herr Indergand wagged his finger. 'Not now, Berlioz. I'm on urgent hotel business. There are guests waiting outside!'

As he turned towards the door he felt something give under his shoe. Looking down he identified a sprig of dahlias that had failed to find favour in the new order imposed upon the basket by Berlioz. Herr Indergand regarded them with interest; he hadn't realised dahlias had bloomed so late this year. How clever of Josephine to procure such a beautiful specimen.

Two things happened then that summoned Meinrad back to the task at hand. Firstly, the doorbell rang for the fourth time. Secondly, his wife appeared at the top of the stairs.

'Good evening, dearest!' he exclaimed. 'I thought you'd gone to bed.'

Josephine Indergand's expression was unreadable.

'What in God's name are you doing, Meinrad?' Her vermillion pyjamas fluttered ominously.

Meinrad Indergand loved his wife and it pained him to see her confused. He guessed her brain must be dulled by sleep.

'I'm answering the front door, darling.'

To Meinrad's dismay this explanation did nothing to assuage his other half who, for reasons he failed to grasp, appeared most agitated.

'And when,' she demanded, 'did you intend to do so, if I may ask?'

'Just now, only you started a conversation a minute ago.'

Josephine Indergand turned the same colour as her pyjamas.

'*I* interrupted *your* activities!? Well, then! I must apologise! I can only assume that, having been roused from my bed and summoned to the landing by the bell, despite having *specifically* told you that we're expecting guests and entrusted you with their welcome only to find you deep in conversation with the cat, I must have somehow misread the situation! It appears the only logical course of action is for me to remove myself to my bedchamber, allowing you to resume your paramount task of *answering the door!*'

Her husband beamed. 'Sounds good to me! Only best do so quietly, you might wake the other guests.'

The doorbell rang a fifth time. Herr Indergand fully intended to answer it, but he grew concerned for his wife: she looked distinctly unwell.

His wife's apoplectic stare came to rest on Berlioz. A moment later she identified the remains of the foyer's seasonal centrepiece, painstakingly picked by her, now lying in ruins upon the carpet.

Wrath inflated her bosom. All feelings of affection fled from her heart.

The lights flickered and dimmed. The woman Herr Indergand loved towered over him like a banshee, her face incandescent with rage. Suzy, roused from her nap, broke into a mournful howl. Several irate guests popped their heads out of their doors and demanded to know what all the commotion was about.

It was some time before Herr Indergand made it to the door.

*****

Richard and Graham listened as a frightful din erupted within the guesthouse.

'You sure this is the right address?' asked Graham.

Richard nodded. 'It's the only hotel in town. I even called this morning, spoke to a very nice woman. She's expecting us.'

'Hm. Maybe I should ring the doorbell again.'

The door opened. A rather flustered little man stood before them.

'Hi,' said Richard, 'er, we have a reservation, I think.'

The two Englishmen entered a cosy hallway. Soft lighting reflected off the dark wooden walls and the innumerable baubles and trinkets on the shelves. Mingling in the air were the aromas of wood smoke, furniture polish, dusty carpets, and warm dog fur: the smells of an old world growing comfortably older.

Herr Indergand assumed his place behind the counter and busied himself with their details. There was a creak in the shadows above them. Richard glimpsed a vermillion trouser leg retreating up the stairs. A door slammed shut.

Herr Indergand kept his eyes on his work, lest the owner of the leg reappear. Graham wondered why there were twigs underfoot.

'Any chance of a bite to eat?' he asked.

Herr Indergand glanced up. 'I am sorry?'

'My friend is hungry,' explained Richard. 'Is the kitchen still open?'

'Ah! No. We are very sorry.'

This displeased Graham mightily. He surveyed the vestibule with hostility and was unnerved to find a large ceremonial mask from equatorial Africa staring back at him. He glanced down to discover an enormous cat returning his gaze with cool detachment. Graham made a rude gesture at the cat, which started licking itself.

Touché, thought Graham.

Herr Indergand produced a key and invited them up the creaky wooden stairs.

'You are here for animal photos, yes?'

'That's right,' Richard answered, 'for a nature periodical.'

'Ah. You are wanting to see the nature, the mountains, the waters, yes?'

'Yeah.' Richard hauled his heavy suitcase up another step. 'Any advice?'

Herr Indergand paused in thought, one hand on the bannister. 'The waterfall, it is very beautiful,' he said. 'Many *gemse*, how you say . . . The chamois, there you can see them. Sometimes *steinböcke*, the ibex also.'

As they passed, Richard noticed several irate faces watching them from the other doorways. The trio conquered two floors before proceeding up a third, narrower flight.

'Unfortunately we are fully booked,' apologised Herr Indergand, 'but your firm is very insistent, so we make up my son's room. It is small, but comfortable. Silvio is away now for *militärdienst* before starting university. He is to study the hydro-engineering.'

The top landing was dark. The panelling creaked as the three men summited the final step. The small unlit space resonated with a dull *bonk*.

'Attention,' warned Herr Indergand. 'The ceiling here it is very low.'

Graham rubbed his head, cursing under his breath.

Herr Indergand groped in the darkness and found a doorknob. There was a squeak and a scrape as he ushered them into a small, tidy room. A recently added second bed crowded the space but still allowed for a large wooden wardrobe, an armchair by the window, and a small bookshelf. A tiny bedside table supported the room's only lamp alongside two mugs, a kettle, and an assortment of tea-related ingredients. Over one bed hung a black and white photograph of a wiry mountaineer with heavy clothes and sinewy hands. Either a trick of the light or faulty exposure marked his eyes with a strange pallor, giving him an otherworldly countenance.

Herr Indergand shuffled aside. 'My wife thinks you will like tea so we include a complimentary pot.'

'Thanks very much, this'll do fine,' Richard assured him. Graham squeezed past them and made straight for the kettle.

'Goodnight, gentlemen,' said Herr Indergand with a little bow. 'We wish you best of luck for your animal photos.' He shut the door behind him.

Graham ducked his lanky frame under the beam and sat on the larger of the two beds, having put the kettle on to boil. 'How does he know what we're here for?'

Richard shrugged. 'The office must have told him. Bit odd, two strangers arriving with big, bulky bags of unspecified equipment only to disappear into the highlands without a word of explanation. I'd prefer people to know what we were about, just so they know we're not a couple of creepy weirdos, wouldn't you?'

'What's a bear doing in this part of the world anyway?' yawned Graham. 'Never heard of bears in Switzerland. They'd disrupt all the skiing and fondue parties, surely.'

Richard sat on the smaller bed and began to unlace his new boots. 'That's the whole point. This is the first time a bear this large has been spotted around here for a generation. Even with the reintroduction programme in Italy and Slovenia, it's considered newsworthy. This one hasn't been tagged yet.' Richard struggled to remove his stiff footwear.

33

Graham raised his eyebrows. 'Shouldn't we keep that quiet? How do the locals feel about a rogue bear wandering through their yards? I've yet to meet a farmer who shares our views on wildlife when it came to creatures that literally eat his livelihood.'

'I've looked into it. There was a local movement earlier this year to have the bear tranquilized and resettled someplace else, mainly from pressure groups who were afraid it might attack livestock or wander into the nature reserve to snack on tourists.' Richard managed to yank off the first boot and set to work on the other. 'But apparently there have been no attacks so far and, with no tag, it's slipped off the radar. It may have gone back across the border.'

Graham leant back and flopped his hands in the air. 'Well, what the hell are we doing then? It's hardly worth sending us here just for some photos of the pretty waterfall, is it? I'm all for a paid vacation but I doubt your department has the budget.'

'Hopefully they're wrong about the bear leaving. Anyway, this time the money's coming from the big office. They even arranged the meeting with the local councillors tomorrow so we can get started as soon as possible. Let's hope they're helpful. The official brief is that if anyone asks, we're looking for marmots.'

Richard finally dislodged the other boot.

'What's that?' Graham asked.

Richard followed Graham's outstretched finger. His box of pills had fallen out of his pocket during the struggle with his footwear.

He put them away. 'Just some medication. I still get dizzy spells sometimes.'

Graham raised an eyebrow. 'I remember those. You once wandered halfway through Brommel Old Court at two in the morning in your underwear before the porter found you. You sure these "dizzy spells" won't impact our work here?'

Richard blushed. 'I'm sure.'

Graham shrugged. 'Okay. You know best. Glad you've got the meds though.' The kettle was boiling. Graham rose and poured it out.

He made a face at his mug. 'This smells awful. We'll have to get some proper stuff at the shops tomorrow.'

Richard was glad the conversation had moved away from him. 'You complain too much. It's fine.'

'And no biscuits either.'

'We shouldn't even be drinking tea this late.'

Graham raised his eyebrows. 'How dare you, sir! A true Englishman knows that tea is to be drunk at breakfast, afternoon tea, and whenever else you want a bloody cup of tea.' He took a mighty swig and winced, but otherwise maintained the composure of a gravely offended patriot.

'Anyway, seeing as there's no food I'm going to turn in early.' Graham plonked his mug onto the bedside table, kicked off his shoes, and stretched out on his bed with a contented belch.

Richard bounced up and down a little on the mattress. 'Don't know how you can go to sleep. I'm much too excited.'

'You're not keeping me up. I'm knackered.' Graham ran a finger over the books on the shelf by his head and pulled out two. 'Here, looks like these are the only ones in English. Spot of reading'll knock you out.'

He tossed them over. Richard picked one up off the homemade patchwork quilt. '*Crime and Punishment*. Not exactly a light read.'

'Literature broadens the mind and nurtures the soul,' murmured Graham, his eyes closed in blissful relaxation.

Richard flicked backwards through the hefty volume until he reached the inside sleeve. There was a dedication.

To Silvio, with love from Laura

'Did the hotel keeper say his son's name was Silvio?'

No answer. Richard reached for the second volume.

'*Central European Mythology & Folk Tales* by Melchior B. Adolphus. This looks more promising.'

A snore of contentment resonated from Graham's open mouth, though whether his sleep was genuine or contrived, Richard couldn't tell. The grizzled man in the photograph on the wall observed the snorer, the strange reflection in his eyes making his expression unreadable.

It seemed a shame to waste the tea after all the fuss that had been made over it. Richard retrieved the abandoned mug from the bedside table and stretched out on his bed. It felt wonderfully soft. The reassuring scent of pine drifted down from the ceiling.

He noticed that the beams were covered in carvings. Even in the dim light he could make out elaborately carved animals, flowers, vines, and fantastical faces staring down at him. He reached up and ran his hand over the old wood, delighting in this unexpected discovery. He made a note to have a closer look in the daylight.

Richard propped himself up against his pillow and, for want of anything better, reached for Melchior B. Adolphus. He allowed it to fall open and, sipping Graham's tea—which was indeed rather poor—began to read. His eyelids started to droop after the first few lines and before he reached the end he was fast asleep.

THE OLD SHEPHERDESS

Deep in the mountains there lived an old shepherdess, who was mortally afraid of death. One night, in the shivering depths of winter, she suspected that the hour of death was upon her and declared 'I will give the very best of my flock if only to be spared one more month!'

As it happens that month was January, who is keen and cunning. Upon hearing the shepherdess's prayer he appeared to her and promised to spare her life in exchange for the best ewe in her flock. The shepherdess willingly agreed and so January departed with the beast.

A month later the old woman felt once more that her time had come, and again cried out 'If I could live but a little longer, I should happily trade the best animal I possess!'

Fair-haired February was listening with her delicate hearing and she too appeared before the old woman to claim her part of the bargain. The shepherdess traded a fine ram, in exchange for which February promised not to trouble her further.

So it went with all the months: March came, squat and irritable under an unkempt cloud of dirty hair, demanding one of these fine animals he'd heard about. Then came April with her deep blue eyes and sweet smile and chose a mild-mannered lamb as her price. By and by May arrived, dancing merrily through the melting snow singing in his clear voice, irreverent and delightful.

Following him were motherly June and fatherly July, who soothed the old woman's aging bones with their smiling warmth. Venerable August visited next, serene and kind, and left too soon. September blew in unexpectedly one afternoon, windswept and witty, and helped the woman light her fire. Then followed October, who was mischievous and laughed heartily as she tossed her flame-red hair. She eventually grew sad, however, and the old woman was lonely when she left.

On the day the last leaves were falling from the trees, November arrived, quiet and mournful, saying nothing and demanding only the old ram that stood in the corner of the shepherdess's hut. It was her last animal and it followed November into the evening twilight without protest.

The old woman was alone now. She spent the darkening days wondering how she would pay the next visitor, as she had no more sheep to barter.

At last one evening he arrived. His name was Old Man Time. 'Come,' he said, 'we have work to do. It is time to use the gifts that you have been given.'

She followed him into the night and with his help did many things.

November had taught her silence and she gave it to the woods. She took the fire from October's hair and put in the cheeks of children to keep them warm. She blew gently on the coals nestling in people's hearths, as September had shown her, to keep them lit through the midnight hours. She used the minutes she wished she could have spent with August to tend to the old and sickly as they slept, sparing no kindness that they might enjoy a *taste of summer's sweet serenity. With a watchful eye she protected slumbering animals in their dens that they might live to see sunlit July and nursed acorns and walnuts deep in the ground so that they might grow in balmy June. She wove the melodies of May into the frozen streams that they might sing again when the ice melted, and smiled April's beautiful smile as she planted the seeds of snowdrops and celandines. When a flock of ravens disturbed her quiet woods she chased them away, waving her hand about like a squall in March. Finally, she took the white gold from February's hair and with January's keen eye she wove it into the canopy of the stars. The threads she discarded fell to earth and broke apart to become snow, covering the mountainside with a deep blanket of whiteness.*

Having completed all these tasks, December—for such, of course, was the old woman's name—returned to her little house. As thanks Old Man Time gave her a new flock of sheep, which she gratefully accepted. So preoccupied did she become with them, she soon forgot all about her visitors and the lessons she had learnt. She fed and sheltered the shy beasts and protected them as best she could. Their fear of all things unknown eventually became her fear and at night she would sit by the fire amongst her animals, eyeing the quivering shadows and pricking her ear up lest she hear an unfamiliar knock at the door.

THE HUNTING PARTY
CHAPTER FOUR

5'900 years earlier

CROSS THE FLOODPLAIN runs a party of five hunters.
The leader is tall and keen-eyed. His breath comes deep and even as he travels swiftly across the plain. A copper-headed axe hangs from his belt. In his hand is a spear tipped with flint, in his boot a knife.

He beckons to the others. Behind him runs a young man with black hair and dark eyes. A wolfish dog lopes at his heels.

Three more follow. The youngest brings up the rear. Their feet skim the earth, legs swinging in counterpoint to the spears grasped in their muscular hands. Together they pursue their prey as it flees towards the mountains.

There are no paths, only the narrow highways trodden by small animals. Occasionally the men cross a larger trail, marking the passage of a boar or a bison. They ignore them.

The tracks lead the hunters away from the floodplain towards the darkening forest. They reach the trees at nightfall and make camp there.

The leader orders the youngest to draw water from the stream and consults the dark-haired man. He in turn observes his dog, sniffing and tasting their surroundings; their quarry passed here not long before.

The chase is postponed until sunrise. One man stands watch as the rest sleep.

They awake in the half-light before dawn. There has been no call from the watchman. They search for him but he has disappeared without trace.

The men quarrel; this should have been foreseen. Next time they shall take more care.

*****

Through the primeval wood moves a party of four hunters.

The leader inspects the earth, his expert eyes reading secrets in the moss and pine needles. Three follow, the dark-haired man and two others. Anger lends them speed. The youngest comes last, the tame wolf races alongside.

The hunt lasts all day. By nightfall they have closed the distance but have failed to catch their prey. Perhaps tomorrow will be different.

This time they make their camp in a clearing, away from the edge of the trees. The leader takes first watch, scanning the woods as the others sleep. Eventually he is relieved by one of his companions and lays down to a fitful slumber.

By morning the sentry is gone. No sign of him can be found, but there are fresh tracks leading into the dark forest.

The hunter's face is set. They have been visited again and now the trail is clear.

He rouses his companions and the chase continues.

*****

Across the rocky moraine climbs a party of three hunters.

The leader bounds across stony crags, ancient landslides, and dry riverbeds streaked by floodwaters from the previous spring.

The dark-haired man comes second, his wolf never far behind. The air carries the smell of snow and the animal sniffs eagerly, tasting it with its red tongue. The warm season has turned and winter is on its way. Behind them trails the youngest.

More than once they think they spy movement ahead; it is only shadows. They race forward, sensing that their quarry is near. But the broken terrain is difficult and slows them down. Hands are needed for climbing and they are forced to leave their spears behind.

Evening finds them tired and empty-handed.

This time, no one sleeps. They crouch in a circle, facing outwards, clutching their axes and knives. There are no trees here. The wind pulls at their clothes and hair but they do not build a fire, fearing the warmth will lull them to sleep. As the hours wear on, their fatigue begins to tell and they slumber despite themselves. Only the youngest cannot sleep. He eyes the darkness fearfully, starting at any sound.

When his companions awake he is gone. His weapons lie where he left them.

*****

Across the wind-swept plateau run two men and a dog, hunting shadows.

39

The wind snaps at their eyes, the rocks bite their feet. Occasionally stones come loose and crash down into the nothingness below. There are no tracks to follow; only the dog can smell the way. They glimpse flickering shapes around every corner and crag, but cannot catch them.

Eventually they find a rocky overhang and rest. The leader is angry with his companion and they argue, but soon both men subside into a brooding silence. The only sound is the wind in the trees far below, like waves on a dark sea. They intend to stay only a while, but exhaustion overcomes them both and they fall into a fitful dose.

In the depth of night there is a noise from the darkness. The leader opens his eyes and reaches for his knife, but too late.

When the dawn comes, only one is left.

He contemplates the pale gleam behind the jagged outline of the mountains. Slowly it lightens, turns to white, then gold. Finally the shining edge of the sun cracks over the crown of snow-capped peaks, black silhouettes against the breaking of the day.

The dark-haired man wipes his bloodied hands on the furs wrapped around his companion's body. As sunlight floods the mountainside he sets off alone.

*****

Across the stony ridge on the flank of a great white mountain runs a dark-haired man, a half-tame wolf at his side. He is no longer following a trail. Around him ribbons of water trickle down from their sources and become rushing white torrents.

He finds a copper axe head in the stream. Someone has used it to pay for safe passage. He steals it and moves on.

He leaps across chasms and swings through the forests. He knows that he has become the quarry and the hunter is now behind him. His mind is fitful, his eyes ever watchful.

He can run a long time. All the same, he suspects it will get him in the end.

But not yet.

THE VILLAGE
CHAPTER FIVE

ICHARD FOUND GRAHAM sitting in the hotel's sunlit restaurant, a pleasant room with large windows, tables at one end and a pub-like bar at the other. He helped himself to a croissant from the buffet and pulled up a chair.

Graham held up a tired-looking slice of ham. 'I must say; the breakfast here is a soul-crushing disappointment.'

'It's Continental,' replied Richard. 'It's what hotels everywhere do.'

'Well, they should do otherwise. That stuff over there was particularly upsetting.'

Graham gestured towards the window. Several sizeable jars occupied a table covered with a chequered tablecloth, each containing something that looked very much like dirt samples; none of the guests went anywhere near the table.

'It's muesli,' said Richard. 'It's healthy.'

'I tried some. It made me extremely unhappy.'

Richard shrugged, his mouth full of cereal.

The piece of ham flopped across the rim of Graham's plate as though trying to escape. He made no move to prevent it. 'So,' he said. 'Day One! What's the program?'

Richard chewed his croissant. 'I need to go to the municipal offices and request official permission to operate within the national park. The brief says we'll be fast-tracked, so there shouldn't be any problems.'

Graham nodded. 'Nice enough day for it.'

Richard glanced out the window and saw the village properly for the first time.

Niderälpli is a minute collection of well-kept houses set in a heavily forested dale. The highest in a series of valleys, it is cradled by some of the tallest mountains in the region, such that it appears to be surrounded on all sides by a great bowl-like ridge of rock. The Gasthaus Meierhof stands at

41

the furthest end of the valley slightly apart from the village, affording its guests a handsome view.

The first thing to catch one's eye is the waterfall. From a spring above the dale a stream of clear water gushes and eventually spills over the ridge. The hundred-foot column falls unhindered before crashing upon the jutting rocks halfway down, forming a series of pools and chutes. From the foot of the cliff the stream's course runs through the wooded valley and the village itself, until the water reaches the dale's lowest end. There the flowing water has carved a V-shaped opening through the rock and tumbles through this gap to the floodplains in an ever-growing torrent.

A rickety railway runs alongside the rapids. Its little red carriages trundle through tunnels blasted through solid rock a century ago, chugging their way up under sheer cliffs and over high-arched stone bridges, the ferocious water pounding below. A paved road—a more recent addition— accommodates those seasonal visitors for whom the leisurely ride up the track is an unattractive proposition. But still the train hauls itself out of the valley several times a day, struggling uphill for over an hour before eventually coming to rest in its tiny station at the heart of Niderälpli.

Richard finished his breakfast, bid Graham goodbye, and headed outside for a closer look.

The road led a short way down the slope from the hotel before splitting into two branches that between them enclosed most of the houses. A narrow church steeple rose in the distance. Richard noted the stone-tiled roofs, the freshness of the air, and the inescapable, overpowering presence of the mountains looming over the village.

Richard stared up at the rampart-like ridge surrounding the valley. To the south was the great cleft in the mountain wall and the narrow twisting road that had led them there the previous evening. On either side the wooded slopes rose up for hundreds of feet.

He turned, following the encircling ridge. When he'd completed roughly half a revolution and was facing north, the mountains' edge arched up into a steepening slant above the treeline, towering into a great horn of barren, wind-swept wilderness.

He craned his neck and surveyed the summit. Wide swathes of snow and ice descended in long white tendrils, groping amongst clefts of the mountain. Even now, at summer's end, its peak was white as bone and the winds teased away the snow in cloud-like filaments.

Richard's gaze returned to the base of the waterfall. The torrent ran past an imposing white building that might once have been a hotel but was now boarded up, and trickled into a small ravine running behind the fields and into the village. Neat stone walls channelled the current through the town, snaking around and occasionally even under the houses.

It was barely nine o'clock. Richard decided to clear his head with a walk around the village. Maybe he'd discover where the river emerged on the other side. Given the size of the place, he didn't imagine it would take him long.

The streets were quiet, save for the sound of Richard's footsteps. It was a matter of minutes to cover the distance separating the hotel from the small cluster of buildings. He walked past whitewashed stone chalets with slate roofs and brass gutters, as well as recently built apartments of a low-ceilinged angular design with large windows, some of which housed small businesses. He saw no one.

Richard experienced the pleasant bewilderment of discovering a foreign place. As he ambled along, studying the tidy chimneys and painted shutters, he felt a strange prickling behind his eyes, as though they were itching to discover all of these new sights at once. The air floated down off the rocks and the coarse grasses high above, carrying the perfume of unfamiliar flowers, the dark aroma of pine, and the chilly scent of ice. He breathed in deeply, as though inhaling his strange surroundings might help him understand their secrets.

Richard enjoyed exploring. When he'd first arrived in London several years before, he'd found it overwhelming. Everything was bigger, noisier, and more aggressive than the village where he grew up. The Victorian facade of his local town hall, which he'd once thought extremely grand, now seemed humble indeed. Exploring London had made it seem friendlier. After work he'd wandered amongst the backstreets and intentionally got a bit lost before making his way back by a different route. In this way he discovered the quiet heart of the city. Often he'd stumble upon something nestled in the shadow of an office tower, or just around the corner from the crowds of suits surging from one air-conditioned skyscraper to the next; old buildings, narrow streets, small and tranquil parks, much as they'd remained for a hundred years or more; unchanged, even as the noise and glass-faced monoliths rose about them.

There, thought Richard, that's what this place reminds me of: somewhere that's stayed the same for generations, no matter what happens around it. It's one of those timeless corners of the world that seems to revolve a little bit slower than everywhere else.

The sound of an approaching vehicle broke his reverie. A tractor rounded the corner, hauling a load of firewood. The wizened driver ignored Richard's friendly wave.

Beyond the road Richard saw the main village square. He recognised it not because it was particularly imposing, but by the numerous red and white flags hanging off various buildings of modest grandeur. He inspected the cobbled space, alone save for a sleeping cat curled up in a pot plant in front of what appeared to be the village's only café. Richard noted the church steeple peeking over a corner and a darkened bar on one side of the square. Next door stood a small shop with a dusty window and a wooden door bearing the inscription *Souvenirs und Antiquitäten*.

In the centre of the square was a fountain. Above it stood the statue of a woman, the stone drapes of a cloak hanging from one slender shoulder. Its hem folded onto a granite stele under her feet. Her blank eyes were turned towards the white summit above.

Richard checked the pedestal for the carved names of those killed in the wars and the thanks of a grateful nation to her dead heroes. But there were none—just bare rock, stained in places by the water flowing from a brass pipe.

Probably some martyred saint, mused Richard.

As if in answer, the church bell tolled half past. This brought Richard to his senses. He guessed that the communal offices must be located within a large building in the southwest corner, which bore the most flags.

Richard pressed the buzzer. Nothing happened.

Richard waited, the morning's optimism beginning to leak away. He pressed the buzzer again: no response. Richard's unease morphed into a sense of dread.

Berlioz woke up in his flowerpot outside the café. He observed Richard with calm misanthropy, waiting for the sun to reach his spot.

Richard stepped back and spotted a small brass plaque partially hidden by a noticeboard. The words were incomprehensible. Richard's mind began to race with horrible possibilities: had he somehow made a terrible mistake? Had he come on the wrong day? Had he come to the wrong *village?*

Berlioz was not alone in observing Richard's distress. Two old men watched from a bench under a tree nearby as he peered into the ground floor windows.

'Look,' said one, 'that young'un seems to be in distress.'

'Hmm,' replied the other, a gnarled old man in a shabby overcoat and glasses busy stuffing an elaborately decorated pipe with tobacco.

Thus ended the conversation.

There was a *schtonk* sound from behind the door. It creaked open. A withered female face obscured by a pair of huge spectacles confronted Richard. The woman's sensible shoes and weatherworn jumper marked her unmistakably as someone who worked in the municipal sector.

'Hullo!' said Richard with relief. 'I'm here to speak with someone from the council.'

The little woman looked at him much as a mother would a leper in her nursery. After a moment she inched aside and Richard was allowed into the building.

Three pairs of eyes examined the dossier Richard had compiled so neatly that morning.

On the left sat a severe-looking woman in a silk scarf, her iron-coloured hair cut executively short. She'd been polite enough during the introductions but so far her demeanour indicated nothing warmer than a ruthless and unforgiving regard for bureaucratic procedure. It was she who first requested his papers.

On the right a large man in a dark suit slouched in his chair. He glanced at the documents but invested most of his attention in a study of Richard himself. Richard smiled politely. The man gazed back at him enigmatically before returning to the papers.

These lay before the gentleman in the centre, a professorial type with a sensible face. He'd welcomed Richard on his arrival and invited him to sit, but for the last few minutes had been occupied with the documents. His only comments had been an occasional 'hmm' or 'aah'.

Richard didn't know quite what to make of them. In his hands he held the cup of tea made by Ursula, the bespectacled secretary who'd opened the door. It didn't taste like it had been brewed with great love. Richard hadn't even been allowed to bring up the subject of his visit until everyone had been introduced and a variety of snacks passed around. The three members of the village council had insisted on asking Richard about his flight, his hotel, where he'd studied, was he enjoying Switzerland, and other banal inquiries.

He assumed this was to make him feel comfortable. It hadn't worked.

Then they'd requested his papers and lapsed into a silence so complete that Richard grew downright uneasy.

His eyes strayed to the cabinet behind them. Its intricate woodwork was extremely fine. Panels had been mirrored using the natural grain of the wood to form patterns like Rorschach diagrams, which Richard found rather hypnotic. The overall effect would have been striking even without the taxidermied fox mounted on top.

There was a rustle of paper as three pairs of eyes swivelled upwards to Richard. The man in the middle removed his glasses and cleared his throat.

'*Also*, Herr Mathern,' he said, 'your qualifications and your documents they are in order. But,' he held up a long finger, 'we would like you to answer some few questions please.'

'Of course,' said Richard. 'Happy to help, Mr . . .' Drat, he'd forgotten the man's name.

'Aufdermauer.'

Councillor Aufdermauer turned to the lady. 'You have questions, Madame Berger?'

Madame Berger leaned forward. 'Tell us more of your firm.'

Richard explained his position at *Nature Magazine*, leaving out the bits about how dirt broke it was. The woman took all this down, nodding, and raised her eyebrows at the mention of Aberfinchley Group Inc. She seemed pleased when Richard spoke of the publicity and investment given to the environmental projects that were being pushed forward.

She nodded to her colleagues. Councillor Aufdermauer spread his hands and motioned to his left. 'Herr Fürgler?'

The large man in the dark suit leaned forward. 'Herr Mathern,' he spoke in a baritone, 'here in the Alps we rely greatly on the visitors for winter sports, the hiking, the wellness, etc. This research, it will be good for the tourism you think?'

'Well, er, I mean . . . It's scientific research. I don't think it has much to do with the tourist industry, really . . .'

The man's expression told Richard this was the wrong answer.

' . . . Unless,' he added, 'you're envisaging some kind of high altitude safari or animal sightseeing tour—that kind of thing. My project will do a great deal to draw people's attention to the imminent threat to the animals' habitat and the importance of wildlife conservation.'

If anything the man's face became even darker.

Councillor Aufdermauer replaced his spectacles and peered at Fürgler. Judging that his colleague was finished, he waved in Richard's direction.

'You permit that we discuss?' he gestured to his colleagues and himself.

'Of course!' said Richard, smiling ingratiatingly.

Aufdermauer nodded. The three officials shuffled their chairs and brought their heads together. Richard understood none of it. However, in the interest of comprehension, we offer the following translation.

'I don't like it,' grumbled Fürgler.

'I knew you'd say that,' snapped Madame Berger. 'Why not? He seems a perfectly nice young man and his papers are all in order. He and his colleague are clearly very qualified.'

Fürgler snorted. Owing to the nature of the Swiss German language, this escaped Richard's notice.

'On paper, perhaps. You can teach skills, but you can't change character. I say we put them on probation, observe their behaviour, and judge whether they are fit to present our community to the world. Then we can discuss permits.'

'We're not Freemasons, Dominik,' said Councillor Aufdermauer. 'Can't we keep this simple?'

'I'm not willing to entrust strangers with access to our community and archives without a proper vetting process. I'm sorry if my concern is unappealing to you, but I guess you have priorities other than the wellbeing of our village.'

46

Madame Berger rolled her eyes. 'You're still mad we didn't approve that disgusting ski lift you want to build on the Gräuelhorn, aren't you?'

'I guess some people don't welcome progress.'

'We've been over this already. It's a money-making scheme that will uglify the entire area.'

Fürgler sulked. 'I guess I'm the only one here who appreciates the urgent need to create more jobs in this town. There's nothing for the kids to do. Is it any wonder they're all leaving?'

Madame Berger raised an eyebrow. 'You think young people want to spend their winters working some crummy lift? We don't need mechanics. We need teachers and doctors! We want to keep them in school so they can graduate and train as something useful!'

'It's not crummy,' muttered Fürgler. 'It's got a toboggan run and everything.'

'Be that as it may,' interjected Aufdermauer, 'we're not here to revisit the ski lift, but to decide whether this young man should have access to our nature reserve. Perhaps we might persuade him to hire a local expert as an advisor?

'Good idea!' said Madame Berger. 'Let's recommend Kaspar to supervise them. No one knows the area better. Besides, it'll give the old coot something to do.'

Fürgler gave another snort that conveyed his opinion of Kaspar, but said nothing.

'I'll get Kaspar on the phone,' said Councillor Aufdermauer. He can give them a preliminary tour of the plateau this afternoon.'

The debate was over. Aufdermauer gathered all the documents, replaced them in their folder, and handed it back to Richard.

'Welcome to Niderälpli, Herr Mathern. Ursula will print off the necessary forms.'

*****

While Richard had been indoors, the square had come alive. People ducked in and out of doorways, greeting their familiars. The two old men on the bench had disappeared into one of the shops and the cobbled space echoed with the sound of voices. Down the side streets Richard glimpsed solid men in heavy jackets minding their own business, tending to the things that constitute village life everywhere.

As Richard hastened past one of the smaller alleyways, there was a sudden flash of colour. He stopped and ducked back.

Between the narrow stone walls, he spotted a young woman in a yellow dress and wide-brimmed hat strolling slowly up the street in his direction, a book in her hand, looking for all the world like something out of one of his

Grandmother's childhood photographs. She was taking a particular interest in the late-blooming flowers hanging over the wall on one side of the street.

She must have dressed up especially for church, thought Richard, though she'll catch her death of cold.

She glanced up and noticed him watching her. At first she paid him no attention and returned to the flowers. A moment later however their eyes met again, and this time she seemed surprised to find him looking at her still.

Richard suddenly felt embarrassed and with an apologetic grin he resumed his walk back to the Gasthaus Meierhof.

THE HIGH PLATEAU
CHAPTER SIX

HAT AFTERNOON FOUND Graham standing by the hotel, visibly irritated.

'What took you so long?' he demanded as Richard emerged from the front door. 'I got back from the shops ages ago.'

'I was waiting for you upstairs. Any sign of our guide yet?'

Graham brandished a receipt in Richard's face. 'Look at what these people charged me for two sandwiches, two packets of crisps, and a few bottles of water. Look at it!'

'Things are expensive here. Everyone knows that.'

'Yeah, well, I didn't know that every trip to the grocer's for the foreseeable future would feel like I've bought a house. I can only assume the pig these sandwiches came from was a beloved local celebrity.'

Richard changed the subject. 'Nice place, this. It's really pretty.'

'Ah, but are they on the National Health Service?'

'Don't think so.'

'Well then, they can never be truly happy,' said Graham.

'What, like you?'

'Piss off. By the way, did you remember those pills of yours? As hilarious as your little episodes were, I'd rather you not experience one halfway up a mountain.'

'Yep,' replied Richard, patting his rucksack.

'Who's this bloke were waiting for anyway?'

Richard scratched his head. 'The council said his name's Kaspar. Lived here his whole life, apparently. He's what they call a weather prophet, or something. I've forgotten the exact word they used but it sounded like a sneeze.'

Graham snorted. 'That's not a thing.'

'Yes it is. They predict the weather by looking at moss and ants and frogs and things. It's an age-old tradition.'

49

'So we're supposed to wait here for this postmodern Merlin to rub his face against a tree and divine where the bear lives?'

'The councillors recommended him very highly.'

Graham shrugged. 'Makes sense I guess. We're stuck up a mountain in a medieval village with sandwiches made from what was, judging by the price, a magic pig. What better guide could we ask for than a self-proclaimed wizard?'

'Speaking of which,' said Richard, 'that must be him now.'

The man coming up the road moved at a measured pace, putting one foot squarely in front of the other in the leisurely, contented way of someone who doesn't need to hurry. He carried a pack on his back and an unadorned walking stick of beech in his hand. A battered, wide-brimmed hat covered his hair, which was white like his beard.

'Him?' Graham blurted. 'He's, like, a hundred years old! We'll have to carry him up the glacier!'

'I hardly think they'd let him be our guide if he couldn't take care of himself.'

'But . . .'

By then the man was within earshot. Graham swallowed whatever else he might have said and watched him approach.

When the man finally reached them he didn't offer his hand, touching the brim of his hat instead.

'Hullo,' said Richard. Kaspar answered with words that made it abundantly clear his English was non-existent.

Richard produced the documents from the mayoral office. The old man waved these aside without looking at them. He raised his eyebrows and gestured up the path as if to say *Shall we?* Without waiting for an answer, he set off up the slope with the same steady pace as before.

Graham looked at Richard and raised an eyebrow. Richard shrugged and set off after Kaspar. Graham followed, grumbling as he went.

Soon they reached a fork. The right-hand branch was the continuation of the road and led towards the large white building overlooking the village. Kaspar took the left, which soon disintegrated into a simple hiking trail.

This footpath led away from the village, winding upwards across the meadows. They soon entered the shadowy quiet of the forest. The pines crowded together tightly. The steepening slope gave the impression that the trees ahead were taller than they actually were, the rise allowing each successive giant to tower over those below.

Kaspar wasn't fast, but he was steady. Under his dark hat the old man was imperturbable and his slow tread carried him upwards like a human funicular. Richard soon found himself struggling in the ascent.

He paused for a moment, allowing Graham to catch up.

'Sometimes I don't know why we bother,' grumbled Graham. 'We get less funding every year. It's all those bloody BBC nature documentaries. Nowadays nobody pays attention to anything that doesn't involve half a dozen film crews and a soundtrack by the London Symphony Orchestra. I bet when we get to the top we'll find bloody David Attenborough wrapping up his latest extravaganza.'

Richard didn't answer, preferring to save his energy for the climb.

Kaspar called from up ahead. He was peering down at them from the next bend, an amused smile lurking somewhere under his beard. He wasn't even out of breath.

They overtook him as he emerged onto something that might once have been a clearing, except there was now hardly any grass growing on the rocks. The sound of their breathing had deafened them to the growing noise of water but when they stopped it hit them full on.

Their gaze rose, following the unbroken gossamer column of water falling out of the sky. Everywhere he looked, Richard saw pools of clear water connected by gurgling rivulets, the rocks glistening with moisture. Most impressive was the pool closest to the falls, a deep basin that exploded in bursts and showers where the plummeting cascade was arrested by the rocks. This, then, was the foot of the waterfall.

The shelf was fringed by a jagged perimeter where a portion had simply fallen into the void. The angled rim resembled a broken windowsill, with a view of the dale beyond. Richard hadn't realised how high they'd already climbed; you could see the entire valley from here.

Kaspar pulled a misshapen cigar from his pocket and lit it with a match from a decorated box. The smoke drifted away on the breeze.

'Come over here!' called Graham, leaning over the cliff edge. 'It's awesome!'

Richard joined him and peered over the edge of the falls. The water spilled over the stone lip and broke into white foam on a ledge some distance below. Then it fell onto another, and another, a staircase of frothing water that tumbled into the dale. Mist drifted upwards off the cascade, carrying the perfume of cool, wet stone.

Kaspar hailed them once more, gesturing to the footpath. Reluctantly they pulled themselves away from the falls and resumed their climb.

The forest began to thin. Then, abruptly, the woods were behind them. This was the treeline, above which there wasn't enough oxygen for trees to grow. It was as abrupt as though the woods had been trimmed with a razor. Except for a few stunted growths, the landscape before them was grassland, rising and plunging into rifts and valleys, at the bottom of which trickled tiny streams. Everywhere was littered with boulders tumbled from the higher slopes.

Richard felt exposed. The forest had housed an almost unearthly calm; here there blew a breeze that he suspected could easily morph into an icy wind if it wanted to.

Kaspar halted to relight his cigar. He blew a cloud of grey smoke and looked to Richard for an indication of where they might want to go. Richard waved Graham over and took out his smartphone.

'We're looking for a large brown bear, gender unknown, last spotted two days ago about sixteen miles from here at high altitude. According to our info its usual route runs right along this pass. No offspring observed yet, but its behaviour indicates it might have hungry cubs to feed. Either that or it's hungry itself. Where do you think we should go?'

Graham thought for a moment. 'Any word from the local farmers?'

'A few unconfirmed sightings in the pastures northeast of here, but nothing definite. The meteorological society positioned a camera but came up with nothing. It's a tricky one.'

'Right, let's start with a patrol along the ridge, then descend to the river and work our way back from there. It's probably lurking at high altitude somewhere but it's got to come down eventually. We'll look for traces of where its usual routes might be.'

'Good idea. Keep an eye out for spots to plant our motion cameras as well.'

'Righty-oh.'

Richard waved to Kaspar and pointed up the ridge. The old man nodded and picked out a narrow track that Richard would scarcely have noticed on his own.

A slope of coarse vegetation rose on their left and descended on their right, flattening out in the distance to meet the rushing torrent of white water that had carved out this high valley. The path narrowed in some places to less than a foot wide, winding up the mountainside like a flinty snake. Occasionally one of their boots dislodged a stone, which would slip off the path and roll down the grassy slope. On the steeper sections these stones would gain speed and bounce higher and higher, sometimes as high as a man's head, as they leapt down towards the torrent. When the trio paused for lunch, Richard watched one rock come loose and accelerate until it seemed to be flying over the earth before hitting the distant water with a *splash*.

Eventually they couldn't hear the stream at all. Looking up, Richard could see they hadn't far to go. Before long they crested the ridge and the valley spread out below them.

They'd climbed the side of the great cliff-sided bowl that sheltered the village. Now they looked down on Niderälpli from a stomach-churning height, much of it already shrouded in the afternoon shadow cast by the mountains surrounding it. Looking up Richard saw the sun-bathed, cloud-capped panorama of the Alps stretching for miles. To one side the great white bulk of the Gräuelhorn towered over the three men. The wind that whipped around them carried the same icy fragrance that drifted off the falls.

As he craned his neck Richard stumbled. Graham reached out and steadied him. A trickle of rock bounced down the slope.

'You all right?' asked Graham. 'Maybe it's time for one of those pills.'

Richard did feel a little dizzy, but shook the feeling off. He found his footing and steadied himself. 'I'm fine,' he said, but checked his bag to make sure the medication was still there, just in case.

The group walked until the sun was low in the sky and the air turned chilly. They crested a stony ridge and dislodged a rather grumpy marmot from under a rock when Kaspar indicated it was time to return to Niderälpli. Richard was reluctant to leave the trail but had come to trust the old man's judgement. Kaspar spoke little and never in words Richard and Graham could understand, but he was a sure-footed guide and they'd gone further that day by following him than they would have alone. Richard made a thumbs-up to show he agreed and turned to Graham.

As he did, he noticed a shadow over Kaspar's shoulder. It was some considerable distance away and moving fast but was very distinctive.

Richard reached for his binoculars.

Graham drew alongside, looking concerned. 'You sure you're all right? You've hardly said a word since we . . .'

Richard grabbed his arm and pointed to the ridge. 'Look!'

Graham looked, as did Kaspar, but the shape had gone.

Richard had only seen it for an instant, but was certain he'd recognised the silhouette of a large, hulking animal. He dropped his pack and rummaged around frantically, looking for his camera.

'It's there!' he said. 'It's right there!'

Graham looked at the horizon and then back at Richard, except he wasn't there anymore. Graham looked back at the horizon to see Richard dashing up the ridge.

Graham turned to Kaspar, who shrugged. As far as he knew, Englishmen did this sort of thing all the time.

Graham swore, struggled out of his rucksack, and pursued.

Richard pounded on. The long grass whipped his legs as he ran, up the slope and down again, only to find that whatever he was chasing had gone. Several times he stopped. Which way? But then out of the corner of his eye he'd spot movement and off he raced again.

It's right there, he said to himself. It's right there, what you came for, the thing you need. It was so easy!

Breathless, he crested a final ridge and found himself looking down at a lake. It sat at the bottom of a lonely valley that was half ravine, half crater.

The wind hardly brushed the water's mirror-like surface. There was no sign of life anywhere.

Where could it have gone? This was a cul-de-sac. The mountainside was so steep, there's no way it could have escaped. He stood on the ridge, swaying and breathless, scanning the blurry moraine for signs of life.

Richard's head was swimming. Behind him he heard the shouts of his companions, but didn't understand the words. He fumbled in his pocket for his pills, then remembered that they were in his rucksack.

I shouldn't have run, he thought. That was stupid. I've frightened it off.

There was a sudden movement at his side. Richard spun around, thinking the animal was behind him. He was more than a little surprised to see a friendly-looking man in a white medical coat sitting on a rock.

'You're Dr Miles,' he said, slurring his words, 'our old family GP.'

'Hiya, Richard!' said Dr Miles. 'Long time no see!'

'What are you doing here?' asked Richard. A good question, he thought to himself, and perhaps wanting a follow-up query regarding the blue-grey horns blossoming from the doctor's head.

'Oh, not much,' said Dr Miles, nonchalantly scratching his ear with a hoof, 'just sightseeing. The air up here is amazing for the lungs, you know.' As if to demonstrate this a couple of multi-coloured gryphons flew by, yodelling delightedly.

'I don't feel so well,' murmured Richard.

The rock Dr Miles was sitting on opened its eyes and stared at Richard disapprovingly. 'That's because you haven't taken your medication,' it said, in a voice uncannily like his mother's.

Richard fell to his knees, fumbling for support. Around him whirled a cast of increasingly bizarre characters, none of whom he recognised now that Dr Miles had run off down the mountainside bleating earnestly. They swam in and out of his vision like a pulsating kaleidoscope, there one minute and gone the next. Wild-eyed beasts, dancing women, bearded troglodytes, and goggled men with faces wrapped in white scarves came and went like wraiths. Suddenly out of the maelstrom swung the huge muzzle of a bear, its eyes dark and sad. Instinctively Richard reached out, but as he did it wheeled away and disappeared like smoke, only to be replaced by a congregation of howling goblins with clipboards, all offering him discounted weekly fruit and vegetable deliveries.

Richard tried to speak, but discovered he couldn't. Never mind, he thought, as he watched a clan of hideous milky-eyed fish-men emerge ululating from the dark waters of the lake; no one could hear me anyway, what with all that noise of pounding hoof beats. Where were those coming from, anyway?

Richard was vaguely aware that the rock beneath him had turned to cream and wondered how it was that the great white mountain now surged upwards as if to crash down on him like a wave.

Then his body hit the ground and the seizure took over.

*****

Richard awoke sweating from a nightmare where he was drowning in a sea of rock and great marbled beasts were swimming through the earth above him, all teeth and spiked, granite fins. Now he saw they'd been replaced by wooden beams carved with dancing animals.

'I should've known this would happen,' said a flat voice. 'Guess we pushed ourselves too far, your brains didn't get enough oxygen and decided to take a vacation.'

Graham's face hove into view. 'You really should've told me about this before,' he said, Richard's box of pills in his hand. 'This is serious stuff.' He gave Richard a concerned look. 'How're you feeling?'

'Like I'm going to be sick.'

'Not to worry. Mrs Indergand has supplied the necessaries.'

Graham brought forth a plastic bucket from under the bed. Richard was about to speak when his stomach heaved.

Graham glanced down at the contents of the bucket. 'Bloody hell, this looks worse than I thought.'

'It's fine,' gasped Richard. 'Just a spot of tummy trouble.'

'Seriously, mate, this doesn't look good. Should I call your editor?'

'No!' Richard's eyes snapped open. 'No, I'm fine. I feel better already.'

'If you say so,' said Graham. 'I'll get rid of this.' He removed the sloshing receptacle, but hesitated by the door. 'You're sure you're ok?'

Richard nodded and pulled himself upright. 'Sure,' he lied. 'It's just nausea from the altitude. It'll pass in a minute.'

Graham remained by the door. 'You'd tell me if something was up, right? One friend to another?'

Richard took a deep breath, and managed a smile. 'Really, I'm fine.'

Graham nodded and, after only a moment's hesitation, closed the door.

Richard sat on the edge of the bed, breathing slowly. He shut his eyes to stop the spinning but the images he'd witnessed on the high plateau flashed before him so vividly that he opened them again.

His hands were balled up into fists. Richard thought he felt something in his right. Opening it, he discovered a number of long, dark hairs that definitely weren't his own.

Richard stared at them for a second. Just before the panic hit he forced himself to lay back and breathe slowly.

His eyes came to rest on the picture of the whiskered mountaineer hanging above Graham's bed. Richard noted once again the strange light in his eyes.

Like many people, Richard heard voices in his head. These are presumably the descendants of those instinctive urges that lived within prehistoric man, blessed with a modern education and dressed in a format we can more readily understand.

Richard found that he got the most out of these voices by projecting them onto various objects in his immediate vicinity.* His thoughts would occasionally get a bit jumbled up and he preferred to deal with them in the form of a conversation.

'I think I'm holding bear hair,' he whispered.

Did he detect a faint trace of mockery in the mountaineer's grizzled face?

Why are you talking to me? Your friend was here a moment ago, yet you told him nothing.

'He wouldn't have believed me,' said Richard, too dizzy to wonder why he was addressing an empty room. 'He'd think it was nonsense brought on by the fit.'

Yet you saw what you saw. There's no denying that.

'Isn't there?' Richard murmured, wincing as a fresh wave of nausea washed over him. 'I've had episodes before but not like this.'

He breathed slowly until the queasiness passed. 'Maybe it was the altitude. But then why didn't it happen to Graham?'

The mountaineer's pale eyes were enigmatic.

The high plateau affects different people in different ways.

Richard lay back and squeezed the patchwork coverlet. Its reassuring softness helped to calm his nerves.

'I wonder if you ever saw something like what I saw today,' he asked aloud of the picture. 'Come to that, I wonder if I really did.'

The room quivered slightly. He closed his eyes again. 'I'm always seeing things that aren't there; I used to go to the doctor about it. People would sometimes go fuzzy, things would blur into each other. It just never seemed this real before.'

Does is it still seem real, now your head has cleared?

Yes, thought Richard. Clear as day. He didn't say the words out loud, but the man in the picture heard them all the same.

Strange place, the high plateau.

---

* This is not as strange as it sounds. People have been doing this for ages. In fact, scripture makes a lot more sense when you remember that most of those claiming to hear the voice of the Lord coming from a gorse bush were malnourished proto-literary shepherds who spent their days standing around in the sun.

Richard tried sitting up again. The dizziness was passing and he began to feel better. He got to his feet. The room wobbled a bit but the worst seemed to be over.

Despite the warmth of the building he felt strangely cold. He reached for his coat and opened the door. The creak of the hinges was reassuring. With a final intake a breath he stepped onto the landing.

Bonk.

Ow. That felt real enough.

Rubbing his head where he'd hit the beam, Richard headed downstairs.

*****

The Gasthaus Meierhof's young waiter Dino had been well trained. He was currently away from hotel school on placement and though he'd hoped for somewhere slightly more exciting than Niderälpli—Monaco, for instance—he nonetheless enjoyed the scenery and viewed it as a chance to hone his people skills. Clad in an impeccable white shirt and black waistcoat he transported a bottle through the air in that special way that announces to the room that one lucky diner has managed to choose, from a host of inferior beverages, the only one in the building worthy of consumption. He sailed between the tables and around an incredibly old woman in a wheelchair by the fire, arriving by the corner where Graham and Richard sat. Since the latter was too busy staring into the flames to pay him any mind Dino directed his attentions towards the former.

Graham inspected the label, nodded, and accepted a splash of the stuff in his glass. This he observed appreciatively, sniffed, and sipped before dabbing his chin with his napkin. He inhaled, allowing the heady aroma to permeate his senses and, leaning over to Richard, announced gravely:

'It's wine.'

He then invited Dino to go away and leave the bottle behind. Dino did so, drawing a wide circle around the old woman in the wheelchair as he passed.

Graham chuckled. 'See her? They tell me her name's Frau Hürlimann. Been here absolute ages. They're all terrified of her.'

He poured out the wine and glanced at his companion. Richard's symptoms had passed but he'd hardly said a word all evening and showed no interest in the glass that his friend slid across to him.

Graham frowned. 'If this is any indication of what the rest of our stay is going to be like, our mountain adventure risks becoming an extremely dull affair, mate.'

Richard started; he'd become absorbed in the flames. He turned to see his friend contemplating him disapprovingly over the rim of a fast-emptying glass.

Richard ran his fingers through his hair. How could he describe the experience, the sheer bewildering weirdness of what he'd seen? It sounded too ridiculous.

'Sorry, I've still not completely gotten over what happened this afternoon.'

Graham was trying to catch the eye of an attractive young woman in well-fitting hiking gear a few tables away. 'No worries. I checked with Frau Indergand—discreetly, mind—and there's a doctor in the village in case you need one. Can't have you flopping around like a beached mackerel when we're hunting bears!'

He laughed rather louder than necessary and grinned in the girl's direction, but she took no notice. Graham burped quietly in frustration.

All through dinner Richard failed to mention what he'd seen, only returning to the subject once the bottle was long since emptied and Graham was halfway through his sorbet.

'Graham,' he began, 'have you ever hallucinated?'

'Wot?' Clearly this conversation was secondary to the task of studying the girl at the other table.

'I said, have you ever hallucinated? You know, seen things that were too strange or fantastic to be true?'

'Tell you what's too fantastic to be true: that girl's calf muscles.' Graham had consumed most of the wine by himself and was beginning to lean to one side like a melting snowman. 'Hey, why d'you reckon they make these dessert spoons so long? S'downright Freudian if you ask me.'

Richard fell silent. It was useless talking to Graham when he was like this. But maybe it would be even harder to broach the topic the next morning, when the vividness had worn off. Even now he had trouble believing it himself.

Richard's thoughts drifted upstairs to his room. He'd put the dark hairs in a sample bag and stashed them in the closet until he decided what to do with them. He wondered if they'd even be there when he returned. He half hoped they wouldn't be.

There was a noise from one side. Looking over Richard saw Frau Hürlimann in her wheelchair. She was poking the carpet with her cane, apparently trying to cause as much damage as possible.

She stopped abruptly and looked up at Richard. One eye had collapsed entirely into the folds of her face, but the other observed him with an icy blue stare. She growled like a Doberman on a chain.

Richard looked away quickly. Suddenly he had a considerable appetite. He even indulged that voice on the fringes of his brain insisting that no meal is complete without at least one dessert, much to Graham's delight.

THE ORCHARD
CHAPTER SEVEN

WITZERLAND'S FARM ANIMALS are among the most sure-footed of all domesticated creatures, and the most docile. And so would you be, were your native habitat about as flat as the side of an erect tent. While their wild cousins the chamois and the ibex favour a brand of reckless athleticism that borders on the suicidal, the various household quadrupeds of the Alps have embraced a more measured approach to life. Dairy cows in particular have knees that don't work when descending anything steeper than a wheelchair ramp, a predicament to which a Zen-like tranquillity of mind is a logical evolutionary response.

By the time Richard and Graham arrived in Niderälpli, most local animals had been herded into barns, awaiting transportation to lower altitudes before the oncoming winter. The day after Richard's seizure, the only four-legged representative still in evidence—apart from Suzy, Berlioz, and a kennel of sled dogs behind the hotel—was a rather bored-looking goat.

This particular specimen was currently harbouring considerable resentment towards his human hosts. Goats are social animals; solitude makes them moody. He didn't understand why he'd been singled out when all his goat companions had been relocated to sunnier pastures. The kind of vegetation that grows at altitude rarely gets around to developing much in the way of flavour and the mouthful of mulch he'd been chewing for the last half hour wasn't improving his mood.

Graham exited the hotel. The goat regarded his preparations with disinterest. Glancing around, he noted the complete absence of entertainment and lamented the downturn in his standard of living brought on by the cold weather. Then, for no other reason than that he was a goat, he burped deliciously. This made him feel slightly better, but not much.

A cloud of morning vapour trailed after Graham as he paced to and fro outside the hotel. Richard soon joined him.

'You look better than last night,' Graham observed.

'Fresh air helps.' Richard looked around. 'Our guide's not here yet?'

'Nope.'

Richard stretched. 'I reckon I might go for a turn, over there maybe.' He gestured up the road at the white boarded-up structure overlooking the village.

Graham shrugged. 'Suit yourself. I'll beep the horn when Kaspar gets here.'

He watched Richard go and popped a mint into his mouth. A bell tinkled to one side. He turned to find a small brown goat watching him from behind a wooden fence. Graham cocked his head and sidled over for a chat.

'Hullo,' he said cheerfully. 'Nice day!'

The goat flared its nostrils, presumably—thought Graham—in greeting, and spat a cud onto the ground.

'You know what would make this even better?' The goat's oblong pupils begged for illumination. 'A cigarette! First thing in the morning, all this fresh air . . . Perfect time for it. Sadly, I've given up. Bad for you and all that.'

Graham leant against the fence, allowing the goat to shove its nose into the folds of his jacket in search of the minty smell he exuded.

'Life is full of hardships, my fluffy friend. If it weren't for the small pleasures we dream up for ourselves, it would be bleak indeed.'

The goat paused in its attempts to remove the mints from Graham's pocket and met his downcast eyes with a look that aroused in Graham feelings of charity and brotherhood. He popped a mint onto his palm, which the goat quickly gobbled up.

'Alas!' continued Graham, 'life is a treacherous old cove. No sooner have you discovered the grace of one of its little escapes than this blessing turns around and deals you a grotesque and agonising death!'

The goat did not respond, its mouth being full of minty goodness.

'For example,' continued Graham, 'take these mints.'

His interlocutor was only too happy to oblige.

'Yes, we're taught that mint's healthy. Toothpaste, Tagines, Mojitos . . . All perfectly proper indulgences for the modern field biologist.' Graham turned darkly towards his chomping companion. 'But how much sugar do they stuff these with to make all that mint palatable, hm? How soon until the occasional minty sweetie does irreparable damage and, looking down in the bathroom one day, I find my nether regions irrevocably disfigured by the ravages of my glucose-related excesses?'

The goat's only response was to break wind spectacularly.

Graham looked on approvingly as the animal made short work of his remaining sweets. 'I admire your hedonistic opportunism, Mr Goat. I shall call you Jerome.'

While Graham was congratulating himself on making a new friend, Richard reached the fork in the road. This time he turned right, towards the shuttered building.

The once elegant driveway was now overgrown with weeds. The building's blank windows seemed to observe him as he approached. Up close Richard saw that the white paint was peeling and the wood had begun to rot, its bygone glory overtaken by decay following years of abandonment.

The gently sloping drive brought him to the foot of a wide wooden staircase. This rose to meet the end of a long veranda-like promenade, level with the first floor and lined with many elegant doors, all boarded shut. Richard put his eye to a crack and peered through the dirty glass, but saw only darkness inside.

He walked along the promenade, one hand on the balustrade. Every few paces there were iron posts set with lamp fixtures, all broken or missing, with only the metal frame where the bright bulbs had once been.

Below him the ground sloped out from under the building into a pasture. A fence bordered the property edge, beyond which Richard could make out the hotel, their bright red car, and a lanky floppy-haired specimen that could only be Graham.

The bannister fell away abruptly beneath Richard's hand. He'd walked the length of the building and reached the end of the promenade. Here was another staircase, mirroring that on the opposite side. It descended onto a quiet, verdant space enclosed by the rock of the mountain on one side and hidden from view by tall firs on the other. Vegetation grew unimpeded, hinting at an overgrown garden or orchard. In one corner Richard could see stones fallen from the wall of the cliff. From the far end came the sound of a bubbling brook.

He descended the steps and strolled amongst the trees, following the sound of water. He soon reached the far end, where the earth fell away beneath the roots of the firs into a steep incline. Nothing but a white wooden fence prevented one from tumbling all the way down to the torrent that raced past on its way into the village.

Richard turned back and was retracing his steps along the green avenue when he noticed something. The stones in the far corner were not fallen pieces of the cliff, as he'd supposed, but headstones. Engraved names and dates materialised from under the moss and lichens, most barely legible after decades of neglect. Half of the orchard was, in fact, a graveyard and, though many of the headstones were hidden amongst the weeds, Richard now saw that they outnumbered the trees.

He'd just made up his mind to leave when a flash of yellow caught his eye.

Next to the fence bordering the meadow was a small sapling, its slender branches stretched out like fingers. On one branch fluttered something the colour of straw. Upon closer inspection Richard discovered it to be a wide-brimmed hat with a golden ribbon tied to it.

He looked at it in confusion: he knew nothing about hats, but he doubted if such a thing could have been fashionable anytime in the last fifty years. And yet it was in good condition, if not exactly new. He picked it off the branch to examine it more closely.

'Excuse me,' called a clear voice, 'I think that belongs to me.'

At the top of the stairs leading down from the promenade stood a woman in a pale yellow dress. She waved and descended the steps.

She moved with an economy of movement that could have been called poise had it not also hinted at some hidden fragility. Her auburn hair was tied in a loose bun. With every step it threatened to come undone and she was constantly tucking strands behind her ear. She was the same young woman Richard had glimpsed in the shadowy alley the day before. As then, she carried a book in one hand.

'Thanks ever so much,' she said when she reached him. 'I wondered where it had got to.' She sounded slightly out of breath as though she'd been hurrying, but there was no flush in her cheeks. Her eyes were brown, but of such a light shade they appeared almost amber.

Richard handed her the hat. 'No worries. You from the UK?'

She replaced the hat, glancing sideways at him from under the brim. 'Pardon?'

'My friend and I are over from London, for work. You from England?'

'I thought so!' she said. 'I overheard you speaking yesterday in the village. I was quite curious to meet you. My name's Eloise, but everyone calls me Ellie.'

'Nice to meet you. I'm Richard Mathern.' She seemed amiable enough. 'Nice costume,' he ventured.

'Thank you!' she smiled. 'I always think one must dress appropriately for the mountains, don't you?'

'Um, sure.'

Richard felt a bit scruffy in his weatherproof jacket and hiking boots. He guessed Ellie must belong to some rich family holidaying in the Alps. That would explain her speech, which sounded to Richard somewhat old-fashioned and over-pronounced.

'Isn't the air here fresh?' she exclaimed. 'My doctor told me it's excellent for the lungs. I've had trouble with my breathing, you know.'

'Sorry to hear that.' Richard assumed an air of sympathetic gallantry.

'Nothing like mountain air for weak lungs,' she continued. 'I'm on a diet too, mostly fruit and vegetables and the occasional bowl of oats with some dried apple on top. The doctors say it will help me get better. It is tiresome though. God knows I long for a roast on Sundays! Boiled cabbage and steamed carrots don't go far when you're famished. But the water! Have you tried the water? It's simply heavenly; so cool it's better than lemonade on a hot day and so clear you can drink it from the spring itself!'

Ellie paused, quite out of breath. She pressed a hand to her chest and steadied herself on the wooden railing. Richard hesitated.

'Are you all right?'

She breathed deeply a few times, then smiled at him.

'Better every day! I haven't spoken that much in a long time and the doctor told me not to exert myself. It's just so nice to meet someone from home!'

Richard found this whole exchange unnerving. The young woman had a way of looking at him with an intensity that made him suspect that she saw more than most. Also—and this became increasingly clear as she moved about—there was something distinctly odd about her, though he couldn't be certain exactly what it was.

'How long have you been in Niderälpli?' he asked.

'Ages,' she answered, facing away from him.

'Going back anytime soon?'

'Oh, I don't expect so.'

He circled around so he could see her face again. 'An extended stay, then?'

'Hmm.' Ellie glanced around her with a vague smile. She seemed to be evading the question.

'When did you decide to stay?'

She thought for a moment, and for the first time her smile wavered. She tilted her head to one side, her forehead creased.

'I . . . I can't seem to remember.'

She looked away across the village. Most of the valley was still shady but the sun had touched the mountain's snowy ridge. It shone like a crown on an ivory head.

'I suppose I just stayed. How funny, I don't remember deciding one way or the other.' She looked back at him in cheerful puzzlement.

Before he could speak she laughed.

'And why not? What a beautiful place, don't you think? It's so magical, and the air so wonderfully fresh! Isn't it wonderful, Mr Mathern?'

Grasping the wooden railing, she closed her eyes and inhaled deeply. As she did the breeze caught her loose auburn hair and teased it out behind her neck, interweaving the trailing ribbon with the thick strands it failed to contain.

'It's lovely,' Richard admitted.

There was something about her eyes . . .

From the hotel came the blare of a car horn, three times in quick succession. Richard glanced over his shoulder. 'That'll be my friend. We're going hiking.'

'What a wonderful idea! Make sure you visit the spring. I hear it's beautiful.'

'Have you ever been there yourself?' asked Richard.

For the second time, a shadow passed over her face. 'No. I never did manage the trip. I wanted to ever so much, but the doctor wouldn't allow it until my health improved. The water is heavenly though. They bring it to me in bottles, clear as the sky.'

Richard still felt an inexplicable sense of unease. He edged towards the stairs. 'I'd better go, they're waiting for me.'

'Of course, I shan't detain you.' She hesitated, as though unsure of her words. 'There aren't many people here from back home and I'd love to speak further. Will you visit again?'

Richard was keen to get away and happy to make promises he didn't intend to keep. 'Sure. Where are you staying?'

'Here.'

Richard looked at the boarded-up building incredulously. 'This place?'

'It's not what it once was, true. But someone has to look after it.'

The horn beeped again. Richard made for the stairs leading to the promenade. 'Well,' he called, 'see you round I guess.'

She watched him go. 'You will come back?'

Richard put his hand on the bannister. 'Sure. Anytime you like.'

There was something strange in the look she gave him, as though she could see straight through him.

'Promise?'

Richard paused halfway up the stairs and flashed her a grin. 'I promise.'

She beamed and waved goodbye, as though she were the happiest creature on earth. 'In that case, I shall expect you anon, Mr Mathern!'

Holding her hat to her head with one hand so it wouldn't blow away again, she skipped back into the orchard grove and disappeared amongst the trees like a mirage in the sunlight.

Richard stood where she'd left him, until Graham's horn broke the spell. He covered the last of the stairs and ran back to the car.

Graham had begun to tire of Jerome's conversation and his mints were history. He glanced at his watch. How much would it cost to get a fancy timepiece while he was in Switzerland? He was just about to get his phone out and check local retailers when Kaspar finally arrived. Graham had beeped the horn as promised and he now watched Richard making his way down the path, running like hell.

Good, thought Graham. It's unbecoming for a man to be late.

'Well, Jerry,' he said, 'looks like this is goodbye. Don't forget to write.' He crumpled the packet and stuffed it in his pocket as he walked away, leaving Jerome to begin a rather interesting hallucinatory experience with strong minty themes.

Richard sidled up. 'Sorry, I . . . got distracted.'

'Anything interesting up at the old house?' Graham asked.

'Nope. Ran into some girl who looks after the place, but it's falling to bits.' Richard avoided Graham's eye and busied himself with his rucksack. He tried to ignore the sounds of Kaspar stretching over by the fence, a mix of grunts interspersed with the occasional creak from his antique joints.

He observed the corner of the package sticking out of Graham's pocket and pointed at it in accusation. 'You weren't feeding that goat sweets, were you?'

'What am I, an idiot?' Graham swung his rucksack onto his back. 'Let's go.'

Richard hesitated.

'Something wrong?'

'I don't know,' said Richard. 'I'm feeling a bit light-headed.'

'Must be the excitement. Got your meds handy?'

'It's not that. I'm fine. It's just . . .' Richard hesitated, not wanting to mention the woman in the orchard. 'I'm not sure I'm ready for all this.'

'Ha!' laughed Graham. 'Rubbish. Was Caesar ready for the Gauls? Was Nelson ready for Trafalgar?'

'If I remember my history lessons he'd had a lifetime in the navy and about six weeks to plan for it. We've had barely two.'

'More than enough.' Graham put his hand on Richard's shoulder. 'Remember what you said the night we arrived? This is a great opportunity! A beast waits for us and we're going to find it. We are embarking on a great expedition. We may be carrying cameras instead of rifles or harpoons, but make no mistake: we are hunters; we are whalers; we are lion tamers! It can't hide from us. Also, we have biscuits. *Ándale!'*

With that he started up the trail. Kaspar followed and, despite Graham's enthusiasm, quickly overtook him.

Richard glanced up at the white building. There was no sign of the woman.

He took a deep breath and followed his two companions up the track.

THE FUGITIVES
CHAPTER EIGHT

The Eastern Road to Agaunum, 286 A.D.

WO YOUNG MEN wended their way across the mountainside. The master walked in front, glancing often at the heavy sky overhead and back at his slave. They moved furtively and with military swiftness amongst the jagged boulders.

Upon reaching the forest they stopped to rest. The slave dropped his heavy pack at the foot of a tree and sat down to catch his breath.

His master gestured for the water gourd, all the while keeping his eyes on the horizon.

'Master Aulius?' asked the slave.

Aulius drank before answering. 'What?'

'Is it too late to go back to the legion?'

'Yes, Olipor.'

'Wouldn't they be glad to have us back,' asked Olipor, 'as we've been missing?'

Aulius glowered at the question. 'No, they would not. We would be punished most grievously.'

The slave was silent for a while.

'What would happen to us if we went back?' he eventually asked.

'We'd be crucified as deserters, Oli.'

The slave thought about this.

'Are we deserters?'

Aulius sighed. Olipor was a simpleton, the result of a difficult birth. Though strong in body and reliable with simple tasks, his mind couldn't handle the strain of letters, numbers, allegory, or sarcasm. He had a talent for observation, a skill somewhat undermined by his tendency to talk about things that weren't there as though they were and his capacity to overlook important details—or so his master considered them—that were right in front of him. Aulius would've gotten rid of him long ago except that his

66

mother back home in Ravenna refused to send him money for a replacement, claiming the new ones just didn't work as well.

'Yes, Olipor. We're deserters. If we're caught we'll be treated as such. But that would be better than being captured by the Heathen.'

'What would happen then?'

The master gave his servant a grim look. 'They would torture us, dispatch us in the most horrible fashion they could think of and, having wrought on our bodies such hideous transformation that even Jupiter himself couldn't recognise us, they'd dump our corpses in the river.'

Aulius wiped the moisture from his lip and scrutinised the jagged horizon. The earth reared up around them, bristling with dark firs and an infinity of cracks and crevasses, each of which might contain an enemy.

They found themselves at the foot of a particularly dark and foreboding ridge. Olipor pointed across the slope. 'It looks like there's a path down there, Master. Surely that would be an easier route than through the trees?'

Aulius shook his head. 'Too dangerous, we must stay away from the road. And don't talk so loud. Sound carries across the valley and we don't want to bring those hairy savages down on us.'

Olipor looked upwards as though expecting a vengeful host of Celts to gallop out of the cloudbanks towering above them. 'Since we're not soldiers anymore,' he mused, 'wouldn't they let us pass safely?'

'Don't be daft. If they found us now they'd still kill us.'

'Why?'

'Because soldiers or not, we're still Romans. Leastways I am. Don't know what they'd do with you. Probably sacrifice you to their hideous blue-eyed moon gods or whatever the hell they do to pass the time. Here,' he added, 'put this somewhere safe.'

Oli took the gourd. 'Was it them who burned the house of Magistrate Verenus?'

Aulius shrugged. 'Probably. Stands to reason, judging by the state of him. Dirty business, and not one we're going to worry about now.'

'What about the others?' persisted Olipor.

'They're not our concern anymore.'

The word *desertion* clanged in Aulius' head like a bell. Then he remembered the bodies of his comrades lying on the cold ground thirty miles west of where he stood. Any man would have done the same.

'Come on,' he snapped. Olipor dutifully rose and shouldered the pack.

The two men travelled fast, covering as much ground as possible. The autumn air was chilly and there was a strong wind coming off the cloud-swathed mountaintops. Aulius refused to descend to easier ground and they remained in the misty forests high above the valley.

The slope steepened. Trees grew crooked in their bed of needles. Below them the forest fell away, opening onto a high cliff and a void beyond. The two men took great care not to stumble, lest they roll down the slope and off the mountain entirely. After struggling up a ridge so steep they were almost on all fours, they emerged onto a lip of bare rock that hung outwards from the cliff and offered a terrifying view of how high they were. They paused on this tiny outcrop.

Olipor glanced upwards towards the treeline. 'If we climbed a bit higher, Master, the going might be easier,' he ventured. 'Trees can't grow there, the way will be clear.'

Aulius was breathing heavily, unused to the thin air. He'd grown up near the sea and didn't like heights. The open space beyond the rocks' edge seemed to exert a horrible pull on him almost as though gravity, like the horizon, was skewed. The wind whistled and whipped through his clothes, as though trying to suck him into the chasm.

'We can't risk being out in the open,' he said. 'We'd be visible against the sky.'

He glared in hostility at the heavens. Then, on a whim, he knelt and stretched out his hands. Olipor recognised this gesture of piety, though his faculties struggled with the concept of Gods and deities.

'Who are you speaking to, Master?'

'I'm praying to Dea Roma to protect us and shield us from our enemies,' said Aulius. 'She will make us invisible and we'll walk unseen across the mountain.'

'Will she appear here? In this wilderness?' Oli had always associated godliness with ceremony and the interiors of the military temples he'd seen. This dark forest didn't seem the sort of place where Dea Roma would be comfortable.

Aulius sighed. 'That's right, Oli,' he said sarcastically. 'Wherever our path leads, the protective shadow of Mother Rome walks with us. Maybe if we're good, she'll ride down in her chariot and carry us into the sky.'

'Really?' Olipor looked around as though Dea Roma might appear over the next ridge.

Aulius didn't bother to respond. Olipor had spoilt things. Whatever pious impulse Aulius may have had was dashed.

The sea of mist had cleared a little. Far below them was a thick forest, becoming leafier and flatter as the slope evened out. Beyond lay the floodplain, its marshes bloated by rain. The river itself was hidden by the dense wilderness that fed off of it, whose tendrils crept across the valley and up the ever-steepening slope to where they stood, surviving even on the barren rock.

Aulius had heard stories of how the barbarians sacrificed their own by strangulation before throwing the bodies into the bog. He turned away from the dullish, grey-green landscape. Olipor, meanwhile, had enveloped himself in his cloak and sat excitedly awaiting the arrival of the Goddess Rome.

'It'll be dark soon,' said Aulius. 'We'll camp here and make the ascent in the morning.'

Olipor didn't think to question the choice of this bleak, windswept location and prepared their meagre campsite as evening fell. After a frugal supper the two men wrapped themselves in their cloaks and waited for dawn.

Aulius found himself thinking of his comrades and his two-day-old desertion: how the legion, dangerously under-equipped for the oncoming winter, had camped on the floodplain; how their officers had failed to organise suitable foraging parties, but commandeered rations for themselves; the harsh discipline and brutal shortages; the subsequent hoarding, the fights and the failed mutiny; the executions; the blood in the river.

Aulius recalled the flight back to his tent as the culling of the mutineers echoed throughout the camp; his orders to Olipor to grab their gear and get the hell out of there and the slave's mute obedience. The memory of their frantic escape through the night still raised his hackles.

He remembered their discovery the following day of the burnt-out house of Verenus, the local official, and the bodies of the magistrate's family. He felt the weight of the silver he'd stolen from its hiding place under the hearthstone, now stashed safely in his pack. He wondered how many of his comrades had escaped, and how many hadn't.

Eventually he fell asleep and dreamt horrible dreams.

Olipor slept soundly, but was woken shortly before dawn by a disturbance in the darkness. He opened his eyes drowsily and looked at his master, enfolded in his woollen cloak. The slave glanced around. To his sleepy gaze the shadows appeared to take the form of a young woman with long hair, flitting silently between the trees. The shadow danced around their camp for a few moments before disappearing into the night.

Olipor closed his eyes and smiled. You were right Master, he thought dreamily; Divine Roma walks with us.

Warmed by this notion the slave fell asleep once more.

Whether in answer to Aulius' prayers or by a stroke of sheer luck, the morning mist had risen again to obscure their ascent. Waves of cloud billowed up like a silent flood, swallowing everything. Soon the men couldn't see beyond a dozen paces. Only the upward rise gave them any sense of direction and they followed it until the ground levelled out.

They came upon a narrow goatherd's track. Despite his reservations, Aulius was forced to follow it, for the mist was so thick that in his blind haste he risked stepping off the mountain altogether. The two fugitives crept along the trail, listening for any sound that might indicate danger.

After several hours they halted at the top of a steep cliff. The trail plunged downward in a series of rocky steps, disappearing into the mist. Aulius wasn't sure he wanted to follow them, so they rested while he decided what to do next. The docile Olipor sat on a stone humming quietly to himself, watching the clouds drift by.

Suddenly the humming stopped. Aulius looked up. Oli had risen and was listening attentively. For a moment Aulius was puzzled, then he heard it too; the faint tap of a shoe on the rocks below, coming up the path towards them.

'Landica!' he spat and dragged Oli behind a rocky knoll. 'I knew we should've kept off the road!' Aulius gripped the hilt of his sword and glowered at the clouds in rebuke.

Oli listened to the approaching steps. 'One man only, Master,' he whispered.

Aulius peered around the rock and beheld a single figure emerging from the mist, labouring up the steep stone steps towards their hiding place. He breathed a sigh of relief.

'It's just a beggar, and an old one by the look of his gait,' he said.

The cloaked figure was barely a dozen steps away now and would discover them soon enough. Aulius made up his mind and tightened his jaw in anticipation. He surged forward onto the path to face the figure.

'Halt, in the name of Rome!' he cried, hand on his sword. 'What is your errand and whither dost thou crawl, o malodorous tramp? Speak!'

The figure paused in its climb. It made no answer save to raise its head, noting the position of the Roman on the ridge.

'I think that's a woman, master,' commented Olipor from behind his rock.

'It is?' said Aulius dubiously. 'How can you be sure?'

'Her arm tattoos,' answered the slave, as though this should be obvious. 'They mark her as a supplicant to the Goddess of Mothers, Virgins, and Healers.'

'I wonder which one she claims to be,' muttered Aulius, before clearing his throat. 'What is your business on Caesar's road, o wretched crone?'

The bent figure lifted its face to get a good look at Aulius. It was indeed that of a woman, though her features were so drawn and dried out by the fierce mountain climate that she appeared much older than her years. Her mouth was firmly set and her grey eyes were hard as she turned them towards the intruder.

Aulius found his resolve wavering under her cold stare.

'Speak, woman! State thy business.'

The woman reached out a bony arm and resumed her climb. Aulius' sword was already half unsheathed but she'd lowered her eyes and kept them firmly on the rocks. She soon drew level with the Roman, walked straight past him, and continued on the path by which the two men had come. If she saw Olipor behind his rock she gave no sign of it and didn't look back. Eventually she disappeared into the fog and the sound of her footsteps receded.

Aulius stood still for a while, listening to make sure that she was gone. He didn't want any witnesses to their passage, but her gaze has paralyzed him and he'd been unable to draw his blade.

'Was she a witch, Master?' whispered Olipor.

Aulius frowned. 'Let's find another way down.'

They continued along the ridge, struggling up and down crags at least as treacherous as the path the old woman had climbed. But Aulius, fearful of pursuit, wanted to cut across the mountainside in search of another valley. The rocks were slippery with moisture and they proceeded cautiously. A stone came loose without warning and Oli slipped a few feet under the weight of his pack before clawing himself to a halt.

'Careful, idiot!' Aulius said. 'If you slip and fall, our food's gone. Would you see me starve before I'm disembowelled by that crone's sons?'

Oli considered this. 'Yes, master. Surely it is better to starve than to be slaughtered?' He ignored his bleeding hands, slashed by the sharp rocks.

Aulius kicked the slave—though not as hard as he wanted to for fear it might send him flying down the mountain once more.

'Get moving and be careful.'

The wind rose and the fog began to clear. The Romans found themselves in a sea of broken rock, a vast moraine of sediment and boulders deposited on the mountainside by a glacier.

Aulius surveyed this new obstacle. The dried-out branches of a stunted tree reached towards him, its roots twisted into the bare rock. All the vegetation had been stripped away by hungry animals, right down to the bark.

The wood was white as the faces of the magistrate's children they'd found in the gardens of his house. Verenus had been left inside and was almost unrecognisable due to the fire. They never found the wife. Aulius had ordered Olipor to move the bodies into the granary where the wolves couldn't get to them and to cover them with sheets.

'Weigh them down with stones,' he'd said, 'so their shades don't walk.' Olipor had done so. Then they looted the house.

Aulius forced those memories aside. He set off across the slew of broken rocks with Olipor following.

They struggled across the moraine until they reached the shadow of an overhang. Scattered patches of greenery hinted at the presence of a rivulet nearby.

'Here.' Aulius tossed the gourd to Olipor. 'See if you can find some water.'

Suddenly he froze. He'd heard the sound of shouting across the moraine.

The last strands of fog were whipped away by the wind. Dark silhouettes appeared on the ridge.

He swore. 'The old hag's betrayed us to the bastard mountain-dwellers!' Why hadn't he killed her? Sorcery, that must be it; she'd deadened his mind with her stare.

Oli trembled, his eyes wide with fright.

'Maybe they haven't seen us,' hissed his master. 'We'll stick to the cliffs until we reach the high plain. They have no reason to search for us there. We'll lose them on the rocks. Let them sound the earth for us; we'll be gone.'

Aulius urged the terrified Oli up the broken slope. They ran, but it soon became clear from the cries that they'd been seen and their enemies, who knew the terrain, were closing the gap.

At last they emerged onto the high plain. The wind tugged at them fiercely as it blew this way and that. Aulius bent over, breathless with exertion. Oli collapsed in a heap, weeping and moaning with fright. The wind carried the angry voices of their pursuers up the slope.

'By the Gods!' Aulius swore. 'For all their height these accursed mountains have not taken us any further from Hades.'

He scanned the desolate plateau and spotted some uneven terrain that might disguise their flight.

'Come, Oli!'

Aulius was the faster runner and Oli fell behind. The slave was weighed down by his heavy pack but it never occurred to him to drop it.

'Oli!' Aulius barked, glancing over his shoulder to see where the slave had gone.

The next moment the ground opened up and Aulius fell through the earth, landing with a splash in a current of running water.

The icy stream engulfed him. He gasped as it soaked his clothes. He'd fallen through a rift, the work of the torrent flowing from the glacier high above. The crevasse was only a few feet deep, barely wide enough for a man—so narrow in fact that Olipor, disorientated and confused by the sudden disappearance of his master, missed it entirely.

'Master!' he cried, 'Master!'

Aulius heard the piteous calls and tried to stand up in the narrow space. He struggled and was about to call out to Olipor for help.

He hesitated.

The torrent raged in his ears and around his midriff. Some of the cold must have entered his heart for when Olipor cried out again, very near to where his master was hidden, Aulius didn't answer. Instead he sunk deeper into the water and hid beneath the weeds that overhung his hiding place.

The shouts of the pursuing war party grew louder. Crouching low in the icy stream, back braced against the rock, Aulius could almost feel the stamping of their boots on the turf. He heard the cries of his slave as they seized him, and winced at the sound of the beating Oli received as he struggled. Aulius pushed himself further into the shadows.

Eventually the grunts ceased and there was only the strange, angular language of the enemy. Aulius lay mute at the bottom of the crevasse, water up to his nose, listening to the argument—presumably over his whereabouts. His heart stopped when he heard the sound of feet crashing through the water upstream, but no one spotted the Roman in the narrow cleft of water.

Eventually the sounds grew fainter. The warriors moved on, presumably taking Olipor with them.

The rushing torrent covered the sound of their retreat. Aulius waited a long time to make sure they'd departed. When he judged the coast was clear he tried to stand, but the current had numbed his legs and he collapsed back into the freezing water with a splash. He swore and pulled himself upright.

A subtle change in the air drew his gaze upwards.

He barely had time to see the figure standing over the crevasse above him—the dark outline of a black-haired head, the flash of an axe at its belt—before a blow to the temple wiped the consciousness from him and he was knocked senseless back into the water.

He floated in the current for a moment until a booted foot was lowered onto his face and he was pushed under the surface for a long, long time.

THE OBSERVATION HUT
CHAPTER NINE

ICHARD CAME DOWNSTAIRS to find Frau Indergand arranging a fresh seasonal display at the front desk. He approached with trepidation, his hostess having made a memorable first impression the night of his arrival the previous week. But Frau Indergand was much recovered from the incident and welcomed Richard with radiant benevolence.

'*Grüezi,* Herr Mathern! Everything is satisfactory, yes?'

'Er, hi. Yes, everything's fine, thanks.'

Richard was halfway into a nonchalant lean against the countertop when he noticed the can of wood polish, the soiled rag, and Frau Indergand's flaring nostrils reflected in its mirror-like surface. He straightened up and put his hands in his pockets.

'You are enjoying the mountains?' she asked, returning to her polishing.

'Oh yes, very nice. Actually there's something . . .'

'You come to *Désalpe?*'

'Excuse me?'

'It is every year the day when the cows, they go down to the valley for the winter. In the village there is a big party. You come on Saturday, you will enjoy.'

'Sounds awesome.' Richard had more pressing things to address than bovine-related entertainment. 'Incidentally, I was wondering if you had any information on hiking shacks, hunting lodges, observation platforms, that sort of thing. Graham and I aren't having much luck in daytime, so we're planning a night-shoot.'

One might forgive Frau Indergand for a momentary lack of understanding. Her trade was hospitality, not natural science, and she made a point not to scrutinise her guests' activities. Her father had been a hunter though and, while she didn't indulge in the sport herself, she considered it a healthy and natural pursuit—provided the proper permits were obtained. Furthermore she knew that two Englishmen had arrived with heavy bags of equipment and were asking where all the big animals were. The distinction between wildlife photographer and big game hunter was not as obvious to Frau Indergand as it might have been.

'You are shooting in the night?' she inquired, setting aside her rag.

Richard nodded. 'Yep. Do you know of a location we could use, a hunting lodge, perhaps?'

Frau Indergand frowned. 'You excuse me, but . . . you have permits from the commune?'

'Oh yes,' answered Richard, glad he'd gone to the trouble of getting them. 'They're upstairs if you'd like to see them.'

Frau Indergand wondered how she might temper this disaster without overstepping herself. Nocturnal gunfire is never an attractive proposition to holidaying families. The least she could do was inspect the weapons. As an experienced armourer she might persuade them not to use too large a calibre.

'You have,' she sought the correct word, *'waffen?'*

'Excuse me?'

'For the shoot, you have *waffen?'*

Richard couldn't help but wonder why she was offering him waffles. Funnily enough, he was feeling rather peckish.

'Ooh, lovely. Do you have some for Graham as well?'

Frau Indergand stared. What sort of hunter doesn't bring his own firearm? Still, too late now. She'd offered, after all.

She ducked below the desk and reappeared a moment later, brandishing a hunting rifle. Richard leaped backwards, knocking over the bottle of polish.

'For the shooting,' she explained, hefting the sinister-looking weapon.

Richard collected himself. 'I think there's been a slight misunderstanding . . .'

At this point the door opened and a rather singular figure entered the hallway.

At first glance the new arrival resembled a collection of woollen blankets and leather belts that had observed the representatives of mankind strutting about, liked the idea, and syndicated into a hominoid-shaped arrangement such that they too might enjoy the benefits of bipedal living. On closer inspection, Richard saw that underneath this outlandish exterior lurked a person, bearded and bespectacled, wearing at least two heavy woollen overcoats and swathed in satchels, side-sacks, and shoulder bags of all sizes. The man hesitated in the doorway, evidently thrown by the presence of a stranger.

Frau Indergand greeted him and beckoned him forward. He advanced, eyeing Richard suspiciously from under his cap. Seemingly unimpressed, he turned away and addressed the proprietor in a gravely baritone.

She attempted an introduction. 'This is Herr Fosco, *und das hier ist unser junger Naturwissenschaftler aus England.*' She followed this with a broken explanation of Fosco's occupation, which Richard missed entirely: he was still recovering from the thought that he might be shot through the head over waffles.

Fosco grunted, reached into one of his bags, and produced two large and very dead birds, which he swung onto the counter by the necks with a *thump*.

Readiness in the face of the unexpected is an important quality in any seasoned traveller. Nonetheless, this sudden and unannounced arrival of death following so closely upon the incident with the hunting rifle would turn even the most robust of stomachs just a little. Richard paled visibly.

Frau Indergand took Fosco's delivery in her stride and began to inspect the animals with small noises of appreciation. Their overcoated owner noticed Richard's discomfiture.

'Hmph,' explained the man, gesturing at the feathered corpses.

'Ah!' exclaimed Richard. That seemed to resolve the matter.

Frau Indergand counted out some money from the till, the cheerful singsong of her conversation punctuated by occasional grunts from the bearded man.

'I am telling Fosco of the night-shooting. He says it is to rain tonight.'

'I think we'll be fine,' Richard answered, smiling at the woollen man's predictions. His mobile app reliably informed him that the following twenty-four hours would remain clear. Besides, he reflected, country folk always obsess over the weather. They dwell on the seasonal comings and goings of rain for the same reason that the man whose job it is to put out traffic cones on the motorway dwells on automobiles: they loom large in the priorities of his universe.

Fosco grunted. He exchanged a few brief words with Frau Indergand then left.

She smiled at Richard. 'Herr Fosco he is saying there is a cabin that no one is using. I will show you on the map.'

*****

A half hour later Richard found Graham in the square under the arcade and told him the good news. Graham's mind, however, was elsewhere.

'Her name's Melanie.'

Richard glanced up from the map. 'Who?'

'The girl from the pub, you idiot. Her name's Melanie.'

76

'I'm trying to show you where the cabin is.'

'And I'm telling you about the future mother of my children. Which do you think is more important?'

'The cabin. I'll be up there alone tonight. If something goes wrong I don't want the helicopter circling endlessly in the dark because you forgot where it is.'

'You'll be fine. Point is, while you're freezing your arse off I'm going to be enjoying a romantic dinner with the woman of my dreams.'

'Have you actually asked her out yet?'

'On my way now, good as done.'

'I'll believe it when I see it.'

'Must you forever play the part of the erratic blowtorch in the paper factory of my dreams? Some support would be nice once in a while.'

Graham turned serious for a moment. 'You sure about this?'

'About what?' Richard folded away the map.

'I know we agreed that you'd take the first shift—cheers by the way—but you had that spell on our first day and, well . . . You'll be all right, won't you?'

Richard smiled. 'Not to worry, I'll take my meds this time. We've got the radios. If I'm feeling at all queasy, I'll just call.'

Graham nodded his head as if to say *if you say so,* then spotted Melanie at the end of the main street.

'Just don't forget to turn the radio on—'

Richard could tell Graham had stopped listening. Graham had developed a particular style of walking designed to exhibit the majority of his rowing muscles to best effect. The trouble was that the key to rowing is in the legs and if someone wants to show off *all* their sporting muscles they must walk in a manner not entirely unlike the exotic birds Richard had studied in biology class. He leaned against the cold stone of the arcade and concluded that the birds had the edge.

Richard was observing Graham's manoeuvring from afar when something peeled away from the wall behind him and blew in his ear. He started so suddenly he completed a full turn and had to orbit back a few degrees to face the entity responsible.

'Hi!'

It was Ellie, the woman from the orchard. She wore the same yellow dress as before and looked extremely pleased to see him.

'Hullo,' muttered Richard, less than delighted. He'd hoped for an opportunity to brief Graham on his meeting with Ellie and to bring him along next time he visited the orchard. He hadn't expected to encounter her again quite so soon.

'How's the hiking coming along?' She examined his equipment bags with interest. 'And whatever is wrong with your friend?' she added, peering around the column at Graham, who was faking nonchalance by the fountain.

Richard sighed. 'He's flirting. I'm afraid he's not as good at it as he thinks he is.'

Graham attempted to lean against the fountain but his hand slipped and his arm disappeared into the water up to his elbow.

Ellie shook her head. 'Sad, isn't it? Love makes fools of us all.'

Melanie and her friends had noticed Graham. He attempted to hide his sodden sleeve by pretending to inspect a shop window, which turned out to be full of lingerie. He swivelled back and found himself near enough to engage Melanie in conversation. She politely ignored his dripping sleeve. Her friends tittered from a distance.

Richard looked away out of loyalty. 'I'm doing a night shoot tonight,' he said to change the subject. 'We've commandeered an old cabin up the mountain. We're hoping to get some good shots of the bear.'

Ellie raised an eyebrow. 'An old cabin?'

'Yep. Little wooden thing, been there for ages, apparently.'

The group of girls passed by the arcade, but took no notice of Richard or Ellie.

'You mean the little goat shed south of the moraine?'

Richard tried to remember the map. 'I guess so. Why?'

Ellie seemed reluctant to say more. Just then a Graham-shaped shadow loomed on the far wall.

'Success!' exclaimed Graham, wringing out his sleeve with his free hand and grinning at Richard. 'Operation Smooth Seduction is on. C'mon, I need to change my shirt.'

Graham skipped away before doubling back. 'Well, what're you waiting for?'

Richard looked pointedly at Graham, then at Ellie, then back at Graham, waiting for a reaction. Ellie stood with her arms crossed, a resigned look on her face.

'Well?' Richard said, 'don't you want say hello?'

Graham looked confused. 'To what, the wall?'

Richard stared at him. He was about to apologise to Ellie when she shook her head and held a finger to her lips. 'Don't bother,' she said, 'he can't see me.'

Graham narrowed his eyes and peered at Richard. 'Not having another attack, are you? I thought you said you'd be fine.'

It was clear that, although Ellie stood in plain sight and within a few feet of him, Graham couldn't see her at all.

There was a sudden chill in Richard's stomach. He tried to compose himself. 'Nope, I'm fine. Never better.'

Had he been standing anywhere other than the relative obscurity of the arcade, and had Graham not just come in from the sunny square, Richard's look of panic might have given him away. As it was, Graham had other things on his mind and missed the tension in Richard's voice.

'Good. Let's go back to the hotel.' Graham set off across the square.

Richard turned back to Ellie, standing in the shadows.

'I'm dreadfully sorry.' She suddenly appeared very self-conscious. 'I'm afraid I've approached the subject in a somewhat roundabout way. It's not an easy topic to broach, particularly on first acquaintance.'

The cold in Richard's stomach solidified, dropping like a ball of lead.

'You're . . . You're not . . .' he mumbled, searching for the appropriate word.

'No,' she agreed anxiously, 'I'm not. If you have a moment I can explain . . .'

Richard was already high-tailing it across the square. He chanced a glance over his shoulder. Ellie was watching him, a look of concern on her face.

This spurred him on to even greater speeds and he reached the Gasthaus Meierhof well before Graham.

*****

Back at the hotel both men were alone with their thoughts. Graham danced in and out of the bathroom while Richard exiled himself to the armchair in the corner and pretended to do some work while dodging the seeds of panic floating around inside his head.

Graham hadn't seen Ellie in the arcade. That was certain. He'd taken no more notice of her than he would a measurement of air.

How was that possible? She was standing right there. There's no way he could have missed her. Yet he clearly had. What's more, she'd known he would.

This was not satisfactory.

Richard felt the chill in his stomach again and knew it had nothing to do with the altitude. Strange thoughts began to creep up and down in his mind, whispering things he didn't want to hear.

Graham broke into song in the bathroom and Richard was dragged back to the present with a sickening lurch. He shut the door and returned to his armchair, feeling foolish.

There must be a perfectly rational explanation. Graham had been standing in the sun; the arcade was dark. The stone column might have been in the way . . . Graham must not have heard him properly . . . Yes, that was it.

By the time Graham emerged from the bathroom, Richard had convinced himself not only that everything was fine but also that it would be silly even to mention it. So he didn't.

As the afternoon waned they headed downstairs, their rucksacks heavy with surveillance equipment. Together they set off up the mountain, following the route Kaspar had shown them. They'd made the trip several times now and knew the way.

Graham hummed to himself. Richard was silent.

High above the valley they discovered their destination: a lopsided wooden hut built on a slanting meadow overlooking a vast prospect of wilderness. Its walls were dried and cracked by decades of exposure to the elements and its roof sagged under its rough slate tiles. It looked like it hadn't been used in years.

The door stuck under the wooden beam but eventually gave way. The inside was a stoic affair, a single room with bare walls and a dusty floor. An iron stove sat on a base of flagstones, a simple stool stood in the corner, and a wooden bench lined one side of the room. A flying beam overhead sported a number of pegs and hooks that must have once held harnesses or tools.

'Here's your Hilton,' said Graham. Richard looked around. The hike had temporarily pushed his worries out of his mind and he fought to keep them there.

'The situation looks good,' mused Richard, his gaze lingering on the line of rusty hooks in the beam. 'I reckon no one's been here for a while; the animals must be used to it by now. We won't even have to camouflage it.'

'Good thing too,' said Graham, 'we haven't got nearly enough leaf netting for the outside.'

'We have leaf netting?' asked Richard.

'Don't we?'

'Never mind.'

The bag misplaced at the airport was still missing, but they had enough equipment to get started. Richard discovered he was unable both to worry and work efficiently and the task at hand soon pushed other concerns out of the way.

Together he and Graham set up their three motion-sensitive cameras in a rough triangulation covering the approaches to the area. There was a brief delay while they argued over which lenses were preferable in low lighting—*Nature Review*'s inventory combined Tom's excessive verbiage with Alan's obtuse approximations to create an exceedingly complicated bit of reading—but the technical manuals soon resolved the issue. They returned to the hut to install Richard's observation post and camping chair behind a broken window, through which the camera and the thermal scope could poke. They disguised it all with a tarpaulin, which also plugged the gap in the broken glass, protecting Richard from the chill. When everything was in place, they piled the empty equipment bags in a corner.

The daylight was fading. Graham had to return to the village to avoid getting caught in the dark.

'Ok, bro,' he said, 'looks like you're all set. See you tomorrow!'

'Hang on,' said Richard, 'aren't you going to wish me good luck?'

'Er, ok, good luck. May you take many very bear-y pictures. Also, may you always walk in sunshine and live with laughter. Now if you'll excuse me, I've got a date.'

Richard watched him lope down the track, whistling a carefree tune. Eventually the bobbing Graham-shaped homunculus disappeared below the horizon and the sun dipped behind the mountains.

Richard was alone.

He retreated into the hut, bolted the door to stop draughts, and took up his position behind the camera. Soon the western sky exploded into reds and ochres, the mountains dark against the glow. Richard watched this celestial fire subside into purple and pink ash clouds until the last golden gleams faded and the flush on the snowy peaks turned a dusky grey. Before long these pale silhouettes melted away into the shadows and not even the mountainside on which he sat could be identified from the surrounding darkness. Night had well and truly fallen.

The first hour or two were not a joy for Richard, whose earlier confidence had fled with the light. The scene in the square played over and over again in his mind and brought him to a worrying conclusion: there was no way Graham could have missed Ellie. She was standing right there. And she'd known that he wouldn't see her.

Richard pondered the implications.

The moon rose until it was high above the landscape and the features of the alpine horizon could be made out by its soft incandescence. Richard felt strangely reassured by its presence. As it hung in the sky in its familiar way he observed the scene before him in fascination. He remembered why he was there and an excited shiver ran up his spine. He'd had been hoping for work like this for ages and the thrill of actually being behind a camera cheered him up no end. Before long he forgot about Ellie and became engrossed in his nocturnal vigil, his thermos of hot tea by his side.

The grasses rustled in the breeze outside as the moon meandered across the pitch-black sky. Ever so often the hut would brace itself against the shifting wind, creaking as it readjusted. Occasionally a particularly strong gust broke on the outside with a *wumpf* and Richard would hear it pass over and around him like a wave. Occasionally there would be a low moan from the chimney pipe as the air passed over it, like breath over the top of a bottle.

Richard glanced at his watch. It was nearly midnight.

Ooh, he thought to himself: the Witching Hour, when the dead awake.

The image of Ellie's piercing stare and drifting walk reappeared in his mind for the first time since the moon had risen. He shuddered; this entire affair carried with it the promise of psychological trauma. Best not to think about it.

He counted down the seconds until the hour changed and one day became the next. He put his eye to the thermal scope and scanned the grey-toned nightscape. Nothing moved. He strained to hear the church bells down in the village sounding the hour, but the only noise was the gentle swish of foliage outside.

So much for witches.

Richard settled down once more to his vigil. Slowly raking across the horizon with his scope, he whispered mock radio transmissions like he'd seen in sniper films. Thus he passed the next couple of hours.

The wind picked up. The beams groaned as it pushed and pulled at the little cabin. A few stray weeds tapped at the window. Richard needed fresh entertainment. He remembered a book he'd enjoyed as a boy where all the objects in the room spoke and said goodnight to each other. He tried to remember how it went.

Tic tic tic goes the clock on the wall
Drip goes the cracked copper gutter
Snore snore snore goes the dog in the hall
Squeak goes the old wooden shutter

Richard frowned as he pressed his eyebrows against the rim of the camera. What was the next bit again? Ah yes.

Tinkledy tink goes the loose windowpane
Cricklety crack goes the ceiling
Swishy swish swish go the leaves in the lane
Bong go the chapel bells pealing

He couldn't recall the rest. He scanned the horizon, wrestling boredom. His recollections had distracted him for a while though, so he continued the game using the sounds around him.

Creak creak creak go the old wooden beams
Whoosh goes the wind in the trees

The hut's too high for any actual trees, thought Richard, but decided to allow himself the artistic license. What rhymes with "beams"?

Splish splash sploosh go the watery streams

Hell yeah, they hadn't named him Poet-Laureate of the Under-12s at St Gertrude's for nothing.

Creak creak creak go the old wooden beams
Whoosh goes the wind in the trees
Splish splash sploosh go the watery streams
Whoosh goes the cold midnight breeze

He'd used "whoosh" twice, but he could fix that in post-production. He continued to compose his rhyme as the hour slid towards half past two.

Yum yum yum goes the sandwich on the bed
Lookety look goes the science man
Boring-dy bored goes the brain in his head

'Baaaaah,' went the goat sitting on the bench behind him.

Pixely grey goes the night-vision scan

Hang on a minute.

Richard turned slowly, his hands still on the thermal scope. The hut was shrouded in darkness, but the shadows appeared to have changed shape since he'd last looked in their direction.

He withdrew the torch from his pocket and snapped it on.

On the previously empty bench lining the wall behind him there now sat a girl, flanked on either side by a goat.

The animals stared back at Richard with looks full of enigmatic judgments. The girl's eyes were lowered. Her hair hung limp and straight, her clothes little more than rags. Her arms were worryingly thin, her feet bare. Her posture was strange, like that of a broken doll—the listless attitude of a simpleton, or a trauma victim.

Richard's first thought was *how did she get here without any shoes?* His second was *how did she get in here without opening the door?*

The girl looked up. She might have been pretty had it not been for her emaciated state and the hollowness of her eyes. She gazed at Richard in a piercing way that reminded him uncannily of Ellie. He began to suspect things, his mind rushing back to places he'd been avoiding all day.

This won't do, he decided.

He was about to speak, but the girl raised a bony finger to her lips. Richard's questions caught in his throat. The girl eyed the torch with a disturbed look, as though she wished he would turn it off. One of the goats bleated again and she put her hand over its mouth, holding it shut. Richard continued to stare.

There was a gentle tap on the roof, followed by another, then several in quick succession. Finally, as the man Fosco had predicted that morning, it began to rain.

Richard made to speak again. The girl shook her head earnestly, her wide eyes urging silence. Richard sat, uncomprehending, wondering what to do.

A moment or two passed, broken only by the steady patter of rain. There was a slight *click*, as though the windowpanes had adjusted to a shift in the wind.

Then Richard heard it: softly at first, obscured by the rain, then louder—the sound of breathing at the door.

There was a light tap on the old wood, as though from a fingernail—or a claw.

The tap became a scratching noise, then a sort of scrabbling. Something was trying to force its way under the doorframe.

Richard stared at the door, then at the girl. She shook her head resignedly and let go of the goat's mouth. It waggled its head and cleared its throat with a mild 'Baaah'.

The scrabbling ceased. For a moment there was only rain.

What happened next was unlike anything Richard had ever experienced.

Something smashed onto the outside of the hut like a train. But the wooden timbers didn't register the impact at all. The air quivered, the shadows writhed, but the hut itself was entirely unaffected. It was like a shock wave at the edge of the material world, one that the fabric of consciousness felt but the senses ignored. The house refused to answer with anything but the mildest of creaks, but the impact made the halls of Richard's mind shudder.

Richard glowered at the girl. This was an unsettling time for him and, at the risk of being ungentlemanly, he blamed her for current events.

If it gets in, her eyes warned, *there's nothing we can do.*

Richard's ears popped as whatever was outside launched itself against the door once again. The silent shock of it rattled his thoughts. The air around him seemed to bend and thrash for an instant before jumping back into place.

That did it.

Richard fumbled for the radio and flicked on the transmitter. 'Graham! There's something trying to get into the cabin, it sounds big but I can't . . .'

There was a great *WUMPF*. This time, the hut groaned under the all-too real force of the blow. A pinch of dust was shaken from the beams and trickled onto Richard's jacket.

'Graham!' shouted Richard into the radio, 'I'm not joking, this is very, very bad. Something's out there. Can you hear me? Say something, dammit!'

Graham didn't answer. He'd forgotten to turn the radio on.

Richard dropped the handset and looked around the room. There were no other exits. He was trapped.

It crashed into the hut again. The falling dust formed a grey snowfall in the light of Richard's torch.

The girl gazed back at him with haunted, hunted eyes. They exchanged a look; one steady and resigned, the other on the verge of panic. Neither spoke.

Then she began to sing.

Her song was slow and soft, the kind one might sing when no one was listening. The goats' furry flanks rose and fell as they snuffled at each other. One even laid its head on the ground and closed its eyes.

Richard watched with incredulity. How could they sleep?

For want of anything better to do, he closed his own eyes and covered his head with his hands.

He didn't recognize the language of the song. The words were indistinct and tentative, but the tune was steady. The soft syllables pattered about in Richard's ears alongside the rain and somehow began to drown out the horror at the door, melting into him like a balm.

He tried to open his eyes but couldn't. He rested his head on the straw next to the goats and no longer heard the creaking beams or the pounding from outside. All around him was a watery stillness and the only sound that lived within it was the song, like a ribbon of sunshine piercing the darkness of a lake and glimmering in the depths.

*****

Richard awoke before he knew he'd fallen asleep.

He jumped up. The girl and the goats had disappeared. The earliest rays of morning streaked across the sky. All was quiet.

It wasn't until the grey dawn transformed into an explosive sunrise that Richard dared to open the door. He circled the hut, examining the damp timbers and muddy ground. The earth was undisturbed, the wooden walls untouched.

Richard re-entered the room and scoured every inch of it from wall to wall, examining his own clothes, the furniture, and the equipment bags. He found not a single trace of goat hair, a scrap of ragged cloth, or footprints of any kind.

*****

Graham heard the hotel room door closing and pulled *Crime &*
Punishment off his face.

'You're back,' he mumbled. 'Anything interesting happen last night?'

'No. Nothing at all.'

Graham grunted, turned over and went back to sleep. Richard threw
down his bags, undressed, showered, got into bed, and failed to get any
sleep at all.

DÉSALPE
CHAPTER TEN

I T WAS NEARING a quarter past nine in the morning when a cab pulled up outside No. 31 Dratford Place and a sprightly man in his mid-eighties stepped out. His once immaculate grey suit was wrinkled and stained, his silk tie gone. He looked like he'd been partying for days, but his face was wreathed in smiles and he moved with the easy stride of a man on the jovial side of sobriety.

'Thank you, driver. How much do I owe you?'

The cabbie hadn't enjoyed this ride one bit. He preferred his customers to look more presentable this early on a Friday morning. He also preferred them to open the door when entering his cab, rather than simply drifting through it.

'No charge, guv,' he replied and sped off in a screeching haze of tire smoke.

The grey man gave a cheerful wave as the cab careened around the bend, before turning and making for the building's entrance.

The doorman didn't appear to notice him so he slipped in behind a distressed posse of paralegals whose commutes had all been ruined by the same cancelled train. He traversed the lobby with the confident air of a man who knew where he was going, though wherever he went he failed to attract any attention whatsoever. The security gates slid open for him, as did the door marked "Authorised Personnel Only". The grey man rounded a corner and arrived in the private entrance hall that gave onto the rear driveway, guarded by the ever-watchful Allerby.

'Morning, Allerby!' he called. Allerby remained unresponsive.

Pity, thought the grey man, and pressed the button for the lift.

Bing.

Allerby looked up in surprise and watched the doors slide apart. The empty lift sat there for a moment or two before the doors closed again.

Allerby frowned. Bloody machine was acting up again. So much for all those new-fangled keypads they installed last year. Cost a fortune too.

He shook his head and returned to his book.

The grey man emerged from the lift upstairs and found himself on a familiar carpeted landing. He smiled as the deputy head secretary Alice appeared with an armful of files. She walked straight past him, sat down at her desk and, with a little sigh, began to leaf through the documents.

'Nice to see you, Alice,' he said gently. She gave no sign that she'd heard.

The open door revealed Dawes' office to be empty, but the grey man spotted a telltale overcoat and scarf on the wall hinting at the owner's imminent return.

Never mind, thought the grey man. I have time.

He strode into the office and settled in one of the comfortable chairs by the window. Eventually Alice closed the door and he basked in luxurious privacy.

He waited over three hours for Dawes to appear.

At twenty-one minutes past twelve Dawes stepped out of the elevator. He was greeted by the sight of his young employer hovering near enough to Alice that she had already begun to reach for the letter-opener.

'Good afternoon, sir.'

Luther looked up. 'Ah, just the man! I was asking Alice when you usually arrive for work. You must have had quite an evening! What was it, too much brandy at the club with the ol' whist team?'

He guffawed and leered at Alice. She in turn eyeballed his jugular and hefted the letter-opener.

'I arrived at half past seven, sir,' answered Dawes wearily. 'I've spent the morning going over some soundings from the financial department. If you'll permit me, I'll elaborate further.' He gestured to his office. Aberfinchley, with a final wink at Alice, brushed past.

'He's no chip off the old block, Mr Dawes,' hissed Alice. 'You wouldn't believe the things he said! I swear if he tries it on with me again I'll . . . I'll . . .'

Dawes placed a reassuring hand on her shoulder. 'Not to worry, Alice, I assure you it won't happen again.'

She sniffed, in a manner hinting that her dismissal was of the object and not the sentiment. 'I wish I could believe you, Mr Dawes. But as long as that man is in the building, nothing is safe.'

'Dawes!' came Luther's voice from the padded sofa beyond the doorway, 'what the hell are you doing? Leave the girl alone. You're too old for her! Ahahahahaha.'

Dawes straightened and removed his hand. 'Carry on, Alice. We mustn't shirk our responsibilities, regardless of circumstances.'

She did so, but not without a rabid look of betrayal at Dawes' back.

Luther had found some mints and lay on the couch attempting to sink them into an ornamental vase on the shelf across the room. Dawes closed the door. 'So Dawesy-Warsey, good news you say?'

Dawes watched a mint ricochet off the vase with a *ping*.

'Indeed. Our lawyers have prepared a convincing argument that the oil spill was not due to the condition of the boat or the sobriety of the captain, but the topography of the coastline itself. The local government hasn't commissioned any geological surveys in over forty years, so there are no up-to-date maps of local reefs or navigational hazards. This is a major risk factor in areas with marked effluents such as the Omboka Delta, which lies several miles north of the accident site. Since no reliable data or navigational markers were available, there can be no reasonable blame.'

Ping. 'Doesn't that mean that the government's responsible?'

'Murumbwanian law does not recognise the phenomenon of erosion. Doing so would mean acknowledging that East Murumbwana—like the rest of Planet Earth—is gradually being drained into the sea through its rivers, thereby negating the local dogma that the size and shape of the country is a physical constant set out by divine will. There can therefore be no change in topography due to deposits in the delta, by law. Our solicitors will argue that the wreck was subsequently an act of God.'

'Wicked. And well done you for compiling that list of environmental projects for us to flood with cash. Wasn't it pathetic how pleased they were?' *Ping.*

Dawes flinched as a mint percussed off a rare and valuable lithograph he'd purchased at Sotheby's, causing it to collapse onto his small collection of conches.

'There is, however, another matter we must address,' said Dawes, somewhat louder than he'd intended.

'Ah, you're alluding to the tragic lack of hot young women on our staff. Incidentally, would you care to swap Alice for Julian? He seems to hate me and I have no idea why.' *Ping.*

'Such a swap would be impractical, sir. Alice is well-acquainted with my ways and Julian is second to none in terms of diligence, efficiency, and loyalty.'

'Spoilsport.'

'I was referring to your recent expansion plans,' continued Dawes. 'It's causing some bad feeling in certain departments.'

'How so?'

'Well, your last email suggests you intend to digitalise the entire seventh floor.'

'Aha, you allude to "Operation Totes Amazeballs"! It would cut costs massively and save lots of hassle. Everyone there is a massive pain in the arse.'

'The seventh floor is where our Human Resource Management staff are housed, sir, and includes some of our oldest and most qualified employees.'

'Precisely!' *Ping.* 'They cost a fortune and look like they died in the Fire of London but nobody told them, so they kept coming to work. Much better to sack the lot and relocate all but the most vital functions elsewhere.'

'And where might that be, sir?'

'My mate Binky's start-up in Dalston, of course. They deal in exactly this sort of thing. Their model's brilliant: they take care of hiring, firing, performance appraisals, complaints, etc. By outsourcing to a proxy we save money, we can set more ambitious quotas, and we put a handy buffer between the employees and us. Everyone's happy!'

Luther flung another mint and succeeded in knocking over a framed photograph of Dawes' late wife. 'Whoops.'

Dawes stiffened. His eyebrows came together much as a line of cavalry might before a particularly nasty charge.

'I don't think that would be wise.'

Luther paused mid aim and turned to Dawes with a look of surprise. 'No?'

Dawes cleared his throat. 'No. In fact, I believe that would be very unwise and not at all in keeping with our vision as a company.'

In the ensuing silence the oxygen in the room did its best to escape through the ventilation system but was thwarted by the minutely calibrated air conditioning units concealed about the place with the aim of creating an atmosphere of perfect stillness.

'Well, Dawes,' said Luther icily, 'perhaps it's time for a change of course in this company. It's stuffy, Dawes. The place is stagnating.'

'Shall I adjust the air conditioning?'

'Metaphorically, Dawes, metaphorically! It's time for a shake-up. We need to reach out to untapped demographics, develop fresh ways of thinking, and explore new avenues of possibility. I have my own vision for this company and I suspect that you're not going to like many of my ideas.'

He swivelled on the sofa to face Dawes. 'Therefore,' he continued, 'I would like you to remember that I am the majority shareholder and it is I who decides what direction we are to take. And,' he added with a smile not many degrees off a sneer, '*your* job—while you have one—is to assist in realizing that vision. Is that clear?'

If the furniture could move, it would have thrown itself from the windows. As it was, it merely quivered on a sub-atomic level.

When Dawes finally answered, it was in a neutral and professional tone of voice.

'Of course . . . sir.'

Instantly Luther was all smiles and the tension lifted like dust from a beaten carpet. 'Excellent! I knew you'd see things my way. Daddy always said you were a proper chum.' Luther tossed the last mint into his mouth and rose from the sofa.

As he drew level with Dawes, he leant over.

'And do take time to consider giving me Alice. I'm sure the girl's ambitious and she's much more likely to be considered for promotion if she works directly for me. Besides, she's not really your type, is she?'

Dawes could smell mint on the young man's hot breath.

'I'll take it up with Personnel, sir.'

Luther gave him a tight-lipped smile and slid the mint around in his cheek. 'Good man.'

Luther's cologne lingered long after he'd left the room.

The office fell quiet. Dawes moved to one of the armchairs by the window. There he sat, contemplating the city before him. Then, slowly but implacably, his face began to change. The mask of servile courtesy he wore slipped gradually off and was replaced with something much more human, and much more ugly. It settled into a contortion of absolute, hideous loathing, such as only the faces of corporate patricians can produce in their most private moments.

There was a discreet noise behind him. Alice stood politely in the doorway, awaiting instructions. She scanned the back of Dawes' head for information, but it remained inscrutable. When at last he stood and turned to face her, his appearance was serene and composed.

'Come in, Alice. Let's address the remaining business of the day.'

Alice stepped through the door, though for reasons she couldn't have explained she lingered a moment or two before closing it. She scolded herself silently and shook her head to wake herself up.

The grey man heard the door click behind him. He was already marching purposefully down the hallway with a worried look on his face. He hadn't liked what he'd witnessed in that office one bit and intended to get to the bottom of this business.

He made for the head office like a shark following a trail of blood. The tread of his shoes made no sound that anyone could hear, save the portraits on the wall. They watched him pass and smiled, recognising an old friend.

*****

Richard's mind was a mess of troubled thoughts. He'd slept little. His ordeal in the observation hut had haunted him into the waking hours the following day. Besides, he still didn't know what to make of the woman in the yellow dress—he avoided the word "ghost" whenever he thought of her for the sake of sanity. Also, he couldn't explain why the Gasthaus Meierhof's downstairs lavatory featured a stained glass window. Who puts stained glass windows in a toilet?!

Richard pulled the chain and watched the water swirl around. He took a deep breath before exiting.

Graham was halfway through his second pint of the afternoon when Richard appeared at his elbow.

'Where've you been?' asked Graham. 'This bland, metallic, characterless Lager isn't going to drink itself. Happy *Désalpe*, by the way.'

'Got caught up,' answered Richard vaguely. He glanced around the room with a troubled look that Graham entirely missed, as he was busy filling his head with fluid.

'Seems quiet in here,' continued Richard. Graham mistook the relief in his voice for exasperation.

'Au contraire, mein Herr. Not ten minutes ago, Suzy the dog farted so loudly the car alarm went off outside. People are still talking about it.' Graham lowered his drink. 'Actually the place was heaving until a minute ago. Everyone's gone outside to see the parade.'

Richard turned back towards the bar. His face burned as though he were blushing. He reckoned it must be windburn—that, or the frustration of another day without results.

He glanced at Graham, slumped over the bar counter. 'You're not looking too cheery. Guess things didn't go too well with the local girl.'

Graham motioned towards an empty stool. 'Melanie had to leave early,' he grumbled. 'Said she had lots of work to do today.'

'What, no kiss, no cheeky footsies under the table?'

'Bugger all. She's somewhere outside now, running about with cows.'

'Bummer.'

'Never mind, let's get some drinks in.'

As if by magic, a muscular man materialised before them so abruptly that Richard leaned back on his barstool.

'HIYA!' shouted the bartender.

Richard immediately wished he were somewhere else. The man wore a shirt that attempted—rather jarringly—to marry the wearer's rugby loyalties and associated lilac chevrons with an astonishing backdrop of pink. Amongst the florid tattoos on his arm Richard could read the name

DARCIE and under a spiky crown of bleached hair he sported the self-satisfied grin of a man who has grown up in Walthamstow—and escaped.*

'What'll it be, gents?'

Graham leaned across. 'Two double absinthes, mate.'

'Right-o.'

Richard watched in mild horror as two glasses materialised on the sticky bar top followed by a reptile-green bottle that screamed *life-shattering hangover*.

Graham gestured across the drinks. 'This is Dave.' There was a distant whoop from Dave, who'd moved down the bar towards the till.

'I see. English?'

'Uh-huh, skiing monitor in the wintertime. Works here when there's no snow. Runs a small accountancy business on the side.'

'How do you know that?'

'Where do you think I was while you had your head inside Mrs Indergand's bucket last weekend? Besides, it always pays to know the barman. Might get drinks for half price!'

---

* The tradition of young Englishmen finding their way to Switzerland dates at least as far back as the early 1800s. The first few, spurred on by a combination of bad nature poetry and the inevitable death wish that came from living in a Victorian metropolis, devised the wheeze of paying cowherds to guide them to the top of the largest local rock so they could admire the view. Following these hazardous ascents it was customary to celebrate the fact that they had entirely failed to die by emptying the nearest inn of any alcohol and/or unmarried daughters currently housed within. Thus, they simultaneously launched the Swiss tourist industry and forever altered the course of the European "Grand Tour", beginning its evolution from the original horse-and-carriage jaunt around the cultural centres of France and Italy to the present-day concept of the "Gap year"; a rail-powered pub crawl masquerading as a language research trip.

These intrepid—though often short-lived—mountaineers were followed by a number of poets and writers, who had either been thrown out of society for having too much naughty fun with each other or caused such destruction to their health through opium abuse that their doctors' only remaining prescription was a monastic alpine retreat and a diet of mineral water, oatmeal, and fresh air. Unbeknownst to the doctors, the members of this second group were routinely met upon their arrival at the station by friendly representatives of the first, and the subsequent treatment of absinthe, orgies, and melted cheese often did more for their health than contemporary medicine would have thought possible.

Perhaps unsurprisingly, more than a few of these pioneers of tourism accrued debts. So as not to alarm the folks back home in Blighty, it became customary to make arrangements with choice local banks who wouldn't inquire into why young Hereward was now living at the Hotel du Lac instead of with dear old Mr & Mrs Diesbach, why he urgently needed to borrow seventeen pounds eleven shillings and sixpence for "French lessons", and who the hell was this "Madame de Sozzle" anyhow.

A receipt was placed before them. While Graham dealt with the mental consequences of a bill that can only be described as not half-price at all, Richard had a moment to himself.

He thought about his night in the observation hut and his encounter with Ellie. He hadn't breathed a word of either to Graham. Come to think of it, he hadn't mentioned the details of what he saw during his seizure either and he had a nagging suspicion that they hadn't been entirely hallucinatory. He wanted to tell someone, but the mood of the bar and the presence of Dave gave Richard pause.

He had, however, sent his enigmatic handful of hair back to London for testing. Depending on what answer came back, well, that would be something.

Over by the fire Herr Indergand was entertaining some guests and their children with stories. He explained how, in the golden days of yore, the rivers flowed with milk. Butter could be squeezed from the rocks, he said, and great orchards of pears and grapes covered the slopes. He explained how these great riches attracted the attention of the giants who descended on the valleys and carried off their bounty to secret hoards in the highest parts of the mountains. The Almighty was furious and caused great lightning storms and earthquakes that killed the giants but also shook all the trees and grass from the tops of the Alps, which remain bare and rocky to this day. Occasionally, Herr Indergand whispered, a hiker would find great bones amongst the rocks, proof that giants had once lived there.

He then proceeded to growl at the children as a giant might. They screamed and giggled until Frau Indergand told him to stop acting so childish and to fetch a fresh keg of beer from the cellar. There was a yelp as someone got too close to Frau Hürlimann's wheelchair and was rewarded by a poke from her stick.

Richard watched the children squirm in delicious terror. The image of the ghostly girl from the hut rose unbidden to his mind. He remembered the creaking of the beams in the wind, the cooing noises she made to her goats as she mothered them, the hideous sounds of whatever had been trying to get in . . . he shuddered.

He remembered the fleeting glances of Ellie in the orchard, though his mind warned him they were best forgotten. Did he believe he'd seen her at all? Did he believe he'd seen any of it?

'So,' said Graham, 'how was your morning?'

Richard looked up, his reverie broken. 'I've been thinking about angels.'

Graham nodded. 'So you've noticed too.'

Richard's pulse jumped. 'Noticed what?'

Graham leaned in conspiratorially. 'I think Melanie fancies me.'

Richard brushed this aside. 'No, I mean actual angels. Well, not real ones, obviously. I was just thinking about them, you know, conceptually.'

'Some profound insights come to you on the mountain?'

'Just wondering. Say, hypothetically, that some people's souls stayed on earth after they died?'

'Like ghosts, you mean?'

'Yeah. What's to differentiate them from angels? As far as we know, they might have all the power and will we traditionally associate with the divine. Maybe there's a crossroads which metaphysics and religion haven't quite got covered.'

Graham raised his eyebrows. 'Only you would bring up metaphysics in a Swiss pub when there's drink to be had. Fine then, I'm game. Let's talk ghosts. What's our central topic?'

'Death.'

'Heavy. Mind if I continue drinking while we discuss the aforementioned?'

'Not at all.'

'Ta.'

Graham drank. 'Ok, shoot. Opening quandary? I'm assuming the introduction will just be a summary of the contents.'

'Is there life after death.'

Graham nodded. 'Good choice: scholarly, invokes the worlds of both natural and metaphysical philosophy, and has no practical application whatsoever—prime essay material.'

'Well,' urged Richard, 'what do you think?'

'No one knows. Anyone who tells you different is either a liar or a fool.'

'But,' countered Richard, 'what if, hypothetically, we could speak to someone who is actually dead?'

'Allowing that everyone who claims they can speak to the dead is, likewise, a liar or a fool, that would be an unprecedented avenue of exploration. But,' Graham added, 'even in this scenario of yours, what's to say that the ghost knows? More people die than become ghosts; otherwise they'd be everywhere. So you couldn't be both a ghost and fully dead.'

Richard thought for a while. 'What if,' he suggested 'we all become ghosts, but the degree to which we can be perceived is a variable, in most cases so minute that as far as everyone else is concerned, we're not there at all?'

'The ability to sense but not be sensed?' Graham grimaced. 'That's not much of an afterlife. I think most people would go mad.' He pulled on his pint. 'Next paragraph.'

Richard dragged himself out of his thoughts. 'Ok, how about this: in the event that there is an afterlife, do we feel passion after death?'

'Hm, not bad. Here's a counter-hypothesis: maybe we feel everything but. Aha!'

'All right, let's be more general. We always assume that death is the end of perception. What if it isn't?'

'Nasty thought, considering what happens to one's body.'

'True. But perhaps, death being the separation of soul and body, the afterlife is merely a different sort of perception; an immaterial kind.'

Graham shrugged. 'We can't know the immaterial. We are matter, we can't understand that which is not matter.'

'What if the afterlife is true matter, and what we think of as being is only one of Plato's shadow allegories? What if "real" life is merely convalescence and the afterlife was real being? Not in some paradise or in the sight of some god, but here on earth?'

'To what end? Life's goal is to reproduce and thrive. The dead, presumably, have other priorities. Life, therefore, must end with death. What comes afterwards is something else. You know, I've never understood the fascination with the afterlife. Seems a pretty morbid way to escape the realities—good or bad—of life, the stuff that constitutes living itself. There are as many heavens as there are people. It's like they're trying to escape into a fantasy. What's the light at the end of the tunnel if not a metaphor for escape from the darkness?'

Richard pondered this. 'Maybe it's understanding. And, having understood, we don't need to worry anymore. Worry is often just as bad as suffering the thing you're worried about.'

'Worry has saved as much as it's destroyed,' Graham pointed out. 'I doubt Van Gogh would have painted much if he'd never been hungry.'

'But what if complete understanding meant we never felt anything at all?'

'Then we'd be observers. Human feeling makes us participants in the game of life. Someone who didn't feel couldn't really live.'

'What about someone who was dead?'

'I suppose they might miss the feeling of belonging, whether or not they felt anything themselves. Like I said, though, that in and of itself would be more than enough to make you mad. Now,' Graham concluded, 'before I massacre the rest of this pint and consign it forever to the state of sweet, delicious memory, tell me something: where's this coming from? You've been moody all week. You got something on your mind that you're not telling me?'

Richard thought of all the things he could say. None of them would sound good if spoken aloud. He'd stumbled on something well and truly mad. Talking about it could only cause alarm. How would that affect the project? Not well, he decided. He needed this assignment. He wasn't about to get himself sent home. Part of him felt strangely exhilarated; it was his secret, and he didn't feel like sharing it just yet. Besides, who knew what was out there to be discovered?

'No,' he said with a shrug. 'There's nothing.'

Graham turned away, distracted, and pulled out his smartphone. A moment later Richard felt his own device vibrate in his pocket. He flicked on the screen and discovered a SqueakSpeak message from Alan, his editor.

Bear hair sample examined by forensics, confirmed genuine. Mature adult, sex female determined from nDNA in root.
Do not balls this up.
-Alan

Richard looked up from his phone to find Graham grinning at him.

There was a sudden uproar outside. Graham downed his absinthe and tugged at Richard's sleeve. Together they went out into the hallway and through the front door. Dave and the other drinkers followed close behind.

The cacophony outside was deafening. Along both sides of the street thronged eager tourists, families, and a scattering of village locals who turned up for old time's sake or just for something to do. The sound of bells drowned out everything else. The booths of sweets, alcohol, and bovine-themed souvenirs were temporarily abandoned as the crowds clustered on the pavement and turned their faces up the road.

Down they came. At the front marched a slow column of men, four abreast. They wore traditional short-sleeved coats of black and red, offset by shirts of white linen. Each man had harnessed to his chest an enormous, oversized bell, which hung down over his knee britches. The bells moved rhythmically up and down in unison as they marched, creating an unspeakable din that caused birds to take flight across the entire valley in the certainty that the Apocalypse was nigh.

Behind the men came the herders and the animals themselves. Months of grazing on luxuriant grass and juicy mountain flowers had made the cows fat and sleek and today every animal looked her best. Each wore an enormous headdress of flowers that swayed as she walked. Around each neck hung a bell only slightly smaller than those strapped to the men in front. Dogs scampered at their heels, yapping and barking whenever one of the beasts tried to escape into the welcoming green fields on either side, forcing her back into the crowd of clanging, rearing, snorting beef. The air was filled with the deafening clangour of metal, the lowing of kine, and the wild whooping cries of the herdsmen.

Richard and Graham watched the procession, fingers jammed in their ears.

'QUITE SOMETHING, ISN'T IT?' Richard shouted.

'WHAT?'

'NEVER MIND.'

Richard spotted Kaspar marching alongside a huge brown heiffer coiffed in a garland of white flowers. He waved. Kaspar waved back and yelled indistinctly.

'WHAT?' shouted Richard, but the procession had already moved on towards the village and Kaspar was lost in the crowd.

Now Richard saw Melanie, driving her dogs forward behind the herd. As the last of the animals passed, the audience spilled into the road and followed the procession down to the square, taking Richard and Graham along with it. As they surged along the road Richard glimpsed a figure dressed in yellow standing on the balcony of the sanatorium, looking down at the crowd. He stumbled and was helped to his feet again by Fosco, who brought up the tail end of the official procession. The masses following behind swept Richard along once again. When he next managed to glance back to the sanatorium, the promenade was empty.

Richard looked around him, trying not to tread in anything organic left by the cows, or accidently slam his knee into one of the many children milling about. Graham had disappeared—presumably pursuing Melanie. Richard saw the Indergands arm in arm a few steps behind Ursula, the communal secretary, looking grumpy as ever. Councillors Berger, Fürgler, and Aufdermauer were there as well, arguing over the layout of the festival decorations. Richard even glimpsed of Frau Hürlimann's glowering face as she was pushed along in her wheelchair by Dino the waiter.

There was nothing for it but to ride the surge. Pressed in by the happy multitude, his nostrils full of the smells of beer and animal sweat, Richard let the swell carry him down the street and through the village in the blinding sunlight of the afternoon.

PART TWO
OCTOBER

THE THREE BROTHERS
CHAPTER ELEVEN

The Schächental, 1498 A.D.

ARIA RUSHED DOWNSTAIRS to see her brothers off to war. She stopped short in the kitchen, disappointed.

'Where's your armour? I thought you'd be wearing armour. Who goes to war without armour to protect them?'

Xavier, the eldest brother, picked up his little sister in his knotted arms. 'Armour's heavy, little bunny, and we have many miles to march before we join the unit in Chur. They'll lend us what we need, don't you worry.'

'I want a halberd,' chimed in Heiri, his brother. 'There's nothing better for killing Austrians. That'll teach them to gallivant around on their stinking horses!'

Maria sulked. Xavier lobbed her over to Heiri who ran around the room holding her in the air until she laughed too.

Their mother wrung her apron as her third and youngest son descended the stairs of the creaky wooden farmhouse with three packs crammed with provisions. Afraid he'd see her eyes welling, she wheeled on her husband. He sat in the corner by the fire exchanging meaningful looks with Kai, their great black- and rust-coloured dog.

'I must say,' said the mother in a steady voice that hid her emotion, 'you're very nonchalant about your sons' departure.'

The man shrugged and ruffled the dog's ears. 'You heard them yourself, wife: the Motherland is in peril.'

'A motherland, yes, but not ours!'

'Well someone's is, certainly. One imagines that they've not lost quite everything since they pay so well for soldiers. Perhaps they have not so many sons to spare as we do.'

'Oh, God!' the mother flung herself on her youngest boy. He was not yet sixteen and possessed neither Heiri's enthusiasm nor Xavier's calm self-assurance.

'Furthermore,' continued their father, rising from his stool, 'it's not the first time we've sent sons off to war. Xavier has seen one campaign already and Heiri's travelled a little. God willing, they'll be fine. They might even bring back some nice helmets for us to use as cooking pots.'

He turned to Xavier. 'Can't say I think much of your choice of road, though.'

'I told you, father; there was a landslide on the Glarus road two days ago. Best we cut south past the Gräuelhorn and make our way east from there.'

'Must we send all three, husband?' cried the unhappy mother.

'What, would you have them stay? You've seen how poor the harvest is. Mark me, there's a famine coming. With six mouths to feed, how long before the grain runs out and we start to go hungry? And even if, God willing, we all came through, what then? You know we can only leave the farm to one son. What of the rest? Shall we see them grow old as rag pickers? Shall we abandon them in the woods to grow their fingernails long and howl like wolves? Or shall we send them to the town to become junk men living in the shadow of wealthy merchants? No, let them go and make something of themselves and, in so doing, secure their futures. Perhaps then they shall marry, and have little mercenaries of their own.'

The father came to stand with his sons. Kai sat next to the youngest boy. Kai was his dog and sensed his discomfort, despite the brave show.

'Don't worry Father,' smiled Heiri, 'my sons shall be wealthy men. I'll skewer five Austrian knights and capture another five. With their ransoms I'll buy a house right in the town square!' He leapt up and hung from one of the beams that ran the width of the room, laughing, before dropping back down.

His father nodded. 'In that case your mother and I can look forward to supper at your house on holy days.'

His wife shrieked a rebuke at him, but now her face was buried in her apron and nobody understood what she said.

'Now then,' said the father, standing in front of his sons while Maria circled his legs, one arm hooked behind his knees. 'You all know Xavier is the eldest, so by God's law and man's, all that is mine will go to him when I die.'

The sons dutifully crossed themselves.

'However,' he continued, 'should Xavier fall in battle, the farm will go to Heiri.' At this his wife wailed inconsolably into her apron.

'I shan't be killed, Mother,' said Xavier, 'I know what to do and my friends will protect all three of us.'

'Nonetheless,' broke in their father, annoyed at the interruption—he'd been up late practicing his speech—'if one of you should fall, your inheritance shall pass to the next brother. We are hardy men, so I dare say you may all live. Reflect on this, my two youngest.' He gripped them both by the shoulder. 'I would rather you earn your own futures than pray for the elder to fall in battle.'

The youngest brother's gaze was sombre. 'We could never wish for such a thing, Father.'

Heiri contented himself with elbowing Xavier in the arm and guffawing. Xavier retaliated by punching him in the gut and Heiri's wheezing made Maria laugh again.

Their father decided it was time to wrap things up while he was ahead. 'In any case,' he announced, 'I give to all of you my blessing. May God keep you and return you to us in good time—hopefully in one piece.'

Their mother kissed them all and blessed them as well. As they shouldered their packs Maria became sad. One by one they knelt to embrace her, before ducking under the low doorway. They strode up the dirt track, heading for the pass over the mountains to the town where Xavier's friends were gathering.

Their father watched them go: Heiri speeding ahead, Xavier following more steadily, the youngest lingering at the back with Kai trotting at his heels. They all looked towards the house before disappearing over the ridge, but the youngest looked back most often.

Their father sighed as they passed out of his sight. 'I'll miss that dog,' he told his daughter, who leant against his boot. 'He works harder than my sons. Still, he'll not be parted from the boy. We'll find another, eh?'

He was about to re-enter the house when his wife rushed out with her shawl. 'Here, whither are you running, wife?'

'I'm going to pray. And you're coming with me.'

'Me, what for?'

'For your sons! Perhaps together we may convince the Lord to pity your unborn grandchildren and forget what a miserable grandfather they will have had.'

'What conceivable use would I be?' he protested. 'If prayers are needed I dare say you're better at saying what's to be said, and knowing how to say it. I'd just get in the way. Tell you what: you run along to church and intercede with the Almighty and I'll go gather the hay for the animals.'

'How can you say such things! Our children gone to meet their end at the hands of some stinking foreigners, and you unwilling even to pray for them! You prefer the barn to God's house, I suppose!'

'You pray in your way, dearest, and let me pray in mine. In my experience, the Lord favours those who love their labour and pray on their feet rather than their knees. Let the hayloft be my chapel and the goats my congregation. I'm sure the Creator has seen worse sinners than them. Ha!'

His wife went red but, before she could summon another rebuke, her husband disappeared through the humble doorway and into the house.

Deciding to save her energy for the members of her family who didn't actively seek to aggravate her, she hurried down the dirt track towards the village. She took Maria with her as an afterthought and left her husband forking hay up in the loft, whistling a hymn.

The three brothers walked for many hours, lifting their weight up the track on legs nearly as sturdy as Kai's despite their heavy packs. Up and up led the path alongside great chasms that looked as though giants had gashed them out of the rock with their teeth. They knew the way—at least at first—and revelled in the beginnings of their adventure. The youngest son said little and left the talk of battles to his older brothers. Kai gambolled quite happily up and down the mountain, urging them on as the sun rose higher in the sky.

'Why so quiet, little brother?' cried Heiri. 'Look where we are! See that peak there? Theresa the cobbler's daughter told me a demon lived there once and none dared climb it. So one day the villagers took the strongest calf they had and fed him the best grains and gorged him on the sweetest oats until he grew into a strong white bull. Then they took him up the mountain and he fought the demon and won. Now it's a holy place!'

The younger was silent. Xavier said that they should keep moving.

Together they crested the first pass, then another. The country became unfamiliar, but whenever they reached a high point on the road they looked back and, by the familiar outlines of various peaks, knew their course.

Around midday they stopped to rest in the shadow of a fir tree. Though they hadn't travelled any great distance as the crow flies, there were now many miles of criss-crossing trails and several towering boundaries of stone between them and home. Their tree stood on the border of a pasture on which grazed a few fluffy goats.

'Too bad about the harvest,' said Heiri, his mouth full of cheese. 'I'd have liked some cherries for the journey.'

'Father needs them for distilling,' replied Xavier.

The younger brother chewed his lunch quietly.

An olive-grey blackcap perched on a bush nearby. The youth observed it thoughtfully, his gaze not leaving the little bird even when it flitted away and sailed off into the blue. Kai sat near him, panting in the unseasonal heat.

Xavier stood and looked across the meadow, shielding his eyes from the sun. 'Perhaps that girl has some fruit we could trade for.'

There was indeed a girl sitting in the grass not too far away. Her clothing was poor, threadbare stuff and her hair hung limp from her head. A goat lay in the grass at her side. She gripped the coarse hair on its neck with one thin hand and stroked its head with the other. Although her face was hidden, even from afar she looked thin and malnourished. The younger brother didn't think she's seen bread or cheese all day, much less any fruit.

Xavier called out to her.

The girl spun around like a frightened animal and regarded the brothers with alarm. Xavier hailed her again, but before he could say anything more she took to her heels like a squirrel and raced away from them barefoot down the grassy slope. Her goats took this as a sign that Xavier was bad news and followed, bleating as they went.

Heiri laughed at his brother's surprised face. 'Ha! Well done, Xavier. You've scared her off, you and your ugly face!'

The youngest watched the receding form of the girl, who was still running full tilt down the meadow. She slipped and fell more than once.

'Did you see?' continued Heiri. 'She stared at us like we were Lucifer's hedge warders. Shame. Give her a bath and she wouldn't look half bad.'

Xavier came back to sit in the shade. 'Don't know what I said wrong,' he grumbled. 'I just asked her if she had any fruit.'

Heiri shrugged. 'Probably a simpleton. I hear the folks round here specialise in producing dull-witted children. Theresa says the clever ones are stolen away by Kobolds in the night and they leave potatoes in the crib that grow into stupid people.'

Xavier muttered to himself, offended by the girl's strange behaviour. The youngest was silent.

The brothers soon crossed the ridge that marked the limits of their familiar territory, beyond which the landmarks of their youth were hidden from view. Xavier was calm and composed, while Heiri rejoiced and looked south. The youngest said nothing, but clung to Kai's fur with one hand. They descended the path as it snaked its way amongst the thistles.

Xavier had made the journey before and led them confidently. They reached a tiny rivulet and followed it. It skirted the foot of a long slope that gradually rose into a great white mountain. Heiri said it was surely the home of dragons but Xavier didn't put much store in this.

Eventually the stream led them to the edge of a cliff over whose edge the waters disappeared in a gossamer waterfall. Together the brothers looked down at the fine curtain of water floating onto the rocks below and beheld how the ridge curved around in what was almost a full circle—save for a deep cleft visible in the far side of the bowl—enclosing a sheltered valley thick with trees, alive with the sound of birds.

At this point the youngest brother spoke at last.

'Listen brothers. Xavier, you're the oldest and by right you shall inherit Father's land and livestock. You're a good soldier and surely will return one day to do so. In any case, Heiri has the next claim and I shall still have nothing to my name. Here is a sheltered valley with clear water. Let me stay and I'll build a life as best I can. I've no wish to go to war and would rather settle here.'

Immediately his brothers protested. Xavier scrutinised the enclosed valley, noting its smallness and questioning the quality of the earth. As for Heiri, he wouldn't hear of his little brother missing out on the glories in store for them in the lowland battles.

But the boy's mind was made up. He would go no further.

Eventually they saw this and, embracing him warmly, they blessed him and wished him luck. They agreed that Kai should stay also, but laughed when they saw how he leant on his master's leg: he couldn't have been persuaded to leave anyway. Both promised to pass the same way on their return so as to visit him.

So saying, Xavier and Heiri proceeded across the plateau, away from the ridge and towards the green valleys waiting beyond the horizon.

Xavier soon re-joined his mercenary unit and set out on campaign alongside his companions. He fought in several battles, always choosing his place in the line carefully so as to have trustworthy men at his side. Even so, he was wounded three times and nearly perished at the hands of an Austrian knight on the second occasion. As it was, he only lost an ear, while the man who'd taken it was pulled off his destrier and dispatched before he'd ridden another twelve yards. Eventually Xavier had had enough and, with a sword at his side and money in his pocket, returned home to tend the farm as he'd promised. The sword eventually rusted, but the farm thrived for many years.

Heiri never returned to the village or his Theresa. His dreams of glory ended at the front of a battle line when, having tripped his adversary, Heiri forgot to stay in formation and rushed forward to finish him off. He was caught from behind and fell forward into the dirt. As the battle raged over him his last thoughts were of his mother and how sad she'd been the day he left. He wondered whether perhaps he should have stayed home after all. Then he wondered nothing.

On that day, however, both Xavier and Heiri were full of life. Their younger brother watched them recede down the track, one racing ahead and the other following steadily behind. When he could no longer tell which was which, he turned and began to make his way around the crested ridge surrounding the hidden valley, looking for a way down. Behind him padded Kai, who occasionally stopped to sniff at crevasses where marmots had left their scent. Eventually the boy found something resembling a path and began his descent.

The way was steep. He was often forced to lower his pack—and occasionally the dog—onto the next ledge with a rope. Below he could see a dark shelf where the water collected in pools, and beyond it the soft slope of a wood. At one point the rocks became slippery where the track passed treacherously close to the waterfall. As the ice-cold meltwater drenched him, the boy thanked the saints it was not winter. Kai squirmed and whined at the end of the rope but soon man, dog, and pack all came to land safely at the bottom. After a brief pause they proceeded together into the forest.

The slope evened out and they found themselves at the bottom of the dale, thickly enclosed within the wood. A startled chamois leapt from behind a clump of vegetation and darted away. The boy could hear the torrent gurgling nearby.

He looked up at the surrounding circle of mountains. The valley was larger and more pleasant than his older brother had feared. But he couldn't discern the cleft he'd observed earlier, only steep rocks surrounded him in every direction.

He decided to climb a tree to get his bearings. As Kai looked on anxiously he scaled a tall pine until the branches could scarcely hold his weight. Glancing around he sighed in relief; there to the south was the opening through which the stream escaped. He smiled, and the singing water below sounded to him like laughter.

By the time his boots touched the ground, he'd decided to stay.

The following weeks were busy. He built himself a modest shelter and hunted on the surrounding slopes. He drank water from the stream and ate the animals he caught. When he'd collected a number of good pelts he followed the river down to the lowland villages and traded them for things he couldn't get for himself. He explored his valley and became familiar with its secrets.

One day he and Kai ascended the far side of the bowl near the great cleft through which the stream exited the valley, a place where the rocks were particularly jagged and steep. This expedition was halted, however, when they encountered a deep rift, too wide to jump, at the bottom of which flowed the torrent. Beyond it the forest loomed as it clung to the side of the mountain, seeming to hang in the air.

Together they skirted the chasm. Before long the boy spied a place where the rocks on either side reached towards each other, nearly meeting in the middle. Seeing this as a place to cross, he made his way towards it.

A moment later he stopped abruptly for, in the time it had taken him to reach the jutting stone bridge, there had appeared on the far side something that had not been there before.

A figure, cowled and cloaked, stood facing him across the chasm. The boy's heart sank; he'd heard stories of men who guarded bridges in the mountains.

The figure spoke to him. Its voice sounded chafed from want of use.

'Who are you, stranger, and where are you going?'

Kai growled at the sound. The boy called back as evenly as he could over the pounding in his heart. 'I could ask the same of you. Nay, I shall:

for I have dwelled in this valley a winter and a spring and have not seen you here, nor any sign of you. Who are you that calls me a stranger in my own home?'

'One who has been here longer than you, I think,' answered the black-bearded stranger. 'I am recently returned from a long journey and would have my valley back.'

The boy clutched his heavy walking stick. 'I shall not leave. I have built my dwelling place here and it is as much mine as yours. More, as you chose to leave it without mark of habitation or ownership.'

'If you will not leave willingly, I dare say you must stay,' replied the opposition, 'though the ground is hard for digging and your bones will be cold.'

Between them rushed the cold water of the stream, as both made ready to receive the other. But before either could make a move Kai, who had stood growling with his hackles raised, saw the preparatory movements of the figure and knew his master was in danger.

The great dog leapt forward, teeth bared. In a moment he'd barrelled across the chasm and was within leaping distance of the figure.

There he stopped.

The stranger stepped forward. The dog's teeth disappeared. Kai stood mutely as an outstretched hand descended on his head and, without fear or hesitation, ruffled his fur. Kai's tongue lolled out and he became quite as amiable as his master had ever seen him.

The boy watched this display open-mouthed.

The stranger smiled at him. 'A strong animal. He would have made a worthy opponent.'

The boy could only look on in astonishment as his faithful dog allowed the stranger all degrees of familiarity, the promise of violence forgotten.

The stranger paused for a moment, then asked: 'You have a family?'

The boy nodded.

The stranger's eyes narrowed under his cowl. 'A family of your own, I mean. You have a wife? Children?'

The boy shook his head.

'But you intend to?'

He nodded again.

The stranger paused once more, continuing to pet the dog.

Finally he said: 'Go back to the valley and build a worthy homestead. Find a wife, have her bear your children. The waters here are strong and the hunting is good. I dare say your line will be healthy. Tell other men of your fortune, bring them here, and let them found families of their own. I give you the valley, but only until this spot. Beyond this river you will never be welcome.'

He looked down at Kai's trusting face and added: 'I like your dog. I'll keep him as payment for my generosity.'

The figure straightened, turned, and retreated into the darkness of the trees beyond. After barely a moment's hesitation, the dog followed him. His owner watched this betrayal in disbelief.

'Kai!' he cried.

The dog ignored him. He trotted after the cloaked stranger, wagging his tail. It seemed to the boy that the dog began to fade and become part of the shadows as he wended his way between the dark trees, flitting and flickering in the undergrowth until he vanished completely.

In later years, when the boy told the story of how he came to the sheltered valley, he would claim that he'd won it at a great price, though exactly what that price was varied in the telling. By and by he learned of one brother's death and the other's homecoming. The returning company, war-stained and peace-hungry as it was, brought to his dale more than one man who craved a welcoming hearth. So the community grew. Wives were had and soon thereafter came sons and daughters. Trees were felled and became houses, and a path was widened alongside the river that flowed down to the floodplain. Before long another stream began to flow the other way, this one comprising traders and merchants.

Eventually some enterprising person sought to include the place on a map and asked what it was called. The inhabitants shrugged, and answered: we call it Niderälpli.

The high trail that had brought the village's founder to the valley could never be made easy due to the sheer rock face one needed to climb in order to use it, but over the years he and others cut steps to make it usable for the able-bodied and sure-footed. He himself climbed it often enough to visit his brother and the old farm. His sister Maria married, and died, as did the others in his life. He grew old.

Some of his children ran off to live their own adventures. Others stayed and enlarged the village he had birthed. By then he'd grown frail and spent most days sitting by the fire, talking little. On occasion he would tell stories, though none so good as that of his encounter with the Devil on the chasm bridge. The memory of that meeting was quieted along with the rest of him one winter, his fire having gone out in his sleep.

FRIENDS
CHAPTER TWELVE

OLLOWING THE *DÉSALPE*, seasonal change in Niderälpli accelerated. The sun rose with increasing reluctance, never making it quite as high as the day before. Temperatures dropped, as though the departing herds had taken the heat with them. In the early hours of the morning the grass was stiff and pale with frost and as people walked through the village clouds of vapour hung in their wake.

In the alley behind the grocery store the air was thick with indignation.

'What do you mean, two months!?' exclaimed Graham. The indignation was mostly his, but Richard was feeling pretty cheesed off himself.

'That's what he said.' Richard nodded in the direction of a mechanic in blue overalls. The little red car had been coaxed into the garage of *Pfister Pneumatique* for some damage assessment. Monsieur Pfister—for the man in the overalls was none other—had the hood up and was elbows-deep in the engine. He examined it intently, a lit cigarette dangling from one side of his mouth, while making French-sounding noises that Richard recognised as indications of deep disapproval.

'Basically, the motor's knackered. He needs to order some replacement parts from the valley that won't be delivered for six to eight weeks.'

'But we'll be gone by then!' exploded Graham. 'What could that car contain that's so rare and important it needs two months to get here?'

'Not sure,' admitted Richard, 'some valve-y thing. I never got to the advanced motor engineering chapter in French GCSE.'

'Let's find a different garage.'

'Can't. I asked at the hotel. It's the only one around.'

Graham threw his hands up in exasperation and stomped out into the street. The mechanic had completed his autopsy and wiped his hands with a rag so greasy it did little except spread the oil around. Richard approached tentatively.

'So . . . you're certain there's no chance of an earlier completion time?'

Monsieur Pfister shrugged as though to say *Perhaps, if I had eleven hands and three heads*. He tossed the rag onto a rusty gas canister in the corner and moved his cigarette to the other side of his mouth.

Richard sighed. 'All right then, perhaps you could lend us a replacement?'

The mechanic indicated a sign on the wall listing rental prices.

Richard groaned internally, but saw no alternative. 'Fine. We'll take something small.' He reached into his jacket. 'I've got some company cheques here . . .'

The Frenchman eyed the chequebook much as he might a long-dead piece of road kill.

Richard sighed, put the chequebook away, and produced his wallet. Monsieur Pfister nodded sagely and reached for the card reader, gratified that Richard had arrived at the same conclusion that the mechanic had known, from the moment of the Englishman's arrival, he must.

Richard emerged into the street some time later to find Graham on the phone. He completed the call just as Richard came up to him.

'Christ, car hire's expensive here. He says the spare will be ready in an hour.'

'Never mind that,' said Graham, 'I've got good news: they've traced our bag.'

'Great! Where is it?'

'Zurich airport. I volunteer to go fetch it.'

'Why so eager?'

'You're a terrible driver. Plus, there's nothing like an unexpected absence to make ladies realise how sexy you are.'

'Fine. While you're there I want you to visit these people.' Richard texted Graham a list he'd been drafting on his phone. 'Those are all the regional wildlife experts I could find online. Apart from those hair samples the last three weeks' surveillance has got us nowhere. We need some advice.'

'Any hot lady zoologists?'

'Well, there's someone called Maja Obladzunova-Guggisberg who runs a clinic just outside Buttwil and apparently spends most of her free time climbing mountains and writing papers on what she finds there. Sounds like our kind of girl.'

'Buttwil, eh?'

'That's what the map says.'

'Say no more. I'm off to cover my shift, after which I shall repair to the hotel and prepare myself for this ravishing scholar from Buttwil.'

'Frau Indergand mentioned there's live music at the hotel on Friday, you could leave the following morning.'

'What innumerable delights these locals provide. What's on the programme?'

'Hang on.' Richard fished out the flyer from his pocket. 'Here we go: "Hodlerjoltz, the Swiss accordion phenomenon. Featuring Jürg Hodler and his sensational music band playing two and a half hours of fantastic Alpenmusig, with a special appearance by Holda Hellenbrau on castagnets".'

Graham did not look convinced. 'We'll see. Anyhow, I've got a bear to find.'

Off went Graham. Richard took out his wallet to see if the garage had left him any lunch money. Despite the business with the car, he was feeling rather cheerful. His daily hikes agreed with him. Since the episode at the observation hut he'd experienced nothing out of the ordinary, glimpsed nothing particularly strange or ethereal, and suffered no unexpected feelings of nausea or vivid hallucinations. Things were looking up.

A car hummed up the road behind him and he stepped aside to let it pass. It didn't.

Richard turned and beheld a huge black saloon, its engine thrumming. Richard recognised Councilman Fürgler from the communal office, waving to him from the window.

'Morning,' called Richard. He remembered the hostility on Fürgler's face when he'd explained the motive of his visit, but today the man seemed perfectly affable.

'A good day,' replied Fürgler, 'but cold. The car is heated. You like I drive you somewhere?'

Richard nodded. 'Sounds good to me.'

Fürgler leaned across to open the passenger door and Richard got in.

'It is the latest model,' Fürgler said almost before Richard was seated. 'The Germans they are making very good cars. I have an arrangement with the company and every eighteen months they send me a new one.'

'Er, that's great. I was just going back to hotel . . .'

'Engineering is a fine thing!' declared Fürgler. 'At my construction company we use only the finest steel parts, for we know that quality is everything.' He smiled companionably at Richard. 'Swiss made! Better even than the Germans.'

'I'm sure it is,' answered Richard, hoping that was the end of it. It wasn't.

'Always we must think of quality and development,' said Fürgler, making no move to actually drive the car. 'We are planning now a ski lift for the north side of the Gräuelhorn. Our parts are made from the best steel. It will be running on twenty per cent solar, so good for the nature too! The environment it is also very important.'

Richard began to suspect that if he was being taken for a ride, it wasn't one that led to the hotel. 'I'm sure your lift is wonderful, but . . .'

'Ah!' cried Fürgler, as though a thought had only just struck him. 'I am thinking, Mr Mathern, you could write about our ski lift in your publication! It would be interesting to your readers, I am sure, to learn about this new enterprise.'

'Ah, er, yes, well . . . the thing is, Herr Fürgler . . .'

'For the title I am thinking, "Technology in Symbiosis with Nature". Good, do you not think? It will look especially nice in online format.'

'Um . . . well, actually we deal excl—'

'Look you here,' interrupted Fürgler. 'I show you some simulations we have made. I have it on the tablet, here!' He thrust the device across to Richard.

'It looks very pretty,' Richard lied.

Fürgler beamed. 'The latest technology. You know North Korea, they are wanting to buy our ski-lifts?'

'How nice.'

'And,' Fürgler enthused, flicking through various digital mock-ups on the tablet, 'there's a toboggan run! For the children, you see; a family-friendly installation.'

'Look, Herr Fürgler . . .'

'Please, call me Dominik.' Fürgler smiled.

'Sure,' said Richard, beginning to wish he'd never got in the car. 'Dominik, if you want to attract visitors with this ski-lift of yours . . .'

'With toboggan!' Fürgler reminded him.

' . . .With toboggan, yes,' allowed Richard, 'then it's up to the council to discuss whatever impact it will have. I'm merely a visitor and couldn't possibly interfere in local politics. However,' he added, watching the clouds gather on Fürgler's face, 'I'd be lying if I said I thought that such an installation would have a positive effect on the local flora and fauna and it would be impossible for me to pretend otherwise in any materials I produce during my stay.'

Fürgler smile faded. 'You will not cooperate?'

Richard spread his hands apologetically. 'I'm here to study wildlife, not to review infrastructure. But,' he added hastily, 'this all looks very promising. I'm sure you don't need my help.'

Fürgler looked like he was beginning to agree with that. Richard took advantage of the awkward pause to press a point. 'Actually there is something you might be able to help us with.'

'Indeed?' Fürgler appeared about as cooperative as a vegan at a hot-dog-eating competition.

'Just a small thing. I was hoping you could put me in touch with Kaspar again, I can't seem to find his contact details anywhere.'

Fürgler frowned. 'You want to talk with the *Wätterschmöcker?*'

'Yes, I was hoping he'd give us a hand finding this bear. We're not having much luck and I thought—'

'No, you do not want this,' interrupted Fürgler with a wave of his hand. 'Kaspar is, how you say . . . the hippie. He is beardy-weirdy. He eats vegetarian and does the yoga and is growing bonsai trees. With him is everything global warming and green cow shit. Sometimes I think he is full of the cow shit! You do not need this man.'

'Nonetheless,' persisted Richard, 'I'd like a chat, if only to probe his expertise.'

Fürgler shrugged but Richard could see he wasn't pleased. 'He has no mobile phone. Call the commune, he will be listed with the tourist board.'

'Thanks.' Richard was suddenly feeling claustrophobic. 'Goodness, is that the time? I must dash. If there's nothing else . . .'

He exited the car before he could be press-ganged into anymore unsolicited ventures and skipped away with a cordial wave, but was called back before he could escape. Fürgler was again leaning out the window.

'There are ways to do things here, Mr Mathern. The community it is important to people and you are a stranger. Remember this.'

The window rolled up and the black car swept off.

Richard walked away, forcing himself not to run. It was only after he'd circumvented the old shop with the dusty window and the sign reading *Souvenirs & Antiquitäten* and ducked down a side street that he allowed himself a sigh of relief. He leant against the wall, enjoying the reassuring solidity of the stones.

After the bright autumn sunlight of the square, the alleyway was dark and cool. Richard's eyes failed to pick out the shape in the shadows until it was right beside him.

'Hullo!' it chirped.

Richard later tried to convince himself that he'd turned to meet the voice's owner with little more than a mild start of surprise. His true reaction could be more accurately described as a sudden, frantic attempt to jump through the wall.

'Why do you people always do that?' he asked, rubbing the side of his head and glaring at Ellie.

'Do what?'

'Sneak up on people. It's childish.'

'I wasn't sneaking,' she answered haughtily. 'You just weren't paying attention. Incidentally, why were you running away from that man?'

Richard wanted to say that he wasn't running away, but suspected that Ellie would know he was lying.

'What are you doing here?' he asked instead.

'Well, you haven't been back to the orchard, so I came to see you instead. Surprise!' She tilted her head and spread her arms wide.

'Wait' she added, 'what did you mean by "you people"?' She lowered her hands. 'Have you met someone else like me?'

Richard told her about his night in the observation hut. When he'd finished Ellie nodded her head in thought.

'Ah yes, the goat lady. I suspected something like this might happen.'

Richard eyebrows flew upwards in indignation. 'You knew about her? Why didn't you warn me? And what was the thing at the door trying to get in?'

'I've only seen her once or twice,' Ellie protested, 'on the fringes of the wood. But they do call it the Goat Shed. I assumed it must once have been hers. I don't know anything about the thing at the door though, just that people avoid the place.'

'Yeah, well, you could have warned me.'

'You were already quite determined to go,' she pointed out. 'Besides, if I'd told you about her, you mightn't have believed me.'

'Why not? I'd already met you, hadn't I?'

'Yes,' she conceded, 'but you haven't returned to the orchard since, have you?' She gave him a sideways, knowing look. 'Maybe I wanted to show you that I'm not the scariest thing out there.'

'You mean there're more of you?' Richard shuddered.

Ellie shrugged. 'Probably. It's hard to be sure sometimes. People tend to come and go. Most keep to themselves. Oh, lighten up!' she said, seeing Richard's expression. 'It's not like we're everywhere! I've only noticed one or two apart from the goat lady and she's never spoken to me at all. Most stay in the ground. Dead is dead, with,' she added, 'only a few minor exceptions.'

Richard eyed her uncertainly. Apart from the disturbing otherness she carried with her everywhere, there was nothing particularly threatening about her.

'I can't decide whether you're a figment of my imagination or not,' he said.

'For all the company you're being today, I might as well be. The least you could do is walk me home.'

Almost before he knew it Richard found himself strolling up the street alongside Ellie, like two friends on a Sunday walk. This act was so incongruously mundane that it overcame his discomfort and, despite himself, he began to relax.

He glanced at Ellie. She appeared normal enough, except that parts of her tended to drift with alarming ease through solid objects when she wasn't paying attention. If she noticed his looks she paid them no heed.

She seemed quite content to walk in silence. This gave Richard time to collect himself.

Strange woman, he thought. Still, if she was willing to socialise—indeed, it appeared she insisted on it—he might as well learn more about her.

They'd arrived back at his hotel. He hesitated.

'Would you like a cup of tea or something?'

'That's very kind, but no thank you. I've rather gone off tea.'

'Something to eat, then? They do rather good desserts here.'

She looked at him pityingly. He reddened. He knew he was going about this all wrong. But then, what do you offer someone who's openly admitted they're dead?

The silence of the afternoon was broken by a burst of flatulence, half-muffled by the copious winter fur covering the tiny buttocks of Jerome.

Ellie was delighted. 'Why, hello!' She stepped over the road and leaned on the fence, her hand outstretched. Jerome sniffed her fingers critically and, knowing her for what she was, induced that no mints would be found in her pockets.

'He can see you,' Richard noted in surprise, watching the animal wander despondently across the field.

Ellie nodded. 'Nothing can fool a goat, or so Grandmother Harriet used to say. They're too smart. If your fence can't hold water, she'd say, it won't hold a goat.'

'Full of information, your granny,' said Richard. 'I wish she was here; she might be able to explain why bonkers stuff keeps happening to me.'

'Is it so very bad?'

Richard wasn't about to forget the night in the hut. Soon, however, his thoughts drifted back to the sunlit orchard instead. 'Not all of it,' he admitted.

Ellie smiled. 'Shall we be friends, then?'

It's amazing how adaptable humans can be. She'd seemed so strange at first, but now Richard couldn't think of a reason not to be. 'All right.'

She gave Jerome a wave, then started back up the road. 'No need to walk me back, I know the way. Come visit soon!'

Graham had already left for his shift and their room was quiet. Richard sank into the old armchair. He reached for *Central European Mythology & Folk Tales* by Melchior B. Adolphus and leafed through it absent-mindedly.

THE WINDS' QUARREL

One day there was a great storm over the lake. White-crested waves crashed onto the rocks and squalls of rain fell so densely that you couldn't see your hand in front of your face. The fishermen cried out in anguish, fearing for their boats.

There was among them a young man called Jora. He recognised that this was no ordinary storm and correctly surmised that the winds were having a disagreement over something or other. Therefore he braved the worst of the gale and walked out over the stony jetty jutting into the lake. Even as the waves threatened to sweep him into oblivion he appealed to the heavens.

First he called the North Winds, who in that part of the world were named Morget, Bise, and Dezaley. Then those in the South; Bornan, Molan, and Foehn . . .

Richard found himself re-reading the unfamiliar names without registering them, his thoughts wandering away from the words on the page. He put the book down and walked over to the window.

At first he couldn't see anyone. Then he glimpsed a flash of yellow disappearing up the stairs leading to the promenade and caught himself smiling without knowing why.

Inside him bubbled a scientist's curiosity. After all, he told himself, why else am I here, if not to investigate anything of potential interest?

His eye wandered to the picture on the wall; the old man seemed to be smiling.

Richard blushed. He returned to the chair and resumed his reading.

QUESTIONS
CHAPTER THIRTEEN

HE FOLLOWING DAY Ellie watched from the promenade bannister as Richard climbed the road to the disused sanatorium. What began as a decisive stride slowed as the way became progressively steeper. By the time Richard surfaced at the end of the veranda, he was moving with that tight-lipped, stiff-kneed gait indicating a shortness of breath that the breather is trying to hide. Clearly he'd just returned from a long hike across the plateau.

'Good morning!' she called.

'Hi,' he wheezed back. 'I promised I'd visit and now I'm here.'

'I'm so pleased. I was afraid I'd scared you off.'

Richard resisted the urge to say something virile like *I'm not easily scared, Sweetcakes,* remembering that Ellie had already twice caused him to try to flee through solid objects.

'Right,' he said instead, 'I've come in the name of science. I've got some questions for you. I want to understand what this . . .' he gestured vaguely in her direction ' . . . is all about.'

'An interview?' she beamed. 'How wonderful! Am I to feature in one of your articles?'

'No. My editor thinks I'm crazy enough already. This is strictly personal.'

'Understandable,' she conceded. 'I suppose it's for the best. In the past I've discovered that photographs of me tend to be terribly unconvincing.'

She sat in one of the wicker deck chairs—or at least appeared to. She certainly adopted an elegant sitting position, but whether the chair was actually supporting her was another matter. If it wasn't, it did an admirable impression of doing so. Richard made a mental note to address that later.

'Right.' He got out his notebook and a pen. 'When were you born?'

Ellie tilted her head to one side. 'That question's of a rather personal nature.'

'True, but the nature of your person is the crux of this interview.'

'It's written down over there somewhere.' She gestured towards the graveyard below. 'I'll show you sometime. Next question!'

Richard glanced at the headstones, then back at Ellie. He couldn't quite read her expression but felt he was on dangerous ground and retreated.

'How do you feel?' he asked.

'Fine, thank you.' She clasped her hands and rested them on her knee. 'Ready when you are!'

'No, that's the question. How do you, in fact, feel? Do you feel anything?'

'Oh, I see. I'm not sure. I certainly don't feel things the way I used to. Mostly I don't feel the need to. Ooh, you can write that: "Does not feel the need to feel." That's sure to bamboozle your readers.' She sat back and grinned. 'This is fun. Next question!'

'Do you eat?'

'That's easy: no.'

'How do you subsist?'

She shrugged. 'I couldn't say.'

'Then how do you reconcile yourself with the laws of entropy?'

'Excuse me?'

'Well, if you don't eat and—presumably—don't consume anything else to create energy, how do you . . . you know . . . live?'

She gave him a patient look. 'I'm not alive. I'm dead.'

Fair enough, thought Richard, and crossed out a subsidiary list of questions. 'What's it like being dead?'

Ellie thought for a moment. 'I suppose that, by definition, it's the opposite of being alive. But in my experience some facets of life are so un-lifelike that one might easily say of them that they're not entirely unlike being dead. Therefore I can only conclude the two are not as mutually exclusive as one might suppose.'

Richard looked up from his notebook. 'If you don't want to answer a question, I'd rather you just said.'

'It's not that simple. The fact that you would think to ask such a question proves you're alive. I'm not. You and I see things from different perspectives. The obsession with "being", for example, is not something I worry about very much.'

'So you've never felt the urge to question your situation?'

'I think to feel urges of any kind you need to be alive. Knowing you're going to die one day gives you a sense of urgency. Once that goes away, everything calms down quite a bit. It's as though the world used to be running away from me and now it's not. Why pursue it? I assume I'll get around to it eventually.'

Richard thought of how to phrase his next question.

'When the impartial observer looks at you . . .' he began.

'What impartial observer?'

'Well, me, for example.'

'All right: when you look at me, what do you see?'

'To be honest, I'm still not entirely convinced I'm seeing you at all. Maybe it's something I ate.'

'Well then, what do you think you see?'

Richard floundered a bit and shuffled his notes. 'Well,' he said eventually, 'you don't seem . . . how to put it . . . you don't seem altogether . . . there.'

'Where?'

'You know . . . *there*. Well, here, I guess.'

She looked amused. 'I suppose I'm not, really.'

'You're not?'

She made a gesture of frustration. 'I'm sorry; I'm not wording it properly. The thing is, I'm not here.'

'Then where are you?'

'No, you don't understand. What I meant was, I'm not here. I am not, here. I'm not, and the place I happen not to be is here. I am nowhere, but I'm not nowhere anywhere else but here. Do you see?

'Not exactly.'

She sighed. 'Let's move on.'

Richard was only too glad to. 'Can you feel the chair you're sitting in?'

'I wouldn't call it sitting, exactly. It's like I said: I'm not here. I'm not sitting at all. It's just that the place in which I happen not to be sitting is this chair. A better approach would be to ask the chair whether it feels that there is anyone in it—or rather, that there is anyone *not* in it.'

Richard considered asking the chair but decided against it. The chair, having only an amateur understanding of metaphysics and little interest in conversing with strangers, was relieved.

Ellie twisted slightly and regarded the chair with an air of sombre curiosity. Richard hesitated, puzzling over whether to interrupt her reverie. A moment later she looked back at him with her amber eyes in that way of hers that was both friendly and deeply unsettling, smiling as before.

Richard took this as an invitation to continue his line of questioning.

'Does death fill you with an overwhelming sense of dread?'

She shrugged. 'Not particularly. Why should it?'

'Just a thought. Now that I think about it,' Richard added, 'that's what being alive sometimes does to me.'

'Cripes. What do you do when that happens?'

'Mostly I invoke the cosmic perspective. The infinite wonder of the space-time continuum helps me to relativize my own problems.'

'I'm not sure I know what that means.'

'Basically I take a few deep breaths and make myself a cup of tea.'

'Is there anything I can do? I'm not exactly an expert on life, but I'd be happy to help. There are plenty of books in the library. I'll show you if you like.'

'No thanks. I came here to talk about you.'

'Of course. Let us proceed.'

'Do you experience cold, hunger, or fatigue?'

'Not exactly.'

'Be more specific.'

'I can't interact with things directly, but I find a side of them that isn't available to you. I suppose I experience the ghost of cold, which actually isn't very cold at all.'

This was more specific, but not much more helpful. Richard soldiered on. 'Do you sleep?'

'I can't be certain. Sometimes I find myself in a different place to where I thought I was, but that's not really sleeping. There are certainly times when I'm not awake. Then again, that's true of almost everyone. Many people are essentially asleep and don't even realize it. And I don't just mean in the metaphorical sense, although there are quite a few interesting psychology books in the library.'

'Sounds like quite a library.'

Ellie nodded. 'It's my favourite room. Are you sure you wouldn't like to visit it when we're finished here?'

Richard glanced at the time on his smartphone. 'I dunno . . . I'm meant to join Graham to compare field notes.'

Ellie peered at the device. 'What's that?'

Richard raised an eyebrow. 'To explain what this is would take a while.'

'Perfect. Next time you visit I'll show you the library and, in exchange, you can tell me what that is.'

Richard hesitated. It didn't seem such a bad suggestion. Ellie wasn't nearly as unsettling once you got to know her. Besides, he did like libraries. 'Ok then, deal.'

She beamed at him. 'Next question!'

'Have you ever tried to leave this place?'

'I don't suppose it occurred to me. I go for a walk in the village occasionally, but never farther. Not much point, really.'

Richard had underlined the next question. 'What happened when you died?'

He'd used a light tone of voice but realised immediately that he'd made a mistake. Ellie's cheerfulness evaporated.

'I don't want to talk about that. And don't ask me about the afterlife,' she added before Richard could say anything. 'I haven't been there and I don't want to discuss where I *have* been.'

Richard sensed that the fun had left her. He sorted through his remaining questions and picked one that seemed least likely to cause offence.

'So, er, what do you do, you know, in your . . . spare time?'

'Very little. Mostly I let everything else get on with its business and I watch.'

'What kind of things?'

She shrugged. 'Oh, you know, all sorts. Flowers, animals, people . . . The most common, insignificant details become fascinating when you're dead. I once became so captivated by the life cycle of bees that I just stood by the hives across the fields, watching them.'

'For how long?'

'I think approximately three months.'

Yikes, thought Richard. No wonder she's bats. Then again, he knew a number of research scientists who would have happily done the same.

'You've been here a long time,' he said hesitantly. 'It must get dull sometimes. Have you ever . . . had a hobby? Ever made anything, or . . .'

She laughed. 'Ghosts can't make anything. Didn't anyone ever tell you that?'

Richard bristled. 'You act like it's obvious,' he muttered. 'Last week I wouldn't have believed there was such a thing. Now I'm expected to know the ins and outs of the supernatural?'

Clearly she found his sulking amusing, but made an effort to look serious. 'I'm sorry. I keep forgetting you're from a different time. Granny Harriet told me all about ghosts, what they could and couldn't do. When I was frightened at night she'd say, "Don't you worry, Ellie, there's no reason to be afraid of ghosts. Some make scary noises and others can move things around a little, but beyond that they're all useless. They can't hurt, change, make, or affect a bleeding thing." And she was right: I can't! Or at least, hardly at all. She'd have a fit if she knew what happened to me.'

Richard pondered this. 'Do you ever get bored?'

Ellie shook her head. 'I've thought about that. I think that in order to get bored, or to feel the urge to create, to achieve, to express oneself, one needs to know that Death might be right around the corner. It's the promise of death that makes a rich life interesting and a poor life dull. Once that threat is removed, there's no reason to hurry for anything, or to fret over inactivity. Making things becomes pointless. Even if I wanted to, I'm not sure I could. My ability to interact with anything substantial is somewhat limited, as you may have noticed.'

Ellie illustrated this point by passing her hand through the tree branches that hung down around them. She seemed to have forgotten her annoyance from before and Richard was glad.

'Are you searching for something? Do you have some sort of mission? Something tied over from your previous life?'

Ellie became pensive. 'I don't often think about my previous life,' she admitted eventually. 'I remember things, of course, but most of it is best forgotten. Becoming this way was surprisingly easy. It was almost like waking up after having always been asleep, as though nothing had come before. I saw my name on the gravestone and it felt right. I saw the orchard in the sunshine and I liked it there. What came before no longer mattered. Perhaps that's why I've never felt the need to leave.'

The bell in the church tower tolled across the valley.

'I'd better go,' said Richard, rising. 'They're expecting me back at the hotel.'

'Thanks for the visit. Sorry I couldn't answer all your questions.'

'Never mind, it's just for my own edification. *Nature Review* is more about owls and unusual pond life. And that's just the editorial staff.'

'That's a shame. I hope you'll come again all the same.'

There it was again, that look that made Richard feel wobbly in the knees. He nonetheless managed a sociable grin before trundling back up the stairs, across the promenade, and down the path. Ellie watched him go, her brow furrowed in thought.

Richard arrived in the hotel hallway and allowed the door to swing shut behind him. His thoughts were jumbled, but a cup of tea would help sort them out.

A noise made him look up. He was somewhat alarmed to see Graham standing at the foot of the stairs, pointing a rifle straight at his face.

Richard threw his arms up to protect himself. Then, as an afterthought, he threw the rest of himself behind the sofa.

'Whoops, sorry Richard.'

Since no shots were whizzing over his head Richard ventured upwards and glared over the armrest at Graham. Herr Indergand was there too.

'What the hell do you think you're playing at?' demanded Richard.

'Nothing. Meinrad here was showing it to me. He was a soldier, you know.'

Herr Indergand raised his hands modestly. 'I only did military service like everybody. But I was good at shooting. My son Silvio is better even. He is doing the manoeuvres but returns in a few weeks' time.'

'I noticed Meinrad's hunting rifle under the counter,' said Graham. 'He offered to demonstrate how it worked.' He placed the butt of the rifle on one hip and struck what he clearly thought was a swashbuckling pose.

Richard emerged from behind the sofa. 'In the hotel corridor?'

123

'Not to worry,' said Herr Indergand, 'the gun is not filled. Live ammunitions are not available in the Swiss stores.'

Richard dusted himself off. 'Glad to hear it.'

'This,' continued the hotelier, 'is why I keep my munitions here, in the desk.'

Richard decided it wasn't the time to address the presence of live ammunition in the building and turned instead to Graham. 'We've got a problem.'

'Hmm?' Graham had raised the gun to his shoulder and was pivoting it around, aiming at various pieces of decorative porcelain and making *pew pew* noises.

'This bear isn't cooperating,' continued Richard. 'Let's have a strategy meeting.'

'Never mind. Only this morning I snapped some shots of a chamois' bottom which border on Pulitzer territory, if I do say so myself.'

'That's not what we're here for. The delay won't go down well in London.'

'Bah.' Graham lowered the rifle. 'We've only just arrived'

'We've been here over three weeks now.'

'Wanna try?' Graham held out the weapon. 'It's easy. Just flick the safety off, pull the lever, aim, and fire. It's fun, makes a kind of *ker-shpling* sound.'

'No thanks.'

'Well then, come for a drink and stop worrying. Anyway, as far as I can see your editor's reacted well enough to the material we've sent in already. As for the bear, there's plenty of time. No need to be concerned.'

*****

'I'm concerned, Dawes.'

Dawes looked over the top of his glasses at Ahmid Sardharwalla, Chief Financial Officer of Aberfinchley Group ltd. 'So I see.'

'This is no joke.' Ahmid fidgeted in his chair.

'Ahmid, I share your reservations. But remember: it's early days. Things will settle down once Luther becomes accustomed to responsibility.'

Ahmid looked doubtful. 'You believe that?'

Dawes hesitated. 'He certainly shows a *willingness* to take his duties seriously.'

Ahmid snorted. 'He may have, initially. Now he appears to have abandoned conventional business hours altogether, preferring to carouse with his "associates". Furthermore, he insists on calling me Amjad Saint-Hardwilly.'

'His ineptitude with names is beside the point. The fact is we owe a debt of loyalty to his father. This company was Des' vision. If he saw fit to nominate his son as his successor, he must have seen something in him that we have yet to discover.'

'Fine, forget the name-calling. What do you have to say about Luther's erratic and destructive staffing decisions?'

'He is attempting to embrace the entrepreneurial zest of his predecessor and bring fresh ideas to the table.'

'And his lamentable strategies?'

'One might argue that our new CEO has a unique vision of the future.'

'Unique indeed! Listen to this.' Ahmid beckoned Dawes forward. Dawes leaned in obligingly. 'We've had letters from Halfcrombe, Wardour's, Spruce, Clyde and several other collaborators. They wanted to say hello and also were wondering if, by any chance, we might have attempted to hack their databases.'

Dawes lowered his paperwork. 'What?'

'It's true. They have reason to believe that there have been targeted attempts to break into their servers, attempts traced to our offices.'

'That's ridiculous. We've worked with them for years. Why hack their systems?'

'Well, we have, at Luther's orders. He views them as competition. In his mind they're fair game. But that's not the main concern. If he was only trying to increase our market share by discrediting everybody else, that would be one thing . . .' Ahmid's fingers tapped fretfully against the desk. 'I believe he's actively trying to undermine this company.'

Dawes looked incredulous. 'Why would he do that?'

Ahmid shook his head. 'I don't know. But he's formed a team to buy up brand name equities across the board and link them to as much negative online content as possible. He's got a competition on in the office to see who can write the most humorous fake reviews. He thinks it's "tremendous fun". And, since we'll need added security for the inevitable counter-attack, he's hired people from outside the company to build a firewall on the cheap.'

'Such sensitive information can't be outsourced to contractors!' protested Dawes. 'We need to vet them individually!'

'He says he has—at least on paper. He's using the privacy of his secure profile so even the board can't tell what he's up to. He took a leaf out of your book and backdated the minutes and made up some interview results. He's ruining everything!'

Ahmid leaned in closer still. 'It's that horrible woman, Dawes, Luther's mother. They must be colluding. Europa never forgave Des after the divorce and now she's after his legacy. Why else would Luther back such delusional policy? She wouldn't even allow Des' favourite song to be played at the funeral!'

'In Europa's defence, "Yes! We Have No Bananas" was an unorthodox choice.'

'Well, unless we do something soon, we'll be short more than a few bananas.'

Dawes considered this dark news, polishing his glasses as he did so. 'I will address this outsourcing business. But as for the rest, we must wait and see. It is quite an allegation, Ahmid, to imply that a CEO is actively undermining his own company. And to what end?'

Ahmid slumped. 'I don't know. We thought Luther's appointment would bring fresh expertise, as well as some of his father's wisdom. We were mistaken.'

He jumped as one of Dawes' ornamental pots on the shelf fell over. Dawes heard the *crunch* of pulverised confectionery and made a mental note to have the cleaners search the shelf for any undiscovered mints left by Luther.

'I don't think we should wait any longer,' said Ahmid. 'Things might reach a point where it's too late to rectify them!'

Dawes shook his head. 'We must wait,' he repeated, 'and see.'

Ahmid frowned. 'I know you set great store in loyalty, Dawes. We all know what we owe Des.' The CFO's eyes were heavy with implication. 'The question, Dawes, is this,' he said gravely. 'Do you wish to see all that Des built ruined out of loyalty to his son?'

He rose before Dawes could answer. 'This can't last, Alistair.'

He shot Dawes a meaningful look before showing himself out.

Dawes sat in sombre reflection. What if Ahmid was right? Was there a secret motive behind Luther's dealings?

No. Luther was an arrogant child with delusions of grandeur and a stunted attitude towards gender equality, but he was no mastermind. He wasn't capable of anything so grandiose.

Over in the corner another one of his ornaments fell over with a hollow *thonk*. Dawes ignored it.

All the same, he thought, access to Aberfinchley's personal investment portfolio might set minds at rest.

Dawes pressed the intercom button. 'Alice,' he said, 'please get that young man in, the one we used for that matter with the automobile company share prices last march.'

'Tall, neck piercing, computer, unwashed?'

'The very one.'

If he accessed the portfolio, he'd be able to reassure Ahmid and the rest and get back to the business of running the company. All would be well.

The grey man observed Dawes from the corner. He glared at the fallen pot and several other things he'd knocked over to get Dawes' attention. He considered the desktop monitor and the engraved fountain pen case, but shook his head. Such drastic measures were not yet called for.

All the same, he pushed over a tiny brass sextant for good measure.

Dawes looked up in annoyance. 'Also, Alice,' he added over the intercom, 'please ask Maintenance to come up to my office. I think the shelves are skewed.'

LARKS AND PROPHETS
CHAPTER FOURTEEN

ICHARD SQUATTED IN front of a pile of dirt and, not for the first time that morning, wondered whether Councilman Fürgler had been right about Kaspar.

The weather prophet crouched in a similar position opposite. He spread his hands, as if the earthen mound was somehow important.

Richard sighed. Before meeting Kaspar he wouldn't have believed that people still walked the earth who spoke literally not one word of English. The two men communicated using a mixture of rudimentary French, bad German, miming and, when that failed, pictures on Richard's phone. Eventually they developed something of a knack for knowing what the other meant, but even so it was weary work. The morning had consisted of Kaspar dragging Richard off the path without warning and pointing at clumps of moss, the undersides of rocks, and—rather memorably—unearthing what appeared to be a large ferret from the undergrowth and holding it up by the scruff of its neck for Richard to examine. After half a minute or so of mad thrashing, the animal realized its struggles were futile. Thereafter it contented itself with hanging in mid-air and eyeing the human face in front of it, waiting for Kaspar's grip to relax enough to allow it to savage Richard's eyeballs.

'It's very nice,' said Richard.

Kaspar grinned. The ferret hissed at him.

Richard looked as closely as he dared. The animal appeared underfed for the time of year, and, though female, did not seem to have borne any young recently.

'Eine schlechte Sommer,' he suggested with help from his phone, *'ein schlechter Winter wird folgen?'*

Kaspar shook his head. You can tell the nature of the summer by the winter, but not the other way around. Winter is always unpredictable.

128

Richard nodded to show he'd understood. Kaspar tossed the ferret unceremoniously into a bush.

Now as they knelt on the ground Richard attempted to divine some meaning from the dirt heap before him. Kaspar wriggled his fingers in what he evidently thought was a helpful way.

'This is an anthill?'

Kaspar indicated that this was so.

Richard looked at it for some time. Nothing happened.

'Nothing's happening.'

Exactly, said Kaspar's eyes.

As Richard watched, Kaspar delicately prised off a piece of the mound and inserted his fingers into the gap. A moment later he held a pinch of ants. He showed Richard the size of the insects, indicating that they appeared muscular and well coloured. This, he made Richard understand, meant that the first snowfall—when it came—would be heavy.

A burst of birdsong made Richard turn. He glimpsed a flash of gold on a branch and identified it as a yellow-browed warbler before it flitted off into the canopy.

'Did you see that?' he said to Kaspar. 'They're rare.' But the weather prophet was too preoccupied with the trees to bother with birds.

Trees were Kaspar's speciality. As they traversed the woods he indicated tangles of roots, some so old and hard that Richard mistook them for rocks. Intermingling with the living wood were the stumps of old aspens that appeared at first glance to be dead, but weren't. Kaspar found traces of green stems from the previous spring, tiny ecosystems gleaning their nourishment from the healthy trees around them. He explained that the plants supported each other, ensuring a dense canopy to protect weaker individuals. Richard learned that although the wood was wild and overgrown in appearance it was actually closely monitored by foresters.

'Shouldn't they clear some of the trees to allow more light?'

Kaspar shook his head. The trees were inter-dependant, relying on each other to share nutriments in times of need. Clear the weaker trees and, with the chain of communication broken, all would suffer.

Everywhere they stopped Richard took careful notes for his reports. They never stayed in one place long. He'd inevitably feel a tug on his sleeve and they'd move on, always upwards.

In this way they crested the treeline and progressed across the high plateau. Richard forgot his fatigue and followed the older man's gesticulations with increasing fluency as they visited various wind-worn features of the landscape; here a bush, there a cross-section of sediment in a rock face. More than once Richard circumnavigated an accumulation of rocks and was met with a sudden drop where the ground simply ceased to exist and valleys appeared in front of him, distant and silent.

Eventually they stopped for a breather. Since the English language had about as much impact on Kaspar as any other language has on the English, Richard resorted to alternative methods. He extricated his phone and produced a picture of a bear, a map, and a calendar. To these he added gestures indicative of *where* and *when*.

The weather prophet made him understand that the bear was far away and would probably not return before November.

Richard nodded but thought this was unlikely, since no sightings had been radioed by any of the surrounding stations. She was still somewhere nearby, he was sure.

They were far above the forest now on a wind-swept stretch of the Gräuelhorn's upper pastures, shadowed by the towering white mountain itself. A gully stretched upwards on one side, bordered by a stream. The slope was treacherously steep and Richard took care not to slip on the rocks.

Kaspar dipped his hand into the water. Richard assumed he was using some age-old technique to measure the temperature, but the old man simply wanted a drink.

A trail of loose shingles and stones led down from the cliff towering above them. Its flow widened from a narrow apex and, by the time it reached the place where Richard and Kaspar stood, its debris was scattered over a wide area. In some places the scree clogged the stream, forming tiny dams. The water flowed quietly enough now but Richard saw the evidence of its power in the channels it had cut through almost solid rock.

Kaspar was smelling the water and making loud, satisfied noises in between sniffly intakes of breath. Richard decided not to disturb him and set off downriver in search of interesting rocks or fossils.

He made his way carefully alongside the shallow water, stepping around the deeper channels and examining rock specimens as he went. His initial search yielded nothing of interest, so he kept going.

He came to a place where the water ran deep and fast, its current squeezed by a narrowing channel. The banks rose up on either side and Richard couldn't advance without wading into the river itself. Prudence dictated he retreat to higher ground.

But just as Richard was preparing to leave the stream something caught his eye; a bright spot in a collection of stones that appeared to have rolled down from the cliff.

He leaned in for a closer look and identified one particular specimen with a bleached, egg-like appearance, criss-crossed with veins of darker stone.

Interesting . . .

Richard held it to the light, rubbing away some loose grit with his thumb. He noted the curious texture and line pattern and stuffed it into an outer pocket of his rucksack for later inspection. Having done so he stepped back, preparing to use momentum to carry him up the bank.

Then his boot slipped.

Richard lost his balance and fell backwards into the stream. Freezing water poured through his clothes. He gasped with the shock, tried to cry out, but his breath caught in his chest.

Kaspar heard Richard fall and hurried over. The old man scooped him up onto the bank and made him stand, helping to remove his rucksack as he did so. Water streamed from Richard's sodden trousers and pooled in his boots.

'Thanks,' he gasped. Lucky the sun's out, he thought, otherwise I'd catch my death of this. His heart raced to pump warmth back into his numbed extremities.

Kaspar called for his attention. Richard looked up and, despite the chill, laughed.

The old man was hopping up and down, swinging his arms rhythmically at his sides. As he leaped about his beard and the brim of his weather-beaten hat rose and fell in flopping unison. Kaspar hopped over to Richard and tugged at his wet sleeve, encouraging him to do likewise. While Richard was jumping up and down Kaspar upended the soaking rucksack to make sure the equipment hadn't been damaged.

Richard laughed at the sheer ridiculousness of it all, but warmth slowly began to return to his body.

Breathless, he stopped bouncing. He raised his face towards the pale October sun before turning back towards Kaspar with a smile, ready to tell him how much good the little dance had done him.

Suddenly Richard turned white and began to shiver more violently than before.

Kaspar was concerned. He'd encountered cold water before and knew that exercise usually did the trick. Evidently these North Atlantic types weren't as water-worthy as they'd have the world believe. He decided to return to the village immediately.

He began to pack away Richard's things; someone would have to dry them later.

Richard made no move to help him. He was too busy staring at the figure over Kaspar's shoulder.

Its face was that of a young man, but its twisted posture spoke of infirmity brought on either by age or extreme suffering. The loose woollen clothing in which the apparition was draped accentuated its gauntness, as did the shaven head and once-olive skin, now turned an unhealthy grey. The ghost—for what else could it be—stared back at Richard with hollow eyes in whose shadows only the most feeble, desperate flicker of life could be found, like the glimmer of moonlight at the bottom of a well.

'Salvete, peregrinus. Vidisti dominum meum?'

It spoke in a hoarse half-voice. Richard was scarcely in a state to answer. The figure's appearance so chilled him he felt like he'd fallen in the river a second time. Kaspar, oblivious, continued to collect Richard's things.

The ashen-faced apparition shuffled closer. Its bare feet were raw and scarred. *'Ego sum vultus pro dominum meum. Vidisti eum?'*

Its voice hissed and crackled from want of use. Richard could scarcely distinguish it from the wind. The figure stood quite close now, bent like a sapling broken by a storm that time had mended, but not healed. It gazed up with a pitiful, pleading look.

Richard found he couldn't answer above an indistinct whisper.

Kaspar heard him. Taking this for a sign of discomfort, the weather prophet grunted as he stuffed the last of the equipment back into the rucksack. His grizzled hand fell on the egg-like stone Richard had recently harvested from the river. Not knowing its purpose, he threw it into the bag along with the rest.

Before Richard could summon up the energy to speak again, the ghost shook its head and stumbled away, following the course of the stream.

Kaspar zipped the rucksack shut and hoisted it onto his own back. He called to Richard, indicating the path.

Richard looked in his direction, startled, as though woken from an unpleasant dream. When he glanced back, the figure had vanished.

The old man pulled at his arm until Richard stumbled after him, still dripping. Together they made their way down the mountain and back to the village.

Richard shivered the entire way. Kaspar grunted, urging him on. Halfway down Richard stumbled, having lost the feeling in his legs. Kaspar shook himself free of his woollen jacket and forced it onto Richard. Then he pulled the unsteady Englishman to his feet and back onto the path.

Rather than following the ridge around the valley to the top of the falls, Kaspar chose to take a shorter path, on the far side of the bowl. This meant that they emerged from the wood near the train station. Only the village lay between them and the hotel, but they'd hardly reached the square when it all became too much for Richard and he stumbled again, dizzy with cold.

Kaspar looked on with concern. The street was deserted. His own house was several minutes' walk away and Richard wouldn't make the hotel without help.

Kaspar grunted decisively, hooked Richard under one sodden arm, and pulled him into the nearest shop. As it happens, this one had a wooden door, a dusty window, and a sign that read *Souvenirs & Antiquitäten*.

The bespectacled, leather-aproned owner looked up in surprise as the door opened and Kaspar entered backwards, dragging a shivering Richard after him. The man put down what he'd been doing and stood up, addressing the weather prophet in a gruff, interrogatory voice as Kaspar propped Richard up against an old chair.

Richard looked around dizzily. The shop was a mess of bric-a-brac, trinkets, odds and ends, bits and bobs, bibelots, and miscellanea of all kinds. Old umbrellas, ancient pipes, second-hand clothes and discarded boots—most full of holes—lay all around on the floor, in the corners, or piled on top of ancient, cracked furniture next to incomplete card sets, tarnished silver cups and much-thumbed old books. The window's yellowed glass gave the room a sepia-like tint. Next to a line of hats hung a grey woollen overcoat, whose ill-sewn patches seemed somehow familiar.

A pair of legs appeared before him, followed by a stern face that somehow seemed more ancient than the junk around him. Richard recognised Old Man Fosco.

'H-h-h-hi,' he managed.

Fosco swung a heavy blanket over Richard's shoulders. He barked at Kaspar, who was pacing back and forth in distress, ordering him to fetch more from the back room. In his daze Richard noted with amusement that Fosco sported a tattoo on one arm.

'S-s-sorry ab-b-bout this,' Richard stammered as Fosco rubbed his icy hands in his own gnarled ones. 'T-t-took a b-bit of a t-t-tumble into the stream. S-s-stupid, really. S-should have been more c-c-careful.'

Fosco looked up, his brow furrowed. He angled his head, as though struggling to understand. After a moment's hesitation he spoke in his low, heavily accented growl.

'Kaspar . . . bring you . . . to . . . river, in mountain?'

Richard nodded. 'Yes, w-we were tracking the b-b-bear, you see. I slipped into the r-river at the foot of the m-moraine. T-totally my fault . . .'

Kaspar returned with more blankets, his brow knitted with anxiety. Richard managed a smile and the weather prophet seemed reassured. After a few minutes Richard felt recovered enough to cover the remaining distance to his hotel. Both old men helped him to his feet and Fosco insisted he keep the blankets.

Kaspar accompanied him to the door but Richard left him there, assuring him he could make it upstairs without help. What Richard didn't mention, and what stuck in his mind as he watched Kaspar retreat back down the road, was the look of shock and mistrust he'd seen Fosco shoot the weather prophet upon learning where he'd led Richard, and the sudden apprehension he felt about his guide.

He struggled upstairs, brushed past Graham—still asleep following an evidently trauma-free night in the observation hut—and had the longest, hottest shower he could remember.

There was unusually high attendance in the Gasthaus Meierhof's restaurant that evening, requiring Graham to use a bit more elbow than usual to work his way through the crowd. Behind him followed Richard, newly fortified by several cups of tea. Graham had insisted he top them up with alcohol, just to make sure the river's cold stayed out. They barely managed to get places at the bar.

'It would appear Hodlerjoltz, the Swiss accordion phenomenon, is not to be missed,' commented Graham. In a far corner of the room the aforementioned phenomenon and his fellow musicians had taken their seats. The sound of tuning violins and wheezing squeezeboxes filled the air. Graham handed Richard a glass of whiskey.

'Thanks. By the way, where'd you put my rucksack?'

'It was wet so I popped it in the car boot. Didn't want to muck up the carpet.'

Richard nodded and took a swig.

The cold from the water had gone, but the chill from meeting the broken man on the mountain remained. The alcohol helped and Richard drank some more, enjoying the burning feeling in his stomach. He'd surprised himself with the speed of his own recovery. This in itself worried him a little. Perhaps exposure to Ellie had hardened him to the supernatural. Still, it was disturbing to discover a darker side to this world that, so far, had contained only straw hats and yellow ribbons.

Oh, and that creepy goat girl. Mustn't forget her.

Graham craned his neck, perusing the room. He spotted Melanie sitting at a table with a friend. His eyebrow rose, much as Caesar's must have at Alesia. 'Looks like the evening just got a lot more interesting.'

Richard followed Graham's glance. 'You going to go talk to her?'

'Better still.' Graham arched his back and shook out his legs. 'I think it's time to introduce the continent to my moves.'

Richard blanched. 'Seriously?'

'Of course. Didn't you know I was a dancer of the highest calibre?'

'I remember you coming third in a college dance-off featuring only one other contestant, if that's what you mean.'

'Exactly. Women love a man who can dance. It's a sure-fire ticket to a night of sleepless passion in the arms of Melanie.'

Richard looked around the busy room. 'You sure this is the right time?'

Graham limbered up in anticipation. 'Sit down, mate,' he said, his eyes on the prize across the room, 'and observe a master at work.'

He turned to the band. 'Okay, boys,' he growled sexually, 'play me a rumba.'

The band did no such thing. For one thing, Swiss folk bands do not rumba. Their genes won't allow it. More to the point, Graham didn't get two paces before his foot met with the immovable cane of Frau Hürlimann—which had not been there a moment before—and he toppled like a drunken giraffe.

A minute later Richard and Graham were standing outside, the sound of laughter still ringing in their ears.

'At least you didn't upset the buffet table,' Richard pointed out. 'That would really have been a disaster.'

'Ha ha. It's bad enough the entire village was there, the old bat had to trip me up right in front of Melanie.'

'In your defence, you made a valiant effort not to hit the floor. It's just a shame that in an effort to postpone your defeat at the hands of gravity you made such a vivid arabesque on the way down.'

'Well, I'm not going to let a small thing like public humiliation ruin my evening.' Graham smoothed his ruffled hair. 'Let's go find something fun to do.'

'But everything's shut.'

Graham raised a knowledgeable finger. 'I happen to know where they keep a set of downhill scooters. Let's go nick some!'

Richard looked aghast. 'Scooters? Are you crazy!? What with Kaspar's animal cruelty and my tumble in the river, I've no wish to net a nature-themed hat-trick by slamming into the ground at forty miles an hour.'

'Spoilsport.'

'It's a stupid idea. Besides, I'm in charge of this expedition and I condemn it as a public health risk.'

'Oh, come on! We haven't had a day off since we got here. We're due some fun. You always were a stick in the mud.'

'What's that supposed to mean?'

'Well, you know, at university while the rest of us were out on the town, you were always buried in work or something. It's like you never bothered to get to know your youthful self.'

'Oh pish. I'm the life and soul of every party.'

'Well then, prove it. Besides, what else are we going to do? Go back in there?'

As Graham said this, an unspeakable cacophony broke out in the restaurant. Richard's first thought was that a small church organ must have somehow snuck into the audience to hear the music, had too much to drink, and fallen over. Then he realised what he was hearing *was* the music.

'Oh, all right,' he said to Graham, 'but just this once. And for Christ's sake be careful.'

Graham grinned and rubbed his hands together. 'Awesome. The sheds are this way. We can use the slope behind the hotel.'

*****

Frau Hürlimann sat in her chair beside the fireplace and sulked. She tended to sulk most of the time, as there was little else for her to do.

Not that this had been a particularly unpleasant evening for her. The hotel staff had given her a supper of soft bread and soup and wrapped her in blankets before wheeling her over to the fireplace. It was a busy night so they'd reserved a special spot just for her.

No one knew quite how old she was. Her ancient face and bulky woollen covers gave her the appearance of a giant piece of dried fruit wrapped in an oversized checked handkerchief. Her reduced mobility meant she relied on the assistance of Frau Indergand, whom she despised.

Then again, Frau Hürlimann despised most people. A life well lived had left her with nothing but absent friends and all too present problems. Her back ached, her hands shook, and her speech was so garbled that nobody understood a word she said.

So much the better for them, she thought. I've got dirt on everyone in the village, and their mothers. The things I could say . . .

She glared as the surrounding crowd clapped along to the music. But over the course of her many years her face had collapsed into such an inscrutable mess of wrinkles that no one noticed.

Look at them, she thought to herself, with their stupid mannerisms and inane grins. Easy enough to smile when there's hot running water and the roads are open all winter!

She looked at each in turn with her single working eye, the dead one lost in the folds of her face. Some revellers gathered in laughing groups while others sat at the tables and drank, bloated from large evening meals. Unable to decide who revolted her most, Frau Hürlimann scowled indiscriminately at all the occupants of the room.

Not a man or woman among them worth a *rappen*, she decided, and sucked her gums in umbrageous disgust. When did people lose their balls? What had happened to the people she'd known as a girl, who could leap up a mountainside steeper than a church roof carrying heaps of kindling on their backs as though they weighed nothing at all? Those pious folks who rose at dawn to milk their hardy cows, who carted goods up and down the treacherous dirt track for a few francs, and still found time to dance and smoke and go to church and raise honest children? These bloody tourists wouldn't have lasted a single winter back when she was young. The turds. If only she could tell the world what she really thought of it!

A man sat at a nearby table, his hair done up in some sort of bleached spiky mess and wearing a shirt so pink it hurt her brain. His entire being seemed to her so offensive she concluded that it was her Christian duty to call him a poop head, but the only utterance of which she was capable was an indeterminate gurgle.

'Huaarghlbrl.'

Frau Indergand looked up from her embroidery, her face a picture of motherly concern. She placed her work on the counter and came over.

'Something bothering you, dear? Did the music wake you from your nap?' She patted the old woman's hand.

Frau Hürlimann turned her icy blue orb towards this new intrusion. Yes, she yearned to say, yes there is something bothering me: the world's gone to shit.

'Weeehurglarbl.'

'Aw, there, there.' Frau Indergand rearranged the blankets so they enveloped the old woman's feet more snugly, every gesture accompanied with a soothing noise or a reassuring smile. Having finished, she crossed the hall and resumed her embroidery.

Sod you, thought Frau Hürlimann. Sod you, sod your smug sympathy, and sod your self-satisfied sodding face.

This made her feel slightly better—but not much.

A shadow loomed over her. Frau Hürlimann looked up apprehensively, noting the tight-fitting sportswear with disapproval. Melanie smiled at Frau Hürlimann as she passed with a drink and went to sit at the table with the man in the pink shirt. She and Dave got to chatting and soon forgot about her entirely.

Frau Hürlimann's scowl intensified and she looked even more like a tartan-wrapped raisin with a grievance than before.

Never trust an Englishman. Klaus had told her that years before, God rest his soul: cads and fornicators, the lot. That's the girl who feeds the sled dogs that live behind the hotel—that pack of mongreloid wolves with their infernal howling. Tcha! Another cheap foreign substitute, imported at the expense of purebred Swiss animals. Admittedly they handled snow well enough. But could they haul a cart full of milk tanks and iron ore up a glacier? Satan's arse they could! She hadn't seen a proper *Sennenhund* in years. What beautiful dogs they'd been, with lovely golden brown and black colours edged with white; an honest coat for a righteous animal that knew how to work, unlike that grey-carpeted pack of inbreds in the backyard.

Her good eye popped open; a thought had occurred to her. Perhaps following the night of unhinged and godless passion that was surely to follow this giggly conversation in the shadows—she knew lust when she saw it, people don't change much—the girl might forget to feed her beasts. If only Frau Hürlimann could then escape her damned wheelchair and set them loose amongst the hotel guests, what a magnificent massacre would follow! How glorious the chaos! What a fantastic way to end the monotony to which she had been consigned!

She groaned with frustration. Alas, it was not to be. Melanie was a good girl, hard working like her father. Nothing would keep her from her work, certainly nothing that spade-faced bartender could do to her.

Frau Hürlimann gazed out the window into the darkness beyond. She remembered when she'd been pretty too. Men had noticed her in the streets of Lausanne outside her finishing school. By God they'd wanted her; more than a few had said so in the shade of this or that lakeside café. Her family had money then, before her feckless relatives sold the pastures for little more than a bratwurst and disappeared.

She gripped her blanket with trembling hands, remembering long summer afternoons in the sun.

Certainly they warn you old age is hard to bear. You lose your looks, your family, your friends . . . But never in her wildest nightmares had she imagined it would be this *boring!* Nothing ever happened. What she wouldn't give for a bit of excitement!

A flicker of movement in the corner of her eye gave her pause.

She squinted, deepening the furrows on her face, peering past the guests, over the musicians and through the large window into the darkness. Something was moving fast.

An instant later a downhill scooter crashed through the window of the dining room in an explosion of glass, chequered curtains, and shredded tires. With a trajectory that carried it over the band, across several tables and past Frau Hürlimann altogether, it came to land in a crumpled heap at the far end of the room. For a moment there was a shocked silence as the assembly recovered from its surprise.

Then the uproar commenced.

Ah, said Frau Hürlimann to herself, that's more like it.

*****

A half hour or so later Richard watched the last of the visitors leave, broken glass crunching underfoot. He and Graham had been handed brooms and were sweeping in a corner with their eyes lowered. A few of the other guests were likewise helping the Indergands tidy up the restaurant.

'Well, that was a disaster,' hissed Richard. He picked up some discarded flyers and tossed them in a bin bag.

'Shut up,' whispered Graham. 'They'll hear you. Besides, it wasn't my fault. One of the wheels on my scooter was wonky. It's a miracle I managed to jump off in time.'

Someone had fitted a board over the shattered window and was hammering it into place. Luckily Councillors Aufdermauer, Berger, and Fürgler were all in attendance and could therefore grant the special dispensation required for hammering after 6:00pm.

'All I can say,' continued Richard, 'is maybe it's not such a bad thing you're leaving for a few days. Hopefully it'll get all this Melanie nonsense out of your head and you won't try any more of this mad bollocks.'

'Shh!' hissed Graham, 'the landlady's coming over!'

Frau Indergand approached, hair up in a practical bun, bin bags in both hands.

Richard paused his sweeping. 'We're very sorry about this, Frau Indergand.'

She waved this aside. 'Don't worry Mr Mathern, it is not your fault. It is no doubt the teenagers. They are always making the trouble!'

Graham nodded. 'Bloody kids.' Richard smacked him in the shin with his broom.

Frau Indergand sighed in exasperation. 'I think it is the television. They see on it the sex and the violence, and they are thinking they are rockstars. Last April a boy is trying to make fire in the church, before that one who is fan of the wrestling is starting a cat-boxing event. The worst,' she held up a finger 'is the motorcycles. Always when I go shopping they are there, crazy driving on the road.' She illustrated her words with a zig-zag motion of her hand. *'Whoosh! Whoosh!* This close to the car! Sometimes—'

She fell silent. Madame Berger had entered the room with more bin bags. Frau Indergand waited until the councilwoman exited.

'I am not wanting to upset Sabine,' she whispered. 'You know, her son Martin is dead in an accident last year.

Richard shook his head. 'I had no idea.'

Frau Indergand gave another brisk sigh. 'Anyway, it is how it is. The children have not much to do here in the mountains.'

She assessed the damage with a critical eye. 'It is not so bad. We will get new glass. Besides, Herr Hodler has agreed to come back and play again for us in a few weeks! You will both come, I hope?'

Richard smiled as hard he could. 'Absolutely.'

As the cleaning process wound to a close the guests were thanked and sent to bed. Curtains were drawn and lights were extinguished, leaving the Gasthaus Meierhof in a quiet darkness. Only the Indergands remained awake, working quietly to ensure that there would be no traces of the commotion by morning.

In the kennel behind the hotel, Melanie's sled dogs opened their eyes and sniffed the air. They rose to their feet and began to growl fitfully. Then, one by one, they set off a howling cry that echoed across the valley.

Meinrad Indergand had rescued those treasures that had been thrown to the floor by the scooter's arrival and was lining them up on the hallway desk for inspection, cleaning, cataloguing, and relocation. Hearing the mournful cry, he muttered something about feeding time, grabbed a torch from the drawer and fetched his coat from its hook.

He stopped on the front step, momentarily unsettled. What with the evening's commotion he'd forgotten to turn on the outside lights and the driveway had been bathed in an inky darkness when the sudden opening of the door lit it up like a spotlight. He could hear the sled dogs scuffling and growling in their kennel.

Herr Indergand held up his torch, shining it on the bonnet of the rental car parked in the driveway. For a moment he could have sworn he'd seen a large, lanky creature standing next to the vehicle, looking as though it was trying to get into the boot.

Torch in hand he inspected the entire street. It was empty. Even Jerome's usual spot behind the fence was unoccupied, the goat having been taken in for the night.

The light of his torch stopped trembling. He must have imagined it. He shook his head, resolving to complain to his doctor about the side effects of his medication.

The dogs' howling brought him back to his duties. He fumbled in his pocket for the key to the kennel, found he'd forgotten it, and went back inside to get it. In the warm glow of the reception hall he forgot his alarm and chided himself for being silly.

All the same, he made sure to switch on the lights before going outside again.

THE MEETING
CHAPTER FIFTEEN

Franz Meierhofer's House — Niderälpli, 1728

IT WAS THAT grey-tinged time of year when it rains incessantly. This was not one of those warm, gentle showers that makes the herb garden smell particularly sweet, nor a dramatic, driving downpour that floods rivers and sweeps away villages. This rain was that monotonous, wearisome dribble that falls in the no-man's weather between autumn and winter merely because statistics require it to, creating a thoroughly unsatisfactory season where every stone is wet, every beam is damp, and no amount of heat can dislodge the shivering in the bones. It created the kind of misery-inducing climate whose effects on the mind and body science has historically made a priority of limiting—except in England, where sitting in damp, cold buildings is considered character-building and remains a popular national pastime.

This rain was not falling in England, although even in those days England was an extremely popular place for rain to fall. Instead, it fell on the house of Franz Meierhofer. The water ran in rivulets off the slate roof onto the unpaved streets of Niderälpli, engorging the stream that foamed in its carved stone bed curving between the houses. Most inhabitants had been driven away from the windows towards the warmth of their stoves, but in this particular house a face stared outwards.

Eva was bored.

Franz Meierhofer's youngest daughter was six and a half years old. She considered this a rather inconvenient age to be. She knew she was no longer a baby, because everyone told her so when she requested more jam at dinner. But apparently she wasn't old enough to work and cook with her sisters, who said the knives were too dangerous, that she'd get to do her fair share soon enough, and that in the meantime she should go and play.

But it's raining outside, Eva explained.

Then play inside, they replied, and shooed her out from under their skirts. The kitchen was bustling and not welcoming at all, as though something important was about to happen.

Eva did her best to entertain herself while waiting for the rain to stop. She found some bits of string and pleated them into a little bracelet, but it was too big and kept falling off. She tried to be helpful by wiping some dirt off the windowsill with the corner of her dress, but nobody noticed. She discovered their tomcat Bubelmütz sleeping in a cupboard digesting his latest rat and spent some time scratching his ears and putting his paws on her nose. They smelled like bread. She slipped her string bracelet over his head like a necklace but this displeased him and he wandered off.

Dejected, Eva moped around and asked her mother if she could go and sit in the barn with the goats. She said no.

But there's nothing to do, Eva explained. Besides, goats are fun.

Goats, her mother informed her, are craven, lascivious creatures that fraternise with evil spirits, and when the Redeemer sits upon the throne of his glory, then before him shall be gathered all nations and he shall separate them one from another as the shepherd divideth his sheep from the goats.*

Sheep are boring, replied Eva. Goats are fun.

Go away and stop bothering people, said her mother.

What little distraction Eva could find never lasted long. By the time evening found her she was sitting in a corner on top of the landing in a very grumpy mood. This, she informed her doll, had been a decidedly mediocre day.

She was still sitting in that corner when the men began to arrive.

This piqued Eva's interest. They rarely had this many visitors.

One by one the men marched past her up the stairs and into the big room behind the wooden door. Although many of them had given her sweets only last Michaelmas, none paid her any attention tonight.

Something was afoot. Eva hid behind the bannister and observed.

Her father entered and exited the room several times, as though looking for someone who hadn't arrived yet. Eva feigned interest in her doll and he took no notice of her. A moment later her eldest sister struggled up the stairs with a heavy tray of drinks.

'How's the food coming along?' their father asked as the girl fought her way onto the landing.

---

* Though eloquent on the metaphorical difference between sheep, those humble and devout followers of the Son of God, and Goats, the lascivious and sinful pleasure-seekers, Matthew 25: 31-33 fails to mention that goats have more distinctive personalities and get invited to way more cool parties than sheep.

She smiled breathlessly. 'Doesn't it smell good? There's bacon, roast chicken and potatoes, a side of lamb with herbs and onions, some dried fruit from the summer season . . .'

Her father raised a hand. 'We'll see it later, no need to stand there all evening telling me about it. Take the refreshments through!'

She made to do so, but he stopped her again. 'Any sign of the gentleman?'

The girl shook her head. 'No, but Mother's watching the road. It's probably the rain. The road's murder when it pours like this.'

Her father gnawed his lip in irritation. 'Everyone's here, we'll have to start without him. Well, girl, go through! Go through!'

She went through. There was an appreciative rumble from the occupants of the room when they saw the drinks.

Franz felt a sudden weight on his boot. Looking down he found his youngest sitting on his foot, looking up at him from under a messy fringe.

'I wanna listen to the meeting,' Eva informed him gravely.

'Go back to the kitchen and help your mother.'

Eva clung to his leg. 'She doesn't want any. I asked. I wanna be in the meeting.'

Her father lifted her up. 'Any more of that and you'll get such a spanking you'll have to eat your soup standing up.'

He put her down and nudged her down the first few steps. Then her sister exited the room with the tray, nearly knocking him down the stairway. In the heat of the subsequent exchange Eva snuck past them and through the half-open door.

A dozen or so chairs had been brought into the room for the assembled guests. The seats closest to the fire held the older, more arthritic persons, including the schoolmaster and the doctor. Eva recognised the man who sold them firewood and the herdsmen who leased their fields for pasture, all conversing in low tones, their faces lit by the fire. A couple of men glanced up, assuming she'd come to clear the empty cups. There was already a small cloud of pipe smoke gathering under the ceiling.

It was the work of a moment for Eva to slip behind the chairs and into the cupboard by the far wall, unnoticed. She pulled the little door closed behind her.

Bubelmütz the cat was already inside and didn't seem pleased by the intrusion. But the cupboard was big enough for two and Eva stroked him into a truce.

A hush fell over the room. A moment later her father spoke.

'Welcome. Some guests are yet to arrive but they're likely to be late due to the rain, so let's begin.'

An elderly voice cut in, coming from a bald man by the fire. Eva recognised it as that of Thomas, the grocer. 'You were right to call a meeting, Franz. I nearly did myself when I heard.'

Franz was surprised. 'Were you, Thomas? I didn't know the news had travelled.'

'Indeed it has!' replied the grocer. He produced a paper from his pocket and waved it about. 'The Bishop wants to annexe our diocese!'

One of the other men put his hand over his face. 'Not again,' he moaned through his fingers.

'Yes! This time it's true!'

'Surely not,' countered another. 'The question of the Prince-Bishop's rights was settled nearly a hundred years ago under Hildebrand Jost.'

'Nonetheless,' insisted Thomas, 'his successor is back. He wants our salt mines I tell you! Read this if you don't believe me.'

The schoolmaster took the paper and searched his pocket for his spectacles. 'This is an invoice for road tolls between Disentis and Visp,' he said eventually.

'Exactly!' spluttered Thomas.

'For the last time,' his neighbour, 'those tolls have been up for years.'

'You always bring this up at market season,' added another man.

'It's unacceptable!' cried Thomas. 'It's highway robbery by the despots in Sion to fill their papist coffers!'

'Who're you calling papist?' shouted one man, rising from his seat.

'Peace, peace!' cried Franz. 'This is not what I called you here to discuss!'

'Then why are we discussing it?' asked the doctor.

'Someone's misspelled "ecclesiastical",' remarked the schoolmaster. 'Should we write back requesting the document be corrected and returned to us for a second perusal?'

'No,' was the unanimous reply.

Thomas the grocer folded his arms. 'I merely express concern for the well-being of our community, tormented as it is both spiritually and economically by the bishops. Remember, the tortures of hell are interminable!'

'As are you,' muttered the doctor.

One of the heavyset herdsmen leaned over and murmured in the grocer's ear. 'Actually Thomas, I meant to ask: had any shipments of drink lately? I gave the last of mine to a sick heifer a week ago. Now I have a healthy cow and no booze.'

Thomas batted him away and brandished his invoice.

Eva rolled her eyes. This wasn't interesting at all! She couldn't sneak out without being seen though. Besides, something told her this meeting was important and that she'd get in trouble if the men knew she was there.

She heard her father's voice again. 'Now, perhaps Elias would describe what he has seen.'

Franz turned to a person sitting with his back to Eva's cupboard, but whom she recognised as a cowherd from the village. He was a young man, pale and nervous.

'Go on,' urged Franz. 'Tell them what you told me yesterday.'

The youth rose unsteadily and stood in the middle of the room. For a few moments Eva could hear nothing save the crackling of the wood in the fireplace and the soft purr of Bubelmütz in the shadows next to her.

'I lost a cow,' began the young man. 'She were a big beast, nice animal but stupid, you know? I let the herd wander up high, to get the grass before the frosts come and ruin all the good eating. I knows I weren't supposed to, seeing as those pastures belongs to Alois who lives down by the mill, but what with the flooding the valley's all flushed out and the animals need fattening up afore winter but how's that to happen what with the blight and all . . .'

Franz interrupted him. 'Please, Elias, stick to the important bits.'

Elias nodded. 'Well,' he continued, 'like I said, this cow gone and got herself lost. I were getting all the girls together afore dark, then up comes the dog, yapping and jumping around, and I sees there's one missing. Really it's the dog's fault, she's got energy sure but no sense, and she doesn't know to fetch an animal back until she's wandered so far she's half gone and I told the man who sold her to me, I told him . . .'

The assembled men shuffled in their chairs. A stern glance from Franz silenced Elias once more. The cowherd took a moment, then started again.

'I found the cow. She'd fallen in a crack and made an awful racket. There she were, bent sideways down a crevasse, water up to her haunches and crying loud as anything. Her leg were broke, see, nothing to be done. It'd be cruel to leave her lying there for hours until she died of thirst or until the wolves came. So I takes my knife and cuts her throat.'

The men grumbled in the affirmative. When an animal stumbled that high in the mountain there was nothing else to do but put it out of its misery.

Eva frowned in the darkness. Poor cow. Elias should have been more careful.

Elias continued: 'Then I says to myself, no sense in the animal going to waste. All this blood on the ground and in the water's sure to attract something or other before too long, but I'm quick and I knows the way. So I leaves the dog to guard her, I takes the other animals back to the barn, and I fetches a saw and an axe so I can collect and salt the meat. It's late, but I'm not having a whole cow go to waste just because she's dumb as dirt and broke her leg, so up I goes with my tools and some gunny sacks, hoofing it fairly sharpish up the track because night's coming on and nobody wants to be up there after dark.'

There was another murmur of assent. Eva rolled her eyes. Everyone knows you don't go back up the mountain once the evening's set in, that's just silly. She was beginning to suspect that Elias wasn't particularly clever.

'So I gets to where the cow fell. The sun's gone behind the mountain and it's dark on the ground already but there's still some light in the sky and I sees her lying there, but there's no sign of the dog. Far as I could tell she'd up and gone. I knew she was slow but I thought she'd know when to stay put. Still, it don't look like anything's had a go at the cow so I gets to work, because it's getting dark and I wants to get home to my fire . . .'

Eva was glad the dog had gone. She hoped it had run away to find someone who looked after their animals better the Elias, and bathed more often. Maybe she would go to the barn tomorrow and find the runaway dog hiding in the straw, and then she could keep it and cuddle it and play with it on rainy days when she wasn't allowed to go outside and everyone was being boring.

' . . . The sound comes from high up in the rocks above me. I don't know what it is, I guessed it's the dog come back after chasing a grouse or something. I calls out her name, when . . .'

Elias' voice caught in his throat. He was invited to sit and someone poured him a glass of spirits. Eva peeked through the crack, wondering what could have frightened him so. Fortified by the drink, he continued.

'Then, just as I've tied the cord on one of the sacks, I hears it again, much closer this time. I looks up and right there in the shadows, not twenty yards away and glowing like lamps, I swear there's a pair of yellow eyes, looking straight at me.'

Eva reached out and touched the cat for reassurance. She held her breath.

'Before I can get up off my knees it comes at me, faster than anything I ever seen, big as a deer and teeth long as barn nails, and goes right for my face. I hardly have time to lift the axe before it's on me. If there weren't that axe between me and those teeth, I wouldn't be here now, I'm sure of that. It gets me down on the ground and I can't see anything in the dark except those eyes. It's going for my throat but I've still got the axe and I'm thinking maybe if I can get a swing in I might stand a chance . . .'

One of logs in the fireplace shifted with a *crunch*, but no one went to poke it back into place. Everyone sat on the edge of their seats, leaning forward.

' . . . next thing you know who should come charging up out of the blue but that old sheepdog. She comes pounding across the grass swinging her head, mad as hell, and smacks right into that thing and they both roll away.

I'm on my feet quick as you can think and just as it's coming back I swings the axe hard as I can and I feels it hit something and there's this horrible howling sound like nothing I've ever heard. Then the dog's back in there snapping and yapping like crazy and I figures this is the only chance I'll get. So I leaves that dog and that dead cow and hoofs it down that mountain like the Devil's on my tail because sure as Hell is hot that weren't one of God's creatures that attacked me up there and I gets down that track as fast as my feet can slide. Then, just before I reach the woods, I turns around to see if it's following me . . .'

Elias shuddered, even though he sat next to the fire.

' . . . I looks up and sees a man, black against the last light of the sky, standing on the ridge, right where I'd been a moment before and no one else had been, and sure as I'm sitting here he were watching me go.'

For a time no one spoke. In her cabinet Eva hardly dared to breathe, listening for what would happen next.

'Was there anything else, Elias?' asked Franz quietly.

Elias shook his head. 'No, sir, that's all I seen.'

Everyone began to talk all at the same time, but Franz hushed them. 'Well, gentlemen,' he said, 'Elias says he met a beast. What is your opinion?'

One of the herdsmen spoke up. 'If Elias here saw what he says he saw, it's like nothing I've ever seen.'

'A wolf,' said Thomas the grocer. 'They descend when the weather gets cold and the calves are wandering off.'

'How big did you say it was?' asked another voice.

Elias shuddered again. 'Bigger than a wolf, sir, big as a mule. It were a monster and no mistake.'

'Rubbish,' said the doctor. 'There's no such thing.'

'But what of the man?' asked another herdsmen, 'how do you account for a man where a wolf was only moments before?'

'We've all heard of such things,' murmured his brother, wide-eyed.

An old man who had not yet spoken was staring into the fire. 'Do you think there were monsters in Eden?' he mused.

'What?' Tom the grocer sounded irritated.

The old man turned his head to look at the room. 'Before the Fall, do you think the Lord made the beasts we call monsters, and that they were gentle like the rest of creation? Is it possible Eden's ruin corrupted them, as Snake corrupted Man? Or were they already evil, lurking on the fringes of Paradise, waiting for sin to deliver them their victims?'

The grocer rolled his eyes.

'The only monsters are in Hell,' the schoolteacher said.

The old man shook his head. 'If the stories are true,' he muttered, 'being created in God's image doesn't save you from monstrosity. Perhaps there are monsters in all of us, waiting for the right time to emerge.'

Elias spoke up again. 'It were no wolf, sirs, and I can prove it.'

The girl pressed her eye against the crack. There was a general intake of breath, but struggle as she might she could not see what Elias was showing the room.

'This is the work of the beast.'

There was a terrible silence. Then her father spoke again. 'Ever seen a wolf do that before, Thomas?'

No answer.

Bubelmütz the cat opened his eyes, stretched, and made to leave the cupboard. Eva coaxed him back into the corner, afraid he might give her away.

'The beast must die,' one of the audience decided. 'But we've so few young men who can land a shot.'

'There's not much to keep them,' muttered another. 'Many have gone to the cities. Others talk of the New World.'

'Tcha!' scoffed a third.

'Can you blame us?' cried one of the herders. 'If we're going to freeze our fingers off hunting snow bunnies we might as well do it for good money!'

The doctor cut in. 'We could request assistance from the Bishop of Sion.'

'What?!' scoffed the grocer. 'That crazed priest who rides around screaming about how Luther and Calvin are servants of the Devil?'

'Besides,' said another, 'he's probably too preoccupied by his property disputes with the Duke of Savoy to receive our delegation . . .'

Eva grew frustrated as this argument continued. Why were they wasting time? Hadn't they heard? There was a monster at large! She had half a mind to jump out of the cabinet and start nominating people herself when her father spoke again.

'Peace, friends, all is in hand. I've found the man for us. He's recently returned from a long voyage, but is familiar with these parts and by all accounts he is a formidable marksman. He's agreed to meet with us to discuss our predicament. I fancy that's his horse we hear now.'

The sound of sodden hoof beats echoed in the street outside and they heard voices from downstairs.

'You invited an armed stranger into our village without consulting the rest of us?' cried one man.

'He might be a highwayman!' cried Thomas, clutching his invoice.

'I've brought him here to judge for ourselves,' replied Franz calmly. Eva recognised her mother's voice downstairs. An unfamiliar rumble sounded in reply.

'What's his name?' asked one man.

Franz told them. Eva couldn't hear very well, but thought it sounded something like Oscar. She didn't know anyone called Oscar.

There was a knock at the door.

The occupants of the room turned with hushed anticipation. No one made a move to open it.

'Enter,' called out Franz.

The door swung open. Eva ducked low so she could see peek at the man who had just entered.

He was very tall. His boots were caked with mud. Under a greying head of hair he sported a dark beard, but his age was hard to fathom. His stance was enough to impress all of the assembled company. Eva thought him frightening.

Franz had introduced him, but Eva had missed the name again.

' . . . He has agreed to track the beast,' her father concluded.

There was a murmur of approval as the council scrutinised the newcomer.

'Well sir,' asked the doctor, 'you think you can hunt this creature and rid our community of its shadow?'

Eva felt, rather than saw, the grim look spread across the hunter's face.

'I believe her blood is as red as mine.' His voice was deep and grating, as though seldom used.

Eva huddled in the dark corner as the meeting concluded. Agreements were made, the details postponed until after dinner. The little wardrobe shook as their boots thumped past on their way out the door.

The little girl waited until she knew the room was empty. She pushed the cupboard door open as quietly as she could, emerging into the room on all fours. She crept behind the chairs towards the landing, hoping to reach it before anyone came back.

When she was a few feet away from freedom, the fire came into view on one side. She glanced in its direction and saw what Elias had shown the room: a large woodman's axe, splintered through the middle, its haft disfigured by uncounted gashes that had split it as effortlessly as though it were matchwood.

Eva decided she'd had enough adventure for one night and turned back towards the door.

A pair of very large, dirty boots stood between her and the doorway.

'What have we here?' growled the hunter whose name she didn't know.

Looking up she saw a greying head with long, uncombed hair and a dark beard, darker eyes, and a smouldering pipe that sent smoke curling up through his moustache in a way that might have been comical had it not also been terrifying.

He exhaled a dank cloud that drifted into the smog lingering under the ceiling. 'Does your father know you're here?'

She shook her head mutely.

The man chuckled and squatted down. 'I'm not going to hurt you,' he said. 'I'm here to hunt monsters, not rabbits.'

Bubelmütz emerged from the cupboard, took one look at the man, decided he was a waste of space, and padded swiftly out of the room.

Eva stiffened her lip in what she hoped was a courageous way. 'There's no such thing as monsters,' she replied haughtily. 'The schoolmaster says so.'

The man smiled. 'Fine, a phantom, then.'

Eva suspected that was the same thing, but she wasn't sure. She watched smoke curl slowly through the man's whiskers and float up in tendrils around his ears.

'What's a phantom?' she asked.

'It's like a ghost.'

'And you kill ghosts?'

The man nodded. 'Among other things.'

Eva held tightly to her skirt with both hands, for want of someone else's. 'Do they fight back with claws and teeth and weapons and guns?'

'Where would they get those?'

Eva thought hard. 'They could make them,' she surmised.

The man's dark eyes reflected the firelight from the hearth. 'Ghosts can't make anything. They're worms who prey on our fear. Remember that.'

A creak shattered the intimacy of the conversation.

'There you are!' cried Eva's mother from the doorway. 'Come here this instant and stop bothering the gentleman!'

Eva was yanked upwards in a vice-like grip and hauled from the room. She glanced back at the hunter and saw him wink at her from under his heavy black eyebrows. She was then marched to the kitchen and spanked until her bottom was sore before being sent to bed.

As she lay under the rough woollen covers listening to her sisters snoring, Eva thought about what the hunter had said. She wondered what kind of monster Elias had seen and whether the hunter would kill it.

There was a creak of wood from the corner. Eva stiffened in terror, but it was only Bubelmütz. He jumped up onto the bed, his eyes glowing green in the darkness. Then he curled up in a fuzzy ball and Eva stroked his fur, feeling the reassuring rumble from his tiny tummy. Before she knew it, she was asleep.

THE SANATORIUM
CHAPTER SIXTEEN

CTOBER WAS STILL young, but as the breeze blew over the shady orchard it already carried with it the metallic smell of snow, as well as the voice of Richard Mathern.

'And if I swipe my finger,' he said, 'all this other stuff comes up. See?'

'It's so colourful!' said Ellie. 'What happens if you push there?'

'I'll show you.'

There was a click and a buzz. Ellie laughed delightedly.

'Here,' said Richard, 'you try.'

There was a pause.

'It must be heat-sensitive,' said Richard eventually.

'To be honest, I didn't expect it to work. Do me!'

There was another click and a buzz, followed by another pause.

'Funny,' said Richard, examining his smartphone, 'the camera can't seem to focus on you at all.'

Richard and Ellie sat together at a rusty garden table in a corner of the orchard. His rucksack lay on a chair nearby. Graham's temporary absence from the village meant Richard didn't have to explain where he was.

'Never mind. What else does it do?' Ellie peered at the little screen.

'Well, apart from calls, photos, the music library, the messaging system and mobile banking, there's also this thing called the Internet.'

'I've heard of that!' she said. 'It's invisible, you need "reception" to get it, and it's difficult to find when you're in the mountains. Tourists complain about it all the time.'

'But do you know what it does?'

Her shoulders drooped. 'Not exactly, no.'

'Well, for one thing, it acts as a repository for the collective wisdom of mankind.'

'Crikey. How does it work?'

Richard shrugged. 'Not sure. Something to do with satellites. But it's great for watching videos. Also shopping. Among other things it allows you to access every book ever written. By clicking a few buttons you can get them delivered straight to your house.'

The look that Ellie gave him then was laden with more raw lust than any he'd yet received from a woman.

'That,' she breathed, 'is absolutely brilliant.' She peered at the screen intently. 'What are all those little numbers?'

'Those are my banking details. You're not supposed to know those.'

'Sorry.'

'Storing information makes it easier to order things next time you visit the site.'

'I see. What's a "Login ID"?'

They strolled around the gravestones as he explained his device's wondrous features. The trees had turned and their leaves glowed red, yellow and orange. As they walked, they trod on a carpet of fire.

'I can't be the only one to come up here,' Richard remarked after a while. 'Why can't anyone else see you?'

'The people who inhabit these mountains aren't romantics, Mr Mathern. I think the everyday dangers of scratching a living from the mountainside while trying to fend off wolves and starvation through the winter are too recent a memory for them to worry about ghosts. Their monsters are all too real.'

Ellie lifted the hem of her skirt with one hand as she walked. With the other she would occasionally stoop and pick up particularly striking leaves from off the ground. Richard noticed when glancing back that somehow the leaves always managed to still be there after she passed. He reminded himself that she wasn't actually picking up the leaves, just the ghosts of the leaves.

'The English,' she continued, 'have long since tamed their countryside. But ours is a morbid race. Our minds cannot accept our relative security. We're constantly on the lookout for new, fantastic monsters to thrill and terrorize us. Where the Scottish sheep herder sees pasture for his flock, the Englishman gazes in delicious horror at a terrifying moor stalked by ethereal hounds and murderous phantoms, ready to drag him back into their swampy abode.' She spoke with a distinctly theatrical relish and accompanied her words with a flourish of her leaf bouquet. 'The story of Frankenstein's monster may have been set in Switzerland, but it needed to be written by an Englishwoman.'

'Are you suggesting I was somehow predisposed to discovering you?'

She gave him that strange, amber look that seemed to peer into his thoughts. He'd become used to it over the past few weeks and it perturbed him less now. But it still stirred up an odd sense of vulnerability and

152

immediately reignited the aura of other-ness that surrounded Ellie, which Richard was increasingly prone to forget.

'I think you were looking for something and you happened to find me.'

'That sounds rather cryptic. What was I looking for?'

'I don't know. Something different, unlike anything you'd seen before. Perhaps you were yearning for distraction. Weren't you lucky that I happened to be here?' She smiled coyly.

'You're making fun of me,' grumbled Richard.

'A little,' she admitted.

'You're saying it's all in my head.'

She shrugged. 'Perhaps it is. But just because something's in your head doesn't mean it isn't real.'

This statement perturbed Richard. There was a lot of stuff in his head.

Glancing around, his eyes fell on the boarded-up face of the white building in whose shadow they stood.

'What's the history of this place? It must have been beautiful once. What happened?'

She looked up at the blank windows, remembering.

'It wasn't always like this. The sanatorium used to house many patients. During the war it was full of soldiers, as well as ordinary people trying to get away from it all. If their families were rich, they would send them here to convalesce. I suppose they weren't quite rich enough, though. One day the money dried up and they closed the whole place down.'

She brushed the peeling white wall with one hand. 'It all happened very suddenly. It was only temporary, they said, but everyone suspected it was the beginning of the end. Some rich man from abroad bought it and wanted to start it all up again, but he lost his money and had to sell it cheap. The commune tried to turn it into a museum for a while but nobody came. Eventually they boarded it up and I've been alone ever since.'

She sighed. 'It's been very quiet. Sometimes I think that if I were still alive I should have died of boredom. Occasionally I come here and talk to the gravestones, to see if they answer.'

'And do they?'

Ellie never seemed to notice cold, but now she shivered. 'Mostly they keep to themselves, but they do stir occasionally. Some nights I'll hear an old man mumbling to himself, or a nurse going on about how many patients she was supposed to visit the day Death grabbed her, or some poor soul calling for their medicine.'

Her gaze fell on the eastern corner of the graveyard, which contained a group of gravestones smaller than the rest. She looked away.

'The children are the worst. Every night there's some poor babe calling for its mother or crying softly in the cold earth. It's downright cruel, bringing them here without their parents to look after them. I hate the people who did it. I can't bear to listen.'

Richard looked at the sad collection of graves, the mountain's tiny nursery of unhappy children who could never leave. 'If their parents had been with them,' he asked hesitantly, 'do you think they'd still cry?'

She looked back, her eyes bright with anger—not with him, but with a world where children were taken from their parents and shut away in cold hospitals away from their families, left to die far from home. 'A loveless life can only end in a loveless grave. Those poor children were cruelly mistreated. If they were unhappy in life, there's no reason death should be any better, is there? I fear they'll cry forever. No one can hear them now, except for me. And what can I do? It's not me they want.'

Richard hesitated. There was a question he wanted to ask.

'Were you unhappy?'

She seemed startled. 'What?'

'In life, were you unhappy? Is that why you've stayed, while the rest have gone?'

She looked away. Richard feared he'd made a dreadful mistake. When she looked back, however, she seemed pensive but not angry.

'Not unhappy, no. A little lonely, perhaps, but not unhappy. I enjoyed life too much to be unhappy for long.'

They came to a gravestone under a beech tree and stopped. Richard realised Ellie must have intended to bring him to this spot the entire time and that she'd been dreading this moment. When she next spoke, she made a poor attempt at disguising the tension in her voice, which had become quieter than usual.

'Well, this is mine.'

Carved in the granite headstone was an inscription in high letters, faded and obscured by bone-white lichens but still legible. It read:

Here Lies
ELOISE LIDNEY
1908 - 1931
Only Daughter of
CHARLES and SUSAN

Lower down Richard could just about make out the words

That which bloomed in days of yore
And blossoms still in people's hearts
Shall flower for them evermore
Though time and space rend them apart

Richard gazed upon Ellie's grave. He tried to reconcile himself with the idea that the person next to him was actually lying somewhere in the earth under this slab of granite and found he couldn't. Ellie kept her eyes on the gravestone, as though she feared what his reaction might be. She fidgeted nervously.

'Some graves are completely silent and you never hear a word. I think I'd like to be one of those; they seem most content.' She picked at some lichen that had got out of hand on one corner of the stone. It clung on stubbornly.

'For some reason I never thought to look for yours,' said Richard.

Ellie couldn't bring herself to look at him. 'Well, here it is. I'm under there, somewhere, I suppose. "Unto dust", etc.'

Richard looked at Ellie and suddenly felt very sorry for her.

'You know,' he said, 'I don't think you're under there at all. I think all of you is right here, right now, with me. The rest is just earth.'

She looked up at him and there was gratitude in her eyes.

They stood there for a moment in silence. He discovered he wanted to hold her hand, but guessed it would be pointless to try. Instead he turned back towards the sanatorium and gazed for a while at its proud gables and high windows, all boarded up.

'Would you like to go inside?' Ellie asked, the mischief returning to her voice.

Hell no, thought Richard. The place gives me the creeps. Then again, he reflected, it might take her mind off things. 'Sure.'

She smiled and skipped ahead, gesturing to him to follow. He ran back to fetch his rucksack and together they mounted the creaky wooden steps and walked along the veranda towards the doors.

'Won't it be locked?' he asked.

She stopped short. 'Crumbs, I forgot. What with our talking, sometimes it's hard to remember you're not dead.' She looked him up and down. 'You're pretty thin. Maybe if you think vacant enough thoughts we could squeeze you through the crack under the door.'

'I'd rather not.'

'In that case, we'd best use the back entrance. They don't lock it anymore. The janitor got shut inside once and had to spend the night. I tried to keep him company but he didn't respond.'

'Tcha! Rude.'

'Quite.'

The back door was unlocked, but it took some pushing and pulling to get it open. Richard was hit in the face by the smells of abandonment: old paper, dust, and stale air. He stepped into a shadowy passageway that had once been painted white but had faded to a crumbly, peeling grey. At least it was dry.

Ellie moved deeper into the building and Richard followed, using the light from his phone to see where he was going. On either side of the passage were empty rooms, all shrouded in darkness behind barred shutters.

'Not much to look at, is it?' Richard's voice sounded very loud in the silence.

Ellie smiled, beckoning him through an unmarked door at the end of the corridor. He followed.

The darkness thickened. At first Richard thought his battery was going, then he noticed the walls were no longer white plaster but dark and grainy, absorbing his light.

The beam glanced off a reflective surface, blinding him. He blinked away the flashing stars and looked around.

He was standing in a wide hallway, panelled with dark wood all along its length. Opposite him was a broken mirror, hence the blinding reflection. He saw that there must once have been many more, but the others were missing.

The panelled walls were interrupted at regular intervals by pairs of glass-panelled doors. Richard counted three on either side of the foyer where he now found himself. In front of him was the main entrance, its doors shut, the conciergerie abandoned. Overhead dangled a great chandelier, which appeared to hang as much from its many cobwebs as from the great chain running through its middle.

This must have been quite a place, thought Richard.

He left his rucksack by the wall and looked around. The plastered ceiling showed signs of previous glories, but the decorative stucco was now crumbling and ruined. In many places it had fallen away altogether, scattering a layer of debris over the floor.

'Come on,' whispered Ellie. She was already halfway up a gilded stairway.

Richard's phone beeped, indicating the battery was low. He put it away and knelt beside his rucksack, feeling around for the torch. His searching finger encountered a rock, which he put in his pocket to get it out of the way. He found the torch, flicked it on, and followed Ellie up the stairs, avoiding the dusty bannisters and walls.

The next floor was also a long corridor, but plain plaster had replaced the mirrors and dark wood. Richard flashed his torch at the deserted hallway's many doors.

'I'm not sure I want to stroll around an abandoned hospital ward,' he said.

'Don't worry,' said Ellie. She pointed to a pair of panelled doors.

Richard peered through the dusty panes. The room beyond was as dark as the rest. He pressed the old brass handle and it creaked open, trailing a tangle of cobweb. He ducked underneath and stepped through the doorway.

A change in the air told Richard that this was a large room. He stood uncertainly a couple of steps from the entrance.

There was a wooden squeak. All at once the room was bathed in bright light. Richard threw an arm over his eyes in surprise. When he uncovered them, he saw that one of the tall shutters had been pulled aside.

'How did you do that?' he asked, squinting against the afternoon sun.

Ellie dusted off her hands and grinned. 'Like I said, I can interact with things to a varying degree. It's easier here than elsewhere. I think of this as my space.' She gestured, inviting Richard to have a look.

The room was lined with glass-fronted cabinets, all filled to bursting with books. At each end stood an enormous fireplace, boarded up but still impressive. The floor was mostly free of plaster, the ceiling having survived better here than in the hallways.

Richard approached one large armoire and shined his light on the dusty spines. There were medical journals, anthologies of poetry, fiction, essays and correspondence, diaries, atlases, and encyclopaedias—all left where they had last been placed with no semblance of classification.

'The English section's over here,' Ellie whispered.

Richard struggled to read the titles through the glass. *The Works of Shakespeare; The Poems of Ossian,* Vol. III; *The Town and Borough of Leominster,* Rev. G. V. Townsend; *The Letters of Horace Walpole; Milton on Christian Doctrine,* trans. Sumner; *Studies in Literature,* John Morley. Reynolds' *Natural History of Immortality* rubbed spines with Byron and Shelley, while Jusserand's *Histoire Litteraire du Peuple Anglais* lurked behind Giles' *Australia Twice Traversed.*

'So many stories,' Ellie murmured. 'Each one is like a little world, dozens of little lives preserved forever. I'm never lonely here.'

Richard marvelled at this secret hoard of literature. 'Some of these are first editions.' He took Darwin's *Vegetable Mould and Earthworms* and placed it next to Lubbock's *Ants, Bees & Wasps.*

Ellie raised a knowledgeable finger and cocked an eyebrow. 'That's not all.'

She beckoned him over to a different cabinet. She produced a small brass key and unlocked it, revealing a dark interior smelling of old newspaper and mothballs. 'This is where I keep my things.'

Richard saw an assemblage of boxes, varying in size and origin. From amongst these Ellie picked a small wooden case containing an ancient pen with a silver nib and a little bottle of black ink.

'It's beautiful,' he said.

She smiled girlishly and replaced it. She took down another box, then another. Each held some different treasure. One was full of old buttons; another housed a small assemblage of ornate picture frames. Within a heavy wooden case she revealed a collection of antique coins, labelled and set in felt, which looked extremely valuable.

'Is all this yours?'

She tilted her head. 'Not exactly. They were abandoned in various parts of the building and nobody thought to collect them.'

Richard must have looked sceptical. Ellie snapped the lid of the box shut. 'It's not like they had any right to them, anyway! Most of these belonged to patients. They should have been sent back to their families. I merely looked after them. When they boarded the place up I brought them to the library to keep them safe.'

Richard smiled. 'You're their curator, then?'

'Precisely,' she replied with dignity and, Richard suspected, the hint of a smile.

There was a noise from downstairs.

Richard stiffened. 'What's that?' he whispered, feeling like a child caught in the neighbour's garden.

Ellie put the box down and tiptoed to the landing. 'I can't see anyone,' she whispered back. 'Nobody ever comes in here.' She grinned wolfishly. 'Maybe it's an angry spirit, come to investigate why two trespassers have broken into their sanctuary. Isn't this fun?'

'That's not funny.'

'What, are you afraid of . . . *ghosts?*' She waggled her fingers and widened her eyes. 'WooooOOOOOoooooh.'

'Stop that!' hissed Richard. 'If I'm caught, I'll get thrown off the project!'

'Oh, don't be so dramatic.'

They listened. There was a scraping sound, as though someone was pushing a rucksack around on the floor.

'It's probably just the janitor checking to see why the back door was open,' suggested Ellie. 'I'll go creep him out so he'll go away.'

She grinned, then walked smoothly into the wall in that way of hers that Richard still couldn't get used to at all. She was only gone a moment and returned almost as suddenly as she'd left, with a surprised look on her face.

'Oh dear,' she murmured, her eyes wide.

'What is it? It's the police, isn't it? I knew you'd get me in trouble.'

'Er,' she began, 'um, it's . . . it looks like . . . Oh dear.'

There was a noise downstairs like the sound of a chair falling over and—though Richard couldn't be sure—what sounded like ragged breathing.

Richard detected fear in Ellie's eyes. What did the dead have to be afraid of?

'Ellie, what's downstairs?'

'I don't know, I only caught a glimpse, but . . . Oh Richard, we need to get out of here right now!'

'What is it?' The sounds seemed to be moving from room to room.

She spoke in a quivering whisper. 'I don't know exactly. All I know is it's bad. Very bad. Let's leave, now.'

Richard looked at her hard. She didn't look like she was joking. 'How?'

'Follow me.'

She led him through a half-concealed door into an empty room that might once have been an office, then through another door into a servant's passage. Ellie looked back frequently to make sure he was following her, avoiding the hallway.

'Look,' said Richard, 'why don't we just—'

'Not now!'

They raced through doorways and small rooms. Once Richard paused and heard the boards creak on the landing beyond the library. They found a staircase winding upwards into darkness. Up went Ellie with Richard close behind.

'Hey,' he said, 'this isn't funny. Let's just—'

She wheeled on him. *'Quiet!'* The fear in her eyes silenced him. She sped upwards.

Richard glanced back. A floorboard groaned in the office beyond the passageway.

He sped up after Ellie. At the top of the stairs the hem of her dress disappeared through a doorway and he followed it. He found himself in what looked like a servant's room; small, square, with a single dark, dusty window.

There was no way out.

A *clunk* behind him made him to jump. A stepladder dropped from a hatch in the ceiling.

Ellie's face peered down out of the darkness. 'This way!'

He climbed into a narrow, dusty attic under an angular ceiling, little more than a cupboard—presumably one of the gables at the far end of the building. Ellie pulled up the ladder and shut the trap behind him.

'Right,' she whispered, 'I think we're safe now.'

Richard tried to sit up, knocked his head on a crossbeam, and swore. Would it really be so terrible if the concierge caught them? What was the worst that could happen?

He flicked his torch on and waved it around until he found Ellie. 'All right, what's going on?'

Ellie was, if possible, even paler than usual. Her eyes betrayed a frayed hysteria that she was fighting to keep hidden.

She took a deep breath, held it for a second, and exhaled.

'Well—'

BAM.

The trapdoor slammed open and a hideous, shuddering snarl filled the air. There erupted from the aperture the head of a creature so nightmarish that Richard screamed in terror. In an instant it clawed its way up and lunged towards them, all yellow eyes and gaping teeth. Richard threw his hands up to protect his face.

As he did he felt a violent lurch, as though the building itself had been turned upside-down. Suddenly everything was blindingly white and a deep stillness reigned in his ears.

THE IN-BETWEEN PLACE
CHAPTER SEVENTEEN

ICHARD SAT UP. An opaque whiteness hung in the air in every direction. He stood up, still shaking from the shock of what had just happened—whatever it was.

He heard a whimper behind him and whirled around. A short distance away he saw Ellie, sitting on what for the moment he was going to continue to call the ground with her knees tucked under her chin, rocking backwards and forwards.

'I'm not supposed to do that,' she stammered. 'I don't know why, I just know I'm not supposed to.'

Richard looked around at the nothingness. 'Where are we?' he asked, his ears ringing from the horrible cry of the apparition. 'Where's that . . . that thing?'

Ellie continued to oscillate back and forth like a child in the dark, except that she was bathed in light.

'We're in the In-Between Place,' she whispered, her lip trembling. 'It's what I call it. It's the place where I woke up after I . . . When I was . . .' She closed her eyes tightly. 'I think it's the place you pass through when you die. I hate it here. I swore I'd never come back, ever.'

Richard looked around again. The In-Between place didn't seem so bad. Already his terror was fading, purged by the surrounding whiteness. Ellie, on the other hand, seemed positively distraught.

'Does this mean I'm dead?' Richard asked. 'Did that thing kill me?' An even more awful thought occurred to him. 'Did you?'

'I didn't think!' cried Ellie. 'I saw that creature and all I knew was we had to get somewhere safe. This seemed like the only place we might escape to.'

'I don't feel dead,' mused Richard. 'Actually, I feel fine.'

'That's because you're not supposed to be here,' she moaned. 'You're body's still there, you're still tied to it. The creature can't touch it. It's after

161

our souls and that's all I am. I shouldn't have come back here!' she cried. 'I shouldn't have!'

Richard perceived a sound in the distance—or was it in his own head?—like far-off thunder, or the pounding hoof beats of many horses.

Ellie looked terrified. 'If we stay here,' she whispered, 'I don't think we'll be able to go back.'

'What do you mean?'

'I only made it back last time because of my books. That, and . . . a promise someone made. But it was difficult, very difficult. If I stay here much longer, I'll be pulled away.' She hugged her knees tightly.

'Pulled away by what?' Richard was finding it hard to concentrate. Though he was unaware of it, he was beginning to forget what had brought them there in the first place. The distant thunder sounded oddly inviting. 'Do you hear a rumbling noise?'

Ellie shivered. 'No. Aren't you cold?'

'Not really.'

The rumbling continued. Richard paced back and forth, trying to get some kind of visual bearing, but the whiteness was uniform and complete.

'Is there anything else here?'

Ellie didn't answer. She'd buried her face in her hands and sat curled up in a terrified ball, shaking like a leaf.

Something odd was happening in Richard's mind. It was as though the whiteness was covering his thoughts, muffling his feelings. He saw that something was wrong with Ellie, but couldn't think what it might be.

He remembered that she'd said she was cold and went to sit with her. He thought of putting his arm around her shoulders before remembering that it would just slip through her. Instead he sat as close as he could without actually touching her and gave her an encouraging smile. She hardly seemed to notice him.

The whiteness began to take on a kind of texture, a gentle drifting downwards. Richard squinted, trying to understand, then it came to him.

'It's snowing,' he cried happily. 'Look Ellie, it's snowing!'

He looked around, only to discover he was sitting next to thin air. Ellie was gone.

This troubled him. Had she said she was leaving? He couldn't remember. The sound of thunder continued in the distance, closer now than before.

A shadow fell over him. Richard looked up.

Before him stood a little desk that Richard suspected hadn't been there a moment earlier, though he couldn't be sure. Behind it sat a man. He was quite bald and thin with strikingly angular features and very long fingers. Richard could not have guessed his age.

The man appeared to be reading from a large book on the table in front of him. By his side stood a heavyset three-legged metal brazier containing an open flame. Both he and it seemed quite unaffected by the curtains of snow falling silently around them, but without seeming to land on either.

The man looked up from his ledger and frowned.

'You're not what I was expecting at all,' he said in a deep voice.

Richard didn't know how to respond to this. 'Oh. Sorry.'

The man peered at Richard over his spectacles. His eyes were an exceptionally bright shade of blue and were striking even when narrowed in an expression hinting at deep misgivings, as they were now.

'You're alive,' observed the man, as though this was not at all satisfactory.

'Yep,' replied Richard. 'She's not though,' he added, nodding at where Ellie had lately been but no longer was.

He stood up and looked around him in confusion. 'Where did she go?'

His interlocutor seemed preoccupied and was leafing through his book. 'She who?' he snapped.

Richard hesitated before answering. 'Ellie.' Yes, that was her name.

The man adjusted his spectacles. 'She appears to be undergoing her own process. I can only assume, therefore, that I'm here for you.'

This made sense to Richard. He put his hands in his pockets and leaned forward, ready to be helpful. He understood that he'd disappointed this person somehow and was keen to help out.

The deep-voiced man continued to leaf through his pages, observing Richard with one blue eye as he did so. 'For a man in your predicament, you seem extremely detached.'

'It's how I register abject terror,' answered Richard, although he didn't so much feel frightened as remember that he'd felt frightened very recently. He couldn't remember why. 'Besides,' he added, 'I've seen some pretty messed-up things the times I forgot to take my medication. This is pretty tame so far.'

There followed a pause in the conversation. For some time the only sounds were the swish of paper, the faint crackle of the flame in its metal cage, and that muffled quivering that air makes when snow falls through it. Richard waited patiently.

'Aren't you going to ask me my name?' inquired the man. 'People usually do.'

'Ok,' said Richard, 'what's your name?'

The man sighed. 'Never mind. I could give you the speech about how I Have Had Many Names and do the spooky voice but I think we'd best sort out this confusion first. You can call me Nubby.'

Fair enough, thought Richard. This guy seemed to know what he was doing. Richard wasn't at all worried.

'Is all this usual?' Richard gestured to the desk and book

Nubby glanced up. 'People tend to get what they expect,' he said shortly.

He lowered his eyes and scrutinised the fine handwriting on the page. A moment later he boomed a satisfied 'Aha!' indicating that he'd found what he was searching for. He smoothed out the page, picked up a pen, and leaned forward to engulf Richard in his cerulean gaze.

'Now,' said Nubby, 'tell me exactly what happened before you came here. What do you remember?'

Richard told him, to the best of recollection. The memories came easily enough, though there was no emotion attached to them. He spoke about himself, where he came from and what he did for a living. He explained where he'd gone to school. He described his parents, his village, and the places where he'd played as a child. He remembered the house he grew up in, the smell of the rooms, the wooden shelves and the itchy carpets, the coldness of the door handles and window glass in the early morning. He relived his earliest memories, his childhood joys, his first kiss, and his favourite toys.

Nubby listened, taking notes in a steady hand. It didn't occur to Richard to wonder why he was saying all these things. He also failed to notice that once he spoke of something he immediately forgot all about it, as though it had never happened at all. As his words were transcribed onto Nubby's ledger they left a void in Richard's mind of which he was innocently oblivious, filled with nothing but the silence of falling snow and the accompaniment of distant thunder.

Richard explained how he'd come to the mountains and forgot that there was such a thing as a mountain. He spoke of his new friendship with Ellie and immediately forgot her name and that he'd ever met her. He recalled his walk through the graveyard with great attention to detail and forgot every single one a moment later. He failed to describe the chilly loneliness of the children's graves and the unsettling insides of the sanatorium, because the whiteness had already erased those feelings. Everything he spoke of had been stripped of emotion. Richard relived his flight up the stairs to the attic without terror. When it came to the eruption of the beast through the floor, he described the horrifying blur as best he could and did so calmly and without fear.

Nubby had said nothing for a while, but raised an eyebrow at the mention of the creature. 'A beast, you say?' He put aside the pen and leaned forward curiously, adjusting his spectacles. 'What did it look like?'

Richard shrugged. It didn't seem important. Had Nubby not interrupted at that moment he would have forgotten the event altogether.

'Not sure,' he said. 'A wolf, maybe?'

Nubby smiled. 'Ah! I love wolves. They used to be called the Guardians of the Dead, you know. Had we met in another time I might have appeared to you with a wolf's head.' He shrugged nostalgically. 'Seems a bit old-fashioned now.'

Nubby scratched his head. 'Come to think of it, it's rather odd that such a thing should occur to you, I must say. Not many people come to me with monster stories these days. Though having heard your case, everything makes a little more sense.' He picked up his pen once more and bent over the ledger, scribbling expertly.

'Why was it following me?' asked Richard.

Nubby gestured in his direction without looking up. 'I imagine it's because of that rock in your pocket.'

Richard had forgotten all about the rock, taken from his rucksack in the corridor of the sanatorium and before that from the waters of the river. He produced it from the folds of his jacket and examined it.

At first he saw only the same dark lines he'd observed that day in the mountains. Then the seemingly random marks took shape in his mind and he saw a faint but distinctive outline—a jagged, primitive caricature of a wolf.

He laughed like a child. 'Well, will you look at that!'

He was astonished he hadn't noticed it before. The lines were meaningless when observed individually, but if one knew how to look at them they came together in a beautiful ensemble, winding around the rough surface in a flowing arabesque. It was as though the animal had curled itself protectively around the stone itself, which now seemed to nestle safely in the linear creature's embrace.

Richard was so engrossed in this discovery he hardly noticed as Nubby rose from his desk and came over to share in his admiration. Though Richard was above average height Nubby was taller still. He bent his angular head to scrutinise the object.

'Beautiful,' he mused. 'Beautiful, but cruel.' Nubby's face turned dark and his blue eyes flashed. 'An act of great cruelty was involved here and something tells me this was not a unique occurrence.'

He held out his hand and Richard handed him the stone. Nubby strolled off into the whiteness, examining the object.

'Such unhappiness,' he murmured, 'such unbearable unhappiness. This creature was duped into betraying a trusted friend, duped by someone I have yet to meet. The poor creature couldn't help itself. And he's not the only one, not by any measure.' He sighed. 'Well, at least for him the journey's over.'

Richard saw something flicker in the distance. A dim shadow emerged, loping through the falling snow, and paused some distance from where they stood. Richard squinted at the distinctly canine silhouette. Eyes that had previously blazed nightmarish yellow were now brown and gazed back at him with primal intelligence, the animal's black and rust-coloured markings unruffled by the snow.

Suddenly it padded away and disappeared into the white nothingness.

Nubby watched it go. 'Much better. How very unkind to keep him locked away for so long.'

He turned and observed Richard thoughtfully, hefting the rock in one hand with the other tucked behind his back. His blue eyes wandered over to the flickering flame in the metal brazier.

Eventually he seemed to arrive at some kind of conclusion. He returned to his seat behind the desk, placing the rock in Richard's hand as he passed. Richard had forgotten it had ever been in his possession and looked at it curiously. All trace of the dark lines had vanished.

Nubby sat down with a sigh. Very carefully he closed the oversized book and removed his spectacles.

'Look,' he said, 'your medical condition has never been the most propitious to long life and we could easily put all this down to some sort of cerebral complication brought on by a sudden and extreme case of the heebie-jeebies. However,' he continued, 'there are rules about this sort of thing, and your friend . . .' he peeked into the book, ' . . . Ellie appears to have bent them ever so slightly.'

Ellie . . . The name rang a distant bell somewhere in Richard's whitewashed subconscious. Yes, Ellie. Nice girl, big brown eyes. Bit on the immaterial side. He smiled at this one remaining image, undisturbed as he was by anything else save the rumbling in the distance, which seemed much closer now.

Nubby continued. 'In these sorts of cases the safest thing is probably to bend the rules ever so slightly back the other way.' From somewhere he produced a gigantic tartan handkerchief and began to clean his spectacles, observing Richard as he did so from beneath his eyebrows, though not unkindly.

'Besides,' he added, breathing on his lenses, 'I don't think you're quite ready for all this. By the sound of it you're dealing with a situation that lies somewhat outside what you would consider ordinary, although clearly you've a part to play in all this. You're doing a fairly good job so far; let's see how you get on.'

Nubby stepped around the desk. Richard felt that something was about to happen and wasn't at all sure he wanted it to. The one remaining image he had, the memory of Ellie, glimmered in his mind. He feared Nubby was about to take it away. The sound of thunder grew louder.

Nubby gestured to him to step forward. Richard stayed where he was and shook his head. 'I don't want to go back. I like it here.'

'Not to worry,' said Nubby airily, 'you won't remember a thing. Or rather, you'll remember everything but.' He gestured again and Richard felt compelled to obey him. 'In any case,' Nubby added, 'you'll be back soon enough. Though something tells me the next time will be quite different.'

A thought occurred to Richard as he stepped up beside Nubby, who adjusted him to face in a certain direction.

'She said she'd be pulled away. Will she be there when I get back?'

Nubby gave him a funny look. 'Oh, I reckon that once you're there it'll be easy enough for her to follow. She's finally discovered that, as far as motivations go, some*one* is better than some*where*. But for me to send you back you need something to connect with, some person or purpose that will bring you back. I need you to think of a reason.'

Richard tried to think, but the whiteness and the thunder were confusing him. 'A reason . . .'

The only image he could conjure up was Ellie.

'Come on,' urged Nubby, 'think. I need something for you to connect with, something material. What about your colleague?' He peeked into the book once more, adjusting his spectacles. 'What about this Graham fellow? He sounds pretty earthy.'

A spark jumped in Richard's mind. 'Graham,' he murmured. 'Graham, our project . . . We're going to make it work.'

'Yes,' said Nubby 'good; you have unfinished business. This project is important to you and must be completed, yes?'

'Yes,' muttered Richard. 'Yes, but . . . Ellie.'

Nubby waved this aside. 'She'll will be along shortly. I'll see to that.'

Richard was reassured. If Ellie was there, everything would be fine.

Nubby removed his spectacles and began polishing them once more with his handkerchief. The rumbling continued to grow.

'Now then, young man, I need you to remember something for me. Namely, where is your friend Graham? Think hard!'

Richard thought hard, fighting the confusion in his mind. Words and names drifted by like phantom shapes in the ocean abyss. As he pictured Graham, a ghost-like memory of green riverbanks of clean cut grass and a tranquil river glittering in the afternoon sunshine floated into his thoughts, along with a name. 'Cambridge, I think.'

Nubby frowned. 'That's a bit of a stretch. Where will he be when he gets back?'

Richard could hardly hear him for the thunder in his ears, but he thought hard. Finally, he spoke.

'The pub,' he said with certainty.

Nubby shrugged. 'That'll have to do.'

With that he reached forward and touched Richard's arm. As he did the thundering swelled around them on all sides.

There was that sudden, horrible lurching feeling again. As Richard tumbled backwards through space he felt as though a surge of galloping horses had crashed over his head like a great wave, plunging across space and through the falling snow beyond.

*****

Richard came to his senses in a dark, enclosed place, his hands covering his face and a roaring in his ears.

He gasped like a man emerging from the sea and struggled to his feet, trying to take in his surroundings. His heart was thumping. He stood for a moment and stared. Then he rubbed his eyes hard just to be sure.

Before him was a little wooden door with a coat hook; to his right, a tiny window set with dimpled stained glass; behind him gurgled an ancient toilet as the last of the flushing water swirled away down the pipes.

Richard emerged from the lavatory and into the restaurant, his thoughts a groggy blur. He smelled food and heard the quiet buzz of conversation and background music. Richard looked around for Graham before remembering that he'd left for a few days. How odd . . . he was sure Graham would be here, somehow.

'You are all right, Herr Mathern?'

Richard swivelled to find Frau Indergand standing nearby, her blue bucket in her hand.

'Hnnnggg?' he inquired.

She looked concerned. 'When you are passing now the door, I see you are walking down from the mountain . . . how you say . . . *irgendwie sahen Sie etwas komisch aus*. I am thinking, maybe you are again feeling unwell.'

'Hmmmmnngr,' reflected Richard. He'd forgotten he'd gone for a walk. Yes, he remembered now . . . up by the sanatorium. In an instant he recalled the feeling of wind on his cheek, the smell of flowers, and the soft give of earth under his shoes.

He waved towards the bucket. 'Hmno, m'fine, thagyou veymush . . .'

Frau Indergand kept an eye on him as he made his way unsteadily up the stairs, then shook her head and returned to the never-ending task of dusting.

Richard slipped and tripped up the stairs to his room, both hands gripping the bannister. The tactile grain of the wood felt strange and wonderful, yet familiar, like the first touch of spring grass after a long winter.

His head had gone strangely blank. He felt dizzy, but a sudden knock on the head from the beam told him he'd made it to the landing. His stomach wobbled inside his belly and he remembered what he'd eaten for breakfast that morning and for dinner the night before, as well as a host of other dishes he'd forgotten he'd ever tasted.

As he unlocked his door he noticed the room was dark. He wondered what time it was, then everything began to spin. He sat down on the bed and closed his eyes for a second. The door creaked shut on its own, immersing him in reassuring obscurity.

He gripped the woollen bedcover to steady himself as images swam before his eyes—the faces of his parents, the view from his grey office window in London, the heavily congested glare of Alan his editor . . .

His hands felt strangely clammy. He wondered if he might be having another seizure but remembered taking his meds earlier that day, and induced that he was simply feeling ill. Had he eaten something strange before his walk up to the sanatorium?

Ellie . . .

Suddenly his mind was filled by a monstrous vision of a lunging wolfish creature and Ellie's terrified face.

Richard's eyes snapped open. He threw himself off the bed, stumbling like a drunken man. Somehow in the darkness of the room he found the door and, half-falling, reached for the handle.

What the hell do you think you're doing? the portrait on the wall seemed to ask, the mountaineer almost invisible in the half-light.

'M'going back,' Richard muttered, 'gonna help 'lie.'

He flailed in the dark, lurching blindly until his searching fingers found the curve of the door handle, the brass cold under his fingers. His hand slipped and he fell backwards onto the floor.

The ceiling swam in front of his eyes. He felt himself drift into a state of half-sleep, though his eyes remained open.

Somewhere in the background the door creaked, followed by a familiar voice.

'Richard? Are you all right?'

He wasn't sure if her voice was in the room or his head, but he heard it clearly. He wondered if he was awake, then decided that he wasn't. Either that, or the ceiling had split open allowing the night breeze in from the outside, carrying with it the aroma of fresh apples.

'There you are,' he said, relieved. 'I was just on my way to find you.'

'Yes, sorry about that. Everything was so confusing and I got a bit lost.'

A shadow came to sit on the bed. 'What are you doing on the floor?' it asked.

'Not sure,' said Richard, 'but I don't think I should move just yet.' The stability of the floorboards was wonderfully reassuring. 'Awfully nice of you to come and visit.'

The shadow tilted its head, as though amused. 'It seemed about time. After all, you've come to see me often enough. You appear to have left your rucksack at the sanatorium. I thought I'd let you know.'

Richard gurgled in gratitude.

'I seem to have caught you at a bad time,' said Ellie's voice. 'I didn't realize it was so late. I guess I drifted off.'

'No problem,' muttered Richard from the floor, his eyes now half closed. 'But I thought you said you never slept.'

'Did I?' She seemed unsure herself. 'Perhaps I do after all. Perhaps I'm asleep now. Perhaps I'm still at the sanatorium, but I'm also in your mind. Do you think ghosts can be in two places at once?'

If Richard had been awake he might have considered this problem. As it was, he simply slipped deeper into sleep, oblivion beckoning from a gently gathering darkness.

'How could you have gotten into my mind so quickly? We only met the other week, surely that's not a very long time.'

The shadow shrugged. 'Who knows? Sometimes people remember a glimpse of a stranger long after they've forgotten their mother's face. I suppose there was too much left unsaid. In any case I guess I'd better be going back.'

'Wait . . .'

His body didn't move, but his mind stretched out and grasped the shadow's hand as it moved away, wishing it to remain. It was warm and exquisitely soft and she gasped with surprise at feeling his touch. In his sleepy state, Richard did not find this strange.

'Would you like to stay?'

The shadow paused. Then it bent over Richard's sleeping body and lowered its face towards his.

'I'm afraid I've grown so used to lying under the stars I've quite forgotten what it's like to spend the night indoors. Besides, I prefer the fresh air.'

Richard felt the most tender of caresses on his face and wondered again if he was asleep or awake. That was his last thought before he drifted into nothingness, where he dreamt of yellow ribbons, curtains of snow, and streams of water clear as the sky.

When he awoke, he remembered nothing.

HEART OF GOLD
CHAPTER EIGHTEEN

ALL WAS NOT well at No. 31 Dratford Place, headquarters of Aberfinchley Inc.

Pigeons roosting in the edifice's lofty nooks sensed a tremor of dread run through the building's steel veins. Many interpreted this as an ill omen but were overruled by their larger brethren who, bloated by a diet of soggy chips and processed street food, told the others in loud and abrasive tones not to worry so much. Tremors of dread were nothing new, they warbled. This was the City, after all. Besides, they added, the data was inconclusive and evidence was insufficient to warrant a change in current pigeon policy. They then returned to their busy schedule of strutting around, cooing, and crapping on the windows ledges of the mighty.

Dawes peered around the corner of his office; the front desk was unattended.

'Alice?'

No response. Dawes' eyebrows twitched in annoyance.

He called again and, met by a deafening silence, went in search of his secretary.

The hallways were empty. Dawes made for the head office—Julian's accustomed location. Here too he was thwarted, for the vestibule was deserted.

Dawes' eyes narrowed. Where was everyone?

He paced the length of the corridor and was astonished to find nobody at work. The glass-fronted offices were unoccupied. He rounded a corner and came face to face with a portly electrician perched on a stepladder, elbows-deep in the ceiling.

'Abelardo! What's going on?'

The electrician twisted to face Dawes. 'Hello Mr Dawes! There is a problem with the cameras, not good, not good. Allerby call me, he says it must be fixed. No worries, I fix it! It is finished by Tuesday, Wednesday latest. No problem. It will be good.'

'Forget about the cameras. Where is everyone?'

The congenial Abelardo looked confused. 'I work alone today, Mr Dawes, no one is here with me. Is only Abelardo. Aberlardo fly solo today.'

'I meant, where's the staff?'

Abelardo glanced around the tomb-like office. 'They are away.'

'Indeed. Where have they all gone?'

Abelardo considered this. 'Maybe they have lunch?'

'At eleven o'clock in the morning?'

Abelardo shrugged and returned to butchering the CCTV system.

Dawes stalked the empty floor. There was something afoot and he was damned if he wasn't going to find out what.

His ear twitched at a clandestine noise down the hall. He peered around the corner just in time to spot a brown loafer disappearing into the supply closet.

With the stealth of a leopard stalking a gazelle, Dawes was across the hallway and standing before the closet. From within came the sounds of secrecy and dissimilation. His nostrils flared in satisfaction. Here, then, was the nucleus of deceit! Dawes grasped the door handle and, pausing only to straighten his tie, erupted into the closet.

'Julian! What on earth are you doing?'

Julian looked out from between the shelves of post-its. 'I have no explanation,' he admitted.

In the shadows behind Julian Dawes spied a second figure, which was soon revealed to be Alice. She stepped out from behind a stack of boxes marked EMERGENCY SHREDDERS with a look of supreme guilt.

Before Dawes could draw any conclusions, he realised they weren't alone.

He pushed the door open further to reveal that the closet currently housed the entire senior staff of Aberfinchley Inc. Behind piles of paper or wedged between the shelves he estimated that all executives could be accounted for, as well as many of the deputies and assistants. They huddled around a small projector humming a felonious hum.

'Ms Spragg,' said Dawes, 'you appear to be giving a presentation in a closet.'

Ms Spragg's eyes flitted. Dawes followed them. The familiar dome of Ahmid Sardharwalla's head loomed beyond the paperclips and it was to this that Dawes directed his next remark.

'What in God's name is going on here, Ahmid?'

Ahmid shifted guiltily. Before he could answer Alice spoke up.

172

'We're having a meeting, Mr Dawes. I wanted to tell you, but they said I shouldn't.'

The others glared at her, but she kept her defiant eyes on Dawes.

Dawes allowed a look of calculated uncertainty to flit across his brow. 'But I walked past a perfectly serviceable boardroom just now, empty and begging to be used. Why the unorthodox venue?' He directed this question at no one in particular, and no one in particular seemed inclined to answer it. Once again it fell to Alice to explain.

'Someone needs to take a stand, Mr Dawes. We're here to discuss what's to be done about . . . about the problem.'

Her assertiveness lent some small measure of courage to the assembled suits. Indistinct mutterings sounded from the corners of the closet.

Dawes turned on Ahmid. 'You convened a staff meeting without notifying me?'

'Well,' mumbled Ahmid, 'it's like Alice said. We've got a problem, Alistair, which needs to be addressed. Only Luther isn't to know about it, if at all possible, seeing as he is, in fact, not to put too fine a point on it, the crux of what could be best described, by those in the know, as the problem itself, more or less . . .'

'Am I to understand,' interjected Dawes, 'that this meeting relates to Mr Aberfinchley?'

'He's crap!' exclaimed an anonymous voice from the back of the room.

All at once the tension snapped and the dike of resentment broke as other injured entities joined in the protest.

'His conduct is absolutely outrageous!' exclaimed a tall hawkish man with round spectacles, formerly from the accounting department. He'd had the temerity to suggest to Luther that a new Rolls Royce might not be a tax-deductible expense and was now tallying paperclip deliveries in a warehouse in Enfield.

'His behaviour is unacceptable!' cried the former overseer of customer services.

'He's driving the company into the dirt!' moaned the former business manager's assistant consultant.

'This would never have happened when Old Lord Aberfinchley was in charge!' lamented the former deputy head janitor.*

'Hear hear!' cried the grey man from a corner, his voice lost in the babble.

Dawes raised a hand and the tumult subsided.

'You're planning a mutiny.' His words fell like lead.

---

* He hadn't been invited, but it was his closet and he'd refused to lend them the key.

Ahmid collected himself at last and stared back with defiance. 'And what of it? Are we to watch our company be destroyed? The competition can smell it, Dawes. Offers are being made! People are leaving! Those you see here are the loyal ones, who do not wish to see this great company gutted and butchered! Are we to stand by and witness all we've worked for be consigned to dirt on the whim of a boy?'

'No!' was the determined, if somewhat muted cry. Corporate types aren't often called upon to provide ovations. Even so, Dawes was not swayed.

'There is procedure for this sort of thing,' he said. 'The board must be convened and all voting partners must register their displeasure as an official complaint, and, should the votes against the current occupier of the position of CEO be in sufficient number, official action is taken. However,' he continued, 'as I'm sure Ms Spragg has just explained to you, Mr Aberfinchley is a majority shareholder and therefore cannot be outvoted by the board, not without extraordinary measures.'

What he didn't mention was that he was still attempting to hack into Luther's private investment platform and didn't want to deal with an uprising until he'd managed it. Once he had the numbers in hand, then he'd know what to do. Until then, he would remain loyal to the late Desmond Aberfinchley.

'The board,' quoted Dawes over the rising protests, 'can typically fire anyone in the company, absent an agreement to the contrary. If there is a dispute over a majority shareholder's actions, then the board may seek to overrule them, within the guidelines set out by corporate governance law and the management agreements.'

'Nonesense!' cried the assembly, or words to that effect.

Dawes could see that the smell of blood was in the assembly's nostrils. He'd weathered many storms, however, and ploughed on. 'It is extremely unusual to suspend anybody with majority interest and such actions should not be undertaken absent extraordinary reasons such as extreme mismanagement, fraud, loss of a required license, or incarceration. In most such cases it is advisable to seek a legal mandate . . .'

'Bollocks!' howled the room, whose occupants were taking rather well to their new role of lynch mob.

'We don't have time for all that Dawes,' said Ahmid, who'd elbowed his way through the throng to Dawes' side. 'The time to act is now. Luther has lost all legitimacy and it's our opinion he should be removed, one way or another.'

The room murmured in agreement.

'Nevertheless,' said Dawes quietly, 'Luther is Lord Aberfinchley's successor and representative. The company must honour Des' values, even if his son does not.'

'Join us, Alistair!' hissed Ahmid. 'You know the system better than anyone. Together we can take him!'

His eyes glowed with revolutionary fervour. The room waited with baited breath. Dawes hesitated.

But Dawes had promised Desmond. And Dawes was loyal.

'I cannot.'

The balloon of expectation was punctured.

'Mr Sardharwalla,' Dawes intoned, 'I call on you to disperse this assembly and report to my office immediately.'

But Ahmid had played his cards. There was no going back. 'If we cannot coax, cajole, or inveigle the directorship back into sanity,' he said gravely, 'then we must at least wrench it from insanity.'

There were mutterings of assent. The flare of mutiny continued to burn in the eyes of the assembled staff.

Dawes looked on with unease: revolutionary rumblings do not lie within the Englishman's comfort zone. It was time to leave.

He turned to Alice. 'Return to your desk and stay there.'

It was an order and not to be disobeyed. Alice glared at him, the colour high in her face. She shoved Julian aside and left the closet.

Dawes moved his gaze onto Julian. Nothing was said, but the message was clear. Julian followed Alice.

Dawes turned to the rest of the room. 'Loyalty, ladies and gentlemen,' he said simply. 'Loyalty.'

He left, closing the door behind him.

'Shame,' muttered the former overseer of customer services.

Ahmid stared at the door ruefully. The hubbub rose slowly once again. 'Quiet!' he snapped. 'Our plan will proceed as discussed.'

'But Dawes will give us away!' cried a voice. Others joined in.

'We're done for.'

'It's all over, lads.'

'Let's trash the place!'

'SILENCE!' screamed Ahmid.

There followed some semblance of silence.

'Dawes will not betray us,' Ahmid said, wishing his own doubts away. 'The plan will proceed as discussed.' He turned to Ms Spragg. 'Please continue the presentation.'

Dawes marched past Abelardo's ladder. The mention of lunch had clearly been too much for the handyman to resist for he was having an early sandwich break. Dawes noted the lifeless cameras with approval; there would be no record of who had entered the supply closet.

He made sure that both Julian and Alice were back in their seats and swept into his office.

He sat at his desk for a time, wrestling with a choice. Then, reluctantly, he reached for the phone.

*****

Among the comfortable residences basking in the Oxfordshire sunshine was a large, whitewashed house benefitting from admirable amenities and an extensive garden. Officially No. 4 Hedge Lane, it was known to anyone who attended garden parties there as "Long Hedge House". It was a sizeable domicile and boasted many enviable features for the out-of-town businessperson.

The outdoor pool had been drained and covered up due to cold weather. Luther was therefore in his mother's sauna instead, recovering from an absolutely masterful hangover.

The stillness was scythed in half by the ringing of a telephone. A groan issued from the sauna and continued until Luther's mother answered.

'Halloooo, Europa Aberfinchley speaking.'

'Europa, it's Alistair.'

'Oh, Ali!' Europa drifted sideways onto the settee. 'It's been such a *long* time! How are you?'

'I'm well, thank you. Is Luther there?'

'You know, Ali, you really should keep in touch more. We all missed you at the garden party last week. Binky did that *awfully* clever song on the guitar. Everyone had a simply wonderful time, I can't imagine *what* kept you away.'

'Things are rather busy here, I'm afraid. Is Luther there?'

'Oh, yes. He's resting now. Had a bit of an old banger last night with some chums from school.'

'I need to talk to him. If,' Dawes added, *'it's not an inconvenient time.'*

'He's technically on leave, Ali,' Europa reminded him.

'It's important.'

'Anything *I* can help you with?'

There was a pause, followed by a polite but emphatic *'No.'*

'Are you sure? You may recall I helped Des with most of the legal work when you were setting up the company. I'm sure your *teensy* problem won't be beyond me.'

'I'm afraid this is confidential. But thank you for the offer.'

'Oh, very well,' hummed Europa, 'but Luther *won't* be pleased.'

She put down the phone and sought out the oaken door of the steamy chamber in which her son convalesced.

'Loo-Loo,' she sang, knocking lightly, 'it's for you.'

'Mmmghgffo way,' was the indistinct reply.

'It's Ali from the office,' continued Europa. 'I think you should take the call, it sounds *rawther* important.'

'Leemee lone.'

Europa drifted back into the drawing room. 'I'm sooo sorry, Ali,' she lamented, 'but there's absolutely *nothing* to be done. Loo-Loo's just *too* woozy.'

'I'm afraid I must insist. We've been unable to reach him on his mobile—'

'Well,' interrupted Europa, 'I will have to insist right back. I know company policy back to front—because I wrote most of it—and Luther is entitled to a total of fifty-eight days annual leave plus bank holidays.'

'Listen, Europa, Luther's upset a lot of people. Explanations are required, he needs to come to the phone.'

'I don't *quite* understand, Ali. Isn't Loo-Loo the majority shareholder?'

'Admittedly, yes. However—'

'Well, then, isn't he entitled to the final word when it comes to disposal of company funds, bonds, investments, etc?'

'That's not entirely untrue, but—'

'Well, then!' Europa exclaimed, 'I don't see why you need to worry about Loo-Loo's enterprising little initiatives, even if they seem a tad unconventional. I'm sure the company can afford a nick or two in the name of progress.'

'But—'

'Besides,' she continued, with a subtle change in tone. 'Luther is, after all, the one who decides on which direction the company should take, as both CEO and majority share holder.' She allowed the words to linger slightly, before adding, 'As you yourself said, Ali dear.'

There was silence down the line following this icy cadence.

Europa rotated languorously at the hips, reached for her drink and missed. 'Oh crumbs, I've toppled the flowers. What an absolute *diffidums* I am! I'm afraid I've got to go now, Ali. I'm sure things will sort themselves out. I'll make sure Loo-Loo gets in first thing! Ta-ta.'

Beep.

Outside the autumn air shimmered as it mixed with the steamy vapours of the sauna ventilation. Things were calm once more.

In his office Dawes was left to wrestle his thoughts.

He stared darkly at the wall for a minute or two. A draft wafted the curtain. Even in this troubled time, Dawes had the presence of mind to note that the glazing required a maintenance check.

He decided that, in order to brace himself for whatever was coming, he would need something to fortify his spirit.

'Alice?' he said over the intercom.

'Here, Mr Dawes,' was the reply. It carried no hint of their last exchange.

'Tea, if you please.'

Dawes watched the gently wafting curtain out of the corner of his eye. 'And Alice,' he added, 'please ask Maintenance to turn on the central heating. I fancy the cold weather is on its way.'

The central heating had not been used since the end of the previous spring and it is fitting that, when the great generator was recalled to life it was done to fuel the deliberations of the great and powerful. Sadly, in the intervening months many of the building's younger pigeons had made their permanent residences inside the mouths of the generator's air vents and were immediately sucked in and pulverised.

The surviving birds interpreted this as a sign that the winds of change were indeed blowing across the parking lot of existence and sowing discord amongst the breadcrumbs of prosperity, as had been foretold; the time for change had come. Since the air vent victims included most of the original naysayers, it was the work of a moment to form a new advisory committee, which embraced widespread reform. It was decided to relocate the entire pigeon population of No. 31 Dratford Place to one of their subsidiary buildings in Hampstead. There, they would be safe.

The migration came off without a hitch and there was much rejoicing. Unfortunately the new colony was tragically wiped out three weeks later when the property was knocked down as part of a redevelopment scheme to build an underground parking lot-cum-swimming complex for the human owner's billionaire offspring.

*****

Richard emerged from the forest and brushed pine needles from his fleece. He breathed deeply a few times, enjoying the pleasantness of the evening. A hard day's work on the plateau had done him good and he'd largely shaken off the wooziness he'd felt that morning.

He descended the path past the sanatorium to his hotel. Graham was due back that evening and Richard intended to get some celebratory supplies in town. Not wanting to take his rucksack, he popped into his room and stored it in the closet. His trousers were dirty from hours of hiking so he swapped them for the pair he'd worn the day before, then grabbed his wallet and went back out.

A few steps from the hotel he stopped. There was something heavy and lumpy in his pocket. He fished about and discovered a stone, the colour of ivory and worn smooth but otherwise unremarkable.

Funny, thought Richard, I don't remember picking that up.

He shrugged and perched it on top of one of the fence posts lining the road before proceeding into town.

Richard took his time, enjoying the end of a long day and peering into shop windows as he passed. He paused a couple of times, once to stretch his legs, and once for a brief internal tussle with the voice that men sometimes have in their heads that assures them that yes, they would look stunning in that fur-lined parka with the paramilitary epaulette-like shoulder pads.* Otherwise he progressed uninterrupted towards the town square.

A few people were wandering about with that gait that suggests they're out for drinks but haven't quite decided where to look for them yet. Richard glanced at his watch. It wasn't even five o'clock yet. It felt later; the sky was already darkening.

Richard found himself in front of the antique shop. It occurred to him that he'd never thanked Fosco for his help during the river incident the previous afternoon. He wandered up to the grimy window and spotted a hunched form, occupied in some restorative task or other. He decided not to disturb the old man and wandered on. Perhaps he'd get a chance next time Fosco delivered the hotel's dinner special.

There was a discrete noise behind him. He knew who it was before he saw her.

'You didn't come to see me this morning,' said Ellie, her back to him as she casually examined the tasteful arrangement of watches in a nearby window.

Richard came to join her. 'I had to be at the cabin early. I hoped to catch the bear on its way back up to higher altitudes.'

He spoke softly and pretended to examine the watches so no one would wonder who he was talking to. The shop exhibited timepieces of all kinds with bracelets of leather and linked chain, some encased in rose-tinted gold, others in silver, all synchronised to the second and ticking away merrily. The names of *La Chaux-de-Fonds* and *Le Locle* were much in evidence.

Ellie cocked her head. 'Did you get any good photographs?'

'Hm. I ran into a rather handsome alpine chough, a kind of raven that lives here all year round. It's got a rather striking yellow bill and distinctive red feet that'll look good in the pictures. Nice glossy black feathers, too.'

'Any bears?'

---

* This is the same voice that routinely seeks to convince you that you are, in fact, a twenty-two-year-old fashion model with cheekbones so sharp they could shave themselves, and whispers conspiracy theories about how your mirror is lying to you regarding your muscle mass and skin saturation.

Richard shook his head. 'Same as last time and the time before.'

'I'm sorry. That must be terribly frustrating.'

She paused, as though waiting for him to speak. But Richard had become distracted by the reflection in the window of the square behind them. An American couple on holiday were attempting to make friends with Ursula, the communal secretary. She in turn had slid along the bench as far as she could and was trying her best to convince them that she was, in fact, a decorative plinth.

Richard chuckled to himself.

Ellie pointed at one of the watches. 'I like that one,' she remarked, 'the silver casing and the white face make for quite a striking complexion. Almost,' she added, 'like a jewel in a snowstorm.'

If there was any emphasis on the last word, Richard failed to notice.

'Nah,' he said, 'I prefer this one. It's got five different dials! I wonder how they do that. Incidentally' he added, 'alpine coughs are supposed to be harbingers of snowfall if they appear near villages, so let me know if you spot one anywhere nearby.'

There was a lull in the conversation.

'Any thoughts on yesterday?' The words had clearly wanted saying so badly that Ellie nearly barked them.

Richard looked down, suddenly sheepish. 'Yes, er . . . I meant to ask you about that.' He glanced at Ellie, but she stared assiduously ahead.

'I had an attack, didn't I?' he asked gravely.

'Hmm?' She refused to look at him, seemingly transfixed by the timepieces.

He took a breath. 'Look, I woke up this morning, and I had . . . Well, I'm having a bit of trouble piecing together parts of yesterday. I remember walking in the graveyard and the sanatorium library . . . Then all of a sudden I was back at the hotel. At least, I think I was. It's all a bit vague. I remember making my way up to my room, and you were there, and I fell asleep, and that's about it. So I guessed I had some really awkward fit and I . . . Well, what I'm saying is, I'm sorry if I embarrassed you, and thanks for helping me, you know, find my way back and everything.'

She turned and looked at him with wide eyes. 'Oh no, it wasn't like that at all,' she cried. 'Don't apologise, it wasn't you, it was . . .' She seemed unable to continue and looked away.

Richard nodded. 'They're weird, the seizures. You don't need to try to make me feel better. Graham told me all about the first one he saw. Was there lots of drooling?'

'You don't remember anything?'

Richard became worried. 'No. Did I do something bad?'

After only the tiniest pause Ellie laughed so gaily that he was taken aback.

'Of course not!' she said, 'Nothing of the sort! It was all very quick, you just went quiet for a while and then you had some sort of dizzy spell. I walked you back to the hotel to see you were all right. That was it. Nothing embarrassing at all.'

Richard smiled in relief. 'Whew, that's good. I'm not sure what I might have done; I've only got Graham's word for it. He once tried to convince me that I'd gone on a neatening rampage and tried to iron all my shirts. Good thing the iron was unplugged, because apparently I did it while I was wearing them. I think he just wanted to save himself the embarrassment of admitting he'd done them himself while waiting for me to wake up.'

He interpreted Ellie's silence as gracious exoneration and smiled the embarrassed smile the afflicted give their carers when they're truly grateful.

'You know,' he said, 'on second thought I think that one's the nicest: the one in the corner with the leather strap. What's it called, *Le Coeur d'Or?* Whoever hand-wrote those labels really went to too much trouble, you can barely read the names.'

Ellie was about to speak when there was a shout from across the square. Richard turned to see Graham swaggering down the street from the station.

'Gotta go,' he mouthed, before striding across the cobbles towards his friend.

Ellie watched the two men embrace in a *poof* of anorak and wander off together in search, presumably, of libation.

She sighed and wandered along the edge of the square by herself. It was mostly empty now. The people it had lately contained had returned to the warm and welcoming indoors. A slight wind had picked up but Ellie couldn't feel it.

She found herself standing in front of the little fountain. She glanced up at the statuesque lady on her plinth, a pensive frown on her pale face.

You didn't ask for him, said the voice in her head.

Her frown deepened.

No, she thought, I didn't. Why should I? That place is best forgotten.

He was there, persisted the voice, *yesterday. Hal. He was there, behind the veil. You felt him.*

Ellie shook her head angrily. Not this, she thought desperately. She wouldn't relive it here, not again, not forever and ever. But the voice wouldn't leave her alone.

He doesn't want to see you.

Yes, he does. He's waiting for me. He promised.

She shouted it in her mind, and yet the whisper was louder.

No. You have delayed. You have stayed here. You never dared return to him, despite his promise, because you know he never cared.

'Yes he did,' she whispered. 'He did care. He loved me.'

181

The breeze blew cold through her, carrying with it a hollow laugh.

He lied.

A leaf blew fitfully across the square, as though trying to flee before the wind, only to have its escape cut short by Ursula. Having remained still as a tomb until she was sure the Americans were gone, Ursula now took a moment to contemplate the leaf entangled in her short curls. Satisfied that she was the only person left in the square, she raised her hand and removed it. She watched the wind carry it away in a loopy curve before whisking it around a corner and out of sight. Only then did she rise to her feet, groaning like a fishing trawler. She made for home, her walking stick clicking on the cobbles.

As Ursula passed the statue she thought she heard something like a sob.

She turned and examined the bronze woman staring mournfully up into the dark sky and the mountains beyond.

Ursula made a wry face and muttered to herself, 'I reckon whatever it is you're waiting for, Toots, it's too late for either of us.'

With that she swivelled and clicked her way homewards, leaving behind her a square that was, now, truly empty.

*****

In his field by the hotel Jerome the goat noticed with alarm that an unauthorised alteration had been made to his fence. Rearing up on his hind legs, he examined a particular post and identified Richard's stone as the culprit.

He huffed and waggled his ears: typical tourists, always littering.

There was something strange about this rock. Jerome sniffed it suspiciously. There was an odd after-smell about the thing that he couldn't quite place.

Jerome's scientific method consisted of two empirical tests, smelling being the first. Since this had yielded mixed results he decided to move on to the second.

Leaning forward, he extended an astonishingly large tongue and scooped the rock into his mouth.

A few minutes' hard sucking told him that whatever unusual life decisions this stone might previously have made, it was now a perfectly ordinary piece of rock.

Since he didn't have anything tastier to put in his mouth at that precise moment he enjoyed another minute or two of sucking. He then spat it out and resumed his circumnavigation of the field.

THE CITY OF CALVIN
CHAPTER NINETEEN

Geneva, 1868

HE ENGLISH CHURCH of the Holy Trinity swung open its doors and discharged its contents into the morning sunshine. The chattering congregation strolled into the square in twos and threes, admiring the waters of the River Rhône glistening some couple hundred yards away and exuding a general cordiality.

Amidst the large hats worn by the women was a pair of particularly impressive circumference, hinting at their newness and cost.

These drew the attention of two moustachioed men. One turned to the other enthusiastically. 'I say, Williams, look over there. It's the ladies from the channel ferry!'

'Why, so it is, Bellows,' agreed his friend. 'Ms Harriet!'

The owners of the hats revolved slowly. One, a severe-looking governess, frowned at the approaching dandies. Her younger, more attractive companion seemed better disposed towards their company.

'How lovely to see you,' exclaimed Bellows. 'We thought we'd lost you after we disembarked at Dieppe. Williams was certain you'd remained in Paris, weren't you, Williams?'

The younger woman flashed the two gentlemen a devastating smile, which thrilled them all the way up their tweed-lined travelling trousers. 'Why Mr Williams,' she chided, 'how terrible of you! I told you I'd make it to the Alps, never mind how many hats Paris had to offer. And by Jove I have! So there.'

She pursed her lips triumphantly. She wore her Sunday best rather than the travelling clothes in which the men had last seen her, hence the delay in recognition.

'I assure you, Ms Harriet,' replied Williams, 'I never doubted you.'

It had taken the English travellers eighteen hours to make the journey from the French capital. Their guidebooks had warned against the

183

apoplexy-inducing 20mph ride, but Ms Harriet and the other women in the group had astounded their male companions by keeping pace all the way from Newhaven. Ms Harriet, who'd scarcely had a chance to leave Gloucester before, found it thrilling. Bellows thought it all tremendously jolly—particularly the flattering travel dresses the ladies wore on the boat. Williams, meanwhile, was utterly lost to Ms Harriet and was already planning an impromptu business trip to Gloucester as soon as possible.

'Splendid, splendid!' said Bellows, beaming through his moustache at whatever ambassadors of womanhood were nearest. 'What a fine day!'

It was indeed. Across the river they could admire the historic bastion of the Old Town on the hill. Beyond it shone the white slopes of the Alps.

'Will you be staying long, Ms Harriet?' inquired Williams hopefully. Bellows was unlikely to leave Geneva until he was certain he'd been seen by just about everybody. 'We're due in Chamonix this Thursday. Perhaps you would like to accompany us?'

'That's where we're headed next! But our itinerary has us departing in two days. I fear we shall have a head start.'

Williams was visibly crushed. Ms Harriet felt for him, so obvious was his disappointment.

'Damn good idea,' interrupted Bellows, 'get ahead of this lot before they nick all the good digs, wot! I myself have taken rooms at the Palace Hotel, reserved months in advance. The owner's promised me a view of Mont Blanc!' He paused for the appropriate gasp of awe at this, but none was forthcoming.

Harriet's severe-looking companion was charitable enough to throw him a line. 'What do you plan to do while in Chamonix, Mr Bellows?' she enquired loftily.

Bellows wheeled on her, his engines re-ignited. 'Climbing, my dear lady! As the way of the proverbial ship is on the high seas, mine is ever upwards. The peaks call to me and I must answer. We have several ascents planned from Mont Blanc to Monte Rosa and beyond. Williams here,' he added, 'is to write about it in his column.'

'Are you a journalist, Mr Williams?' asked the governess, even as Bellows inhaled for another burst of verbal energy. Williams blushed as Ms Harriet turned towards him with genuine interest. Bellows' moustache twitched in frustration at having lost centre stage so soon.

The square was full of expatriates now; most lately arrived as part of the tour group, a few travelling on their own steam as Williams and Bellows were.

An urchin lingered a short distance away and caught the eye of the ladies.

'Poor child,' said the governess. She fished out a penny and handed it graciously to the boy, who darted away. 'Doubtless his parents have succumbed to famine or disease. It is shocking how destitute the people of this land are, and how poor the earth under its mantle of shining beauty.' She wheeled on Williams. 'I wonder, sir, have you read the recent publication by Mr Joseph Parkinson on social injustices in our capital city? Similar miseries are rife in our own country. I would be happy to tell you of our work with St Verena's Charitable Foundation. A man of your position could be of great aid to us!'

'By all means,' said Williams, already picturing Ms Harriet's admiration as he ladled his meagre savings into her lap to do away with as she wished, be it on diamonds or beggars.

Bellows had stopped listening and was trying to engage another young woman in a conversation about horses.

The child, meanwhile, raced across the cobbled street to where his mother sat, very much alive, begging for alms from the passers-by alongside other women. 'Look Mummy, the foreign lady gave me a coin!'

His mother inspected the penny, unimpressed. 'Cheap cow,' she muttered, 'this is the smallest piece they have. You run off quick, over to that lady by the lindens with the gullible face and the stupid-looking husband, and see what you can get. Don't get dirt on her dress, mind, or you'll feel the back of my hand after you feel theirs!'

Off trundled the urchin. With dextrous feet he danced between the legs and skirts of the congregation until he reached the edge of the crowd. It was a hot day and he fancied feeling a breeze on his face. Deciding he had better things to do than beg for coppers, he abandoned the congregation and made his little way down to the harbour.

At its western point the great lake narrowed and squeezed into a fast-flowing river, on either side of which sat the city. The little boy stood on the northern shore which housed, in addition to the small Anglican church, the train station—scarcely ten years old—and most of the newer hotels. More and more tourists were welcomed every year.

Firmly rooted atop its hill across the Rhône stood the stone buildings of the Old Town. Having joined the Confederation fifty years earlier Geneva had become the country's gateway to the West, but still retained much of the severity it had acquired and indeed cultivated during its history of political and religious independence. At the top of the city stood its crown, the Cathedral of St Pierre; a building of mixed architectural heritage, which nonetheless made no excuses for itself as it loomed over its subjects from its seat on the hill. Around it clustered stately grey buildings, glowering disapprovingly like a grim congress of stone at the cheerful sunshine that flowed—uninvited—through their iron-framed windows.

From the edge of the lake where the waters gathered pace and flowed swiftly under the city's bridges came the pealing of a bell, announcing the imminent arrival a ship. She could already be seen making her way around the promontory and into the harbour, sitting low in the water under the weight of many passengers. The steam-powered vessel cut a swathe through the fleet of lateen-sailed market boats jostling like white-winged birds for the best wind, her great red wheels pulling her through the water.

'Shall we walk down to the docks and watch her come in?' suggested one of the assembled tourists.

The congregation agreed that this was a marvellous suggestion and made for the lakeside. Williams stayed close to Ms Harriet while Bellows pursued a sporting-looking redhead and her friends heading for a nearby apple stand.

A number of men stood by the gunwale of the *Helvétie* as she steamed into the harbour. These included the aforementioned urchin's father, Kurt, alongside a number of other men and their wares. Many had been travelling for hours, although—as the bells of St Peter would shortly confirm—it was only just approaching midday. Kurt stood on deck beside a small academic-looking gentleman, who'd been questioning him for most of the journey.

'Would you mind going over that last part again, please?' asked the little man.

Kurt mopped his forehead on his sleeve. He'd been standing in the sun all morning and could almost taste the cold beer on the quayside.

'Anyone who sees the ship whereupon the lady rides,' he recited wearily, 'will see her grant their heart's deepest desire, whatever it may be.'

'And the ship navigates the lake at twilight, did you say?' The little professor leafed backwards through a notebook containing page after page of tiny, meticulous writing.

'Yeah, that's right. Big old sailing ship, kinda like those ones over there.' Kurt nodded at the twin-sailed barques. They drifted past the steamer like gigantic swans, riding the swell from her paddle wheels.

'Fascinating.' The professor scribbled away in is book. 'I particularly enjoyed your description of the Lady of the Lake herself. Golden locks, with . . . melting . . . blue . . . eyes, and . . . cheeks . . . Oh, what was it again?'

'The colour of sunset on the water,' repeated Kurt.

'And wherever she sets foot on land, flowers bloom?'

'Yep. Roses and lilacs, mostly.'

'And you heard these stories from your grandmother, you say?'

'Pretty much, yeah.' Most of them, anyway. Kurt couldn't remember all the details, but he had a vivid enough imagination to make up the rest. He felt the weight of the coin in his pocket and was about to hint that another like it would be much appreciated when a whistle sounded.

The little man glanced around in surprise. 'Are we here already?' he cried.

'Looks like it,' answered Kurt.

'I'd best get my trunk ready. I've left it so late! Thank you for speaking to me, my good man. Farewell!'

The professor tried to stuff his notebook into his pocket but dropped it on the deck. Kurt grunted, stooped, and picked it up. He couldn't read but he knew letters and, as he returned the book, he noted the initials M. B. A. stencilled into the back.

The professor thanked him again, turned, and made his way back through the crowd. Kurt watched him shuffle across the crowded wooden deck towards the body of the ship where the luggage was piled.

One of Kurt's companions came over. 'You've been talking to the little doctor all the way from Lausanne,' he remarked. 'What did he want?'

'Would you believe, he wanted to hear stories. Paid me a handsome price, too.' Kurt hefted the coin, more than a labourer made in a week.

'By God! That much for a tale?'

'That and a few other things. He asked me to name the winds on the lake, but I'm not sure he'll remember them.'

Others had noticed the flash of silver in the afternoon sun and gathered round.

'Here, Kurt! Where'd you get that?'

'The little German paid him to tell stories!'

'What, clean ones?'

'Yeah,' said Kurt, proud to be the centre of attention. 'He wanted to hear fables like my grandmother used to tell. He was mostly interested in the ones about monsters and mountain creatures.'

'Reckon he'd pay me to tell him some of my own?'

Kurt shrugged. 'You can ask, though we'll be ashore in a minute. Besides, he pressed me so I doubt there's any you'd know that we didn't cover already.'

'Ha!' cried the first man. 'I know way more stories than you. What about the one where the Kobolds give lumps of coal to climbers as gifts, which turn into diamonds when they take them home?'

'Old hat,' scoffed another. 'I heard one about a tree that sang everyday at noon, because it contained the soul of a saint who'd died nearby. The townsfolk liked it so much they cut the tree down to make an altar and put it in the church, after which it never sang again'

A third man leaned forward. 'Did you tell him about the *Benandanti*, the followers of the Dame Abonde, who are born under the sign of the caul and join with the dead to fight witches at harvest time? That was always my favourite story, when she rides out of the sky . . .'

'Rubbish,' interrupted a fourth. 'I prefer the one about the lady who lived by the lake and walked on mist and every night she would dance by the waterside in her undies until this bloke sees her, and then . . .'

His voice was lost in the hubbub of competing stories. They were all silenced a moment later by the shrill whistle of the boat itself, which had heard enough for one day. With smoke billowing from her smokestack of black iron, the vessel slowed as she approached the pier. It was already lined with people. Several thick wooden posts stood in the water a full foot or more beyond the end pier itself, reaching higher than the heads of the assembled crowd.

With the shore fast approaching, two sailors climbed onto the gunwale, hands heavy with the thick ropes that fed from coils on the deck behind them. They hefted these as the boat swung in, steaming within a couple of feet of the pier.

The boat's master gave a piercing shout. Immediately the pressure to the engines was cut, a cloud of steam was released from a valve, and the red wheels stopped turning. The vessel drifted onwards, carried forward by her own momentum. As she passed by the pier the crewmen swung their hawsers over and around the wooden posts, once, twice, and braced themselves. The ropes snapped taut and the posts groaned as their water-clogged bases felt the weight of the heavy-laden boat.

The sailors had done their job well; the lines held and the vessel juddered to a foaming halt. A less experienced throw would have missed the post entirely, or failed to coil the rope in the necessary way, or—worst of all—tripped the thrower, bringing him down between the boat and the pier. As the steamship swung sideways and ground against its much-worn wooden anvils, the assembly breathed a collective sigh of relief at the passing of this mundane peril.

A hinge creaked as a gate was opened in the side of the bulwark. A ramp was thrown over the gap and her human cargo stomped across without ceremony onto the causeway. Miners, furriers, shepherds, and other visitors from higher altitudes dragged their wares ashore. It was a long way to come, but commerce was good in the city. Many a tourist paid top franc on the boulevards of Geneva for some local curiosity, only to find a week later than these could be had in most villages for half the price.

As the deck began to clear, Kurt and his companions found that they could breathe a bit easier. But there was little time to rest.

'C'mon lads,' said Kurt, 'let's get this stuff onto the cobbles.'

The men began passing boxes, bundles, sheaves, and packages along a line and across the water to the shore. One man reached for a barrel that sat near the front of the boat, about stool-height, but at the last minute thought better of it and took up a different bundle instead. The barrel could wait, he thought vaguely.

The voice of l'Éveil began to sound high in the cathedral tower, soon followed by the chimes of her sisters Bellerive, Accord, and others. The deep tones of Clémence were lacking, as she'd suffered a crack earlier that year and was awaiting repairs. A grave matter to all noble Genevans when the minister had announced it, her absence went largely unnoticed by the multitudes down by the shore of the Rhône.

With much discreet manoeuvring Williams managed to position himself beside Ms Harriet as they watched the men pouring off the boat.

He cleared his throat. 'What rugged-looking fellows, eh?'

'Indeed,' she agreed, 'but dignified. I fancy these are the last true remnants of those noble peasants we read about in the stories; men who survive by their wits in the wilderness, who fought with Robin Locksley and witnessed fairies dance in the woods.'

Dear me, thought Williams, what a frightfully vivid imagination. She must read a lot of novels.

Harriet noticed his doubting looks. 'You think me naive, Mr Williams?'

He stammered some hasty excuse, which she waved away. Taking him by the arm, she pointed at the boat. Most of its cargo was already ashore and its iron hull floated higher in the water, but a collection of small barrels remained.

'See there, Mr Williams. There is a group of men on deck who seem to have come straight from the mountains. See the old father who sits by them? What a noble face. I dare he say he could tell a story or two!'

Williams was so thrilled by her touch he could scarcely drag his eyes from her but look away he did, searching for the old man. He couldn't see anyone of that description on board, and told her so.

Her brow furrowed. She pointed out the greybeard's position once more. 'Surely you must see him? Look! Even now he stands to allow the removal of the barrel on which he sat.'

Williams looked earnestly for the man. He saw the assembled group, observed the wiry men carrying kindling and large bundles of wool, identified the barrel as it was carried away. Nowhere could he see the man she described.

He looked away and was silent.

Harriet could see he wasn't joking and her brow furrowed in confusion. She hardly heard as Williams made his excuses and sheepishly walked away.

She stared back at the old man. He stood in clear view on the deck, now emptied, looking down into the water with eyes that seemed to see in the green water the reflection of sunken cities and the flicker of mermaids.

He glanced up and, noting her stare, smiled politely and touched the brim of his battered old hat.

Williams made his way through the streets away from the harbour, feeling guilty. Was it discourteous to abandon a woman when she was having a fit? No, he decided. Best leave her among friends; they'd bring her round. In all probability she'd had too much sun, that was all. But then why did he feel so shaken?

Williams found a quiet street and paused to light a cigarette, one of the expensive ones he'd bought in Paris. As he exhaled the white smoke his mind dwelled on Ms Harriet. He felt a mix of disappointment and guilt run through him, as well as a variety of less easily worded emotions.

The Englishman gradually became aware that he wasn't alone.

In the alcoves across the street he noticed a discreet shadow move from behind a pillar. It stepped closer and he saw it was a woman, with a confident look and an easy affability he could sense even from where he stood. She smiled at him and thereafter he was in no doubt as to her employment.

Ordinarily he would have tipped his hat and moved on, but today didn't feel like just another day. He was young and he was in a new and foreign country with the sun shining on him. Furthermore she was a handsome woman with a fresh-faced and healthy demeanour, a rarity in her London counterparts.

Williams hesitated and stood there a while, smoking. The woman waited patiently across the street for him to finish his cigarette.

Immediately following the disembarkation of the passengers and cargo, the waiting men assembled on the shore began loading their wares for the return trip. Condiments, medicine, tools, and various assorted luxuries were piled below deck for delivery further up the lake. Some would proceed upriver on barges to the small towns nestling in the shadow of the Alps, where mule-drivers would take over from the sailors. They in turn would cart the merchandise up into the blue wildernesses and quiet villages where people laughed in private at the stooped, bow-legged gait of the bearded men who brought them traces of the luxurious lifestyle in the valley and went to bed envying the fineries that Genevan ladies wore.

Once asleep the villagers' minds grew wings. In their imaginations the mule-drivers became stunted and bright-eyed, their wares metamorphosed into great riches, the ladies in the far-off cities were transformed into fair princesses, and the villagers dreamt of a world where dwarves turned coal into diamonds, where fairies rode through the sky, and nymphs danced amongst the lilies while swan ships sailed past on the silent moonlit waters of the lake.

ALL SAINTS' EVE
CHAPTER TWENTY

ALLOWEEN, IN ITS modern transatlantic incarnation, has never truly caught on in Central Europe. These are countries steeped in centuries of tradition whose calendars are already filled with public holidays. In some parts one can scarcely move for equinoxes, solstices, and anniversaries of this or that saint's murder.* Any modern festival wishing to be deemed worthy had therefore better be bloody brilliant.

You'd think the candy would be enough. In conservative communities, however, few are inclined to embrace an institution involving such liberal use of the colour orange and welcoming the children of strangers onto your front doorstep. That this invasion of privacy is supposed to be rewarded with treats, that these treats are by nature the last thing you should give a growing child, and that the whole affair is America's fault does little to ingratiate the holiday with Europeans.

---

* Popular forms of historic martyrdom include burning, drowning, impaling, and sudden divorce of the victim from one vital organ or another. Other practices grislier still were occasionally used: St Lawrence, for example, when ordered by the Emperor Valerian to produce all the wealth of the church on pain of death, thought he'd be clever and brought forth a host of orphans and cripples, declaring 'Behold the treasures of the Church!' One can judge how hilarious witty the Romans thought this was by their response, which was to stuff him into a waffle iron and grill him. He is said to have retained his love of one-liners well into the experience, at one point declaring 'I am well done, turn me over!' The Vatican later demonstrated that it was itself not without a sense of humour by making Lawrence the patron saint of cooks, chefs, and comedians. Thus was born the first—and probably last—documented case of state-approved irony in the Catholic Church.

Switzerland has more masked carnivals than any other country. There are torchlit midnight parades when cities echo to the sound of bells. There are marches to celebrate the arrival of spring in which ancient guilds juggle flags and compete to see who can hit their drums the loudest, where cloth snowmen are burned in effigy as cavalry plunge and rear dangerously close to the crowd, and the ground shakes as entire villages dance in the public square. When masks are worn they aren't made of plastic but of plaster, cloth, wood, and leather, human skin having fallen out of fashion of late. Scarcely a month goes by without seeing some kind of celebration, especially in those parts of the country that lean towards Catholicism.*

With so much to celebrate it took a while for the ecclesiastic judiciary to decide when to schedule what, but eventually the first two days of November became, respectively, All Saints' Day and All Souls' Day. Pagan rituals predate both, however, and for centuries preceding the arrival of the Christian faith the darkening days of autumn have been a hallowed time that marks the waning of the year.

It's the time to remember the Dead.

That is what Graham was doing that evening, in his own way. He was dining in the hotel restaurant and had spent a poignant moment commemorating the animal whose sacrifice had allowed it to become his pork chops. A minute later he'd devoured the forkful entirely and forgot all about the pig it came from, turning instead to the fried potatoes on the other side of his plate.

The hotel was busier than usual, filled with the evening hubbub of clinking plates and cutlery. Richard sat opposite, his food untouched.

'Hey, Graham.'

'Hmm?'

'Does it worry you that we've been here over a month and we have nothing of what we were actually sent here to film, while we're up to our ears in extraneous detail of things we weren't meant to cover at all?'

'What's your point?'

---

* While Protestantism took advantage of the Reformation to jettison some of Christianity's more opaque rituals as well as ditching the saints and their gag reel of original deaths more or less altogether, rural Catholicism retains many vestigial elements from its struggle with paganism. The new religion overtook the old by assimilation as much as by straightforward replacement, for early Christians were much happier celebrating the resurrected Son of God if they were allowed to keep their old ways, or at least the fun bits. Hence why people burn Yule logs at Christmas, why they paint eggs at Easter, and why every February young Swiss men dress up as demons and run around their villages with blazing torches shaking chains at terrified virgins; all heartwarming family traditions of which Jesus would certainly have approved.

Richard leaned forward, his brow furrowed. 'My point, Graham, is we're telling ourselves that all this extra material of marmots and goats and dramatic scenery is important for the project. But we're forgetting the bottom line.'

'Which is?'

'Which is, sooner or later we're going to need something bear-related to send back. Right now we've got nothing.'

Graham waved this aside. 'What, did you think we'd get everything we needed in a few weeks? Good material takes time! We're conducting important research into the diminishing fauna of a vital European biosphere. They're not going to cut our funding. We'll get the shots. It's just a matter of time.'

'I still think we should move it up a gear. I say we bring back the night shifts.'

Graham swallowed his mouthful of potato and reached for his pint. 'Fine,' he said, 'but I'm taking the day shift this time. You can do the night ones.'

Richard recalled his first sleepless night in the observation hut and the sounds at the door, as well as the pale figure of the girl and her haunting song. Though the room was full of people, he suddenly felt cold.

Graham took Richard's silence to mean he'd thought better of the idea and dug into a fresh pile of food that Dino the Waiter had brought. 'By the way,' he said, his mouth full, 'you haven't seen my copy of *Crime & Punishment*, have you? I put it on the bedside table yesterday and now I can't find it.'

Richard shook his head. He was busy drafting an email to his GP in his head, requesting that his medical tests back in London be rescheduled . . .

'Strange,' said Graham, looking around, 'you wouldn't know it was the thirty-first. There are hardly any decorations up at all! Then again, they don't need any when they've got her.' He inclined his fork in the direction of Frau Hürlimann. She was looking particularly grim that evening, possibly because of the pointy black hat someone had placed on her head for the occasion.

'Halloween isn't big here,' said Richard, looking out the window. 'Apparently the tradition is still to celebrate All Saints' Day. It's technically tomorrow but Frau Indergand told me that there's going to be some kind of candlelit display.'

'Sounds like fun. Let's go!'

Richard raised an eyebrow. 'We have work in the morning. Besides, we won't understand anything anyone says.'

'Who cares? It's a festival, and festivals are for socializing.' Graham waggled his eyebrows suggestively.

Richard was about to say that taking time off was the last thing they should do when he noticed something worrying. All the tables were occupied and latecomers could find nowhere to sit. Some of the more enterprising guests, as though acting on Graham's advice, had decided to mingle.

'Oh no,' whispered Richard, 'the Americans are coming over to our table!'

'Oh, don't be so grumpy,' Graham replied. 'It's Halloween! Americans are all about that stuff. Be sociable.'

A moment later the Americans were upon them, teeth gleaming like porcelain.

'Hi there! I'm Kaitlyn, this is Chase. We're from Grand Rapids, Michigan!'

'Pretty busy, huh,' said Chase, pulling up a chair. 'Mind if we join?'

Richard groaned inwardly. Graham, however, was all smiles.

'Greetings,' he answered congenially. 'I am Graham, this is Richard, we're from London and may I say how smashing it is to meet our cousins from over the pond.'

'Hullo,' said Richard.

Kaitlyn clasped her hands. 'Oh will you listen to that, Chase! Aren't their accents wonderful? I told him you were British! I've always loved the accent, so elegant.'

'Er, cheers.'

'I just love being in the mountains. Apparently there's a Halloween party later tonight in the village! Won't that be fun?'

'Is there going to be an actual party, then?' asked Richard.

'More sort of a traditional thing I understand,' answered Chase, taking a bite of cheese. 'My guidebook has a whole section about the festival. Wanna read it?' The volume was thrust upon Richard before he could refuse. 'This bit's really good. It's about the Wild Hunt, where all these ancient warriors come riding out of the sky all dead and howling and summoning the souls of fallen men, galloping through the skies behind some lady in a winged helmet called Bertha and her brother Berchtold.'

Richard winced at the combination of cheese obstruction and Chase's accent.

'It's a great read,' chimed in Kaitlyn, 'wonderful translations and lots of really interesting facts. Got it down in the village, if you're looking for a good guidebook.'

'Lovely, thanks for that.' Richard handed the book back.

'We'll make sure to pick up a copy. Nay, two copies!' added Graham.

'So,' said Chase, having cleared some of the cheese. 'What're you two boys doing in the mountains? You into cycling at all? I love cycling. I was just telling Kaitlyn, I spend the whole year looking forward to my vacation so I can come here and rattle up and down the trails. I just live for it!'

Kaitlyn put her hand on Chase's wrist and smiled. 'He does, he *so* does,' she crooned. Graham nodded rapturously.

'Actually,' said Richard, 'we're here for work. We're writing a paper for an environmental journal.'

Kaitlyn's mouth made a large O. 'Oh, you're scientists! Just like Richard Attenborough!'

'Sort of.'

'Actually,' Graham took over, 'we're here to track big game. We're doing a piece about large animals returning to the Alps.'

This delighted the Americans. But then, thought Richard, Americans always seem delighted. Why was that? Maybe it was all the sugar in their cereal.

Kaitlyn tugged on Chase's sleeve, inhibiting his cheese consumption. 'Chase, you gotta tell these guys about our adventure!'

Graham leant forward. 'What adventure is this? Tell us, Chase!'

Chase folded his napkin and spread his hands to conjure the scene. 'Ok, so, we're driving up the road late at night down in the forest somewhere.'

'It's awfully dark,' contributed Kaitlyn.

Chase nodded. 'Dark as pitch, our headlights barely reached the trees.'

'That does sound dark,' said Graham. Richard kicked him under the table.

'Suddenly,' cried Chase, 'what should emerge from the woods but the biggest wild boar you ever saw!'

Graham gasped. Richard looked up in genuine interest. 'How big do you reckon?'

'Yes Chase,' said Graham gripping the edge of the table, 'how big? Was it absolutely colossal or simply massive?'

'It was HUGE!' Chase spread his arms, nearly knocking over the flowers. Richard lunged forward to catch the vase. Chase hardly noticed. 'Tall as the hood of the car!'

Kaitlyn whispered to Richard across the table. 'More like knee height actually.'

'It was gorgeous,' continued Chase, 'big as a pony. It stood there in the middle of the road, looking straight into the headlights. I'd stopped the car, obviously.'

'Of course,' said Graham, chin cupped in one hand while with the other he topped up Chase's apple juice.

'There it stood, fur rippling and steaming in the cold air.' Chase was nearly whispering now. 'Its bristles were shining in magnificent reds and golds and greens. And then—and this is the really amazing bit—'

'I'm afraid Chase has a weakness for the melodramatic,' interjected Kaitlyn.

'I made a slow sign with my arm,' continued the imperturbable Chase, 'and, as if in response, the boar turned, and slowly—majestically, even—walked away, real dignified, submerging itself in the bracken.'

'Now Chase,' said Kaitlyn, 'you're exaggerating just a tiny bit. It was a big, dangerous animal and we were lucky to be in the car. You make it sound like some kind of spiritual experience!'

Chase frowned. 'Well, I'm not saying it was like a vision or anything. But I really felt like there was some connection, a moment of understanding between me and the boar. You know?'

'Oh, Chase,' breathed Graham, 'I *so* know.'

Chase clasped him firmly by the shoulder. 'I like you, Graham. You're a solid guy. Now, tell me something. Do you believe in spirit animals?'

Kaitlyn sighed in contented exasperation. Richard excused himself. Taking his coat and scarf from the hook on the wall he made for the door, while a conversation about how many gears Chase's mountain bike had continued without him.

*****

It's only natural at a time when the world of the living approaches that of the dead that the division between the two should dwindle ever so slightly.

Ellie was experimenting. Councillor Aufdermauer was setting up torches in the street and she'd discovered that if she blew in his ear he would glance around in confusion and scratch his earlobe. He couldn't see her, but on this particular day she felt more solid, more *there* than usual.

She pinched his bottom and he whirled around, worried he must have backed into something. Ellie danced away, giggling to herself, satisfied that she had thoroughly confused the councillor. Aufdermauer returned to his work, muttering to himself about draughts and the dangers of pneumonia.

Ellie ambled along the street, passing the arcades on the side of the square.

'That was a bit cheeky of you.'

She started. Richard emerged from the shadows. 'It's not nice to tease people.'

'Oh, don't be such a stick in the mud.' She blew playfully in Richard's ear, but he turned his head to avoid it.

'He still couldn't see you, could he?' he asked.

'No. Why would he?'

196

Richard shrugged. 'For some reason I expected something to be different this evening. Maybe I thought that everyone would be able to see you too.'

'My, I shouldn't think so. Can you imagine their fright!' Ellie laughed.

'You didn't seem so concerned the times you made me jump,' said Richard, just a touch ruefully. 'Besides, isn't that a bit inappropriate?'

'It's more appropriate than you might think,' she said, a mischievous glint in her eye. 'All Saints' Day has its roots in old pagan festivals, back when divinities weren't so solemn all the time. The church wanted to make it a "Commemoration of the Faithfully Departed", but the rituals themselves are older. I dare say if you went into the mountains this evening you'd see more than you might bargain for, and not very much of it Christian.'

As if prompted by her words, Richard saw a light flicker high up on the mountainside. He wondered if someone had been foolish enough to light a fire in the woods, when another appeared. These were followed by many more until there appeared on earth a constellation to rival those in the sky, its stars less numerous but burning with a golden flame that threatened to outshine the pale light of the heavens.

'Walk with me?' suggested Ellie.

'All right.'

The evening was dark. Other couples wandering slowly around the streets, some holding candles. A signpost decorated with a white ribbon pointed towards to the church.

People seemed to be going that way, so Richard and Ellie followed them. She gestured to the old building with its dark-tipped bell tower and rust-coloured clock face, illuminated against the night sky.

'It's nearly three hundred years old, apparently. Wouldn't know it, would you? Decidedly they take better care of it than the sanatorium. Let's visit the graveyard!'

Richard looked at her. 'Is that . . . I dunno, allowed? For you, I mean.'

She laughed. 'I don't see why not. Dead people are pretty much the same everywhere. So are the living,' she added, 'though they won't admit it. I guess they have more to prove.'

It might've been meant innocently, but to Richard it felt like something of a dig.

'We have more to lose, certainly.'

If she heard anything in his voice she didn't let it show.

The cemetery was lit with torches in honour of the day. Its wrought iron gate had been pushed open, beckoning people in. To one side an open flame burned in a three-legged metal brazier, though it gave off no heat that Richard could feel as he passed.

The graveyard was playing host to candlelit gatherings of people huddled near gravestones, under arches, and in the shadows of hedges. Many had brought flowers to decorate the graves. Some dipped soft pine branches in bowls near the headstones and proceeded to shake them over the graves, anointing them with droplets of water. Others grumbled about how various estranged cousins hadn't contributed to the grave fund recently as they weeded away stray growths and other signs of neglect.

Some burials featured framed portraits set in bronze of the occupants, which Richard found particularly compelling. He inspected the sepia-coloured faces with interest. Solemnity must have been the watchword in the early days of Swiss photography; there weren't many smiles.

He glanced over at Ellie. She was older than many of the ground's occupants, but she displayed none of the harshness in the portraits. She strolled with the lightness of a wraith, which—he had to remind himself—she was.

It gave him pause to watch her progress through the groups of mourners, surrounded by her perpetual and otherworldly cheerfulness. He noted how people seemed to sense her without seeing, how they parted before her. It was as though she, being apart from the natural order, manifested herself as a rift in the fabric of nature, and nature attempted to shield its children from her otherness as she passed.

Richard noticed something else: Ellie made way for no one and paid little or no regard to the people around her. All her attention was given to the flowers decorating the gravestones and the features of the stones themselves. An elderly man began coughing a few feet from her and had to sit on a bench. His grandchildren fussed and worried over him, but Ellie didn't even glance in his direction.

How many ghosts had Richard made way for in this same unknowing, servile way? How often had his actions been affected by the whims and fancies of the long deceased? How many of his dreams had sprung from the achievements of great men? How often had he adopted the philosophies of history as his own? And yet, how little thought of him his heroes must have had in their lives.

Richard wondered what would happen when his work was done and he returned to London. Would Ellie stay behind? Or would she haunt him forever?

His thoughts drifted into dark and uncertain waters.

Ellie completed her inspection and walked back towards him between the rows of candlelit headstones. Her smile further widened the rift between her and the solemn faces of the departed in their bronze frames. But where before Richard had only seen affability and charm, he now spied the shadow of something else: a kind of hunger.

He shivered slightly as Ellie drew level with him.

'I think I'd better go back to the hotel,' he said.

She gave him a surprised look. 'All right then.' She sounded disappointed but made no move to stop him.

Richard walked away, his feet crunching on the gravel path. At one point he glanced back to see if she was following him, but she wasn't. He felt relieved.

He wasn't watching where he was going and bumped into someone. Richard stumbled and blushed with embarrassment, unnerved by a tall man in a leather jacket and motorcycle boots. He apologised in broken German and the man assured him in a reassuring bass that it was all right and not to worry.

Richard hastened on, his thoughts more mixed up than before.

Maybe he should make some new friends. He hadn't made any real attempt to socialise with the locals since he'd got here. Even Graham was making some kind of effort to integrate. Then again, Richard hadn't had to look far to make new acquaintances: they sought him out from beyond the grave.

He looked around. It was a large graveyard, divided into sections by low walls. The burials here looked more modern. The other visitors were grouped amongst family or friends, not looking to include a stranger in their moments of remembrance.

Richard turned towards a quiet corner at the edge of the torchlight. There he spotted a young man sitting alone on one of the gravestones, smoking a cigarette. Deciding that this was a time to reach out to the living, Richard wandered over.

The sound of the gravel under Richard's feet made the young man look up. Richard raised a hand in greeting.

'Special day, eh? Day of the Dead and all that . . . Bit spooky I'd say.'

The youth offered nothing by way of reply, save to exhale a lungful of smoke. His jeans were too large for him and his hair was done up in spikes. He was much younger than Richard had first supposed.

'So,' he ventured, 'you come here often?'

The youth answered in Swiss-German. Though Richard couldn't identify the words he recognised the tone as one that implied that whoever Richard was, he might be happier somewhere else.

Richard decided he'd had enough of socializing for one day and struck out for the hotel at a brisk pace.

The smoker watched him go. He threw his cigarette butt onto the gravel and, for lack of anything better to do, reached for another.

The wind was picking up and began to blow out the candles. Only the iron brazier by the gate continued to burn steadily in its metal frame.

The graveyard was almost empty now, everyone having gone home. The only remaining presence was the youth, still smoking by himself in a corner. Though he'd not stopped all day his pack never seemed to run out.

He'd heard the sound of a motorcycle pulling up outside the gates some time before. Now the youth glanced up and saw a tall figure walking down the path.

He lowered his eyes and focused on his trainers, smoking furiously. His hand trembled as he took another drag but he kept his eyes fixed on the ground, listening to the steps in the gravel coming towards him.

A pair of motorcycle boots appeared in his vision. He feigned disinterest and continued to smoke.

'Hello, Martin,' said a deep voice.

Martin remembered that voice. He concentrated very hard on his cigarette and didn't answer.

'I've come to fetch you,' continued the voice.

'Don't care.' Martin's voice was even younger than his face, which had aged beyond its years.

'That's what you said last time. I thought perhaps you'd changed your mind. People are asking after you.'

Martin's eyes betrayed a world of feelings that his face was trying to hide.

Before him stood a very tall man with an angular face in black leather biking gear, a motorcycling helmet under one arm. His bright blue eyes gazed back at Martin with intensity, but there was warmth in them as well.

'Come on,' he said. 'Time to be on your way.'

The boy hesitated. Then, with a few final drags for courage, he stood up.

'Sure, I guess. Whatever.'

He tossed away his cigarette and slouched off. The tall man followed a couple of steps behind, writing in a small notebook he'd taken from his jacket. Together they walked past the flickering torches towards the gate, where a large black motorbike was parked. A second, smaller one stood beside it.

As they passed the brazier by the entrance the man tore out a page from the notebook and dropped it in. It lay amongst the embers for an instant, until the flame caught and burned it away in moments.

PART THREE
NOVEMBER

THE MOURNING MONTH
CHAPTER TWENTY-ONE

IGH ON THE mountainside there grew a bush. It hung precariously over the edge of a rocky outcrop, a footpath on one side and gaping emptiness on the other. How it had come to be there was anyone's guess. The ground beneath it was brittle and threatened to give way every spring when the ice melted. Unlike the forest far below the bush had no shelter from the wind, which over time had so maligned and mistreated it that it now grew permanently sideways, as though suffering from an ill-healed back injury.

It was in fact an extremely old bush. Dynasties of marmots had lived and perished in the tunnels beneath its roots. Its unobstructed view of the valley made it a favourite perch amongst the local hawks, who came there to spy on rodents, discuss avian politics, and—during the more romantic times of year—ensure the arrival of the next generation of hawks.*

The bush didn't mind. Perhaps it preferred solitude, or found trees altogether too intimidating as neighbours. In any case it continued to survive, if not thrive, sitting mostly undisturbed on its inhospitable knoll.

This venerable plant had enjoyed a largely stress-free day thus far. Its foundations hadn't shifted in any particularly alarming way recently and the air was mercifully devoid of lustful birds. There was a minor moment of concern when two colourfully clad bipeds with matching baseball caps and American accents had paused on the trail to gush about the view, but they'd moved on. The wind, while not so strong as to erode any precious soil, was nonetheless doing a good job of clearing away the furry debris left by the family of marmots now hibernating beneath its roots. The bush rustled comfortably in the breeze.

---

* This was one neighbourly tradition the marmots could well have done without.

Suddenly there was an alarming *whoosh* as something sped along the track, mere inches from the bush's outstretched boughs. Had whatever it was not leapt aside at the last second, the bush would have surely seen a precious twig or two snapped clean off. Something was in a tremendous hurry and didn't care who knew it.

A young marmot awoke to the pounding of feet overhead and needed to be cuddled back to sleep by its mother. There was no one to offer such comfort to the bush, however. The event left a hairline trauma in its growth rings, which, to anyone capable of interpreting it, might have translated into something very like "Well, *really!*"

Richard Mathern raced ahead, gathering foliage as he went. He travelled light, with nothing but his weatherproof for protection from the elements and his small rucksack on his back.

This was not the same man who'd collapsed on his first day. Richard's boots carried him along the narrow track with ease. Weeks of daily hikes had made him sure-footed and strong. As he crested the last ridge and looked down into the rift below, he was scarcely out of breath.

His shoulders slumped in disappointment; the bear lure was still there, untouched. He'd already checked the trip-wires and motion-sensitive cameras. It had been the same for weeks.

Richard's routine had changed along with his new fitness and familiarity with the terrain. The reports which landed on the desktops of *Nature Magazine* three or four times a week now overflowed with data and photos, alongside insightful annotations about where his findings came from and how they reflected the changing state of the local flora and fauna. But the thing Richard truly yearned for, the missing piece in every file he sent, continued to elude him.

He followed his usual route along the mountainside, using the track where he could and finding his own way where he couldn't. The ground was hard, the greying foliage stiff with frost. Clouds of vapour trailed in his wake.

It froze often now. The valley still awaited its first real snowfall, but a permanent dusting of hoarfrost coated the mountainside and every sunset was swifter than the last.

Even the rushing torrents had slowed and were beginning to freeze. Soon the waterfall itself would solidify into an enormous icicle running down the side of the cliff. Kaspar could often be found by the pools near its base, testing the thickness of the ice and muttering to himself through a fog of cigar smoke. Old Fosco roamed the plateau draped in his many overcoats with his gun and pipe, waiting for the cold to drive chamois down from the higher slopes. The Indergands no longer indulged in evening walks because of the chill and Madame Berger frequently berated

Councilman Fürgler for forgetting to shut the doors of the Communal Offices.

Richard saw no one today, however. There was little sign of life anywhere.

Funny, he thought to himself. If things go on like this I'll be seeing more of the dead than the living.

He hadn't seen much of Ellie recently, mostly because of work. Time hung over Richard like a cloud and he spent increasingly lengthy shifts crouching in bushes or hanging over crags—waiting, listening, hoping.

He paused on a ridge, feeling the grass crunch under his boot. There was a warbling sound from below. Richard looked down and spotted the tell-tale red crest and white tale feathers of an alpine grouse, waddling amongst the rocks.

Not you, he thought: I've already done a piece on you.

He sniffed the air and scanned the horizon with his binoculars. Nothing.

Richard's thoughts dwelt on potential failure and what that would mean for him. The snows would spell an end to his efforts, yet still the bear evaded him.

He put away the binoculars and prepared to retrace his steps. He'd had enough of being alone with his thoughts for one day.

And, just as he thought that, he ceased to be alone.

'What ho!' cried a voice from Richard's right.

Up the slope climbed a man dressed almost entirely in tweed, a leather rucksack on his back, a white silk scarf trailing in the breeze, and a wide-brimmed hat flopping about his ears. The hand not holding a wooden alpenstock waved gamely in salutation, the man's moustachioed face flushed red with exertion.

Two months earlier Richard would have marked this curio down as an eccentric period re-enactor out for some commemorative stroll, but he'd become adept at reading the signs.

Oh no, he thought. Not another one.

The man covered the last bit of ground and drew alongside Richard, beaming. 'What ho, what ho, what ho. Lovely day for a climb, wot!'

'Yeah.' Richard kept a wary eye on the stranger. 'You come up here often?'

'Often as I can,' responded the spectre. 'Which is to say, almost every day. To be frank I'm not overly engaged at present.'

He straightened, having regained his breath. 'Allow to me introduce myself: the Right Honourable Lord Frederick Urquhart Bellows-Wicklesworth, Gentleman and Mountaineer Extraordinaire, at your service. Call me Bellows.'

There was little Richard could do but respond in kind. 'Charmed. I'm Richard, Richard Mathern. Call me Richard.'

'Ah, Richard! Good English name. Richard. Riccardo. Reichhart. Dick. Lovely to meet you I'm sure, Dickie.'

'Richard. So, what brings you up here, then?'

Bellows leaned in with a conspiratorial air. 'I'm glad you asked me that, Dickie.'

He whirled around, gestured dramatically to the surrounding mountains. 'Behold! The Alpine plateau, the noblest mountain range in the world. These lofty peaks are like the ogres of legend: massive, terrifying, monsters in plain sight begging to be subdued. They used to be feared once, but now, like the heroes of myth, men make short work of them. Yet they are predators! Some would say the untamed snakes of Abyssinia and the ferocious tigers of Bengal are deadlier, possessing as they do the gift of stealth. True, for most mountains, haughty pride has been their downfall. They've had the life sucked from them by generations of climbers and the onslaught of tourists that followed. This one, however, is untouched, its face unbesmirched and its roots unmoved. It stands unyielding and loves neither Christian nor Heathen. Fear it, Dickie, for it cares nothing for you and will destroy you utterly without a thought, burying your remains forever!'

Richard listened, only half-interested. He'd seen enough ghosts for one holiday and was preoccupied by other matters. 'What's it like on the summit? Windy, I expect.'

Bellows deflated somewhat. 'Couldn't say. Never made it, old chap.'

'What, not even once?'

'Alas. The first time I tried I took a rather nasty fall. I blame the guide—told me to cut across a ledge instead of following him, insisting the trail was too narrow. Bloody fool! I slipped and the rope snapped on the rocks. Thought that was the end off me. Turns out, it was!' He laughed.

Richard managed a weak smile.

'But did I let that stop me? The dickens I did! I got right back up again, didn't I, old boy?' The alpinist prodded the mountain's flank as though it were a gigantic horse. He craned his neck, beaming up at the towering whiteness of the Gräuelhorn. 'You beautiful bastard!' he shouted through his moustache, 'I'll have you yet!'

'Look,' sighed Richard, 'would you mind doing that somewhere else? Only I've had a series of fairly stressful encounters with the undead these past few weeks and I was rather hoping to have a quiet think on my own.'

Bellows looked affronted but soon regained his composure and good humour. 'Understood. Nothing like sublime nature for a bit of solitary cogitation, wot?'

'Something like that. Lots to think about, and everything.'

'Zounds! Not all jocundity in the life of Mathern, eh Dickie? Anything I can help with?'

'No, thanks.'

'Not to worry, I shall be moving on presently. Posterity calls! In any case you know where to find me: right here on this confounded slope. Perhaps another time when you're at leisure?'

'Whenever you like,' said Richard. 'I'm here most days.'

'Splendid. Anon anon, then!'

And with that, off went Bellows, his white scarf and a cheery whistle trailing through the air behind him.

Richard listened to the receding *crunch crunch crunch* of Bellows' footsteps. He lingered a while, allowing the echoes of their conversation to clear, before proceeding down the track and back to the village.

*****

Dawes knew something was wrong before he entered the lift. There was muted tension in Allerby's greeting at the door.

The ride up was a long one. Dawes dwelled fitfully on the progress of Ahmid Sardharwalla's plot and his own ongoing battle to hack into Luther's private server, whose security wall had so far stumped even his most resourceful goons. He resolved to entreat Ahmid to abandon the scheme, at least until they saw the numbers.

Dawes emerged from the lift and almost walked into his secretary.

'Oh . . . Good morning, Alice.'

For the second time that morning Dawes suspected something was amiss. Alice exuded the same tension as Allerby.

'He's waiting for you in your office, Mr Dawes.'

'Who is?'

'Aberfinchley,' Alice replied, as though the name itself were poison.

Normally Dawes would have reprimanded her for her omission of the customary English honorific, but something in her voice convinced him to postpone the discussion. What was Luther doing in the building this early?

'Thank you, Alice.' Dawes made for his office.

Luther was standing with his back to the door gazing out the window as Dawes entered. Before any greetings could be offered, Luther spoke.

'It's sad, Dawes, when a CEO can't trust his own staff.'

Dawes paused, his coat still over his arm. 'Excuse me, sir?'

'You mean to say you don't know?' Luther turned and advanced slowly. 'The omniscient, omnipotent, and immovable Alistair Dawes isn't up to speed?' He stopped a pace away and looked into Dawes' face.

Dawes was a seasoned player. He sensed a change in the wind and suspected ill tidings. But a true veteran never folds when he can bluff.

'I don't think I follow, sir,' said Dawes in a voice so innocent even his mother would have believed it.

Luther smirked. 'Well, I'm afraid your reputation for infallibility has taken quite a blow. I happen to know something you don't.'

He turned and strutted back to the window, brandishing his mobile phone. 'There's a plot to overthrow me, Dawes.'

'Sir!' replied Dawes with suitable helpings of shock.

'Indeed. Those worthless farts on the senior staff disagree with my vision and have attempted to stage a coup. Good thing I outsourced our cyber security! I've got the whole system on lockdown. If anyone comes near my private portfolio without authorisation, I'll know.' He threw himself into an armchair. 'I dare say they excluded you from the conspiracy because you don't hold any part of the ownership and therefore were of no direct use to them. Arse-heads.'

'It beggars belief, sir.' It was all Dawes could do to not let anything show.

Luther scowled at the window. 'There's a smell in this building. Betrayal does that to places. I smelled it on my first day, literally as I walked in the door.'

'Shall I inform housekeeping?'

'It's a metaphor, Dawes! What's wrong with you?'

'Nothing sir, only you used the term "literally" so I failed to recognise the figurative nature of your comment.'

Luther scoffed. 'Overthrow me! Never mind. I've taken measures.'

Dawes cleared his throat. 'Might I be permitted to inquire exactly what these measures were, sir?'

Luther laughed without mirth. 'Suffice to say we unexpectedly find ourselves severely under-staffed. Best let HR know, they'll need to start hiring. Amjad Saint-Hardwilly and his minions won't be coming into work today, or indeed tomorrow.'

Dawes felt his heart sink, but retained his imperturbable mask of professionalism. 'Very good, sir.'

Luther rose. 'Oh, by the way,' he added, 'I've launched an initiative that I'm hoping will allow us to acquire a number of important franchises hitherto owned by rival firms. Print, online reference sources, that sort of thing.'

'Indeed, sir?'

'Yes. I thought that, should something like that mining plant incident reoccur, I'd like most of the coverage to come directly from us.'

'Most ingenious, sir.'

'Unfortunately that meant withdrawing funding from other, smaller ventures. Needed the money. We can take those up again later.'

Dawes' face fell. 'If I may ask, sir, which funding projects have you discarded in favour of this . . . initiative?'

'Not sure, some of the boring ones. I left a few on your desk, I'll get Julian to dig up the rest if you want.'

'Very advisable, sir.'

Luther shrugged. 'Fine. Too late now, anyway.'

He departed. Dawes sat down slowly, taking in the documents on his desk. Alice slipped inside and shut the door.

'Shall I follow up that guy with the tattoo and laptop again, Mr Dawes?' she whispered. 'He nearly cracked the security wall last time!'

Dawes' hand fell on one of the papers before him—an official retraction of the Desmond Aberfinchley Scholarship for Natural Sciences.

'I think not, Alice.'

Alice stared. Had her boss not been Alistair Dawes, the omniscient, omnipotent, and immovable, she would have sworn his voice trembled.

The grey man watched from a corner, his presence unnoticed. He was to them as unremarkable as the wall, his expression as invisible as the gust from the air-conditioning unit. Had they been able to see it, though, they would have found it a great deal more chilling.

The grey man rose and passed into the front office. Alice soon followed, though unlike him she bothered to open the door.

He summoned the lift and stepped inside, noting the absence of his reflection in the mirror.

The lift was not entirely sure what to make of its contents. It was clearly no longer vacant, yet it nonetheless fell somewhat short of being occupied. The lift found this unsettling. It was a functional piece of infrastructural hardware, seldom called upon to do any hard thinking, and was relieved when a button was pushed. It resumed the familiar task of vertical motion, on this occasion a gentle descent to the IT department.

*****

Later that same afternoon Ellie watched Richard climb the road to the sanatorium. She'd been waiting by the bannister on the off chance he might.

He hadn't combed his hair, she noticed, or shaved. Richard had allowed himself to get rather scruffy over the past few weeks. He ascended the slope easily, but his expression was moody. Ellie surmised he'd once again returned empty-handed.

Richard disappeared briefly behind the corner of the promenade before emerging at the top of the stairs. The wooden decking creaked under his boots, the cold having sucked all the moisture out of the boards. His gait was heavy, his gaze lowered in disappointment.

'We haven't seen you for a while,' Ellie said. 'How have you been?'

'Busy. Work's not going well.'

Ellie noticed bits of foliage sticking to Richard's jacket. She resisted the temptation to reach over and brush them off. 'I'm sorry,' she said, and meant it.

'It's all right. We're not giving up. I found a guy in Andermatt who owns a state-of-the-art thermal camera. I'm thinking of hiring it.'

Ellie's brow furrowed. 'I've been thinking about your mission . . .'

'Nothing like a thermal camera to flush out wildlife,' continued Richard. 'Works over huge distances.'

'I'm not sure you're meant to find that animal,' said Ellie.

Richard looked confused. 'What do you mean?'

'Well, perhaps it's just not meant to be.'

'Things are what you make them.'

'Sometimes things don't go to plan.'

'Well then, they must be made to go to plan,' Richard countered. 'Everything is achievable. It's just a question of time and effort.'

Ellie looked at his tired face. 'Do you know what your problem is, Richard?'

He raised an eyebrow. 'I hadn't realized I had a problem.'

'Now, don't be like that.'

'Ok then, what's my problem?'

'Your problem is that you've found a solution in your head for how the world works and you expect everything in it to adhere to your philosophy. You want the whole universe to agree with you, Richard, and I'm sorry to say it just doesn't. Look at me.'

He looked. A sullen petulance lurked at the corner of his jaw.

'It doesn't,' repeated Ellie. 'And in situations like this, you sometimes have to take the good with the bad.'

Richard sulked. He'd thought Ellie would cheer him up, but lately their meetings were less fun.

His phone rang. He turned away to answer it.

'Hello? Richard Mathern speaking.'

'Mathern,' came a familiar yap. *'It's Alan. What the hell have you been doing?'*

'Excuse me?'

'You must have done something. Otherwise why would they decide to dump us like a bag of cat shit?'

Richard curled his nose. He hadn't spoken to Alan in weeks and had forgotten how much he loathed him.

'You're not making sense, Alan. What are you talking about?'

'The bear project! The thing that was going to bring in all that money!'

Richard could almost hear the background silence at *Nature Magazine* as people stopped typing and glanced over to the head office to see what was happening.

210

'What are you saying? What's happened?'

Alan groaned. *'Bloody hell, he doesn't know. Why am I not surprised?'*

Richard froze. 'Has our funding been cut?'

Alan sniffed. *'Might as well have been. We received a note saying that major cuts are being considered and that some projects are shortlisted for termination, pending final assessment. Yours is on the list.'*

Richard felt his stomach land with a sickening *thud* somewhere near his ankles. 'But they can't do that! We haven't found the bear yet!'

'No shit! That's why they're considering shelving the whole thing. You were sent to find bears; you haven't found any. I guess they're sick of waiting.'

Richard's mind worked furiously. Being on the shortlist wasn't the final word, was it? It was probably just a temporary decision; he could still make it work. All he needed to do was find the bear. Publicity would take care of the rest.

'How long is the assessment time?'

'They say four weeks, but to be honest it's pretty vague. The bottom line is, you've got a month to get your together. What have you been up to all this time, Mathern? Swanning around the mountains and . . .'

Richard didn't hear the rest. He was too busy hanging up.

Ellie watched as Richard turned a shade of pale rivalling her own. 'Something wrong?'

'Can't stop,' said Richard. 'Gotta run.'

'But you've only just arrived!'

'Something's come up. Besides,' he added, throwing on his rucksack, 'it's not like you're going anywhere, right?'

She didn't appreciate this last comment but was unwilling to start a confrontation. 'Well, all right then . . .'

Richard was already legging it across the promenade. He vaulted down the stairs and raced down the track to the hotel. A cold breeze filled the space he'd lately occupied.

'Bye, I guess,' muttered Ellie to the air. She turned and looked up at the ivory peak behind her. She'd seen dozens of winters in the mountains; she knew it wasn't long before the snow came. Time would run its course.

She tilted her head in thought. The beginnings of a smile tugged at the corners of her mouth. Off she went on an impulse following the same track as Richard, not towards the hotel but into the village.

Ellie made for the large building housing the communal offices and peered through the window. Inside she spotted the hunched figure of Ursula, the secretary, her gnarled face illuminated by a computer screen.

Ellie smiled and, unobserved—indeed, to most potential observers, unobservable—slipped through the door.

*****

Richard entered the hotel lobby and headed for the stairs. He found Graham slumped on the bottom step, scratching Suzy's ear.

'Hey,' said Richard. 'Gotta send some emails.'

He waited for Graham to let him pass, but today his companion seemed uncharacteristically depressed.

'Aren't you going to ask me how I'm doing?' Graham asked mournfully.

Richard wasn't keen to discuss his talk with Alan. Feelings of dread were knocking about inside his head and he worried that if he let them out, everything would be over. Four weeks to save the project . . . Maybe if he wrote to the right people he could buy himself more time.

'Ok, how are you?'

Graham sighed. 'Not great. There I was, a paragon of virility, and all it took to reduce me to a quivering adolescent was a few harsh words from a woman.'

'I see. Melanie turned you down again, did she?'

Graham sighed again and ruffled Suzy's fur as she inspected Richard's shoes for interesting smells.

'Yep. I have therefore, in my shame, decided to forego all hopes or dreams involving womanhood and shall instead seek happiness among God's less fickle creatures. Take my relationship with Suzy here; easy, simple, a bond of true friendship founded on our shared appreciation of country walks, cuddles, and Dostoyevsky.'

He nodded towards the corner under the stairs. Amongst a pile of dusty suitcases, bits of timber and a heavy-looking wood axe, Richard made out the remains of the missing book, bearing the teeth marks of many hours' satisfied perusal by Suzy.

Richard had calmed down just a little. The best thing would be to give Graham a little information while concealing the bigger picture. Besides, he had an idea.

'I got a call from the office. They're not happy.'

'Why should they be?' lamented Graham. 'Everything's so sad.'

'For God's sake, pull yourself together. I want you to go and talk to Melanie. We need to borrow her dogs.'

Graham looked horrified. 'I can't do that! She's spurned me! It'd look like the desperate attempt of a scorned man.'

'So you're just going to sit here and mope?'

'Excuse me,' countered Graham. 'I think you'll find that, in situations such as this, I'm entitled to a suitable period of mourning involving drugs, alcohol, and, hopefully, a dark-haired foreign beauty who practices yoga and likes craft beer.'

Richard rolled his eyes. 'Fine, I'll do it. Where can I find her?'

'She works mornings at the sportswear shop on the high street.'

'I'll call her tomorrow. Can I go upstairs? I need a nap.'

Graham moved aside. Richard mounted the stairs, forcing himself not to run. The landing seemed miles away. After knocking his head on the beam as usual he sat down heavily on the bed and began to undo his bootlaces, reliving the phone call in his mind. He resolved to ring Melanie first thing in the morning.

His eyes wandered along the beams until they reached the picture of the old man on the far wall.

'I don't suppose you know where I can find a bear, do you?' Richard asked the black-and-white photo.

The old man seemed to consider this.

I hear they've got some in a pit in Bern.

Richard sighed and turned to the wall, his thoughts mixing together.

It had become his habit over the past weeks to reach for a book whenever he was preoccupied and he did so now. Invariably his hand fell on *Central European Mythology and Folk Tales*, by Melchior B. Adolphus. He leafed through the stories until he found one he hadn't read yet.

THE DEVIL'S SEAT

In olden days a spirit made its abode in the mountains east of Aigle. As long as people kept the old gods this spirit was simply one among many, but the gradual introduction of Christianity so angered the spirit that it soon cultivated a magnificent loathing for the new faith. Most of all it despised the sound of bells, which caused its head to ring such that it screamed with rage.

The spirit grew malevolent and dangerous. The local people became afraid of it and learned to avoid certain roads said to be its highways. Unwary travellers risked being caught high in the mountains and flung to their doom or would disappear altogether, never to be seen again.

In the village of Griuns lived a man with two sons and a daughter. The eldest son was angry because he always had to take the long way around the mountains in order to avoid the evil spirit that plagued the area. One day he decided to seek it out and kill it. The entreaties of his family and friends did nothing to dissuade him, so they gave him their blessing and off he went in search of the demon. He did not return and was soon given up for lost.

Some time later the second son also tired of wearing through his shoes on the long mountain roads. He announced his intention to complete the task his brother had started. All the prayers and supplications of his father and sister would not hinder him and he followed the same path into the mountains. When he disappeared in turn there was much grieving in the town.

One day the daughter came to her father and said, 'Father, I too wish to confront the spirit that lives in the mountains.'

Her father was horrified. 'You, kill a demon? Absurd! Besides, I've already lost two children. To lose a third would be too much to bear. Stay with me and mourn your brothers from the safety of home. The mountain road is accursed.'

'Nonetheless,' insisted the girl, 'I wish to go.'

Her father sent her to bed without her supper. But, whilst the village slept, the girl stole a piece of cheese from the kitchen, wrapped it in her apron, and crept out of the window. She followed the road into the mountains with nothing but starlight to guide her.

It was a long way and the sun rose faster than the girl. But she was resolute in her purpose and walked with a steady tread. By and by she came to the crest of the pass high above the valley.

All of a sudden she heard a thunderous noise like that of an avalanche and spied a dark cloud descending from the peak. As it came near she saw that it was no cloud but a dense flock of ravens within which flew the demon, horned and cloven-hoofed. So terrible was his appearance that the girl identified him as the Evil One himself. Fearing the worst she knelt, picked up a heavy stone from the ground, and hid it in her apron.

With a roar the spirit came to land on the path in front of her. Seeing the girl he threw his head back and laughed.

'Ha! Is this the terrible creature of whose trespass the stones whispered to me? I shall eat you in two bites!'

The girl was very frightened, but spoke quickly lest the demon keep his word. 'I have come to challenge you,' she said, 'and to demand that you go away and leave this place in peace.'

The demon laughed all the more and rushed forward to devour the poor girl. She reached for the stone that she might throw it at him, but in her haste she flung the piece of cheese by mistake. This turned out to be a stroke of luck, for the demon had not tasted cheese before. He sniffed it, nibbled on a corner and, finding it exceeding good, devoured that instead.

'That,' he declared, 'was quite the finest thing I have ever tasted.'

'I am glad,' said the girl. 'It is called cheese.'

'What's more,' continued the demon, 'I have decided not to eat you.'

'That is good,' said the girl.

'Instead,' the demon announced, 'I will carry you off to my lair where you shall be my slave and make me cheese forever.'

'That is not so good,' replied the girl.

The demon's brow darkened. The girl feared he might consume her after all.

She cried, 'At least give me a chance to save myself. I shall tell you a riddle; if you know the answer then I shall be your slave. But, if you guess incorrectly, you must leave this place without harming me and confine yourself to the summit of the highest mountain you can find, to live in exile forever.'

The demon smiled an evil smile, for he knew all the answers to all the riddles ever told.

'Ask your riddle,' said the perfidious spirit

The girl thought a moment before asking, 'What is a kindness?'

This angered the demon no end, for what could he answer? He knew precious little about kindness, and what pleasures he did know were evil and perverse.

'That is not a fair question,' he said. 'Ask me something clever and I shall answer.'

The girl mocked him with pitying looks. 'I do not think you know the answer,' she said. 'You could not show me a kindness if you wanted to.'

The demon became furious. Nothing angers a spirit more than mockery, most of all that of a girl. 'Test me!' he demanded. 'Ask of me one kindness and I shall grant your request or else admit defeat.'

'Very well,' said the girl with cunning in her voice. 'Submit to the exile I have requested voluntarily. Then shall I concede that I have known your kindness.'

Then the demon knew he was undone, for one way or another he had sealed his own fate.

With a cry of anger he rushed forward but, bound by his promise, he could not touch the girl. She returned to the village with the happy news that the pass was now safe to travel, and there was much rejoicing. Before long there appeared on the road the lost souls ensnared by the spirit, including the girl's two brothers. There was merriment and thanksgiving in the town of Griuns and for three days the bells rang every hour in celebration.

Driven away by their hateful sound, the demon retreated to the summit of the Diablerets where, as far as I am aware, he remains to this day, brooding and as full of malice as ever. The natives insist that when the north wind blows of an evening, one can still hear his mournful cries echoing across the valley. These speculations are usually accompanied by repeated and fervent signs of the cross.

N.b: There are some who contend that the mountain in question is not the Diablerets, but Monte Rosa, the Eiger, or even Mont Blanc. Others say that no demon reigns there, but Berchtold the Bringer of Winter and his sister Perchta, the White Lady, and that the cries carried by the wind are *those of the Wild Hunt; that great cavalcade of lost souls that rides through the sky on the Ember days of the year. One must note the resemblance to the story of Lord of Grimmelstein, who is condemned to leave his grave on holy days and hunt in the woods as punishment for breaking the Sabbath, and the White Lady's similarity to the Dame Abonde and her followers the Benandanti, who are said to do battle with witches for the fate of the harvest. Besides the aforementioned lord almost every valley and hillside in Switzerland is said to be visited at times by some similar wraith, sweeping by on the wings of the wind, if not by the Wild Hunt itself.*

[M. B. Adolphus]

Richard didn't find this story very relaxing. Instead his head now teemed with images of perfidious spirits and nightmarish witch dances in the sky.

He set the book aside, lay back and stared at the carved ceiling. This merely replaced the monsters in his head with real ones carved from wood. A human-faced lion leered at him from a corner, its features forever contorted in a mocking grin.

Richard turned over and lapsed into an uneasy sleep.

On the lower landing the dejected Graham continued to scratch Suzy's neck. High in the mountains the spectre of Frederick Bellows laboured onwards and upward, towards a summit he would never reach.

Only the bush, high on its rocky knoll, had nothing to complain about. Nevertheless, it kept a wary eye out for the shadow of any approaching birds.

AIRBORNE
CHAPTER TWENTY-TWO

IDERÄLPLI'S KENNEL HAD housed many variations of canine-themed animals for generations. As he stood beside it in the alleyway behind the hotel, Richard shifted a couple of steps to where he judged upwind to be.

'So, let me get this straight,' he said: 'when a dog dies, you give its name to the next puppy that's born so its spirit lives on in different bodies?'

Melanie nodded. 'Yes! Also, you shouldn't name a puppy after a dog that's still alive, otherwise the spirit gets confused and kills one of the dogs.'

Richard scratched the head of a large malamute who was investigating his groin. 'You believe all that stuff about reincarnation?'

Melanie shrugged. 'I don't know. Maybe. Tradition says that the dogs' spirits can be traced all the way back to their ancestors, that memories are passed on from dog to dog. By changing the name, you kill the lineage.'

'Your English is amazing, by the way.'

'Thanks! I spent a year in Edinburgh for my Erasmus.'

It hadn't occurred to Richard that animals might inherit names. Then again, there must be farms in England whose barns had housed a cow named Bessie for a thousand years or more. Perhaps it made sense for the herd to outlive the herdsman. Farmers would come and go, but in their various succeeding manifestations their beasts would endure.

Richard wondered if animals inherited a shared consciousness from their ancestors, some primeval instinct that humans had lost. Maybe each Bessie remembered things the previous Bessies had learned. Perhaps the collective mind of the herd stretched back through time immemorial, before farms, before domestication, even before man. Did cows dream? In sleep did they relive an age when they weren't merely ambulatory milk factories, but rearing, galloping, horned behemoths? Perhaps, within every cow chained up in a barn, there beat the heart of an auroch.

And within every dog, a voice in Richard's mind added, that of a wolf.

Melanie was giving him an inquisitive look. There reigned around them a concerned silence.

'Sorry.' Richard felt the blood rise to his face. 'I must've drifted off.'

He'd been tired all morning, though he couldn't have said why. Graham had still been in bed when he'd left.

'Sure you don't want to come and help me convince Melanie to let us borrow a dog or two?' Richard had asked as he laced up his boots.

Graham had shaken his head, his eyes still closed. 'No way, man. I'm living under a shadow.' He pulled the duvet cover over his face.

'Come off it,' said Richard.

'I'm serious,' Graham replied from under the duvet. 'My dreams were full of strange omens: I dreamt that a spirit appeared at the foot of my bed, skin black as charcoal with an other-worldly glow shining through the cracks and lectured me on the importance of recycling; I dreamt that an eagle circled the room three times before logging onto my laptop, taking screenshots of my browser history, and sharing them on social media; I dreamt I was visited by the ghost of a young woman . . .'

In the bathroom, Richard's electric toothbrush switched off. 'Really?'

Graham threw off the duvet. 'No, not really, you berk. I'm just sick of you pushing me to talk to someone who's clearly not interested, so can we just drop it?'

Graham rolled over and faced the wall. Richard went to find Melanie by himself.

Her voice cut into his train of thought. 'They tell me you want a smelling dog to track the bear, yes?'

'Um, yeah, if that's, you know, all right with everyone.'

Unexpectedly, Melanie shook her head. 'I'm afraid it's not possible.'

'Why not? It seemed like such a good idea.'

'I understand. But I don't own these dogs. The owners would not allow them to be used in this way. The other problem is this: the dogs, they're very independent in spirit. The huskies don't obey me half the time. They won't agree to work for you.'

Richard slumped.

'But the idea is not bad.' Melanie smiled. 'In fact, there is another dog I could recommend. Perhaps the owners would lend her.'

This is why, two hours later, Richard found himself standing atop a windswept knoll alongside Suzy. Her beloved copy of Dostoyevsky was in her mouth—Richard had been unable to persuade her to leave it behind—and her jowls salivated at the thought of an afternoon's delicious chewing.

218

Getting her up the path had been hard enough. Suzy's tracking was leisurely at best and all she'd unearthed so far was a disagreeable old marmot who'd sent her packing with a hiss and a swipe of his sharp claws.

Richard eventually lost heart and decided to call it off. 'Sorry for dragging you up here, old girl,' he sighed. 'Guess I got overexcited.'

Suzy shook her floppy head and adjusted her weight to ease her arthritic joints. She missed her carpet and was eager to get back to it for a spot of reading.

Richard was about to leave the knoll when he heard a buzzing noise overhead.

A spindly little drone hovered in the air about two dozen yards away. By the glint of a lens hanging amidst its four propellers Richard knew he was being observed. Despite the ominousness inherent to remote-powered robot beetles, this one managed to hover in a way that was almost congenial.

'Nice, isn't she?' called Chase, appearing from behind a hummock. You, sir, are looking at the PXB Falcon Sky Eye, max speed 35 mph, battery-powered flight time thirty-three minutes, iOS and Android compatible, currently streaming live footage to my cell phone. Isn't she a beaut?'

Richard hiked up the short distance and joined the American, the PXB Falcon Sky Eye buzzing merrily around his head.

'I rented it from that Dino kid from the restaurant. Awesome stuff!'

Richard stared at the drone with growing interest. 'How far can that thing see?'

'Far as you like. Actually, you can help! The camera relays live images back to me, but I'm an idiot and didn't bring my tablet. What with this sun, I'm having trouble seeing where I'm going on my phone screen. I've been keeping the drone in sight so far, but I think between the two of us we could pilot this thing and use the camera at the same time. We could send it miles away! Wanna help?'

Richard did want to. He wanted to very much. 'Do you mind if we send it over some tracks I've covered? I'd be curious to see what it can see. It might just be what Graham and I need.'

Chase was thrilled. It was the work of a moment to hand Richard his phone and sync it with the drone.

The screen presented Richard with several touch-sensitive controls that commanded the angle and focus of the camera nested between the drone's rotors. Richard gave the dials an experimental swipe and was afforded a detailed view of himself from above. The drone bobbed around in the air but the picture remained reasonably steady.

Chase winked at him. 'Miniaturised triple-axis stabilisers.'

The screen was cracked in one corner, but Chase's face was recognisable as a mosaic of grinning white teeth.

'Let's go!' he cried. The PXB whizzed into the sky and was soon lost to view.

'I'll need directions now,' said Chase, 'I don't want to crash this thing.'

'Ok, hang on.' Richard screened his eyes from the sun and peered at the phone. 'Gain a little altitude and head towards the mountain.'

'What mountain? I can't see where I'm going.'

'Oh, right. Sorry. Go left.'

'What, like this?'

'No, not like that, you'll smash right into the cliff!'

'Dang it! Which way?'

'The other way!'

'Which other way?'

'Dammit, there are rocks everywhere!'

'Aaaargh!'

'Aaaargh!'

'Aaaaaaaaaaaaaaargh!'

This continued for some time. Suzy grew bored of all the screaming and found a patch of moss on which to snooze.

Eventually Richard and Chase regained control of the machine and overcame the difficulty of having one man flying blind while the other could only see what a cracked smartphone screen would allow him to see.

'Okay,' said Richard, steadying his frayed nerves, 'move forward slowly, maintaining a constant altitude.'

'You got it.' Chase edged the levers on his control panel forward.

Richard watched the image shift. The ground fell away as the drone carried its tiny payload into the sky.

He experimented with the controls on the screen, and the camera swivelled around. Pointing it down he saw himself and Chase both looking upwards, already far below. He brought the camera up again and rotated it, scanning the horizon.

'This is amazing, I can see for miles! Want to have a look?'

'Not now. At some point we'll bring her back and I'll show you how to fly her so we can swap.'

'Ok. Turn to the left a bit, I can see the treeline.'

The drone rose higher, its camera sweeping over the expansive landscape.

'There's the track leading down to the village! I can see the scrub where Graham hid one of the tripwires.'

'Anything moving?'

'No. Amazing view though. Let's go up the mountain a bit.'

'Tell me when the light flashes red. That means we're running out of battery.'

'Sure thing. Let's go higher.'

The trees thinned as the ground continued to rise. Richard directed Chase to rise with it and soon the flanks of the mountain filled his view.

Great boulders and ice sheets drifted silently underneath the drone as it climbed, trying but failing to encompass the sheer size of the thing in its little lens. No matter where you looked there was more of it, yet the mountain's vastness seemed somehow diminished by the small, cracked screen of the phone.

Richard glanced up just to make sure the Gräuelhorn was still there in real life. It towered over him as it had done since his arrival, white and terrifying, nothing like the neat, trim picture on the screen. It dominated his field of vision like some monstrous, icy creature and its scent filled the air.

'Eyes on the prize, Richard,' said Chase.

'Right.' Richard looked back at the screen. 'Whoops, we're heading for a cliff, best move away.'

'Which way?'

'To your right a bit.'

'How's that?'

'Perfect.'

Walls of black rock drifted across the screen. Richard swivelled the camera to point forwards again. Chase's careful piloting pulled them away from the white giant and back out over the open plateau. For a little while the only sound was Suzy gnawing contentedly on her book.

'Right,' said Richard, 'we're over that high valley at the base of the glacier, where the stream is. Let's make a pass over to the right and . . .'

He stared at the monitor. Then he stared harder.

'Move down a bit.'

'What is it?' asked Chase. 'You see something?'

It couldn't be. 'Slow down!' Richard cried.

'I'm trying! What is it? Is there something down there?'

Richard peered at the screen, trying to find the dark patch he'd glimpsed a moment before.

'Make another pass over the valley.'

There it was again. In the time it had taken Chase to turn and make another sweep, the shape had moved.

Richard felt the same sensation creeping up on him that he had on the first day, not wild this time but disbelieving and hesitant, his exuberance tempered by weeks of failure. He was desperate not to be wrong.

He recognised where the drone was hovering, one of several high valleys squeezed between the sharp crags jutting outwards from the mountain, places he and Graham had visited several times already. For some reason the camera was having trouble focusing for the first time since take off. Still, Richard could make out a familiar trail running straight past one of their motion-sensitive cameras hidden in a rock pile.

He jumped. There it was again: a blurry yet distinctive silhouette, barely noticeable in the shadow of the crag but unmistakable, moving steadily along the track.

'Bloody hell!'

Chase failed to recognise the sheer ecstasy in this exclamation and became agitated. Richard insisted everything was fine and told Chase to fly as steadily as he could. He thumbed the controls, willing the lens into focus.

The drone lurched suddenly to the side and the dark shape slid off the screen.

'Damn! Arse! Sodding hell!'

'What?' Chase cried. 'What happened?'

'The stupid thing swerved away. Did you jerk the controls?'

'No. Maybe it isn't responding properly. Is the battery running low?'

'No,' Richard lied.

Chase saw the red light blink on the phone. 'Sorry, I'll have to bring her in.'

'Don't you dare!'

'I'm bringing her in!'

Richard watched in agony as the picture swung away and the drone set a course back down the mountain. He wasted precious battery power swivelling the camera to face backwards. The silhouette was still there, getting smaller every second.

He desperately tried to focus in on the dark patch, already half-invisible against the mountainside. The phone was so close to his face it was almost rubbing against his eyeball. A minute motion of his thumb centred the lens on the dark spot. Almost there . . .

There.

An instant later the drone swung around a cliff and rocks obscured his view.

Richard swore, but the maniacal grin stuck to his face. He'd seen her. Not only that, he'd ascertained her position. To get there she must have walked straight past his cameras, all set to a hair trigger: not only did he have the shots, he had them in close-up and high definition.

'I've got her! The bitch is mine!' He laughed out of sheer glee.

The drone reappeared above them, buzzing in the distance. Chase piloted it down onto the grass where it flopped in exhaustion, its battery spent.

Before Chase could stop him Richard descended on the machine and was clawing it open.

'Hang on,' said Chase, 'I'll help.'

He got out the memory chip and handed it to Richard. The Englishman's hand trembled as he took it.

'Lemme get you some water,' offered Chase. 'You seem a bit shaky. I've got a bottle somewhere. I've also got these awesome energy bars with no added sugar. Want one?'

There was no response. Chase looked up: Richard was racing down the slope towards the village. Suzy laboured after him, struggling to keep up but relieved that he was finally heading in a direction she favoured.

Chase watched them go, shrugged, and began to pack up the drone.

The hotel door clattered as Richard erupted into the hallway. He raced upstairs, the precious memory chip in his pocket. The beam gave his head a customary *bonk* in greeting but Richard didn't even slow down. Without stopping to remove his jacket he rushed to the table and yanked open his computer. He fumbled for the chip and swore when he couldn't find it before remembering it was in his other pocket.

At last he inserted it into the port and watched the film upload.

*****

Chase returned to the hotel to find Kaitlyn waiting for him. He told her about the afternoon's excitement.

'So he's found his bear, then!' cried Kaitlyn. 'And you helped him! How nice for him and his friend.'

Chase's face was clouded. 'Well, that's the funny thing. I looked at the screen a couple of times and I couldn't see anything.'

'Well, that's normal with those drone things. Didn't you tell me yourself that you need one person to drive and another to look at the monitor? You must've lost control of the camera angle when you tried to look.'

'That's what I thought at first, only . . .'

'Only what?'

'Well, I'd synced the drone wirelessly with my phone to record the footage. You know, for my video blog. So both the drone and my phone were simultaneously downloading the footage. I thought I'd give Richard the chip from the drone and use the copy on the phone for myself.'

'Yeah?'

'So, after Richard left I uploaded the phone footage onto my laptop so I could see the animal for myself. I also wanted to test the camera to see how it all came out.'

'And what did you see?'

Chase leaned forward. 'Nothing. Just mountains.'

'What do you mean? You couldn't see the bear?'

Chase shook his head. 'There wasn't any bear. There were loads of tracking shots of rocks and gullies and stuff. But no bear.'

Kaitlyn looked confused. 'Maybe it was away somewhere in the distance?'

Chase shrugged. 'It'd have to have been pretty far away. All I saw was dirt. Great quality footage though, the dirt looked amazing! Here, I'll show you.'

'Later, honey. Why do you think he saw if there wasn't anything in the shot?'

'Beats me. English people are weird. Sure you don't want to see the dirt?'

'I've got a better idea. What say you to some fondue?'

Chase gasped. 'I love fondue! I can't believe we haven't had any yet.'

'I know! There's a panoramic restaurant about twenty minutes away down the mountain that has great reviews. It's in an old building with traditional décor and great views and everything!'

'Lead the way, honey.'

Twenty-two minutes later they were down the mountain filling themselves up with melted cheese, having forgotten all about Richard and the mysterious footage.

*****

Human beings are remarkably good at dealing with hardship. Were you to take an average person, maroon them on a desert island, and announce that they wouldn't be rescued until they'd spent exactly one year in solitary exile, you'd be surprised by how well they'd cope with the news. Granted, initially they'd demand to know who put you in charge, threaten to sue the pants of you, and attempt to fling any number of coconuts in your general direction while screaming hysterically. But this first phase soon passes, as does the second—usually characterised by the maroonee spending several days kneeling on the beach and pleading with the waves. Eventually people see sense and pull themselves together.

The island soon becomes home to a number of innovations including a primitive grass dwelling, the only working fireplace for several hundred miles, and a newly domesticated crab named Ian. The maroonee will devise many cunning methods of assuring survival, like basic fishing implements and Thursday night karaoke sessions down by the tide pool. A particularly talented exile may come up with something original, like an irrigation system for the mango trees, some sort of personalized art form dedicated to expressing ennui, or a new religion based on half-remembered television documentaries about Ancient Mesopotamia.

Occasionally things get a little bit out of hand and the island witnesses the beginnings of a violent sect wherein its only human representative anoints themself High Vizier of the Crab People and terrorizes their crustacean subjects with regular seafood barbeques on the beach. This is a particularly high risk when the marooned person was previously a high-ranking corporate official or the member of a royal family and usually ends with the High Vizier declaring that they are immortal, diving into the lagoon to do battle with a shark, and losing. It is then customary for Ian the crab to inherit the late Vizier's responsibilities.

These occurrences remain the exception, however. Mankind's natural resilience usually pulls through—if occasionally assisted by modest spells of temporary insanity. In most cases, once the full year has elapsed, the architect of this experiment will be met on the beach by a castaway who, though hairier and smelling strongly of singed crabmeat, will likely be wiser and more compassionate than when they arrived.

If, however, the point of the arrival was not rescue but the announcement that, due to a general strike affecting air traffic over French Polynesia, the rescue flight would be a week late, the crushing anguish of a whole year would slam through every neuron in the maroonee's brain like a home-made stone hammer through crab shell. Even the most stolid person in the world would immediately descend into such a raving and irrevocable maelstrom of madness that no doctor in the world could ever hope to coax them out of it, regardless how many PhDs they had.

The point is; humans are generally fine with hardship. It's disappointment we can't stand.

When trying to describe what Richard felt as he looked at the film uploaded from the memory chip to his laptop, the word disappointment falls short.

His state worsened when he retrieved the footage from the motion-sensitive cameras on the trail he'd overflown that afternoon. Each frame had been lovingly calibrated to capture the approach of any animal; the exposure was timed exactly right; he'd considered the time of year, temperature, phase of the moon, probable cloud formations, and humidity when he'd set them up. Indeed, every image was exactly what he could have hoped for, except that absolutely none of them, not one, showed even the slightest trace of a bear.

*****

Dawes sat at his desk, impeccable in dress but crushed in spirit. He looked like a penguin that had lost its egg in some distressing encounter with a sea lion and had taken up business in order to forget its tragic loss, only to find that there, too, lay only emptiness and despair.

Bing.

Dawes frowned at his email server. He'd always hated electronic correspondence. As he clicked on the envelope he yearned for the feel of expensive stationery and the reassuring weight of a letter opener.

Strange, he thought: this email appears to have been sent from the secure server. Stranger still, it was headed with Dawes' personal priority code, which he hadn't used in years.

He froze.

'Alice!'

The aforementioned appeared. 'Yes, Mr Dawes?'

Dawes turned an accusatory glare on Alice. 'Who has been accessing my computer?' he demanded.

Alice looked confused. 'I . . . I don't . . .'

'Who has been accessing my computer? Who?'

Dawes rushed around the desk and stared with wild eyes at his secretary.

'WHO?'

Dawes' voice raised in anger was a thing unheard of. The office, ordinarily a haven of monastic calm, reeled at the noise. For the unsuspecting, overworked Alice it was like being yelled at by her favourite grandfather.

Dawes watched her collapse to the floor in a wailing heap, her papers cascading onto the carpet in an arabesque of white. The moment of madness had passed and he was himself once again. Too late: Alice's meltdown had begun.

He stooped, attempting to raise the quivering figure to her feet. 'I apologise, Alice. That was very wrong of me.'

'Mmmmmh,' was the tearful reply.

'Come sit down.'

Dawes helped Alice to a chair. He perched on the end of his desk and waited for her hiccoughs to subside.

'M' sorry, Mr Dawes, (hic) it's just (hic) I wa-wasn't ready f-for (hic) for th-that . . .'

A fresh wave of tears erupted and Alice tried angrily to expunge them. Dawes felt like a brute. But there were more pressing matters to attend to.

'I need to know, Alice,' he urged, 'has anyone had access to my email?'

Alice shook her head emphatically.

'Are you certain?'

Alice glared at Dawes with the wounded look of the betrayed. His outburst was bad enough, but such an implication as this bordered on veritable injury.

Dawes saw that he had gone too far. 'Of course,' he said, 'of course you are. When have you ever been otherwise? Thank you Alice, that . . . that will be all.'

Alice rose and made for the exit. She paused by the door and looked back, her red-rimmed eyes reproachful and yet full of concern for her employer. Dawes had returned to the desk and was staring at the screen.

She shook her head sadly as though to say *this is truly the end*, and returned to her desk to have a good sniffle.

Some moments later Dawes picked up the phone and dialled.

*****

Beep.
Beep.
Click. 'Lady Crowley speaking.'
'Hullo, Lettie,' said Dawes.

In the Master's Lodge of Brommel College, Leticia Crowley sat up in surprise. 'Alistair! Is that you?'

'Yes, Lettie, I'm afraid so.'

'Well, this is a surprise, I must say. Not a word in what, four years?'

'I always was a rather poor correspondent.'

'I'm so sorry about Patricia, Alistair. I never did get a chance to say.'

After only the most minor of pauses he answered, *'Thank you.'*

'So,' Leticia continued in a lighter tone, 'still encased in that gigantic glass phallus of yours, presiding over the dealings of mice and men? Or are you finally free for tea and a catch-up?'

'Actually, Lettie, I'm calling on business. I require some advice from an expert in family law and private wealth.'

'What's happened to your private army of solicitors?'

'The ranks have been somewhat thinned of late. It's a long story, one best discussed in person.'

'I see. Finally making that one-way trip to the special clinic in Switzerland are you, you old scoundrel? I always knew the law would catch up with you eventually. Probably best to take the easy way out; less paperwork when things get messy.'

'That's not it. I'll explain later tonight, when you come to the office.'

'Can't. My brother's on holiday and George and I are looking after his two girls. We're treating them to dinner.'

'Cancel it.'

Lady Leticia swivelled in her leather chair so she was facing the window. A punt laden with drunken teenagers drifted past the bottom of the Master's Garden, their discarded essay papers floating down the river behind them. 'Why should I?'

'Money. That, and the satisfaction of bringing the wrath of justice down on someone who deserves it.'

'How much money?'

Dawes named a figure. Eyebrows rose.

'My, my, Alistair, this must be important.'

'It is. You'll find out more when we speak tonight.'

The door to Lady Leticia's office swung open. Her youngest niece rushed in and grabbed her leg, waving a piece of paper.

'Auntie, look! I drew a caricature of the Prime Minister being trampled by a bison!'

'Not now, Darling,' said Leticia, gently disengaging herself, 'Auntie's negotiating a truce with the Patriarchy.' She returned to the phone. 'I'm on my way, Alistair.'

'Excellent. Use the back entrance. Allerby will let you in.'

Beep.

Leticia looked at the phone as though Dawes might have shared with it some crucial piece of information that was being withheld from her. The device offered no illumination, so she replaced it.

'I used purple as well as red,' continued her niece, waving a lurid illustration, 'so it's a metaphor for both the government and the opposition. My next one is going to be one of Anubis, the God of Death from that book on Ancient Egypt you gave me, where he weighs the Chancellor of the Exchequer's heart in judgement, deems it unworthy, and feeds it to his cat.'

'How wonderful,' said Leticia. 'Listen, dear,' she added, 'I need you to go and tell Uncle George that Aunt Lettie can't come out tonight. Something's come up.'

The child was desolated. 'But we're having pizza,' she pointed out.

This ironclad argument very nearly floored Lady Leticia, but through tremendous exertion of will she stood firm.

'Next time, I promise. There's something afoot in London and I suspect whatever it is will fund the entirety of your university fees. Then, when you're a QC, we can have pizza every night! Won't that be fun?'

Her niece considered this. 'I suppose,' she admitted.

'Good girl. Now, run along and fetch Auntie's mink.'

THE IRON MONSTER
CHAPTER TWENTY-THREE

Niderälpli Railway Station, 1919

AYING THE TRACK had taken the better part of eight months. Great swathes of earth had been either carted away or dumped down the cliffs into the river. Any boulders too large to dislodge had been dynamited and the icy torrent had been bridged several times to bring the narrow gauge railway up the mountain to the sheltered valley of Niderälpli.

It was a cold, sodden afternoon when the townspeople spotted a plume of steam rising from the ravine, mingling with the heavy mist. Before long the line of carriages appeared, pulled by a sturdy black locomotive with green siding. The tracks were icy, but the locomotive's immense weight bore down on them and the wheels' grip held. Though the air was filled with a dismal sleet, when the train pulled into the station it was met there by most of the villagers, who managed a convincing if slightly damp cheer.

The ceremony was brief, as it was already late and many of those gathered in the icy drizzle held invitations to the banquet to follow. The formalities dispensed with, the mayor led the way back to the town hall, leaving the workmen and the miners to shunt the engine into its new depot.

All—save one—were Italian. Most came from the poor valleys south of the Alps, though a few hailed from as far as Basilicata and Sicily. The German-speaking mechanics and engineers having joined the celebrations in the village, the only Swiss now remaining was Müller the Foreman.

He climbed into the engineer's booth and issued instructions to his workers. The men set to work on levers and valves, gloved hands struggling with pins and turnbuckles, hurrying to unhook the chains before the slush on the couplings froze solid. Before long they'd separated the carriages and backed the locomotive carefully through the big wooden doors to its designated spot at the far end of the depot. The high-ceilinged

229

space was wreathed in great clouds of steam from the engine that curled around the legs of the men as the boiler hissed and settled.

Their job done, the workmen crowded round to admire the machine.

'*Che bestia, eh, Capo?*' said one worker.

'*Si, Angelo.*' Müller had dug tunnels on both sides of the Alps and spoke Italian nearly as well as German. The foreman stood smiling beside the black locomotive, enjoying the *plink* sounds of her sleet-soaked metal as it cooled. 'She was a long time getting here, too.'

'None too soon, by God!' cried a voice several men to his left. 'I count eight months of sleeping three to a bed on five francs a day!' To underscore his point the speaker held up various combinations of fingers, all of them incorrect.

'And they made us work Sundays, too!' growled another.

'Well she's here now, boys!' cried Angelo. 'Tonight, we're celebrating!' From his gunnysack he produced from among the tools a hidden cache of wine, to deafening acclaim.

Müller continued to inspect the train as the bottles were passed around. As part of the engineering team he'd spent many months planning the extension of the railway line, the greater part of whose execution had seen him in the company of the hired labourers blasting the machine's path out of the mountainside. He had little use for dignitaries or ceremony and was in no hurry to attend the party thrown by the village's governing body. His workers, though by no means subtle in their wit and occasionally over-enthusiastic in their quarrels, had shown themselves to be dependable in their work and truehearted in their friendship. He was an engineer first and foremost and prized the men who made his work possible.

The wine continued its circumvention of the depot, whose freshly tarred roof echoed with bouts of raucous singing and good-natured quarrels. The men took turns climbing into the engineer's box to move the levers and tap the pressure gauges with their fingers. Müller looked on, making sure nobody accidentally loosened the brakes.

The great wooden doors had been left ajar. One of the miners noticed the tip of a tiny blonde head and a single blue eye observing the festivities.

'Look here, boys!' He retrieved a little girl of five or six decked out in clean shoes and a blue dress from her hiding place. 'A visitor! And a mighty pretty one, too.'

The men cheered. The girl clung shyly to the miner's calloused hand.

'Approach, Giovanni, that we might greet this vision!'

'She's a beauty and no mistake.'

'She wants to see our train! As well she might. Behold, *Principessa*, the triumph of our labours!'

The crowd parted and Giovanni led the girl towards the train. Müller jumped down from the box and waited for her at the end of a corridor of booted and moustachioed Italians, who raised their bottles in salutation as the child passed.

When the girl and her chaperone had come quite close to the machine, she stopped as though afraid. Giovanni knelt to comfort her.

'She's saying something!' he said. 'Bah, it's German; I cannot understand it.' He turned to Müller. 'Will you translate for us, *Signore?*'

The assembled workers joined in.

'Yes, translate! What's she saying, Signor Müller?'

'Huzzah, the lady speaks!'

'Tell us what the little one has to say about our beautiful machine!'

'Quiet!' shouted Giovanni. 'How's he supposed to hear over you lot?!'

Remonstrations flew thick and fast.

'Yes! Shut up, Paolo, the lady speaks!'

'Shut up yourself. You're louder than my mother-in-law!'

'*Silenzio,* buttheads!'

Eventually the hubbub died down and Müller knelt down in front of the girl. 'What is it, my dear?' he asked in German.

The girl whispered something in his ear.

'What does she say, *Signore?*'

'Tell us!'

Müller's brow creased in an effort to understand the girl's child-speak. She pointed a worried finger at the locomotive and he swivelled on his heel to follow her gesture. When he returned his gaze to the assembled workmen he looked amused. 'She asks, "Is it a monster?"'

The crew laughed. The girl continued to look with fright at the blank face of the mechanical beast. Vapours rolled off its iron flanks as moisture boiled away from the heat of the engine.

'A monster, she asks. Ha!'

'I'm not surprised: look at the snout on it! What an ugly bastard.'

'The Swiss may be good engineers but they have about as much sense of style as the Germans.'

This was met with hoots of approval and the pouring of more drinks.

Müller smiled at the girl's anxious face. 'Don't fret, child. It may look like a monster, it may even carry some monsters, but remember: it's *your* monster. It'll do what you tell it to and I reckon it'll serve your village well. Real monsters don't look this ugly.'

One of his workers leaned over, already half drunk. 'And we all know what to do when the real monsters come to call, eh boys?'

'Fetch a gun!'

'Loose the dogs!'

'Unleash Paolo's mother-in-law!'

More raucous laughter. Müller glanced around to make sure no one had started a fight yet. The rail depot was hardly the place for a child.

231

The stalwart, dependable Giovanni stood protectively between the girl and the iron machine. With his free hand he patted one of its bumpers. The heavy *thunk* reassured the girl of its innocuousness and she returned Müller's smile, though she didn't let go of Giovanni's hand.

The men began to lose interest and returned to their celebrations.

'We'd best get her back to her family,' said Müller. 'My guess is, they're at the fancy party.'

The big miner nodded. 'I'll come along. Anyway, she's hanging on to me so hard I couldn't get her off without a lever-iron.'

The crowded depot was becoming unbearably loud. Müller shuffled closer so the girl could hear him. 'What's your name?' he asked.

The girl hesitated. Giovanni gave her hand a reassuring squeeze. She leant forward and in a little voice whispered in Müller's ear.

'Anna Hürlimann.'

Müller nodded. 'Well, Fräulein Hürlimann, it's time we found your parents.' The foreman stood up and cast an eye around him. He took in the merriment of his labourers, worrying what might occur in his absence.

'I'll supervise until you get back,' volunteered Angelo. 'There'll be no trouble.'

Müller nodded, doffed his cap, and motioned to the girl. After a minor prompt from Giovanni she followed and together the three stepped out into the night, the tiny figure of the girl trying to keep pace with the men on either side.

The paving stones around the train station glistened with patches of ice and they steered the girl so as to avoid them. When this became impossible, they hoisted her into the air. She giggled, her tiny feet pedalling through nothingness. The two men proceeded carefully so as not to slip and fall. Like their black locomotive they were solidly built and their boots' grip held.

Further on, where the dirt thoroughfare had turned to mud, the ground offered more of a foothold. But rather than put her down the two men continued to swing the little girl so as not to dirty her shoes. In the darkness overhead great clouds billowed, heavy with the promise of snow.

The trio beheld the gas-lit windows of the Town Hall in the distance and heard the rowdy festivities within. The bright lights shone on the houses of the village square, their golden glow reflected in the tinkling waters of the fountain. As they approached, their shadows lengthened until it appeared that the girl was adult-sized, flanked by two lanky giants.

These fantastic shapes danced and flickered around the square until their owners disappeared into the building itself and the visions were absorbed. The only shadows remaining thereafter were those hidden behind the corners of the old stone buildings and in the flickering darkness of the water in the fountain basin.

NOVEMBER FLOWERS
CHAPTER TWENTY-FOUR

OU ARE LISTENING, Monsieur Hayle?'

'What? Oh, yeah, totally. What does this one mean again?'

Councilwoman Berger looked displeased that Graham hadn't been paying closer attention. But he made such a show of inspecting the framed articles on the wall that she forgave his momentary lapse of concentration.

She gestured to another picture, one of many that hung in the tiny museum squeezed into two rooms behind the post office.

'This is a photograph of the train station when it was completed. You see, behind there are maybe five, six houses? Today there are many more. This is but one example of the, how you say . . . *bénéfices* of rail travel.'

'Interesting,' muttered Graham. He snuck another glance over towards the far corner when he thought Madame Berger wasn't looking.

Richard was sitting alone on a bench. He showed no interest in anything the councilwoman said, leaving Graham to summon what gushiness he could all by himself.

'What's that old building there?' Graham inquired. 'I don't recognise it.'

Madame Berger inspected the photo. 'This is the old school,' she said. 'It is destroyed twenty or so years ago, after they are building a modern building in the valley. Now our children must travel for their classes.' She sniffed disapprovingly. 'Monsieur Fürgler and others send their children to the private schools. Is it surprising that the local establishments have no money if the commune does not support them?' She huffed in bureaucratic outrage.

'Yeah, totally. Listen, Sabine, thanks very much for the tour. I think it's time for my colleague and me to talk business.'

'You are making progress? It is taking a long time.'

'Well, as the saying goes, Rome wasn't built in a day. Thanks again for the tour.'

Madame Berger nodded and turned away. She noticed Chase and Kaitlyn admiring the pictures in a corner and bustled off in their direction.

Graham sat down next to Richard. 'You all right?'

'Hmm.'

'Only, you seem a bit down. You've hardly said anything since yesterday.'

Richard managed a thin smile. 'I'm fine.'

It wasn't wholly convincing and Graham was less than wholly convinced. 'Maybe you should go on one of your walks around the sanatorium,' he suggested. 'They always seem to cheer you up.'

Richard shook his head. 'Not today. Not in the mood.'

They sat in awkward silence for a time.

Graham spoke first. 'Still thinking about that video of yours, eh?'

'It doesn't make any sense,' muttered Richard.

'Yeah,' said Graham, 'but those drone things are notoriously unreliable. Having an American at the helm would just make things worse. Even if the bear was where you thought it was, I expect Chase pointed the thing in entirely the wrong direction.'

'How could I have seen it on the monitor if the camera wasn't pointing at it?' demanded Richard. Before Graham had a chance to resolve this conundrum another thought struck him. 'Wait, what do you mean, "If the bear was there"? Don't you believe me?'

'Course I do. That is, I definitely believe you *think* you saw it.'

Richard snorted. 'Now you think I'm delusional, do you?'

Graham gave him a hard look. 'No, I don't. The fact is, though, there was nothing in the footage that looked even remotely like a bear.'

'I saw it!'

'So you say. But this wouldn't be the first time you've seen weird shit that wasn't there, would it?'

Richard shot to his feet. 'I think I might take that stroll after all,' he said and walked out the door.

Graham watched him go and sighed.

Someone cleared their throat. Graham looked up to see Councilwoman Berger eyeing him from the other end of the room, some eco-tourism flyers in her hand.

He sighed again.

Richard stormed through the village, stomping his boots and huffing into his collar. He'd treated Graham unfairly, but what the hell. The disappointment of yesterday weighed on him. He was in no mood to make allowances for what, from Graham's point of view, must have seemed a perfectly reasonable question. Richard had adopted the role of the abused party and sulked accordingly.

Richard glared into the shops as he passed. Everywhere he looked—except in Fosco's antique shop, whose dusty window remained cluttered as ever—he saw fake snow and plush polar bears staring back at him. The village had seen a proliferation of winter decorations, but the long-awaited snowfall still hadn't arrived. This was unusual in Niderälpli for that time of year. On most nights the hotel restaurant now hummed with dark mutterings about Global Warming.

Richard stopped at the lights to allow a lorry to pass. His eye was drawn to the sportswear shop on the corner. Its window housed a large stuffed bear wearing goggles, a ski helmet, and a t-shirt sporting the words A VERY BEARY CHRISTMAS!

One of the great tragedies of adulthood is that grown-ups can't turn to stuffed animals for personal appeasement. His mood worsening for want of fuzzy bear hugs, Richard moved on.

Outside the communal office Ursula was arranging a display of holly branches and other assorted foliage. Richard stomped past without speaking to her. He rounded the corner like a man-sized pyroclastic flow and nearly collided with Councilman Aufdermauer. The older man jumped back a pace in surprise.

'Herr Mathern!' gasped Aufdermauer. 'You appear so fast! You surprise me.' He caught his breath and adjusted his glasses. 'You are well?'

'Been better.' Richard pulled up his collar against the rising cold.

Aufdermauer nodded. 'It is the changing of the seasons. Always the winter is bringing with it the melancholy.'

He turned towards the fountain in the square, now silent. 'We are shutting off the water, so it does not freeze the pipes. The fountain it is very old, you know? A famous French sculptor is making the statue. I forget his name. The books are saying the statue she is St Verena, who died down in the valley many years ago, in Roman times. I think she is very beautiful, no?'

Aufdermauer must have noticed that Richard's attention was not entirely his. He regarded the young man with a new hesitation. 'Your work, it goes well?' he inquired.

Richard glowered. 'Well enough.'

Aufdermauer concluded this wasn't the day to talk about statuary. 'In this case,' said the councilman, 'I will not detain you.'

He moved on. Richard acquired both the satisfaction of having communicated his displeasure and the guilt of having inflicted it on an innocent.

'Richard!'

Melanie was crossing the street towards him. Her friendly face brought a fresh reminder of the futility of his plans and his ludicrous plan to use sniffer dogs.

'How's it going?' she asked.

'I'm fine.'

'Great. I've brought your book. Chase gave it to me when he brought the Indergands' dog back from the mountain.'

She held out Suzy's copy of Dostoyevsky, a mangled and drooled-stained ruin. 'I hear it didn't quite work out,' she added.

'No,' agreed Richard. 'Anyway, that's not mine. Graham borrowed it from our room. I think it belongs to the Indergands' son Silvio. His name's in the dedication.'

Melanie opened the book to read the barely discernible handwriting on the inside sleeve.

To Silvio, with love from Laura

She stiffened and turned stony-faced. 'I see. Well, in that case, you'd best return it.' She tossed the book to Richard, who fumbled it in surprise. He stooped to pick it up off the ground as Melanie stormed off.

Berlioz the Cat watched Richard crossing the square. He extended himself over the edge of his flowerpot in the most beguiling way he knew, but Richard sailed past without offering so much as a scratch under the ear. This slight caused Berlioz to view Richard with a new coldness. Having formulated a plan to use the Englishman's underpants as a toilet at some undetermined point in the future, he went back to sleep.

Richard had covered nearly every street in the village, save the one leading back to the hotel. This he climbed with waning energy, tired out from the effort of being disagreeable. Finally, more from habit then any actual decision, he turned away from the hotel, making his way alongside Jerome's pasture towards the sanatorium.

When he reached the orchard he sat down on a bench and looked out over the valley. He closed his eyes and sighed, allowing his furrowed brow to relax. It wasn't long before he detected the familiar shimmer behind him.

'I was wondering where you were.'

Richard opened one eye. 'Went up to check the cameras again this morning. Still nothing. Half of them hadn't even gone off.'

'I'm sorry.' Ellie circled the bench and sat down. 'When I spotted you running downhill yesterday I was certain you'd got it.'

Richard shook his head. 'It was a failure, just like this whole thing.'

'But you've done so much.'

'We haven't got what we came for. That's all they care about back at the office.'

It's hard to shimmer compassionately, but Ellie managed somehow. 'I'm sure they appreciate all the work you've done.'

Normally this would have soothed Richard but today everything had a strange aftertaste. The bells that morning had sounded tinny and unpleasant. The wind gusted about, prodding at him with its cold fingers. Even Ellie's voice began to annoy him.

'Perhaps Mr Hayle might take your mind off things?' she suggested. 'You're always saying how funny he is.'

'Not today. He's been acting like a massive pain in the—' It felt wrong to swear in front of Ellie. 'He's being annoying.'

They sat without speaking for a moment. Richard noticed that Ellie chewed her lip in a nervous way. She also appeared to be hiding something behind her back.

She noted his curiosity and, blushing, brought forth her hand. 'I brought something. It's for you.' It was a box tied up with a yellow ribbon, which she allowed to drop delicately into his palm.

He looked at it for moment, puzzled, then opened it. It contained a shiny, brand-new watch. Inside the lid of the box the words *Le Coeur d'Or* were inscribed in delicate silver letters.

'You said down in the village that it was your favourite. I was taught it's bad manners to offer a man a gift before he gives one to you, but I assumed you wouldn't know that rule. I don't suppose it matters anyway— it's not like you could.' She smiled.

Richard swallowed. 'How did you get it?'

Ellie smiled cunningly. 'The computer at the communal offices. Took me an absolute age. At first I couldn't make it work at all. I tried to get Ursula to help but no amount of blowing in her ear could get her attention. I'm afraid I used your login bank details; I remembered them from your phone. Technically I owe you quite a lot of money but I wasn't sure how else to go about it. Hopefully the receipts from the coin collection in the library will make up the difference. I wrote an electronic mail letter to Christie's in London. Apparently it's quite valuable!'

She waited for a response. Richard gazed down at the watch without saying anything, his face unreadable.

He closed the box and put it down on the bench. Ellie's smile faltered and she flushed with embarrassment.

'I'm sorry,' she said, picking up the box. 'I thought you'd like it.'

'No, it's lovely. It's just . . .' The words caught in his throat.

'Well,' said Ellie in a resolutely cheerful voice, 'no matter. I made some enquiries on-the-line. Those customer service agreements really do go on and on, don't they? In any case, we're entitled to full reimbursement on any items within one month of purchase as long as they're returned with all the labels. We can pick out something else together!'

'Stop it,' said Richard. 'Just stop it.'

Ellie looked at him in surprise. 'Stop what?'

'This!' cried Richard. 'All this! The presents, the smiling, pretending that everything's normal. It's not!'

He got up and began to pace. 'I can't accept this,' he said. He was pulling at the hair on the nape of his neck and swung his hand away angrily. 'This has to stop, this whole thing.'

'Richard—'

'You're a ghost, Ellie. Christ, I don't even know what you are. Are you even here at all?' He shovelled around in his pocket for his medication before remembering that he'd left it at the hotel. He swore inwardly and continued to pace.

'Look,' said Ellie, holding up an appeasing hand, 'there's no need to get excited. I made a mistake, but it's fine, we can—'

'I mean, what the hell were you expecting?' Richard shouted. 'You're dead, for fuck's sake!'

In the silence that followed not a sound was heard. It was as though someone had thrown a rock through a church window.

Ellie had gone very still. Her trembling hand tightened around the box.

Richard held up his hands apologetically. 'Sorry, I didn't mean to shout. Only, this is crazy. I didn't realize it until now. It's got to stop. I'm going to concentrate on my job and forget all this madness.'

'I'm sure I don't know what you mean.' Ellie's words were glacial. She rose from her seat. 'Perhaps you'd care to explain yourself, Mr Mathern.'

Richard took a deep breath. 'Look,' he said, 'I didn't—'

'I didn't realize that our association was causing you so much distress. I apologise for not having had the insight or awareness to notice. Our conversations must doubtless have been very trying for you.' Ellie was standing very still and upright, both hands gripping the box tightly in front of her.

'That's not what I meant . . .' began Richard.

'When I showed you my gravestone you said the only thing beneath it was earth, while the true me, my soul, was walking by your side. And I believed you! What am I to think now?' Her vehemence shocked Richard. 'In all my sleepless hours I did not wish for life, or love, or even a peaceful rest. All I wanted was someone to talk to, someone who recognised what I thought you did when you said those words: that I was here, and that I was a person.'

'It's not natural,' Richard muttered. 'It's not right.'

She whirled on him, and spat through her tears. 'Not natural? Not right!? Perhaps you can tell me what is natural and right, Mr Mathern: is it people coughing their blackened, bloodied lungs out by the thousands because they'd spent the entirety of their short lives in a cellar or a mine?

Or the countless millions blown to pieces by war over a piece of dirt, or the poor souls frozen to death for want of a piece of coal? I, I at last have found someone to talk to, someone who despite everything can see me for the shade, and here you are throwing away my gifts and reproaching me for not rotting away silently like I ought to. But no, *I'm* the unnatural one.'

'What do you expect me to do?' Richard cried, 'Come and live with you on a mountainside forever?'

She shook aside her furious tears. 'What have you thought of me this whole time? Perhaps even now you don't believe what you see! You must think I'm merely some apparition conjured up by your mind as a pleasant distraction. Have you enjoyed having a phantom lady prance around on your arm and point out the pretty sights?'

Her form was fading at the edges, losing its solidity. But her eyes blazed like torches in a mist.

She threw the box aside. Richard didn't dare look where it landed.

'Who are you to say what I am? I still think and speak and walk, don't I? Who are you to say I can't feel! I was once as real as you and soon enough you'll be a shadow like me. I doubt anyone will notice you, though, back in the city smoke where everyone's a ghost anyway!'

With this, she turned and vanished amongst the leafless trees.

Richard stood bewildered. Then his temper returned with a vengeance and away he went in turn across the promenade past the sanatorium, stomping his heavy boots onto the decking as he went.

Any moisture not frozen in the earth had been sucked from the air by the November cold, leaving it dry and lifeless. In the shadowy gully where the stream passed close to the sanatorium, the torrent had slowed to barely a trickle, running quietly over the smooth stones of the riverbed. Its edges were iced, even in the daytime, and any vegetation was coated in tiny crystalline blossoms of frozen water.

The box containing *Le Coeur d'Or* had fallen open and the watch lay tangled in its yellow ribbon. Calm descended upon the orchard above it. As evening began to darken, its round, white face stared up at the sky, as though wondering how it had come to be there.

A shadow fell across it, temporarily blotting out the evening sky. Once the shadow had passed, the watch was gone.

REMORSE
CHAPTER TWENTY-FIVE

ARLY THE FOLLOWING morning a deep calm reigned in the Gasthaus Meierhof. Suzy snored in the hallway. Berlioz returned at dawn with a bellyful of mice while the guests were still abed. Josephine Indergand bustled about in her boudoir, preparing for the day. The stairs squeaked as her husband Meinrad snuck downstairs to see if he could rustle up any cookies for breakfast before his wife discovered him and forced him to eat muesli instead.

Richard's dreams had been turbulent and confusing. When he awoke he momentarily forgot where he was. He stared blearily at the face of a three-horned goat sticking its tongue out at him from the beam overhead. Then he remembered his conversation with Ellie the day before.

He hastily pulled on his boots and jacket. Pausing only to knock his head against the landing beam, he raced downstairs and out the door.

He went first to the sanatorium, but Ellie wasn't there. Even when she wasn't immediately visible, he could usually feel her presence; it was nowhere to be felt today. He didn't need to check inside the building to be certain, but he did anyway.

He was appalled by what he found there.

The library was dark, dusty, and abandoned. Rotting books sagged in their cases. Cabinet drawers yawned open, their contents strewn across the room. Richard forced open the cracked shutters, scattering cobwebs and crumbling plaster. The brass work was tarnished and dull. The whole place stank of decay and neglect and anyone would surmise that not a soul had been there for years.

As Richard hurried past the hotel on his way into the village, a voice hailed him. He ignored it, hastening down the road with the single-mindedness of a remorseful man. Monsieur Pfister watched in confusion, one hand hanging in the air in greeting. The other rested on the newly waxed bonnet of the red car, whose glorious renovation Richard had disregarded completely.

The little cobbled alleyway was cold and empty, the wall garden devoid of flowers. The shadows of the arcade yielded only more shadows. With every place Richard visited, the chilly feeling in the pit of his stomach turned chillier. Before long it felt like he'd swallowed a bucket full of ice. But he dared not stop.

He scoured the village until the sun was high in the sky. After that, he searched the mountain.

He followed his usual trail, powering upwards through the trees, across the plateau, circumventing the lake, over the ridge, past the observation hut, all the way to the foot of the moraine. It was the same route he'd followed for weeks but this time instead of the bear he searched for Ellie.

Eventually he stopped by the frozen stream. It was that or keel over. His ribs ached, his face was half frozen, and he'd eaten nothing all morning.

He bent double, feeling dizzy for the first time in weeks. He didn't know why he'd come up here, except that there was nowhere else left to look. He remembered Ellie's words from the first day, about how much she wanted to visit the spring.

Well, here it was.

Richard looked around. Nothing. He gulped, his breathing steadier now. It had been a long shot, but he was bitterly disappointed.

There was a shimmer to his left and he whirled around. But it wasn't Ellie; it was the Right Honourable Lord Frederick Urquhart Bellows-Wicklesworth.

'Ah, young Dickie!' exclaimed the apparition. 'As promised, I was just on my way to pay you a call. How are you this fine morning?'

'Sod off, Bellows.'

Richard sped away, leaving the spectral mountaineer speechless in his wake.

*****

Graham awoke to the sound of Richard pounding down the stairs. This would have been enough to arouse some degree of alarm in most people, but Graham was not most people. He told himself that if there was something he needed to know, Richard would have told him.

He was about to go back to sleep when Richard's mobile phone rang.

Graham opened one eye. It's uncharacteristic of anyone in this modern day and age to leave a building without their phone. He surmised that Richard would return soon enough to collect it and that the situation didn't require any direct input from him. He rolled over and snuggled into his pillow, ready to enjoy what slumber remained him.

It was only several minutes of uninterrupted ringing later that Graham re-emerged from beneath the duvet, dishevelled and irritated, and answered the phone.

'Hullo?'

'Mathern, you idiot, where have you been?'

'Excuse me, who is this?'

There was a moment's hesitation at the other end as Alan checked the name on his screen, suddenly worried he'd insulted someone important by accident.

'Is this Richard Mathern's phone?'

'Speaking,' replied Graham with a yawn. 'To whom do I owe the pleasure?'

'It's Alan from Nature Review. Where's Richard?'

'I'm afraid he's temporarily unavailable. But I'd be happy to take a message.'

'Right. You tell him—'

'Hang on, I need a pen.'

Graham went to fetch one from the desk, returned to the bed, decided he didn't like the pen, and went to fetch another.

'Right,' he said cheerfully, 'got it.'

'Good. When Richard gets back you tell him—'

'Atatata, gotta get some paper. Won't be a mo.' Graham shuffled some discarded receipts on the nightstand with his free hand for a while, humming as he did so.

'Sorry about that, all ready now.'

'You just tell Richard—'

'Whoops, I forgot your name. Who're you again?'

There was a crackling down the line as someone smothered the receiver in order to swear with more freedom.

'Alan,' snapped the voice.

'How do you spell that?'

Alan told him, in a tone that implied he wished he were carving it onto Graham's forehead. *'And by the way,'* he added, *'the message is fairly simple. I don't think you'll need to write it down.'*

'I'm afraid I will,' answered Graham, who was rather enjoying himself, 'I have an appalling memory. What would you like me to tell Richard?'

'Tell him he's fired.'

Suddenly, Graham wasn't enjoying himself any longer.

*****

242

Richard stumbled out of the woods late that afternoon, exhausted. His tread was that of a man whose life has taken a terrible turn and who knows it's his own fault.

Beneath him the Gasthaus Meierhof's windows glowed amber. Instead of going there straightaway, he cut across the field to the sanatorium. He knew she wasn't there, but he went anyway. He crossed the promenade, stopping halfway along the bannister to overlook the village. The sun hung low in a cloudless, golden sky.

Richard winced. He'd not given much thought to his body during his search, but now it clamoured for attention. Everything hurt, and his insides ached with hunger.

He scowled about, looking for somewhere to sit. His eye fell upon a familiar wicker chair. Its emptiness seemed all the more singular to Richard because it had once held—or appeared to hold—Ellie's form.

The chair absorbed the clouded ferocity of his stare, somewhat at a loss for how to respond. To be the object of someone's displeasure is terribly confusing for furniture. The chair's talents lay mostly in muted stillness and stability, yet this individual seemed to expect something more. It suspected it didn't possess the power to resolve the situation, but nonetheless it hated to disappoint.

Richard decided he didn't want to stay there any longer.

He and his cloud of hostility moved on. The chair gratefully resumed the business of being a chair, happily decomposing on the ruined porch.

Richard entered the hotel corridor and realised just how tired he was. His boots hadn't felt this heavy since he'd first put them on.

As he passed the door to the restaurant he noticed Graham sitting by himself, his face turned away. Richard was relieved; he didn't want to talk to anyone.

He laboured upstairs to his room and made straight for his bed. He unlaced his boots and kicked them into a corner before flopping backwards onto the woollen coverlet.

In the golden light of the setting sun the creatures carved into the beams were outlined by deep shadows. Richard's eye wandered up the line of one monstrous serpent's tail searching for the end, only to find that there was none; it simply became a second serpent winding around the body of a bucking stag.

He glanced around the empty room. The grizzled old woodsman in the portrait on the wall stared back, but not with his usual pale glare. In fact, his face appeared almost sympathetic.

What's up?

'Oh, you know,' sighed Richard. 'There's this girl.'

Ah, I see.

'No, you don't. This girl died a long time ago.'

So did I. Dying's not as bad as people think. In fact, sometimes I'd go so far as to recommend it.

'Well, until now she's, you know, been there. I could see her, talk to her, hear her laughing. I could feel her presence before I knew she was there and after she'd left. But now, she's just . . . not there anymore.'

Where exactly is this "there" you speak of?

'Everywhere!' Richard covered his eyes with his palms and rubbed hard. 'She was everywhere and now she's gone. I can't find a trace of her anywhere.'

Then where is she?

'I don't know.' Richard watched the last of the daylight slide up and out of the room as the sun dipped below the ridge. 'She's disappeared.'

I'm confused. First you complain about too many visions, now you complain about too few. Which is it to be?

Richard glared at the picture, then turned away. He thought about making tea but decided he didn't want any.

Something dug into his leg and he looked down. It was Melchior B. Adolphus. He didn't particularly feel like reading but he picked it up all the same, hoping for distraction. The book fell open of its own accord.

THE YOUNG MAN AND HIS DESTINY

Richard launched himself from the bed and heaved the book across the room. It ricocheted off the closet door with a *thwack* and spun into the corner, where it lay in a crumpled heap.

Richard stood in the middle of the room, breathing heavily. Eventually he walked towards the book and leaned forward as if to pick it up, but changed his mind at the last minute and returned to the bed instead, where he rolled over and switched off the light.

When Graham returned later Richard pretended to be asleep. Graham didn't try to wake him.

SHUTDOWN
CHAPTER TWENTY-SIX

HEN RICHARD ARRIVED at the observation hut the next day, Graham was unusually subdued.

'Hey,' said Graham, his breath misting.

'Hey. Anything?'

'Nah. Checked the forecast though, fog's on its way.'

'Anything else?'

'They're expecting snow by the end of the week.'

The expression on Richard's face became, if possible, even darker. He slumped into the camping chair. Graham shook his thermos invitingly. Richard nodded. Graham busied himself with preparations.

'Any news we can use?' he inquired.

'What?'

'You know, phone calls, emails about the project?'

'Oh. No.'

Damn, thought Graham. He doesn't know.

Richard rubbed his eyes and stared out the little window. The mist that had been lingering over the horizon had begun to seep into the valley. Having collected over the distant lakes into a towering mass of cloud, it now bled over the surrounding ridges like a vaporous glacier. Richard watched the great white soup pouring in over the mountains, pooling and frothing silently between them, rising by the hour. Eventually the valley would be buried in cloud and would stay that way until spring. The observation hut would remain above it, to be alternately crushed by snow and baked by the unbridled winter sun.

'I can't believe we've still got nothing,' muttered Richard.

Graham shrugged. 'Meh, who cares? I reckon we're overestimating this whole business. The important thing is, we're having a good time.' He was wondering how to bring the conversation round to Alan's phone call.

245

'What are you talking about?' Richard snapped. 'You know how important this is, Graham. I've told you again and again. I need this to work. Stop pretending it's some sort of game.'

Graham snorted. 'Well, if it were a game, I know who I wouldn't want on my team: Alan, that humongous berk from your office.'

Richard looked up from his tea. 'How do you know Alan?'

Graham suddenly seemed very interested in the stove. 'Oh, you know, from emails and things. You left a couple of messages from the office open on your laptop. Sounds a right arse-face.'

There's nothing like a common enemy to bring people together, but Richard didn't have the energy to lambast Alan. The very mention of his name spoiled his mood further.

Graham fiddled with the camera. For a while the only sounds were the *tink* of teaspoons on tin mugs and the sipping of hot drinks through cold lips.

'You can go back to the hotel now,' said Richard, 'it's my shift.'

Graham didn't seem particularly inclined to go. 'I dunno,' he yawned. 'I feel pretty well-rested. Maybe you'd like an extra pair of eyes today.'

Richard was anything but well rested. He was also irritable, upset, and filled with self-loathing. 'What, you think I can't do the job on my own?'

Graham looked up in surprise. 'No, course not. I just thought, you know, two eyes are better than one.'

'I've got two eyes. Two is the usual number of eyes to have.'

'I meant two pairs.'

'What you meant was, you don't think I can do my job properly.'

Graham put down his mug. 'I meant nothing of the sort. Bloody hell, what's wrong with you today?'

'Nothing. Everything's fine.' Richard fixed his eyes on his steaming mug.

Graham bristled. 'Quite some nothing you've got going on there, mate. Something wrong?'

'I'm fine.'

'Bollocks you are. What's the matter?'

Richard didn't answer. Graham swigged his tea, made a face, and put it down on the bench with a *thunk*. 'It's not like it matters anyway,' he muttered.

'What do you mean?'

'Nothing,' replied Graham flatly. 'Everything's *fine*.'

'Why doesn't it matter? What's happened?'

'What's happened to you is what I'd like to know. Maybe we should ask someone else. Like Alan.'

'The hell's that supposed to mean?'

Graham threw back the last of his foul, tepid tea. 'All I'm saying is, if a friend's in trouble he should tell another friend. Otherwise, what good is being friends?'

'If we're such good friends,' said Richard, his voice rising, 'where've you been for the past four years?'

'What? Where's this coming from? I've been busy!' Graham slammed his mug down. 'I may not have a "real", job like you, Mathern, but I work bloody hard. And London isn't exactly next door.'

'Don't give me that, you come down whenever the mood takes you. You never thought to visit me, I guess!'

'You never invited me! Are you too busy sipping expensive drinks with your fancy new friends?'

'No! Actually, I hate the place! Everyone's rude, everyone's broke, anyone who isn't a sodding oligarch lives in a shithole!' Richard didn't remember standing but he now loomed over Graham and the camping chair was on its side. 'Even before this project went sour, everyone at the office acted like I'm slow or something and all my so-called friends never passed up a chance to remind me that I work a rubbish job for no money. I live in a dump with rent I can barely afford. I thought this project was going to make some kind of difference but it's all messed up and I've got sod all to show for myself!'

Graham was staring up at him, his tea mug forgotten.

'And all the work we've been doing hasn't earned us a single bloody "well done" from Alan and those bell-ends at the office and you know what? You know sodding what? They discontinued our funding three weeks ago. I didn't tell you because it was all too bloody humiliating, so I've been paying for everything since then and soon there'll be no more money and I'll have to go back to that mouldy little flat in London and the whole thing will have been a great big sodding waste of time!'

Richard paused for breath, his throat ragged and sore.

'Biggest city in Europe,' he breathed, 'and I'm lonely all the time.'

He sat down on the floor and wiped his nose on his sleeve. For a while both men were silent.

Graham came to sit with Richard. 'I'm sorry.'

Richard sniffed and breathed deeply. 'I should've told you before.'

Graham lowered his head. 'There's something I've been meaning to tell you, too.'

'What?'

Graham told him about the phone call. Outside the billowing clouds assumed fantastic shapes, drifting past like airborne icebergs in a celestial fjord.

When Graham finished he stood up and leant on the window, looking out. Richard tried to take in what he had just heard.

'This whole thing's just a cover story,' he said slowly. 'They never cared at all.'

Graham punched the wooden frame, but said nothing.

A further moment of silence went by. Then Graham heard Richard laughing through his tears.

'You know,' said Richard, 'that's just perfect. We never even had a chance.'

Graham sat down again and put a hand on Richard's shoulder. 'Let's go on a trip,' he said, 'just you and me. Like we used to. Rent's paid here but we can take the car and go off somewhere for a few days. What do you say? We're at the crossroads of Europe. We can go wherever we want and be home in time to scrap the car. Italy, France, wherever the hell we like.'

'No,' Richard said at last. 'Might as well stay. I don't feel much like travelling.'

'Ok.' Graham rose. 'Then let's go back to the hotel and have a drink.'

Richard rubbed his face in his hands and exhaled. Graham offered his hand. Richard took it and Graham pulled him upright. Together they collected their equipment, locked up the hut and, shoulder to shoulder, strode back down the track toward the silent torrent of towering white.

*****

Anna Hürlimann tugged ineffectively at her blanket in an attempt to better cover herself. The heavy wool would not comply, however, and displayed a talent for tying itself into knots the old woman's hands were unable to undo.

Eventually she gave up and turned to observe the room, growling softly.

The restaurant was bustling with activity. The oncoming winter festivities were Niderälpli's biggest attraction and the hotel brimmed with holidaying families, as well as the few youngsters who weren't already off skiing in one of the high altitude resorts. Guests came in large numbers, and they came hungry. This was the one time of the year when the villagers saw a real influx of tourist capital and they made the most of it.

Dino scurried to and from the kitchen, balancing plates piled high with schnitzels, rösti potatoes, barley and onion soups, roast lamb with boiled vegetables, minced veal in cream and mushroom sauce, sausage and leek stew, and of course the obligatory pots of fondue with mountains of fresh bread. Alongside these were served pickled onions and gherkins, cured meats, and a complimentary shot of kirsch provided—reluctantly—by Herr Indergand. His wife Josephine bustled about ensuring that no table was without copious amounts of cider, mugs of hot spiced wine, and cold beer in chimney-like glasses, with apple juice for the kids. The hungrier families had already devoured their first few courses and moved on to the sliced cheeses. Eagerly they dug into boards of Gruyère, Emmenthal, Appenzeller and Montfort while those with a sweeter tooth contented themselves with sugared apple cakes, sweet walnut pie, and heaps of ice cream drowning in chocolate and raspberry sauce.

Frau Hürlimann did not approve of ice cream. Anything that tasted that good had to be sinful.

Memories of her younger days floated by; sunny afternoons spent down by the lake shore, where handsome young men would call to her from cafés, offering her sugary treats in the hope she'd sit with them.

She gnawed on her piece of cheese, contemplating the dishes being consumed around her. She found it harder to chew than she used to. Her gums couldn't take it.

I'll be damned if I'm going to that confounded dentist again, she thought. Stabs me in the mouth with a metal wire for fifteen minutes and then has the balls to tell me my gums are bleeding . . . When did people decide you needed all your teeth? My gran managed fine with dentures. Never saw a dentist after that. Smart woman.

She took another nibble off the corner of her cheese and found it tasted rather good. What had they given her tonight?

She held it up to her good eye and nodded in approval. Alte Schweizer was always a safe choice, but the old man in Sumvitg who provided the wheels used in the Gasthaus Meierhof's kitchens sourced a particularly good one. It had a rich, nutty, and slightly charred taste that Frau Hürlimann loved. She chewed with enthusiasm, ignoring the pain in her jaw.

Alte Schweizer . . . There had been a rhyme about the old Swiss, hadn't there? She'd heard it many times as a girl. Slowly the words came back to her.

Who were the ancient Schwyzer men
Our brave and pious fathers?
A rough and wild brethren
Each fighting with the strength of ten
Like thunder as cloud gathers

Those hardy souls who tamed the rocks
As hard as beech wood joints
As closed-up as a church alms box
As cunning as the mountain fox
And sharp as sabre points

Their youthful hearts were free of sin
Though theirs was humble fare
Their low-clung beams would force their kin
The bend the knee to come within
But outside, who would dare?

How such a folk endured so long
Nobody truly knows
These brothers lived in mirth and song
Their hatreds fierce, their friendships strong
And slow to pardon foes*

Frau Hürlimann chewed smugly to herself. Ha! she thought. Beat that, the Internet! Mind's sharp as it ever was. She grimaced, wishing she could say the same for her teeth.

The door creaked open and the two Englishmen entered the restaurant.

Frau Hürlimann marked them. They looked dishevelled and glum, but there was an air of fraternal support in how they carried themselves. They managed to find a table, grabbed Dino as he passed, and ordered what looked like a long list of food. Clearly theirs had been a rough day.

One slumped over his elbows, staring vacantly into nothing. The other gripped him by the shoulder. Frau Hürlimann couldn't hear what was said over the din of children slamming desserts into their faces but it must have been a word of encouragement, for the other managed a weak smile.

The old woman grumbled, still chewing. These cubs think they've suffered, she thought. They think they know what Hell is! What a couple of bozos.

The scrape of cutlery on porcelain made her wince. She growled half-heartedly at Dave the barman as he passed with a crate of empty glasses.

What do the young know? All their hardships are tempered by optimism. Life's rough edges are softened by laughter and love. They haven't seen their friends decay and die. They haven't watched the world change until you don't recognise anything or anyone anymore and people treat you like a museum piece. Or worse, don't notice you at all.

Hell isn't other people. Hell is a world of strangers, silence without peace, solitude without intimacy.

Hell is loneliness.

---

* The English edition of *Central European Mythology & Folk Tales* by Melchior B. Adolphus offers this translation of Meinrad Lienert's poem *Wie sind die alte Schwyzer gsi.* Although in an effort to streamline its prose it fails to include some entertaining imagery regarding sheep, it nonetheless gives a good idea of the overall gist.

Frau Hürlimann thought of the village as it had been when she was little. She couldn't remember what her house had looked like. It had been torn down years ago. What was there now, was it the post office?

She looked down, hoping for another morsel of cheese, only to discover she'd finished the last of it. She sighed.

When had everything got so bad? There must have been shortcomings to being young, but she couldn't remember specifics. Time had made it all relative. What had seemed awful then now translated as merely character-building.

Her frown deepened as one particular memory came to her. The day Klaus was buried; she remembered that.

That was a very bad day.

She sighed again, deeper this time. I should've married that man when I had the chance, she thought. As for the rest, who can say? The bad didn't matter now. And for all the good the good did me, I'm still here in this chair, with nobody worth talking to and nothing but memories.

But what memories!

There is in every country an older country, one where the air smells sweeter and it's always springtime. There is beauty in the innocence of a young country just as there is in the face of a child. So it is with memory. And, as child ages and contemplates itself later in life, one looks on that same land of memory in ones twilight years and thinks one sees it for what it truly is: fleeting, futile, and short.

She hadn't thought so at the time. The young never do. They're too busy enjoying things to weigh their worth. Who's to say that's not a kind of wisdom in itself?

Her feet were cold. She ruffled the blanket with one hand, but this only dislodged it further and it crumpled on the floor, leaving her sulky and uncomfortable until Frau Indergand noticed and wrapped her up again.

*****

Julian entered the office on the top floor of Aberfinchley's headquarters and was met with the interrogatory stare of Dawes, who sat with steepled fingers and closed eyes in the dimly-lit room.

'We're ready,' said Julian breathlessly.

The hawk-like eyebrows behind the desk settled into a grim and determined formation, like dreadnoughts on the North Sea.

Dawes took a deep breath and exhaled slowly.

Very well,' he intoned, 'let's begin.'

*****

251

In the darkened corner of Richard's hotel room, the discarded book lay where he'd thrown it. As evening slipped by it sagged and settled, the battered old cover bending under its weight. Eventually it flopped onto its spine. Its crumpled pages fluttered open, as though inviting a reader to peruse them. But there was no one there except the old man in the picture and he'd never been much for reading.

THE YOUNG MAN AND HIS DESTINY

There was once a youth who lived in a small and unremarkable village. His people were poor, but he knew in his heart that he was destined for great things.

'My life story shall be worthy of remembrance,' he said. 'First, I shall garner a following of valiant heroes, who shall become my loyal companions. Then I shall embark on many perilous adventures, surviving numberless dangers. Lastly, I will marry a princess and found a dynasty of kings, that my name might live forever.'

Thus assured, he bade farewell to his family and friends and set off down the road. By and by he came to a riverside house alive with the sound of laughter. Inside was a party, with music playing and many young people dancing.

'Excuse me,' he said to one of the girls. 'Do you know were I might find a brotherhood of heroes, awaiting a fearless leader to whom they might pledge their loyalty?'

'I'm afraid not,' laughed the girl. 'We are simple country folk. It is a feast day and the celebration is in full swing. Linger with us awhile, for we are good company.'

'I cannot,' said the youth. 'I have sworn to surround myself with champions, that our great deeds might live in everlasting memory.'

'A valiant aspiration,' said the girl. 'But I think you'll find that true community and comradeship such as ours outshines the bloody fraternities of the battlefield.'

'Can you direct me to the nearest battlefield?'

'I'm afraid I can't.'

'In that case,' said the youth, 'I'm afraid I must be on my way, for I am destined for greater things than this.'

He travelled on. On the cusp of a great forest, he discovered a second house with high windows and a garden of many wondrous plants. He knocked on the door and was met by a wise man, bearded and bespectacled.

The boy asked, 'Is this the home of a giant? Are you the ward of a cruel ogre, detained against your will?'

'I should say not,' replied the wise man. 'This is my home, a place of study and scholarship. Tarry with me awhile. I am a learned man and can teach you all the rare and wonderful things I know about the world.'

'I cannot,' said the youth. 'I am destined to accomplish great feats of arms.'

'A fine endeavour,' agreed the wise man. 'However, I think you'll find that knowledge, sagely wielded, yields a power greater than that of the sword.'

'Do you have a sword I could borrow?'

'No.'

'In that case, I must be on my way, for I am destined for greater things than this.'

The youth travelled on again. By and by he came to a third house by a field with a stout chimney and a dog curled up by the door. Inside he met a husband and wife sitting by the fire.

'Is this a royal hunting lodge?' he asked. 'Are you a king and queen, attired like the common folk to better survey your subjects and domains?'

'Can't say we are,' answered the wife, 'more's the pity. We are honest working people. It has been a good year and the harvest is due. Bide with us awhile. Eat, and rest your weary feet. If you wish, you may stay and make a life here, for we have many daughters but should dearly love a son to call our own.'

'I cannot,' said the youth. 'It is preordained that I should marry a princess and found a lineage of royal blood.'

'An enviable legacy,' acknowledged the husband. 'Though I've heard it said that while every girl worthy of love is a princess, not every princess is a girl worthy of love.'

'Do you know any princesses?'

'I fear not.'

'In that case,' said the youth, 'I must be on my way, for I am destined for greater things than this.'

In time the youth became a young man, and the young man grew older. Wherever he went, he was dissatisfied. Whatever he did, he was discontented. Whoever he met, he was disappointed. When at last his hair had turned white he wandered the roads still, stick in hand, convinced as ever of his immutable destiny.

Night was falling one evening when the old man came upon a stranger, even more venerable than himself, sitting by the side of the road. His shoes were tattered and full of holes.

'Stop, stop!' called the stranger. 'Look, my shoes are ruined by the road and I cannot get up. Will you help me?'

'I cannot stop,' replied the old man who had been a youth. 'I am in a hurry, for I am destined for great things.'

253

'Please,' pleaded the stranger. 'It will be dark soon and I am alone. Help me up, then you can be on your way.'

Out of pity, the old man extended his hand. In an instant the stranger seized him and said, 'Do you know who I am? I am Death. Look at the holes in my shoes, worn to shreds from chasing you! I have visited the men who would have been your friends and the women you might have loved; they had never seen you. I looked for you in the houses of learning and the halls where the powerful sit; none there knew of you. I searched for your face by the light of countless hearths where greybeards sit and tell their stories; you were not among them. In your quest for greatness you have left your life unlived. But now I have found you, as I find everyone—in the end.'

With that Death led the old man away; unfulfilled, companionless, his name already forgotten, his only remaining journey the one that would lead him into the silent anonymity of Never.

HIS COMPANY OF ANGELS
CHAPTER TWENTY-SEVEN

Niderälpli Sanatorium, 1931

HE SUN, HAVING spent the day trundling across the sky in the customary fashion, settled into its westernmost position and hung there with an air of self-satisfaction.

A number of the sanatorium's guests had come out onto the promenade to enjoy the crisp November air. Some, wrapped in sheepskins, lounged in deck chairs equipped with adjustable shades to shield their faces from the sun. Others strolled up and down in front of the glass-paned doors. Friends and acquaintances congregated in twos and threes, sharing parts of the promenade and chatting companionably next to the ornate iron lamps.

Some processed the length of the building and descended the steps to the garden, immaculate after a summer of attentive care. The few leafy trees that survived at this altitude had shed most of their crowns and the breeze was carrying away whatever isolated leaves remained on the branches. These had scarcely hit the ground before the fastidious gardener, who'd been observing the weakening foliage from a bench near the rose bushes, descended upon them with a rake and whisked them out of sight.

Those patients for whom nature's charms were less appealing enjoyed the cosiness of the large sitting rooms inside. Some sat in armchairs reading, others played cards or wrote letters at tables near the fireplaces. Those who weren't asleep appeared visibly drowsy and what little talk took place was languorous and genteel.

Other than the tinkling of teaspoons and the murmur of polite conversation there was no music. A handsome young gentleman from Krakow had made a foray at the piano some minutes earlier at the insistence of two French sisters, but he could only play one song and that song was "God Who Hast Embraced Poland". This brought on such a chill from the Muscovites in the Russian corner that he lost heart and took up a hand of cards instead. A polite calm resumed.

A moustachioed major was holding forth from one of the more comfortable armchairs. A round-faced woman listened with rapt attention to his accounts of the war and all the reasons why the Kaiser had been pre-destined to lose. He spoke safe in the knowledge that there were no Germans present, as they were all attending a lecture on physiognomy in the library upstairs. A dowager and a pale bespectacled professor attended from couches nearby, while a goateed Austrian viscount did a wonderful job of ignoring everybody from behind a leather-bound volume.

The Major paused for breath and the round-faced woman jumped in.

'Is this your first visit to the sanatorium, Major?'

The Major had only arrived a few days before and was still being introduced to the other guests. He coughed to clear his throat. 'Yes, my doctor advised me to take the air.'

'This is my fourth year in Niderälpli. Every time I leave, I think myself cured at last, yet I always seem to return! But it is so very pleasant up here after all.'

The Major harrumphed in a vaguely affirmative way, but found the prospect of convalescing for four years somewhat unsettling.

Across the room someone told a joke and the Russians chortled. The Franco-Polish card game continued nearby.

'Will you be staying with us long, Major?' inquired the pale professor.

Before the Major could reply, there was a *BANG* as someone allowed a door to slam shut, causing everyone to jump. Activity halted as the room's occupants looked up to see who'd made such an indelicate entrance.

The culprit was a large man in sturdy but unfashionable clothes and an old woollen overcoat. This was odd, as he'd just come from the corridor where it was rather warm. The most striking thing about him was the look of intense bewilderment on his face, as though he'd expected to find himself somewhere else entirely, or was altogether lost.

He gazed at the room. It stared back.

'Oh, er . . . Very sorry I'm sure, er . . . Oh, God . . .'

This unprepossessing introduction marked him unmistakably as an Englishman.

The Austrian viscount returned to his assiduous study of the leather volume. The Russians resumed their conversation as if the man weren't there.

'*Bonjour, Monsieur,*' said one of the French ladies by the fire. 'I do not believe we 'ave made your acquaintance.'

The man hardly seemed to see her. He mumbled some incoherent excuse before exiting brusquely the way he had come in.

There was a moment of silence. Then a buzz of comment began in several languages simultaneously.

'What a strange fellow.'

'Did you see ze look on his face?'

'Didn't recognise him. Is he a patient?'

'With such a countenance, 'ow could he not be? I 'ave not met 'im myself.'

The Major turned back towards his companions. 'I fancy that's the same chap with whom I shared a coach from the station when I arrived. We travelled together from London, though we never exchanged more than a word or two.'

'I can well believe that!' cried the professor. 'No one with a complexion such as his could have been here for longer; else he would appear more rested. Such a countenance is not to be seen in a healthy man.'

'His affliction must be severe indeed,' chirped the small woman. 'I do not imagine he has much hope of recovery. I dare say he has waited too long. Has he any friends here?'

'*I* should not wish to make his acquaintance,' huffed the dowager, 'not until he improves his manners, that is.'

With mutterings of satisfied agreement the game was taken up once more. Everyone agreed the intrusion had been most disagreeable.

The Major was the last to turn away from the door, wondering what had so disturbed the stranger. Soon the others drew him back into the general chatter and his mind had to make room for more pressing distractions.

About a half hour before the man in the overcoat burst into the sitting room, he'd emerged from the doctor's clinic in the lower levels of the building and, hat in hand, made his way slowly up the stairs. Though not himself a patient, a room had been prepared for him on the upper floor. It was towards this that he made his way.

The stairs brought him up from the medical level into the lavish hallway that ran the length of the building's ground floor. He saw none of its delights—the gleaming mirrors or expensive side tables with their decorative vases and fashionable statuary. All he saw was the carpet, which alone amongst everything else was old and worn. His head remained lowered as he made for the main staircase.

Another man was sweeping the floor. He looked no older than thirty but he too moved with an almost painful slowness. When the two met they started, each taken unawares by the other. The man in the overcoat seemed to find this encounter upsetting for he walked past without acknowledgment and ignored the sweeper's stuttering greeting.

The man climbed the stairs to his room. Any inmates not bed-ridden were either downstairs or outside enjoying the weather. Here the corridors were plain and whitewashed, opulence giving way to practicality. The smell of disinfectant was omnipresent, but not strong enough to mask the other scent: a musty, unhealthy background odour that permeated the walls and hovered behind each of the identical numbered doors.

Eventually the man found his room and went in. He shut the door behind him.

He threw his hat onto the bed and sat down at the desk. A small pile of second-hand books sat at his elbow. He moved them aside. A moment later he rose again and paced before slumping back into the chair. He remained there for a while, listening to the laughter outside his window.

Then he took pen and paper and began to write.

My dearest Susan,

It saddens me beyond measure to tell you that your daughter passed away last night. I can only imagine the grief this will cause you and poor Charlie, but believe me when I say that I share in your sorrow and grieve over the desolation my niece's passing is sure to wreak in your lives. Eloise was a dear, delightful girl and I know we all hoped this cure was the answer to our prayers. I'd scarcely arrived two days ago when I was informed of the gravity of her condition. I scarcely left her side—indeed, I'm still in the clothes I wore upon my arrival. But she worsened so that even now I can hardly believe it. I hope and pray that in time we shall see that all things are for the good, difficult as they may be for us to bear. Meanwhile we must trust that she is now in the house of Almighty God and that his company of angels is brightened by her arrival.

He paused and blinked hard before continuing.

She spoke of you only yesterday. She was glad that her father had someone to look after him during his own illness, and was certain that she would see both of you before too long. I fear she was being brave, even then.

The man struggled to think how to continue. All he knew was that he couldn't possibly tell his sister the truth; it would hurt her too much. So he lied.

By the time I arrived she had settled in and been made comfortable.

As he wrote, his memory echoed with what his niece had actually said, her voice small and diminished by her illness.

258

'No one will speak to me, Uncle. I don't understand a word of German. No one from home seems at all eager to know me or acknowledge that I'm here. I don't know why.'

He continued to write, his lips white and thin with effort.

She was well received and during her stay made the acquaintance of several other guests.

There it was again, he thought; the echo of her voice in that hateful room downstairs.

'One day the doctor left my door ajar and an Italian gentleman saw me sitting all by myself and came to talk. I think he does odd jobs for the hospital. He couldn't understand me any more than the next fellow and spoke hardly a word of English. But he liked to talk and I was more than happy to listen. To tell you the truth, I nearly wept with relief at having company. He was in the War and I understood that a shell blast had rendered him nearly deaf, poor soul. Now that I'm bedridden no one else comes to visit, except for the doctor. He doesn't say much.'

The man included some vaguely consoling details about the competence of the doctors and how diligently they'd tried to tend to his niece. As he did he caught himself hoping they would all die in solitude and agony, as Ellie had.

He dismissed these vindictive thoughts. Though Ellie's words were painful to remember he clung to what vestiges of her remained to him, such that they were burned into his memory even as his letter contradicted them.

'When a patient passes away, they're never spoken of. Nobody even comments on their absence. Indeed, they're careful not to, as though it's a rule one is expected to abide by. It's the most beastly thing I've ever seen.'

The sanatorium is very peaceful, and much of the day is given over to rest so the patients lead a very calm and tranquil existence.

'It hurts so much, Uncle. Every night I wake up from the coughing and can't get back to sleep for hours afterwards.'

I was by her side in the end. She went peacefully.

He had not been by her side. She'd died alone in the night and he couldn't bring himself to believe it had been easy.

She was happy here . . .

'I'm so unhappy here.'

. . . and had friends to keep her company.

'I'm so lonely.'

The man became so violently overcome by grief that he ceased writing and just sat there and wept. The silence in the building around him was so profound he might as well have been alone. In his anguish he didn't care who heard.

He sat at the desk for several minutes until the storm passed. The sanitised, immobile air made him crave the outdoors.

He rose and opened the French windows. These led onto a balcony that ran the length of the building, with a deck chair in front of each room. He stood there for a while with his eyes closed, inhaling the fresh mountain air until he was ready to go back in. The curtain wafted gently as he passed.

He resumed his seat at the desk, haunted once again by his niece's voice.

'I want to come home.'

Under the previous line he wrote

She missed you very much.

That much at least was true. The next part he wrote swiftly.

I understand from your letter that arrangements have been made for her boy. I am compelled to say that I cannot approve of this adoption. Can we not adequately care for him ourselves? I refuse to feel gratitude towards these people after how they treated my niece, their money be damned. If Lord and Lady Aberfinchley think that this gesture atones for the appalling behaviour of their son, I dare say they'll be disappointed. It was enough that our Ellie was taken in by the scoundrel, even after her illness and his own loathsome nature led him to abandon her, to the point that to the last she swore her Hal—as she called him—was a good man and that he was waiting for her to return, healed. Let us not waste our time and tears attempting to force familial responsibilities on the fellow. Rather, let us forget him entirely and entrust his retribution to God. Far better that Desmond be fostered by a loving family than be consigned to a wretch who couldn't bring himself to care for his mother.

The final decision must be yours and Charlie's. I say, let us not hope to see the rogue ever again.

The last few lines were hard to read, the letters angular and smudged. He allowed himself a moment to gather himself before finishing.

As such a great portion of our funds has been spent here, I'm afraid there can be no question of a burial at home. But do not worry, my dear, I have found a spot of such natural beauty and calm that you could not help but be happy were you to visit it. Perhaps you will one day.

I've made arrangements for my immediate return following the funeral. I will write again soon.

He signed, folded, and slid the letter into an envelope bearing the monogram of the sanatorium. He picked up the meagre collection of books—dwarfed by his large hands—and slipped them into his overcoat. Then he reached for the pen, snapped it in half, and threw the pieces at the wall.

He left the room and walked along the corridor like a man who scarcely knew where he was going or cared. He descended the stairs heavily, deliberately, his bleary march carrying him past the many mirrors. Upstairs he had smelled the musk of death soon to come. Now from downstairs rose the tang of the morgue; the icy aroma of death recently visited.

He suddenly felt ill, and rushed through a door he hoped led to a lavatory. It was then that he burst into the drawing room. The slamming door, loud as a gunshot, startled him.

'Oh, er . . . Very sorry I'm sure, er . . . Oh, God . . .' He stared around, disorientated. People were speaking to him, only he couldn't hear what they were saying.

His insides heaved and he erupted into a cold sweat.

He mumbled something, anything, and rushed from the room. Across the hall he glimpsed the half-open lavatory door and rushed for it.

He emerged a few minutes later, pale and haggard. In his rush he'd dropped his letter and books onto the carpet. He retrieved it and retraced his steps, arriving once more in sight of the great staircase.

The sweeper was again attending to his duties. This time the man in the overcoat paused, out of sight, as though considering whether or not speak.

The sweeper failed to notice the man's footsteps. He laboured across the carpeted floor with painful slowness, like an old man, or someone who knows that no one is waiting for his company.

261

Eventually the man appeared to make up his mind and moved on without a word. He placed his letter in the tray next to the concierge's office marked AUSGANGSPOST and exited the hateful building with a calmness of demeanour he had not thought he possessed.

There came from within a deep, ringing, metallic sound.

'Ah!' exclaimed the dowager in the front room, 'dinner at last. I'm famished. This mountain air has a way of kindling the appetite, it's quite remarkable.'

The Major roused himself from his armchair, took the dowager's arm, and led her through. The others followed and together they made their way to the refectory.

Inmates across the grounds heard the gong. Whether because of the air or the disease gnawing on their insides, they had prodigious appetites and came swiftly.

No one paid much attention to the man in the overcoat. He pulled his hat down low over his face and walked alone down the road towards the village. Soon enough nobody remembered that he, or his niece, had ever been there.

PART FOUR
DECEMBER

THE WINTER FÊTE
CHAPTER TWENTY-EIGHT

EROME THE GOAT was not having a good day.
To begin with, the temperature had dropped again overnight and his knees were giving him gyp. This always happened during the changing of the seasons and inevitably aroused in Jerome feelings of melancholy, as he was reminded of his increasing age and the meaninglessness of his existence. Also, there was frost in his beard.

Furthermore, he hadn't even had breakfast before his plans for the day were irrevocably ruined. He'd gone to bed with the intention of sleeping in—the mornings were getting darker after all—then going for a late morning stroll across the field to the fence. Instead, he was rudely awoken at the crack of dawn when a host of men descended upon him and hauled him away for some kind of perverse medical examination that included a de-lousing shampoo and several shots.

Lastly, his morning constitutional thus denied him, the afternoon found Jerome lashed to his fence wearing a pair of felt reindeer antlers and a necklace of sleigh bells. This could only mean one thing: the village council had drafted him—without prior consultation—to play the part of Rudolf in the Winter Fête's St Nicholas display . . . *again*.

He broke wind hoping it would cheer him up, but his half-hearted efforts were disappointing and floated away without giving him any pleasure.

From somewhere in the leafless meadow above he heard two dejected voices in conversation.

'So, what're you going to do with your life now that we've been cast off by society?' asked Richard.

'Dunno,' answered Graham, 'maybe run off to Scotland and go fishing.'

'I didn't know you fished.'

'Had to. I needed subjects for my paper, *Neurological Dysfunction and Erotomania in Catfish*. It's what I was working on before we came here.'

'Sounds interesting. Been put on hold, has it?'

'Discontinued for the foreseeable future, I'm afraid.'

'Sorry to hear that.'

'To be honest I might've had something to do with it. Anyway, I wasn't coming up with anything truly earth-shattering. All the groundwork's been covered already.'

'I'm surprised. Yet, for some reason, also not surprised.'

'Hm. Subsidised publishing in academia has resulted in an absolute deluge of obscure research. Still, mustn't disappoint the faculty, so I guess it's back to the aquarium for me. Either that or I'll see if anyone's hiring for one of those mad polar expeditions where everyone starves half to death and loses a few toes. How 'bout you?'

'Well, I've been jacked from *Nature Magazine*, so I guess I'll have to start looking for something else.'

Richard and Graham, unlike Jerome, had risen late that day. There was, they agreed, little reason not to. Following a meal that was neither breakfast nor lunch they strolled up to the orchard, allegedly because Graham had never visited it but really because Richard hoped for a glimpse of Ellie. She was nowhere to be seen.

'Nice view,' commented Graham. 'I can see why you came up here so often.' He waved down at Jerome. The sleigh bell collar jingled mournfully back at him.

Together the two men wandered into the village. It was a cold, clear day and Niderälpli thrummed with activity. The streets echoed to the sounds of locals and visitors alike basking in the glow of the fairy lights strung between the buildings, though Christmas was still three weeks away. Customers bundled in winter clothes ranging from the matching fluorescence of Kaitlyn and Chase to the unfathomable antiquity of Fosco's old army coats bustled in and out of the shops. Preparations for the fête were already under way. As Richard and Graham wandered to and fro they were surrounded by people carrying wreaths, bells, torches, and other sundries. Everything around them spoke of excitement, unrestrained anticipation, and the general goodness of being.

Wherever Richard looked he saw the flushed and happy faces of holidaymakers. But nowhere did he see the one face he was looking for—or rather he saw it everywhere. He saw her in the whitewashed walls of the houses and the branches of the trees that lined the square, now bare and empty of birds; he saw her in the flitting shadows of the alleyways; he saw her in the sad face of the statue above the fountain and heard her laughter in the trickle of the water.

It was as though the whole village, the entirety of creation, knew the one sight he wished to see and was mocking him—a poor joke made even more mirthless by the certainty that, in all likelihood, hers was a face he would never see again.

He was surrounded by people. Yet, even with Graham at his side, he felt alone.

In the square stood a large horse, breathing steam and leaning against the brakes of the decorative sleigh to which it was harnessed. The driver called to them, offering a ride. Richard shook his head and they continued on.

They halted to allow Dino the waiter to mount the pavement in front of them, hauling a hand cart with several large kegs juddering about inside.

Graham gave his companion a sidelong look of concern. 'I was thinking about what you said the other day.'

'Yeah?'

'Do you really hate London that much?'

'I don't hate London. I just hate living there.'

They strolled past the shops, most decorated in the winter theme. The more expensive ones exhibited bronze statuettes of rearing ibex and fur throws, while the more modest establishments made do with fake snow and plush polar bears.

'Maybe you should come and visit me up in Cambridge some time. We could relive the rare old times.'

Richard shook his head. 'Those days are over. They're not coming back.'

'Come on, it's not so long ago as all that.'

'You never left, Graham. Once you do, things change. I remember passing through a year ago and walking into town from the station like I used to. Everything was familiar: the smell of the river, the view of the library, the rainwater collecting under the paving stones . . . But it didn't feel like a homecoming anymore.'

'And London doesn't either?'

Richard shook his head again. 'When I lived in Cambridge, it was my home. I had a place there, somewhere where I felt I belonged. I felt valued. I haven't found anything like that since leaving.'

They came to one of the little bridges that crossed the channelled torrent. Richard leaned over to watch the water. 'Maybe that's why going back makes me sad. I miss the feelings Cambridge used to give me: safety, belonging, home. Now it's just full of memories.' He threw a stick into the river. 'And ghosts,' he added.

Graham watched the stick float away. 'Is that why we lost touch?'

Richard turned to look at him. 'No, we lost touch because secretly I always hated you and I never wanted to see your hideous, nauseating face ever again.'

Graham looked shocked, then collected himself and punched Richard in the stomach. Richard rolled with it, grinning, and both men sparred playfully for a moment.

'Growing up hasn't been everything we hoped for, has it?' mused Graham. 'Still, I guess it's not entirely our fault.'

'Maybe we should have become hedge fund managers instead.'

'Ew. Anyway, we'd have been rubbish at it.'

'Turns out we're rubbish at this, too.'

'Bullshit,' retorted Graham. 'Even if we didn't pin down that sodding bear, we documented just about everything thing else on this mountain to within an inch of its life.'

Richard kicked a stone across the road, his hands in his pockets. 'If you say so,' he muttered. 'Far as I can see, it's been a huge waste of time.'

'Pish. I don't care what the office says. I think we did a jolly good job. Our content is being picked up by platforms worldwide. I even read some of those reports of yours, cracking stuff. Jolly good material.'

'What do you mean, "some"? I expressly gave them to you to proofread.'

'Doesn't really matter now, does it?'

'I guess not. That bear's probably curled up a nice cave somewhere for the winter by now anyway. Besides, this way we get to take everything we've done and sell it to the BBC.'

They shared a chuckle as they rounded a corner and saw the woods where the fête was to be held. A line of poles had been hammered into the ground and strung with lights to mark the way. Monsieur Pfister was driving a lorry piled high with firewood piled into the trees.

Graham rubbed his gloved hands together for warmth. 'Funny old thing, this fête of theirs. Reminds me of the Lewis Bonfire.'

'It's probably much the same thing. Or at least it might have been, originally. I guess both have been tempered by a thousand years of the Christian church saying "Right: no human sacrifices anymore, but you can still make big fires and dance around them ominously covered in paint" or something.'

There was a jingle and the clip-clop of hooves as the sleigh *whooshed* past at the top of the street. They caught a glimpse of Kaitlyn and Chase's happy faces and then it was gone, giggles trailing in its wake.

Graham nodded at the little village. 'In any case, I'm glad we came. Nice place, this. If I weren't so ruthlessly virile I might suggest the scenery was positively romantic.'

He looked Richard up and down. 'I don't suppose you'd like to enact the part of a tall brunette from the Planet Earth team for the duration of a sleigh ride just to humour me, would you?'

'Don't get carried away,' Richard raised a gloved finger. 'Any monkey business and I'll twat you.'

Graham scratched his three-day-old stubble. 'You'll agree though, there's a desperate shortage of women in the world of wildlife photography. Makes these shoots rather dreary in the long run, no offense.'

'None taken.'

Graham pointed his thumb over his shoulder. 'I was thinking of going down to the woods and watching the preparations, might be fun. Care to join?'

'I think I've had enough "fun" for one visit. I might go for a walk instead.'

'You'll miss the Glühwein.'

'I'll just have to find consolation in the knowledge that you'll be here, drinking enough for two. Maybe I'll join you later.'

'Suit yourself. Give me ring if you change your mind.'

*****

Dawes' office was a hive of activity. The air buzzed with excited muttering. Even the biscuits were honey-glazed.

'Right,' said Dawes, 'everyone here?'

'Nearly,' replied Alice, 'just waiting for the big guns.'

Dawes poked his head round the door to assess the crowd. He withdrew it again promptly. 'Alice.'

'Yes?'

'Why are they all wearing fake moustaches and spectacles?'

'Well, HR revoked their passes and though we managed to get them all visitor's badges Julian and I thought it best if they wore disguises.'

'Ah.'

'To be honest, it was mostly Julian's idea.'

'And where is young Julian on this fine day?'

'He's bringing up the heavy machinery.'

'And the sing-song?'

'It was Lord Aberfinchley's favourite. I think they've adopted it as a sort of anthem.'

In went Dawes. A roomful of moustachioed myopics paused halfway through a spirited rendition of "Yes! We Have No Bananas" and turned to greet him.

'So, Dawes!' cried one figure, whose baldness marked him as Ahmid Sardharwallah. 'Have you come over to side of light after all, then?'

'Don't gloat, Ahmid.' Dawes gave him a stern look. 'This is happening on my terms, not yours.'

A few unidentifiables whispered to Dawes through their false moustaches. 'Is this it, then?' they asked, 'are we doing it?'

Out in the corridor a cheerful *ding* announced the arrival of the elevator.

'Show her in directly, Alice.' Dawes turned to the room. 'May I introduce Lady Leticia Crowley, QC LLM M.A (Cantab.), our solicitor and one of the finest legal minds this side of Oxford.'

'And indeed the other side,' added Leticia, appearing in the doorway. 'Don't bother getting up, lads. You there!' She pointed to a hapless intern. 'Is there any tea to be had in this palace of the Patriarchy?'

Alice appeared with a trolley and a kettle. 'Here we are, Lady Crowley.'

'Ah! Lovely lovely lovely. Thank you, my dear. How nice to meet someone who knows what they're doing. This one,' she waved at Julian, 'kept me waiting at the lift for two whole minutes.'

Alice beamed. Julian sulked. Dawes interrupted.

'There is still one more thing we must do,' he said.

Leticia curled her lip. 'Must we? He doesn't deserve it.'

Dawes nodded. 'For Des' sake.'

Leticia shrugged. 'If you wish.'

Dawes went to the phone, but there he hesitated. Two-dozen moustaches bristled, two-dozen pairs of fake spectacles quivered.

There was a collective exhalation of relief when he picked it up and dialled.

'Hallooo?' cooed Europa Aberfinchley.

'Europa,' said Dawes, 'what I have to say is very important, so listen carefully. You know how much I admired Des and how close we were. I'm doing this for his sake. Luther needs to go on vacation.'

'Whatever is going on, Alistair?' Her voice rose and fell like a duck in a wind tunnel. Dawes could almost hear the ice cubes in her G&T.

'I'm serious, Europa. Call Luther and tell him to take a couple of days off. And if at their conclusion he should find himself west of the El Hierro Meridian, that would not be a bad thing.'

'Come now, Ali, you're not making any sense. Luther wouldn't leave London now; he's so very excited about all his new projects! Why don't you discuss it with him yourself in the morning?'

Dawes hung up. 'Well,' he said briskly to no one in particular, 'I tried.'

'So you did, Alistair,' acknowledged the grey man from the corner. Nobody heard him.

Leticia stepped forward. 'Ready, Alistair?'

Dawes looked up. 'Yes.'

'Good.'

Leticia tossed her scarf to Alice and sat down at his computer. Dawes turned to face the window, smoothing his hair absent-mindedly with one hand.

In his corner, the grey man smiled.

*****

In Niderälpli, the festivities had begun. Fires were lit in the forest and the lights marking the path twinkled merrily, inviting people to follow them.

The revellers needed no encouragement. The smells of mulled wine, grilled cheese and roast pig had been wafting across the meadow all day. Scarcely had the announcement been made that the fête was open before the little clearing was overrun. It now teemed with people buzzing with the anticipation that precedes all good old-fashioned fun.

Richard gazed down at the village from above. Though it was only afternoon the vale had already slipped into shadow and he could see the lights flickering amongst the trees. A dense fog had gathered in the valley below. From where Richard stood it looked as though a great woolly glacier had rolled in overnight and covered the lowlands. The skyline was inundated with heavy clouds. These battleship-grey harbingers of winter congregated en masse behind the horizon, held back by the crest of the mountains. Soon they would spill over and muffle Niderälpli in a cold darkness.

Richard checked his phone: the forecast promised clear skies at high altitude until evening. The villagers would have to wait a little longer for their snow. Besides, it would be a few hours before the mountains lost the light and Richard was confident in his familiarity with the plateau.

Out of habit he followed his routine patrol along the ridges, taking time to appreciate the views and familiar landmarks. After all, he might not see them again.

The walking was easy. He'd grown used to it and it felt good to use his legs. He could have covered the ground swiftly, but today he took his time. Under his jacket he wore several extra layers. Even so, the icy wind gnawed at whatever bits of skin weren't well covered. He picked up his pace and felt warmer.

A familiar bush hove into view. It rustled as Richard passed, though whether in greeting or with apprehension he couldn't have said.

He traversed the ridge until he reached the rock where he'd first encountered Bellows. Here he lingered, half-hoping the ghost would reappear and accept his apology. When he didn't, Richard carried on.

His walk carried him high above the treeline to the wind-swept slope where the little wooden hut perched. Emptied of equipment, it was as they'd first found it: aged, solitary, and empty. Richard passed without going inside.

The black lake at the bottom of its bowl had sunk into the rock, as the springs that fed it froze and the trickle slowed. It appeared shrunken and dead. Richard wondered what might lurk at the bottom. He didn't linger though, remembering what had happened the first time he'd come there and not wishing for his own demons to return.

He came at last to where even the weeds started to wither. Here the ground was almost entirely rock. What grass did survive looked tired and grey at the edges. It was as though the colour had gone out of both the mountain and the sky. The indigos and rich greens Richard had admired upon his arrival were now pale and faded, like a child's picture taped to a window, the colour fleeing before the oncoming winter.

Richard found himself in a familiar spot; a rocky moraine fringed by high crumbling rocks, littered with debris. In the middle of it Richard recognised the rift through which flowed the cold stream, now silent where before it had leapt and bubbled. The ground on the far side of the stream rose sharply in an avalanche of broken terrain towards the foot of the cliff. At the bottom of the moraine yawned the omnipresent void.

Richard twisted, observing the rocks above him. They towered overhead like a wall. Had they stood to the south instead of the north-east, the riverbed next to him would have never seen daylight. Even so, the noontime sun had sunk so low in the sky that its beams now hardly ever reached this spot, and what little water remained was frozen solid. Richard felt the cold through his boots. Not for the first time, he was reminded of the similarities between these mountains and a great, petrified sea of solid rock. Like every ocean, its edges were rimmed with everlasting ice.

Richard was tired. He hitched up his rucksack in preparation for the descent to the village. It was as though his thoughts were turning away of their own volition, dragging him back with the promise of a cosy bonfire and a steaming mug of something or other. He stepped away from the stream, his mind full of promises of hot food and raucous company.

As he did his foot caught on something and he stumbled, catching himself at the last moment.

The sudden fall took Richard by surprise and he needed a moment to collect himself. He'd come worryingly close to losing his balance completely, which would have meant a painful tumble down the rocks and—unless he'd been able to stop himself—off the rim of the cliff below. His heart was thumping hard. He remained on his side for a minute without moving, waiting for the dizziness to pass.

He craned his neck in search of what had tripped him and discovered something white and oblong sticking out from the ground, like a dead branch. Sodding thing, he thought.

His foot hurt. The thought of putting his feet up by the fire seemed more attractive than ever, but something about the object's appearance made him pause. The earth was loose and, with a bit of digging, he exhumed it. It helped that the ground was rocky and hadn't frozen together, unlike the soil lower down.

Richard held the object in his hands. It was a bone, long and cracked, but unmistakable. It must have belonged to some large animal—a mule perhaps, or a cow. It looked very old. Richard guessed it must have been uncovered by the torrential flow of the river the previous spring.

His stomach growled but he ignored it.

He looked more closely. The bone's surface was rough to the touch. He brushed off the dirt and discovered a number of lacerations.

Hullo, he thought; this animal's been tampered with. It felt as though something with a sharp edge had cut straight down to the bone.

Richard looked at the cliff again. Predators were known to drag parts of their kills back to their dens for later . . .

He suddenly remembered falling in the water, here, with Kaspar, several weeks prior. How could he have forgotten? Hadn't he discovered something then as well?

The bone wouldn't fit in Richard's rucksack, so he placed it carefully to one side. He rose and went to stand on the edge of the stream again. He put his hands on his hips, assessing the other side and the steep climb to the foot of the cliff. The words *horrifyingly* and *unsafe* sprung to mind.

After a moment he drew away and retraced his steps.

Then, as though on an impulse, he wheeled around, raced to the edge of the water, and leapt.

THE CAVE
CHAPTER TWENTY-NINE

ICHARD LANDED ON the slope with a *thump* and seized the grass to keep from slipping backwards. For a moment he clung there, fumbling for a foothold in the frost with his boots.

If he hadn't known better, he might have believed the ground didn't want him there. It felt like the rocks themselves had tried to tip him backwards into the water. He supposed he'd become overconfident and resolved to be more careful.

Richard was not what one might label a "city boy". He'd grown up in a small country village and his childhood had included lots of playing outdoors with sticks and getting his knees dirty. Even after moving to urban areas for school and work, he remained fairly at home in the great outdoors. Thanks to his training as a biologist his familiarity with different types of plant, soil, and the mating habits of small animals were considerably above average.

On the other hand, he remained a contemporary man. There are certain things that such men will invariably miss, if only because they don't think to look for them.

Richard did not, for instance, notice the subtle drop in temperature that occurred the moment he set foot on the opposite side of the stream. He also failed to perceive a different smell in the air, as if one wind had suddenly been replaced by another. The sound of the stream itself seemed altered and the rocks made a different music as the thread of water trickled over them. The light, the air, even the ground he stood on, all underwent an almost imperceptible shift, as though the sun had effectuated a slight but sudden jump, or the cardinal points had been tweaked by some unknown power.

Richard failed to notice this, though he mightn't have had circumstances been different. He might have looked just a little bit closer at the shadows on the cliff face or listened more attentively to the rustle of the wind in the grass. As it was, he heeded none of these things, for his attention was entirely drawn to the great vein of stone above him, in whose shadow there had appeared the mouth of a cave.

Richard gazed up at the dark aperture, thin and twisting but unmistakable, so discreetly tucked away amongst the boulders and crags that, had he been standing even fractionally to either side, it would have been invisible.

Something beckoned him up the slope. Not the cave itself—a dark, narrow, unfriendly cleft in the brooding rock—but something within him. The promise of something unfamiliar and fascinating lifted the depression that had weighed on him for days.

After a couple of deep breaths and a slight adjustment of his rucksack to steel the nerves, Richard began his ascent.

His boots carried him over the rocky turf, not reading the age of the stones or telling him what was buried beneath his feet: the skulls of animals, polished and darkened by the passage of time; flint arrowheads of various sizes and shapes, still sharp; scraps of bronze and tin, meticulously shaped and beaten by ancient hands; countless tokens, trifles, and treasures, all hidden deep in the earth, sentinels guarding the looming cliff face and marking the way to the entrance of the black cave.

The rise evened out onto a carpet of pebbles that appeared to have fallen out of the gap in the rock, barely wide enough to accommodate a man. A frozen thread of moisture ran through them under Richard's soles to join the stream that flowed below.

The mouth of the cave didn't resemble the ones in picture books, those big, round openings like a giant's mouth. This one was jagged, twisted, squeezed painfully between two massive boulders that jostled unevenly for space. The opening itself was so veiled by these two lumps of stones that Richard was amazed he'd noticed it at all.

He stepped into the narrow space. His rucksack got in the way so he removed it, but not before he'd extricated his torch. He leant in again and shone his light into the dark, twisted hole. After the initial squeeze the mouth widened, curving out of his line of vision.

Almost before he knew it, he'd pushed through the gap, staggered forward a few steps, and was standing inside the mountain.

Richard gazed at the time-stained walls of the cave, which met in an arch several feet above him. The gloomy passage wound away like an uneven corridor, its walls smooth from erosion. An unearthly silence reigned. Richard assumed that, come spring, melt water would pour out of the glacier above and flood the tunnels. His eyes adjusted to the darkness, which, even only a couple of steps in, was like ink.

He turned, blinking at the bright light behind him, and felt a tremor of doubt. He was dangerously under-equipped for this sort of thing. Late afternoon was no time to start exploring unfamiliar caves. He decided to allow himself but a short foray—no more than thirty paces—before returning the way he'd come.

He closed his eyes for a moment until the flashing blue-white image of the entrance had faded from the inside of his eyelids. With one hand on the wall for safety, he advanced into the darkness.

Richard tested the floor with his feet. The walls of the corridor surged in and out erratically, blocking his torch beam from penetrating any great distance. After six paces he couldn't see the opening anymore. After twelve, the daylight had dimmed such that he depended on the torch alone. At twenty paces, the ground rose up and he was forced to duck his head so as not to crack it on the sharp ceiling. At twenty-four paces, the walls came together so tightly that Richard was forced to stop and consider once again the safety of what he was doing.

This was far enough. Time to go back before his hiking excursion turned into one of those horror stories from television documentaries involving a gruesome and painful death. But then, thought Richard, twenty-four paces was not yet thirty. It didn't look that dangerous. With a minimal amount of wriggling he could easily overcome this obstacle. Steeling himself, he turned sideways, inserted his body carefully into the crack, and eased himself forward.

The obstruction was roughly a foot or so in depth. Only a couple of steps were needed really, but as Richard inched his head and shoulders carefully between the walls of rock it began to feel very tight indeed. The thought crossed his mind that he shouldn't like to get stuck here, for in all probability no one would find him until the mountain itself wore away and the melt water washed his bones out.

Now, he thought to himself, that's exactly the sort of negative thinking my mother warned against.

Gripping the torch between his teeth Richard wrapped his forward hand around the far corner of the gap and, holding his breath, pulled himself through.

He stumbled, caught himself, and flashed the torch in front of him.

After the narrow gap the corridor widened. Some five paces on it arched into a natural doorway almost as tall as he was, speckled with what appeared to be dark seams of rock that wove over and around the opening.

Well, thought Richard, by my reckoning I've allowed just enough distance to have a peek at what's through there. Then it's back the way I came.

By the glow of the torch he saw that the floor continued fairly evenly beyond the aperture. In his curiosity Richard forgot the mile of solid rock above him. With his few remaining steps he reached the doorway.

He ducked and was about to step through it, when the dark lines on its frame-like edge caught his attention and in them he suddenly recognised the hand of Man.

Richard froze, staring in astonishment.

His eyes moved up and around the archway. Here was the outline of a body, there the curve of running legs, the jagged edge of a bestial maw. The dark traces he'd taken for impurities in the rock were now revealed as markings, a multitude of black images drawn onto the stone. Even in their faded state, he recognised the pointed ears and curved tails of canine animals, their likeness preserved through years beyond count by these images on the wall.

His mind racing, Richard's gaze washed over the pack of painted wolves surrounding him, which seemed to stare back at him. They spiralled overhead across the ceiling and walls and covered many of the loose stones on the floor, some of which glowed white under his beam.

Richard stepped through the doorway and into the space beyond. Once inside he stood up, flashed his torch around, and his breath caught in his throat.

He'd entered a small cavern with a dome-like ceiling. Though in the open air its size would have appeared modest, after the slender passage and rocky overhangs, Richard felt as though he'd set foot in a small church. His torch illuminated the domed cavern and he perceived a multitude of shapes and forms all over its interior in a variety of colours: red, black, ochre, and white abounded, with an occasional splash of green. Some had faded but most retained an astonishing brightness, as though this hidden place had preserved in them an inner life.

Richard revolved, his mouth hanging open with wonderment at the richness of the pictures, his heart thumping in the deathly stillness.

He beheld figures of people, animals, strange shapes and symbols flowing across the stone. Their vividness amazed him. Many looked as fresh as if they'd been painted the week before. How long it must have taken! How painstakingly the artist had laboured over these likenesses!

Richard's heartbeat quickened. This was a far greater discovery than anything he could have written for that crummy magazine; it was something remarkable, unique. This changed everything! He couldn't wait to tell Graham.

He wished to flood the place with light, that he might appreciate these works of art in all their splendour, but it was almost certainly the absence of light that had saved them from perishment. This realisation nearly made Richard turn off his torch, but the thought of finding himself in the dark, alone and encased in rock, caused a trickle of fear to run through him.

He allowed himself another moment or two, then turned and ducked through the stone doorway. The painted walls were plunged into darkness once more.

Richard retraced his steps and, in what seemed like no time at all, he'd squeezed through the narrow gap, ducked under the low overhang and followed the winding corridor until he burst out of the crack in the rock into the blinding radiance of the evening.

He shielded his eyes against the glow of the sun, now low in the sky. Only just remembering to pick up his rucksack from where he'd left it, he set off down the track into the fiery west, hurrying towards the village to share the news.

In his haste Richard forgot about the black wolves whose intricate and sinuous bodies guarded the arch deep in the shadows. Had he thought to re-examine them in greater detail, it might have struck him that the markings now appeared a great deal clearer and more vivid than when he'd entered.

The shadows lengthened. Touches of gold and pink streaked the sky, and the white caps of the tallest peaks radiated incandescence. The evening light retreated up the slopes, sliding over the rocks, followed inexorably by the encroaching night and, far below, the thick, rising fog.

Inside the mountain, the darkness shifted. In the unlit corners and crevasses, so lately illuminated by Richard's torch, the inky lines that had been given such clarity by his brief presence twisted, lifted, and slid off the rocks that held them. The air along the twisting corridor quivered as they passed.

At the mouth of the cave, the evening light had risen above the crack in the rock. As the twilight deepened the shadows emerged; one at a time in a dreadful line the keen-eyed spectres came, trailing smoke and hatred. They sensed the man who had visited the hallowed ground of their master's sanctuary, who had seen the sacred images, the transgressor who even now was making his way down their mountain. They also sensed another presence, more familiar, one that gave them strength and made them bare their horrible fangs in the dying light.

In the shadows below the white peak they gathered and, noiseless and terrible, set off in pursuit.

*****

Richard hurried across the high plateau and counted the ridges, aiming for the forest and the familiar dirt track. He knew the swiftness with which he'd lose the light and pressed onwards. A breeze had risen and it tugged at him.

He stopped to catch his breath. The mist was still rising. That he might have to deal with fog as well as darkness gave Richard pause. Still, it was not rising particularly fast. He would make the village in time.

Something in the air shifted. Richard felt the hairs on his neck twitch, as though sensing some unseen presence behind him.

He turned, but could see nothing.

He continued on his way, followed by a growing collection of indistinct shapes flitting amongst the rocks.

Richard reached the waterfall as the sun was dipping below the horizon. For the first time since he'd first made the climb with Kaspar, he couldn't hear the sound of running water. The pools were all frozen, save the largest. The remnants of the stream still flowed through it, preventing the ice from settling.

Richard paused for a minute and once again experienced the twitching sensation on the back of his head.

He wheeled round, scanning the crag. He eyed the frozen waterfall clinging to the side of the cliff and strained his ears against the sound of the breeze.

Nothing.

Chiding himself for lingering, Richard set off once again. The village lights appeared through the trees and the excitement of his discovery swelled once again, but he couldn't shake that sense of unease.

It was only once he stepped off the rocky ledge and onto the forest's soft carpet of pine needles that Richard realised he'd been holding his breath.

He stopped to listen, but could discern little save wind in the treetops; a great whooshing, like a slowly crashing wave that never reached the shore. He shivered and wished for the presence of a friend by his side.

Something caught his eye amongst the shadows that framed the icicle-like column that had once been the waterfall. He squinted at the sharply inclined horizon, half hidden by the swaying pine branches.

A few seconds later Richard was running full tilt through the woods, trees flying past him, pursued by the ancestral fear of yellow eyes in the darkness.

He hurtled down into the gathering night, never taking his eyes from the track for fear of slipping, of falling, of being caught by what followed. Pine branches lashed at his face, his woollen hat slipped over one eye; he ignored it. His only thought was to run, to run, to—

A shadowy figure erupted out of the darkness ahead and only by slamming his boots down hard did Richard curb his speed so as not to barrel into it. He stumbled and fell in a panting heap amongst the pine needles. Looking up he found himself staring straight into the mouth of a rifle barrel.

THE AIRMEN
CHAPTER THIRTY

On the slopes of the Gräuelhorn, 1943

IETER YANKED AT his harness, heat from the burning engine scorching his face. Flames licked the soles of his flying boots as he hauled himself from the wreckage and tumbled off the fuselage into the pitch darkness.

For a terrible moment it felt like he was falling from a great height. Then he landed in the snow with a *wumpf* and found himself at the bottom of a Dieter-shaped hole. He wondered vaguely whether someone knew he was coming and had already dug his grave to size.

'Dieter!' cried a voice from the cockpit.

'Coming!' he answered, thrashing in the deep snow.

The flames from the engine were spreading fast. Dieter forced himself not to think what would happen when they reached a fuel cell.

'Dieter! I can't move!'

At last Dieter caught one of the mangled wheel struts and hauled himself onto the half-intact wing. The pilot was fighting the harness holding him in his seat, blood dripping from a gash on his forehead.

'Get this off me, I can't see with all this damned blood in my face.'

'Keep still!' said Dieter. He quickly undid the belts, as the fire crept along the side of the plane.

'I think my leg's broken,' said the pilot, trying to sponge away the blood with his sleeve. All that did was spread it across his face in frightening crimson streaks.

The last buckle gone, Dieter straddled the cockpit, slipped his hands under the pilot's arms, and hauled him out. The man cried out in pain as his leg was wrenched free and together they tumbled into the snow bank.

Dieter dragged his companion away from the plane, now totally ablaze. When they'd reached a safe distance he let himself fall backwards into the welcoming softness of the powdery snow. The two Germans lay there awhile, breathing heavily.

Eventually the pilot spoke. 'Where the Hell are we?'

'No idea,' Dieter replied, his eyes closed. 'The navigator's still inside, along with the other gunner. They've been dead for an hour.'

'Looks like we overshot and landed in the Alps. Question is, where? What with the curfew and no lights, I got completely lost.'

'Damned Italians,' grumbled Dieter as he lay in the snow. 'All it takes is one or two communists in the woods for them to get scared and turn the lights off.'

The fire found a fuel tank and a jet of flame flew into the sky as the wing exploded. The pilot tried to pull himself upright but fell back with a groan.

Dieter opened his eyes and watched the burning wreck of their Dornier crumble and crack. The high flames obscured all trace of the stars. The snow hissed as it melted in the searing heat.

'How's the leg?' Dieter asked.

'Feels a mess. Can't tell how bad though . . .'

Before he could continue they heard a noise in the darkness.

Dieter struggled upright. 'Sounds like footsteps,' he whispered. 'Someone's coming!'

The pilot peered into the darkness. 'I can't see a damned thing. Where?'

Dieter pointed. 'There! They're coming towards us!'

The pilot squinted, blinking away his own blood. 'How many? Are they soldiers? What shape are their helmets? Christ, I hope it's the army and not the communists. That would be just my luck.'

'It looks like he's alone,' whispered Dieter. 'No helmet, but he's armed.'

'Shit! I knew it. Italian commies, I bet. Wait, what are you doing?'

Dieter had unstrapped the pistol from his hip and trained it on the oncoming figure.

'Halt!' he shouted. 'Not another step! We are soldiers of the Reich and demand to know your allegiance!'

'Du depperte Arschgeige,' moaned his companion. 'You've blown it now!'

'Sshhh,' hissed Dieter, 'he's saying something!'

The men couldn't make out the words, but they did recognise the language.

'He speaks German!' said Dieter, lowering his weapon. 'Ha! We're saved!'

'Where in hell have we landed?' asked the pilot again, trying to turn towards the oncoming figure. He could hear footsteps in the snow now, muffled by snowshoes.

Dieter advanced towards the figure emerging from the penumbra.

'Greetings, friend, are we glad to see you!' He stretched out his arm. *'Heil H—'*

There was a flash and a crack in the darkness. Dieter's head snapped back. He teetered for a moment, before falling very slowly backwards into the snow.

'Dieter!' yelled the pilot.

The blood had begun to crust around his eyes, the swelling making it impossible for him to see. He wrenched his body painfully around, trying to make out the shape in the darkness.

The snowshoes padded past Dieter's body towards the prostrate pilot. Through the blood and swelling on his face the German could make out a figure in heavy clothes and, in its hand, a very nasty-looking rifle.

'Bastard,' he breathed.

The wooden butt of the gun came down hard and that was that.

Some time later a detachment of guardsmen from the militia approached the still-smouldering wreck of the German plane. A small distance away they found the body of the pilot. The impact wounds on his face accounted for the cause of death. They guessed he must have pulled himself from the wreckage before succumbing to his injuries. Two others lay amongst the ashes, but the heat meant there would be no chance of recovering them until morning.

In the darkness they missed the wide, shallow prints leading away from the wreck, the abandoned pistol in the snow, and the bloody rut marks of another body being dragged away from the burning circle into the wilderness beyond.

SHADOWS
CHAPTER THIRTY-ONE

WITZERLAND IS NOT renowned as a warlike nation. The fact that it has one of the most hard-won battle records of any European nation and that conscription remains compulsory there, causing railway stations to be perpetually crawling with soldiers, does little to dispel the world's general unawareness of the Swiss military machine.* Indeed, most countries look at Switzerland nesting in its mountain redoubt much as they would a cat in a basket and go, 'Naaaw, isn't it cute?'

Switzerland, however, consoles itself with the knowledge that even if the most highly developed and digitally weaponised superpower stuck its hand into that basket, the sheer viciousness it could unleash coupled with the element of surprise would allow it to slice off a few fingers before being brutally crushed by superior hardware and overwhelming numbers. The practice of active duty for all male citizens has therefore survived and shared experience of mountainous mud-related misery remains a popular icebreaker at parties nationwide.

Richard had been only partially aware of this fact when he arrived. Now, lying in a breathless heap at the foot of a tree with a gun pointing at his left eyeball, it was quite forgotten. All he knew was that he was being held hostage by foliage and that an argument was taking place between various elements of flora dotted around the vicinity. Had he understood Swiss German, he would have heard the following:

---

* This armed presence is particularly obvious on Fridays and Saturdays, when most of the Swiss armed forces are travelling either to or from their parents' house. Military service is largely a gap-year activity for young men and the top brass have made the tactical decision to rely primarily on the nation's mothers for laundry duties.

'Sarge!' exclaimed the bush. 'Sarge!'

'What the hell is going on? Who's broken cover?'

'Over here Sarge, I've got him! He ran straight into me!'

A sturdy shrub shuffled over to where Richard lay and examined him.

'Who the hell is this?' demanded the shrub.

'Isn't he the target?' inquired the bush.

'Of course not, idiot! He's not even wearing the sash!'

The bush was devastated.

'Have we won?' inquired a nearby hedge of holly.

'Silence!' commanded the shrub. But it was too late, other voices were already sounding from the shadows.

'I think Silvio's got him!'

'Not a minute too soon. We've been out here for hours!'

'If we hurry we can still make the party in the village. C'mon boys!'

'Qu'est-ce qui se passe les gars?' asked a currant hedge who appeared to be smoking a cigarette. *'On a terminé la manoeuvre?'*

'Someone explain to the *Romands* what's going on.'

'What *is* going on?'

'Dunno. I think the Sergeant got over-excited and broke cover.'

The shrub bristled. 'Silence!' it shouted. 'Nobody moves! This is not the target, the manoeuvre is still on-going, and the unit will sustain three casualties as a result of breaking cover.'

There was an uproar as various bits of the forest stood up in protest.

The shrub turned back to the bush and pointed an irate finger at Richard. 'Right: who the hell is this ass-head and why isn't he saying anything?'

'Dunno, Sarge. Maybe he hurt his head when he fell.'

'Well, find out if he's conscious and ask him what he's doing up here after dark.'

The bush leaned over. 'Hullo there! You all right?'

Richard had followed this exchange as well as someone on the verge of a panic attack can be expected to follow a conversation apparently carried out by vegetation, in the dark, and in a foreign language. Richard had little enough time to pull himself together before the bush carrying the weapon aimed at his face addressed him directly.

'Excuse me?' Richard's voice sounded small in the darkness.

The bush—now flanked by a dozen leafy comrades—reached up and pulled aside some leaf netting to reveal the face of a young man painted in crude green and black strokes. The soldier turned to the shrub, which in turn was revealed to be an indignant man in his middle years.

'Sarge, I think he's a tourist, maybe from the village.'

The sergeant rolled his eyes. 'Just what we need. There goes the mission.'

The young man knelt and scrutinised Richard amiably. 'You speak English?'

'Yes,' said Richard with relief, 'yes, I was out for a walk when . . .' He faltered.

The soldier nodded sympathetically. 'Yes, it is confusing. We are doing the manoeuvres, you see. We are training for the military service and we are not allowed to go to the village until we catch the target. We are laying an ambush for him here. We think you are him, so we stop you. We apologize.'

Richard glanced over his shoulder. The forest was dark and foreboding, but the flash of yellow eyes was nowhere to be seen. His heart was still thumping and he was grateful to be surrounded by armed men.

'You stay in the village?' asked the soldier as the rest of the unit shuffled up.

Richard nodded. 'The Gasthaus Meierhof.'

The young man nodded. 'Good choice! This is my parents' place. I'm Silvio!' He held out a gloved hand. 'Now we are finished, we can go back together!'

The sergeant had been listening to this conversation with suspicion. His limited English was sufficient to alert him to hints of dissent. 'What's that you're saying, Corporal Indergand?'

Silvio slung his rifle over his shoulder. 'Well, Sarge, since the exercise is ruined, I thought we'd call it a night and send the men home. I can accompany this guy back to his hotel. We're going the same way.'

The sergeant inflated like an angry balloon, his eyes popping from his face in a way that would have alarmed his ophthalmologist.

'You'll do nothing of the sort! I've never heard anything so utterly insubordinate in all my life! The target has not been acquired, you have not selected your three casualties, and you've spent several minutes in full view of the enemy! Un-shoulder your weapon, Corporal, and take charge of your section!' The aggrieved N.C.O. turned to address the rest of his command, many of whom had removed their helmets and were snacking on treats from their ammunition packs. 'The exercise continues!' he bellowed. 'Regroup and resume positions!'

One can only empathize with the unfortunate sergeant. The responsibilities of command are a burden to even the most level-tempered of men and the sergeant could not in all honesty be described as such a man. One cannot rely on the loyalty of twenty tired young recruits who've already spent several hours clothed in pine needles within sight and hearing of their own homes while a party's going on under their very noses. Consequently, rather than re-establishing discipline, the sergeant's command caused an immediate mutiny to break out amongst the vegetation.

As the sergeant struggled under a barrage of abuse, Silvio turned to Richard.

'You can go,' he said. 'I think we will be some time.'

'You're not coming with me?' asked Richard. He hadn't forgotten the yellow eyes in the dark.

Silvio gave him a thumbs-up. 'We are sorting this out between ourselves, then we are following behind you. You come for a beer?'

Richard nodded. 'Sure.'

Silvio saw him back onto the track before returning to the confrontation. The sergeant had already handed out several court-marshals when another company descended on them in a carefully timed mock counter-attack, using the chaos as an opportunity to savage the rival brigade. Any discipline that might have remained evaporated and mayhem ensued.

It was truly dark now and the track was treacherous. Richard was accompanied by the reassuring shouts of company sergeants who, having taken a lot of trouble to hide their soldiers convincingly, were demanding to know why the exercise had been interrupted. The relief this gave Richard as he made his way down the track was indescribable, for though he understood nothing of what was said, their tone of voice was not the kind used to herald the approach of shadowy monsters. He could still hear them as he emerged from the wood, twigs cracking underfoot.

Just as he exited the trees he encountered a stony-faced Fosco, fully equipped with exercise moderator's map, torch, and special sash. Judging by the look on his face, he was not at all pleased with the disruption.

'Hi!' said Richard.

'Hrmph,' was the disapproving response.

Richard hastened past Fosco towards the village and the hotel beyond. The butterscotch glow of the lights had never seemed so welcoming.

Because of his mad flight through the woods he approached Niderälpli from an unusual angle. He emerged onto the station road to find the village deserted and guessed everyone was at the fête.

The silence reminded him of the cave. He looked around him. All seemed quiet. Nonetheless he didn't feel like hanging around and made for the safety of the houses and brightly lit streets.

BANG.

Richard jumped, but it was only a firecracker bursting in the woods. As Richard crossed the empty square he heard festive music and the chatter of happy people. He considered joining the safety of the crowd, but his fear had passed. He decided to make for his hotel, resolving not to set foot near that cave again.

A sliver of moon appeared at the edge of the mountainous ridge encircling the village, as though checking to make sure there wasn't any unwelcome company lurking there.* Evidently it was reassured by what it found, for it continued to rise in the usual fashion. Meanwhile the great white fog, which had been steadily rising since the afternoon, finally brushed the lowermost houses of the village and began to seep through the streets.

Richard arrived at Gasthaus Meierhof having met no one since leaving the soldiers. He'd just entered the light pooling outside the hotel's windows and resolved to take an extra dosage of meds and a hot bath when he stopped.

He turned, but saw nothing except silent darkness. Like all shadows that lurk at the edge of the warmth-tinted lights of home, it was indiscernibly black.

His mind was playing tricks on him, Richard decided. Then he heard it again: an indistinct shuffle.

He turned, his eye drawn towards the shadowy alley to the side of the hotel. The road towards the village was empty. The sled dogs were eerily quiet.

Richard stepped back, suddenly not wanting to be too close to the hotel. He moved sideways to bring the alleyway into view. Bracing one hand on the wooden fence by the road, he leaned forward and gazed down the side of the building. There was nothing there.

All at once he realized that where there definitely *was* something was the space immediately behind him, and that whatever currently occupied that space was breathing down the back of his neck.

'BleeuuuaaAAHRrrgh.'

Jerome watched Richard spin away from the fence like a drunken ballerina in an earthquake and chewed his after-burp pensively.

Richard returned to the fence and glared at the goat. 'You massive arse! You nearly gave me a heart attack.'

Jerome stopped chewing and turned into the wind. His sleigh bells jingled as he sniffed the misty air.

Richard turned just in time to see the gaunt silhouette of something long-legged and angular slide across the wall a building as something passed in front of a street light, following the scent that had led it from the cave straight to where Richard stood.

Jerome saw wolf, but since he didn't smell wolf he decided that this was simply something that appeared to be a wolf, but wasn't. He did not wonder further. Whatever had persuaded what he was looking at to

---

* Scholarship disagrees on what might constitute unwelcome company for the moon. Guesses vary between A) one of those annoying rocket-powered deliveries of helmeted hominoids who always leave their footprints everywhere, and B) a hitherto undiscovered and more attractive moon.

resemble something else was not his business. It presented no danger to him. Like most goats Jerome had a generous spirit and he didn't question people's motives.

He turned to see if Richard had any tasty mints, but Richard wasn't there anymore. Jerome watched the dust settle in the road leading up to the hotel's front door, heard the frantic slamming of bolts, and sighed.

Something told him he wouldn't get much sleep tonight.

THE MIST
CHAPTER THIRTY-TWO

ICHARD ERUPTED INTO the foyer and proceeded to employ as many locks as the door could offer him. Niderälpli being a quiet village many of the bolts had never been used and revelled in their new importance.

Having achieved a status as near to impregnability as he could, Richard bent double from terror—that, and the effort of sprinting the length of the driveway. He clutched at the counter for support.

Warn someone. This thought, which had given him wings in the woods, had been subdued during his meeting with the soldiers. It returned to him now with a vengeance.

Something caused him to look up. A wheelchair appeared in the doorway containing the blanket-wrapped Frau Hürlimann, cane poised.

Richard gestured towards her, but was still too overcome to speak. She recognized him and the cane lowered a few inches.

It's that bloody Brit again, she thought. Looks like he's in a spot of bother too. What could it be this time? Whatever it is, serves the bugger right, I say.

She scrutinised the lad with her good eye. Something was genuinely wrong.

Richard caught his breath at last. 'Danger . . . the cave . . .'

What's this, thought Frau Hürlimann, something kicking off, eh? She wheeled herself closer to the hyperventilating Englishman and poked him encouragingly with her cane.

'From the mountain . . . Black wolves from the cave . . . Everyone's in danger! We have to tell them!'

A gnarled claw shot out from beneath the tartan blanket and grabbed Richard's jacket. It dragged him downwards in its vice-like grip and he found himself face to face with the old lady's icy blue orb. It bore through his skull and her voice was suddenly edged in steel and clear as a bell.

'*Wölfe?* The wolf he is here?'

Richard nodded furiously.

The old woman kicked her chair forward with astonishing alacrity, slammed back all the bolts, unlocked the door and, still clutching Richard's lapels, dragged him out into the night. By now the fog had engulfed the village almost entirely and its uppermost tendrils were drifting up the road towards the Gasthaus Meierhof.

In his astonishment Richard allowed Frau Hürlimann to pull him halfway around the Gasthaus before digging his heels in. He yanked at the claw that still clutched his jacket, but she would not let go.

'You don't understand. There are monsters coming. Real monsters! We have to tell people!'

Frau Hürlimann ignored him.

'Listen you mad old bat, you may not believe me but I've seen things, things you couldn't even . . .'

Frau Hürlimann swung her cane into Richard's stomach, taking away what little breath he'd managed to recover. He swore wheezily. Before he could retaliate however he suddenly understood her intention. Before him stood the wooden gate to the kennel, its iron lock faintly illuminated by the lights of the restaurant.

Richard heard the dogs' ragged breathing as they growled through bared teeth. He'd never heard them make such a sound. Their breath steamed under the wooden gate as they thrust their muzzles through the gap.

The old woman tugged at his sleeve. '*Die Hunde!* To loose the dogs, to loose them!'

That didn't sound like such a bad idea. Better yet . . .

Richard lunged for the front door and the desk where Herr Indergand housed his ammunition. The ruthless claw dragged him inexorably backwards.

'Dogs!' insisted Frau Hürlimann.

Richard suddenly remembered what Melanie had said: the dogs had borne the same names for centuries, successive individuals carrying those names over generations since the first ancestral pack. These dogs had outlived every master they'd ever had. What better way to hunt a spectral wolf than with a pack whose lineage stretched back all the way to when the wolf was the primordial enemy of man?

Richard snapped out of his daze to find that Frau Hürlimann, clearly exasperated by his behaviour, had wheeled herself over to the kennel and was thrashing at the lock with her arthritic fists.

Richard rushed back into the deserted hotel. He wrenched the heavy axe from amongst the discarded timber in the corner under the stairs before dashing outside once more. He wheeled the old woman out of the way, took a deep breath, and swung the axe through the night and down onto the ancient padlock.

The ear-splitting impact of metal rang out from the alley and echoed back at them. Richard stumbled backwards from the momentum of the swing, but was surprised to see the padlock still very much in place. There was, however, a hideous white scar on the adjacent wall, hinting at the less-than-true aim of his swing.

He raised the axe for inspection. The ancient blade had crumpled under the force of the impact.

Frau Hürlimann closed her one eye, allowing her head to fall backwards in the timeless gesture of an exasperated woman faced with yet another example of male incompetence.

Richard was wondering what to do when he felt that tingling sensation on the back of his neck again. He turned in time to see a pair of yellow points appear in the mist at the corner of the alley.

The shadow let out a blood-curdling howl, akin to that Richard had heard in the sanatorium attic, and lunged towards him.

Richard's mind raced for solutions to this bowl-loosening turn of events, but his legs refused to move. It was like his synapses had melted under the heat of fear. The beast bore down on him like a phantom nightmare.

He raised the ruined axe out in front of him and shouted as loud he could, less a demonstration of courage than a desperate effort to drown out the snarling before those horrible teeth snapped shut inside his throat.

There was a *whoosh*. A grey canine streak flew past Richard, shattering the momentum of the oncoming wolf with a sickening *thud* of muscle. On its heels followed what appeared to be an avalanche of furred fury as several teams of dogs exploded out of the gate, which Frau Hürlimann had opened with a lethal swing of her heavy cane. The rusty lock never stood a chance.

The pack tore into the phantom, their teeth somehow finding a hold in its insubstantial form, and ripped it to pieces. Something in this apparition had stirred in them an ancestral and instinctive hatred and all cuddliness disappeared as they gashed and bit and skinned their enemy with brutal efficiency.

A second howl sounded from down the road. Save for the dogs that were actively savaging the now motionless remains of the wolf, the entire pack sped off into the night to deal with the plague of shadows invading their home. Within moments snarling fights had erupted throughout the fog-smothered town. Every street was full of flying fur and shadowy death as the dogs wreaked righteous retribution everywhere they could find one of the ghostly trespassers.

Richard would have happily fled back into the hotel to the safety of his duvet but as the slobbering dogs pounded off into the night he witnessed a singular sight, one he would subsequently struggle to describe in all its stormy glory. Frau Hürlimann, fresh from her victory over the padlock and flush with inhuman vigour, had seized the collar of one dog and was careening out of the alley swinging her cane and whooping like a Valkyrie, her wheelchair flying like a chariot towards the carnage in the town.

The proud and manly cortex somewhere at the back of Richard's mind suspected that he might be judged rather severely if he allowed a centenarian to charge into battle while he stayed behind. Then again, he thought, I'd prefer it if future generations, when watching the DVD box set of my life, didn't have to balk at a huge red disclaimer on the front reading *Contains mild peril and occasional disembowelment.*

Still . . .

His legs were already moving. He followed on the heels of the sled dogs sweeping from the hotel into the village, now alive with the howls of the undead.

*****

Graham burped contentedly, wondering what to do next.

The fête was in full swing. People jostled for room in the crowded clearing. Steam billowed from the food stands filling the wood with the salty smell of outdoor cooking. In the music tent Jürg Hodler and his band squeezed their accordions as though their lives depended on it, pausing only to drink the many beers offered up by fans. The casks of mulled wine and cider from the lowland breweries had already been replaced once and everywhere gloved hands clasped hot drinks against the chill.

Revellers had already attended an event held amongst the trees advertised as *Das Hotschrennen*, soon revealed to be a pig race. For a short time the din of Hodlerjoltz was drowned out by the shouts of spectators and the squeals of the athletes. The winner trotted across the finish line to deafening acclaim and was carried away in a shower of torn-up betting slips to receive her title and ribbon.

Graham spotted Melanie standing by the sausage hut, but quickly looked away. He'd spent weeks running after the girl and he'd had enough. Her tenacity had been enough to dampen even the resolve of the Hayles.

He inspected his pint for a moment before glancing back. Melanie was looking at him. Was that the shadow of a smile at the corner of her mouth?

The power of a woman's smile is without equal in a man's heart. The mere hint of a favourable disposition in Melanie's face was enough to ignite in Graham the emotional equivalent of a sparkplug going off inside a

Rolls Royce Merlin engine. The pistons of his heart roared into life as hope surged once again.

He stood up a little straighter, cleared his throat, and raised one eyebrow in what he judged was a seductive manner. His brain sent messages to his rowing muscles to engage immediately as Graham prepared to saunter over towards her.

Hullo, he thought, what's that noise? He was sure he'd heard a howl—and not from a dog either. Melanie looked at him curiously, wondering what was wrong with him.

It came again. This time others heard it and the hubbub died down. Some were puzzled, others anxious, none more than Herr Indergand who suspected he'd soon be on the receiving end of a great deal of annoyance for forgetting to lock the kennel.

A few men went to investigate. They were followed by most of the children and their families, who thought this was some exciting surprise event. Melanie joined the men. Graham followed, anxious not to miss an opportunity.

Seeing most of their audience departing, Jurg Hodler and the rest of Hodlerjoltz abandoned the stage. They made up the rear of the marching column and broke out into a medley of oompah favourites. The festive group of revellers, chatting and singing to each other in the wintery evening, set out to joyous musical accompaniment. As they emerged from the wood they encountered the dense fog rolling up out of the valley. The column progressed along the lit path, torches sputtering in the damp. It was the work of mere minutes to cross the fields and arrive in the village.

The children raced ahead, curious to discover what new festive treat was in store. Some of them, despite earnest supervision, had come into the possession of several lit torches and waved them about their heads as they ran. It was this tiny vanguard that arrived first in the foggy streets.

One of the smaller children wandered down a back alley, thinking he'd seen a cat. He stumbled on the cobbles but was saved from injury by copious layers of winter clothing. The boy pushed himself back up and looked around for the animal.

There was a sound behind him and he turned.

Of all his friends at school the boy was, so far, the only one who wore glasses. Through these fine optical enhancements he beheld a muscular malamute skidding into his lane. The dog was transformed beyond recognition—a wild-eyed, bloody tangle of mauled fur, its tail up and quivering and its red tongue dangling from slavering jaws.

The little boy stared wide-eyed at the panting animal, paralysed with fear.

Then a yellow-eyed shadow smashed into the dog from behind and the boy screamed as loudly as he could.

That was when chaos truly broke out.

*****

Richard raced across the village square, brandishing his axe. The blade was bent and useless but the heavy handle passed for a club and steeled his nerves. Every street in the village was alive with snarling, howling, yelping, growling, yapping, snapping, and yowling. Teeth flared in the darkness. Feral yellow eyes raked across the night leaving hellish vapour trails behind them. Creatures emerged repeatedly from the billowing darkness and made for Richard, but each time one of the dogs slammed into them from the side, from behind, and once even from between Richard's own legs, punching it out of the air and setting on it like a hellhound. Everywhere he looked Richard saw four-legged combatants pursuing each other through the streets.

He rounded a corner and found himself in the village square. All was anarchy. The foggy streets teemed with howling infants. Parents everywhere were screaming for their misplaced offspring. Wild eyes flashed amongst the shadows, pursued by the snarling sled dogs. Tufts of fur blew across the square and discarded torches sizzled and fizzed on the damp cobblestones as panicked revellers clattered over them, sending them flying in a spray of sparks and smoke. A bass drum, abandoned when the members of Hodlerjoltz took to their heels, rolled slowly across the cobblestones and collided with the fountain with a hollow *bong*.

Richard spotted Kaspar, brandishing his walking stick at the shadows. Dino the waiter was trying to calm some hysterical children. An apoplectic mother ran into Meinrad Indergand and knocked him over, only to find herself met by Josephine Indergand's indignant wrath. Fosco, still wearing his high-visibility sash and army reserve fatigues, shouted to Richard across the square but Richard couldn't make it out. Fosco started towards him, but tripped on a discarded torch and stumbled.

Richard was about to go help him but a noise behind made him stop.

He turned. By the light of a streetlamp he spied one of the wraith-like wolves, half-visible in the shadows. It raised its ragged muzzle, sniffed the air, then fixed its yellow gaze on Richard. A ripple of anticipation ran down its flanks.

Suddenly the haze around Richard turned blinding white. From across the square came the roar of a freshly renovated engine. Richard had time to identify Graham, white-knuckled and grimacing behind the wheel of the little red car, before the entire thing flew through the air and careened into the wraith. There its flight was arrested by the wall of the building with a sound like a portaloo being hit by a freight train. The noble vehicle staggered backwards in a mangled heap and crumpled onto itself with an air of definite finality.

In the second it took Richard to collect his senses, the wolf had vanished.

'Graham!' he yelled.

'SAINT GEORGE AND ENGLAND!' was the enthusiastic if somewhat disorientated response from the ruined car.

'Are you all right?' Richard grappled with the door handle.

'Did I get the thing?' asked Graham. Richard managed to yank the door open. 'What the hell was that anyway? And why are all these bloody dogs howling in the streets?'

Amazingly, Graham was intact. The car, however, was a tragedy. The force of the impact had pulverized everything that wasn't welded together and shattered everything else. The vehicle lay bathed in mist like a corpse on a battlefield. From the cracked fuselage came a feeble hiss. A single remaining headlight flickered, then went out with a *plink*.

'I think the car took most of the damage.' Graham prodded himself. 'Good thing I remembered to wear my seatbelt.'

His movements were unsteady and he needed help from Richard. They staggered a short distance and collapsed onto one of the benches lining the square. The death throes of the engine mingled with the faint tinkling of running water in the nearby canal.

Richard's heart skipped a beat when he spotted one of the wraiths a short distance away. But it fled, pursued by a hissing, demonic silhouette that looked suspiciously like Berlioz the cat. The shadow wolf tried dodging down an alley, where a team of sled dogs was waiting. It didn't have long to regret its mistake.

There was now such uproar that they had to shout to be heard.

'Wolves, you say?' yelled Graham.

Richard nodded. He could explain the specifics later. Maybe.

Graham stared at the mayhem. 'I didn't think there were this many wolves west of Poland. And what's this about the old woman?' He cupped his hands around his ears as a team of dogs galloped past, howling as they went.

'The huskies were her idea.' Richard grinned breathlessly. 'She saved us all from the wolves!'

'Rabid dogs, more like,' retorted Graham, though not without admiration. 'Never seen such nasty-looking mongrels. Must be a pack of escaped strays. Where's the old bat? We should congratulate her!'

'Dunno. But I think I saw old Fosco take a bit of a tumble. Where's he got to?'

Both men jumped as several deafening gunshots rang out across the square. Silvio Indergand's platoon had appeared amongst the villagers and, instead of delighted surprise and embraces from various family members, encountered screaming children and lunging feral shadows. Rather than awaiting orders the young men had used their initiative and begun to shoot wildly into the fog, ignoring the bellowing from their commanding officers. This did little to calm the terrified populace and the din rose in a crescendo of screams, whizzing bullets, and growling streaks of grey fur.

Across the square Councillors Aufdermauer and Fürgler tried to quell the commotion—in vain. Silvio found himself separated from his unit and bumped into Melanie, who wheeled on him with surprising ferocity. The two now appeared to be having an argument.

Richard and Graham sat on their bench, contemplating the chaos. With sightings of the hideous wolf-like creatures becoming increasingly infrequent, many of the dogs retired from the fight and reverted to their innocuous natures. One of them took advantage of a lull to urinate on the fresh carcass of the car.

Graham watched a toddler run screaming past their bench, closely pursued by its frantic mother. 'You know,' he said, 'I reckon these village fêtes aren't all they're cracked up to be.'

Across the square Melanie and Councilwoman Berger had collected a group of weeping children and were trying to herd them into the communal offices, but were being prevented from doing so by the soldiers. Silvio wanted to help but Melanie kept batting him away with harsh words and obscene gestures, clearly wishing the young man gone.

Graham inhaled sharply and flexed his shoulders in a manner usually carried out on screen by someone talking about "stiffening the sinews" and similar things.

'My lady love is in peril,' he announced. 'I must go to her.'

He stepped forward in a vigorous, decisive, and extremely heroic manner, right into the empty space above the dwindling stream. He then proceeded to hurtle to the bottom with such majestic swiftness that the icy water couldn't help but receive him with due deference. The resulting *sploosh* was gratifyingly celebratory.

Richard rushed to the edge and beheld the sodden wreckage in the darkness below. 'Bloody hell, are you ok?'

'Eeuuuarrgh . . .' was the as-yet undecided reply.

Richard was trying to figure out the best way to descend the steep sides of the canal when he looked up and saw Melanie running towards him, torch in hand. She reached the opposing ledge and gazed down in turn at the ruin of gallantry, gurgling as the water splashed around him.

'Er,' Richard began, 'I think he's had a bit of a fall. How do we . . .'

Melanie ignored him, crouched down, and jumped the entire five-foot drop in pitch darkness, landing expertly in an inch of water. She waded over to inspect Graham.

A familiar whoop drew Richard's attention to a tartan-wrapped figure framed by the light of the café across the square.

Frau Hürlimann watched the chaos with indescribable satisfaction. At last! The massacre she'd dreamed of had come to pass. Admittedly it wasn't the guests who were being torn to shreds, but unleashing righteous destruction upon the Devil's hounds would have to do. Her grip on the dog's collar had slipped and she'd come to skidding halt a few paces from Fosco's shop. Loath as she was to miss out on the fight, she'd obtained for herself a front-row seat. She observed as the horrified crowds milled around in the dark and was delighted by the occasional flash of teeth in the darkness and the bullets whizzing past. Any rabid creatures that came too close received a skull-shattering blow from her cane. Nobody paid her the least bit of attention and she had an absolute ball.

As the last wolfish howls were silenced and replaced by screaming, the old woman judged the best part of the evening to be over. She began to think of returning to the hotel. Her arm ached from the effort of smashing the lock and her eyesight had begun to blur.

Dammit, she thought, as a screaming child darted past her still clutching a half-eaten gingerbread man; all this excitement's made me dizzy. Still, beats sitting alone by the fire.

Someone came to stand at her elbow, though with her fuzzy vision she didn't recognise him. She'd already decided to ignore him when the man addressed her directly.

'What a mess, eh?' he remarked.

She grunted. She was enjoying herself and felt unusually predisposed towards conversation. 'Yep. There'll be a hell of a mess to clean up tomorrow.'

The man laughed. She liked his laugh. It was nice.

'You said it! And it's all thanks to you, Annie.'

This gave her pause. No one had used that name in a long time. Twisting in her chair she beheld the man standing next to her. As her vision cleared she recognised him at last. Her mouth popped open with astonishment and he grinned at her.

From across the square Richard recognised Frau Hürlimann and pointed. 'There she is! Told you she'd be fine, look at her: sitting there cool as a cucumber.'

Graham burbled nonsensically as Melanie dragged him from the canal.

Richard squinted in the darkness and frowned. 'Hey, does she seem all right to you? She looks a bit weird . . .'

Frau Hürlimann was taken aback by the appearance of the man, but quickly found her words. 'You sodding fool, where have you been all this time? I've been waiting for sodding ages!'

He smiled apologetically. 'Sorry about that old girl, couldn't be helped. Can't rush this sort of thing you know. Still, I made it in the end, didn't I?'

His voice warmed her heart but she continued to act annoyed. 'Well, you took your sweet time about it, I must say. Bit rich to be gone so long and then to suddenly pop up out of nowhere and expect me to be all pleased. Look around you! Look at these useless clods you left me with, running about in the dark like clowns!'

'Oh really? And where are they all now?'

She looked around. Where before there had been a darkened village square streaked with hurtling shadows and chaos, she now beheld a magnificently lit room full of laughing figures. Someone was playing a fiddle. Her eyes widened as she watched them dance, their icy blue softening as she heard the music.

How very like Klaus, she thought. He knew she could never resist a good party.

In his corner the fiddle player looked up. The candlelight reflected off his bald, angular head and his blue eyes glinted knowingly behind their spectacles. He struck up a new tune, a fast and merry dance that brought the room roaring to its feet.

Despite herself Frau Hürlimann smiled and, as the man beside her caught the glint in her eyes, he laughed all the more. The next moment her hand was in his and her newly youthful legs had kicked aside the blanket.

Richard barely managed to catch her before she fell forward out of her chair and onto the pavement. In another minute the doctor had been called for, but by that time she was too busy dancing to care.

BEGINNINGS
CHAPTER THIRTY-THREE

Royal Hallamshire Hospital — Sheffield, 1993

R MATHERN IS it? John Mathern?'

The man turned around. 'Yes?'

'Hello Mr Mathern,' said the nurse. 'I thought it was you!'

'I'm sorry, have we met?'

'Well, dear, you might not remember. I'm Jackie, the nurse who helped deliver your son. You know, following that whole tricky business with the membrane.'

'Oh! I'm sorry.' John gave Jackie a distracted smile. 'Didn't recognise you, what with the surgical mask.'

'Makes sense. Tell you what: I'll take it off so we can have a proper chat. How are you, love?'

'Oh, very well thank you. Helen's been offered a post at the university and we've finally had our mortgage approved. We found a little house just outside Dungworth, about a half hour's drive away, with lots of space for Richard to run about.'

Jackie beamed. 'How lovely! How is the little darling?'

'Well, actually that's why we're here.' John gave the ward a preoccupied glance. 'Richard's been suffering from what seem like dizzy spells. We're worried it's some kind of allergic reaction. He and his mother are in there now with the doctor. I just popped out to make a call.'

'Poor thing. Can I get you a cuppa while you wait?'

'No, thanks. They've been in there a long time. Maybe it's more serious than we thought.' John scratched the hair at the nape of his neck. 'We've known Nick since before medical school; he seemed the obvious choice. But he's asked for my neurological records . . .'

'Don't you worry, Love.' Jackie patted his arm. 'Dr Miles will sort out your little boy, sure enough.'

'I know, it's just . . . He's always been a little—Nick!'

299

'Hullo John!' The white-coated doctor waved. He turned to the worried-looking woman beside him. 'Over here, Helen, I found John.' He knelt to smile at the small child holding her hand. 'There, that wasn't anything to be afraid of, was it lad? Jackie, would you mind popping down to EEG and giving this note to Bruce?'

'Right you are Doctor, back in a tick.'

'Ta.' Dr Miles rubbed his hands. 'Now, Mr and Mrs Mathern . . . Funny, it's odd saying that out loud. Seems only yesterday that you were just John and Helen, necking in the college bar. And now you've got a sprog of your own! How time flies, eh?'

John leaned forward. 'Is it serious, Nick?'

'Probably not, but I want to give young Richard here an MRI just in case.'

Helen wrung her hands. 'Oh, John . . .'

John put his hand on her shoulder. 'It's all right, Helen. Richard, why don't you go play with the dusty window over there, ok? Now Nick, why does he need an MRI if it's not serious?'

'Ah, well, let's see here . . . Your records indicate that your father was prone to seizures?'

'I think so. I was too young to remember much before he died.' John's gaze strayed across the hallway to his son, who was dutifully inspecting the windowsill.

Dr Miles flipped through his clipboard. 'Well, what with the family history I think Richard might have a mild case of epilepsy. I want to poke around inside his brains a little to have a better look.'

Helen gripped her husband's hand. 'Oh, John!'

'It's fine dear. Yes Richard, that's a very nice dead spider. Why don't you go show it to the other children? There's a good boy.'

Dr Miles stepped aside to let a gurney pass. 'Don't worry, John, the basic tests indicate a healthy constitution. We'll just pop him in the big tube and have a wittle around for anything abnormal. You know, aneurisms, signs of brain trauma, a cheeky tumour maybe . . .'

Helen seized her husband's arm, too appalled to speak.

'Listen, Nick,' John growled. 'If you don't stop scaring Helen we're going to need a new doctor and so are you.'

Dr Miles took a step back. 'I was only joking! Christ, but you people have tightened up since school. Must be parenthood. Mind you, I always believed marriage was the death of youth.'

John rubbed his temples. 'Just give us the diagnosis, you berk.'

'Relax, Richard's absolutely fine. Probably. Almost certainly.'

'Dear God.'

'There's very little reason for concern. We're just doing some routine procedures. At the very worst your son might have to take some medication once in a while to stop himself from falling over and dying.'

'Well, thank God you did eight years at medical school,' muttered John. 'Otherwise you might've turned out to be totally unprofessional.'

'Ah,' exclaimed Dr Miles, 'there's Jackie. That probably means Bruce has got the EEG ready. And here's young Richard. Look, he's brought a friend! Now laddie, want to take that big syringe of yours and come down to the lab to ride the fun machine?'

John wheeled around. 'Richard, put that down! You don't know where it's been!'

'Your father's right, best give it here, lad.' Dr Miles took charge of the offending item. 'Here, Jackie, perhaps you'd better return it to the ward. Come on then, chaps! The lift's down the hall; we can all go together. It'll be fun! Look, Richard's already excited.'

'At least one of us is.' John eyes followed his toddler as he wandered around the ward. 'I can't believe they actually gave you a licence.'

'Ah,' sighed Dr Miles, 'the mysteries of modern medicine. I like to think I bring a certain *je ne sais quoi* to the tedium of clinical practice.'

'Whatever. We're going to wait by the lift. Christ, Richard! Leave that alone! Helen, get him away from the body bag!'

'Anon anon, dearest John.' Dr Miles turned back to Jackie. 'Now, where did I put those files?'

'Right here. You know, sometimes you can be a cruel man, Doctor.'

'The world is a cruel place, Jackie. And yet, we must all soldier on. By the way, did anyone enter my office while I was examining the boy?'

'I don't believe so, Doctor. Why?'

'Well, I stepped out for a second to fetch his parents' records and when I came back he was babbling about some bloke called Jones or James or something. Said he walked in just after I left and was asking for directions.'

'How odd. I was standing just outside the door. Not a soul went in that I didn't know about.'

'Vivid imagination, I suppose. Sign of a sound and healthy mind! Let's hope so, anyway. I can never remember, are hallucinations bad? Guess we'd best pop downstairs and find out! We'll be back after the scan. Please have the records ready on my desk.'

'Right you are. Don't scare them too much, now.'

'Wouldn't dream of it.' Dr Miles turned and nearly bumped into a tall young man in scrubs. 'Whoops, excuse me Alex! Didn't see you there.'

'No worries, Nick.' The intern smiled. 'Hullo Jackie, where's the B-O-D-Y? Someone said he was scaring the kids.'

301

The nurse pointed. 'Just over there, Alex. Probably one of your fellow interns, you're always leaving things where they ought not be.'

'Cheers. Don't know what he's doing in the paediatric ward. Some wazzock probably popped up to the roof for a fag and forgot about him. Bloody interns! Speaking as an expert, obviously.'

'No need to rush, dear, I know for a fact that the people currently waiting for the lift wouldn't want to share it with this bloke. Take the next one.'

'Sure thing, catch you later.' Alex sidled over to the gurney when he heard the sound of high heels striding down the corridor and glanced up. 'Hey, hey Lilly! A pleasure as always, and may I say you're looking particularly ravishing today.'

The head of paediatrics skidded to halt before him. 'What in God's name is that thing doing in my paediatric ward?'

Alex flashed her his most winning smile. 'No idea, Lilly, looks like someone forgot about poor Mr Jones here on their way down to the fridge. I'm taking him there now.'

'See that you do. I don't know what we'd say if the parents saw it.' Lilly pointed imperiously towards the lifts. 'Get it out of here!'

'Anything you say. Any thoughts about Saturday?'

Lilly rolled her eyes. 'For the last time, you Australian creep, I'm not going on a date with you.'

Alex gave her a hurt look. 'I'm from New Zealand.'

'Whatever. Leave me alone.'

'Why Lilly, why must you break my heart like this?'

'Well, for one thing you're too young for me, and for another you're a moron.'

'I love you, Lilly!'

'Shut up and go away. Now, has anyone seen my big syringe?'

GOODBYES
CHAPTER THIRTY-FOUR

ICHARD STOOD UNDER the arcade of the village square, watching the funeral procession. Behind the white-robed priest six men bore Frau Hürlimann's coffin on their shoulders. Dino the waiter was one; his cheeks were wet. There followed a crowd of thirty or forty, small enough until one realised that all were from the village and therefore by sheer scarcity their presence augmented in value.

Madame Berger brought up the rear of the procession, but soon broke away and hastened back to the communal offices. There were several vehicles parked outside, including a van bearing the logo of the Historical Preservation Society. News of the cave paintings had spread fast and various entities had descended on the village clamouring for access. The councilwoman looked positively radiant.

'Herr Mathern!'

Richard looked up to find that Herr Fürgler too had retraced his steps and was standing before him.

'Councilman,' Richard replied warily.

Fürgler held up his hands in appeasement. 'Not to worry, I am only wanting to congratulate you on the discovery of the cave. It is wonderful, wonderful! I am visiting it this afternoon. They have shown me photos but I must see it myself. Such history! Such prestige! Such tourism! All thanks to you.'

'No threats about interfering with local business then?'

Fürgler smiled. 'On the contrary. I am chairman of the local council for farmers and owners of livestock, acting on behalf of the commune who owns the land. We are already planning a visitor centre and archaeological museum—with souvenir gift shop!'

Richard's expression softened. 'Sorry your ski-lift project was cancelled.'

Fürgler waved this aside. 'Who cares? This is better, less dangerous for the ecology. My colleagues are very pleased.'

'Glad to hear it.' Richard turned to the procession. 'Where's Fosco? I saw him fall the night of the attack.'

'A small abrasion, nothing more. I believe he has left for a recuperative holiday.'

Kaspar nodded at Richard and Fürgler from amongst the crowd as he passed. So affable was the councilman that he overcame his dislike for the weather prophet and returned his greeting with a wave.

A small group of people rounded the corner and approached. 'Ah!' exclaimed Fürgler, turning towards the assembled faces. 'Meet my family!'

His wife greeted Richard regally from under a cloud of blonde curls and five children mumbled in greeting. Only four were standing. As Richard looked down at a smiling little girl in her wheelchair, Fürgler's insistence on the importance of a toboggan run suddenly made sense.

Fürgler sniffed the air contentedly. 'Our first expenditure is a family holiday. I am thinking the ocean can be beneficial for the limbs, yes?'

Richard nodded. 'So I hear.'

'You will be leaving us soon?'

'Graham and I are going today.'

Fürgler nodded. 'In case I do not see you,' he reached out a large hand, 'goodbye, Herr Mathern. Safe travels.'

Richard shook it and managed a smile.

He returned to the hotel to find Graham lying on his bed, clothed and ready for their imminent departure. Various bits of him were wrapped in bandages that the doctor deemed "utterly unnecessary", but there had been a tacit agreement that Graham deserved some mark of distinction for his bravery during the night of the attack. His packed bags stood by the door.

Richard perched on the end of the bed. 'How do you feel?'

'I've felt better.'

'Does it hurt much?'

'Only when I breathe, so about ninety-nine per cent of the time. Otherwise it's like being on holiday.'

'Well, at least you're not complaining about it.'

'I know, I'm positively stoic.' Graham struggled into a sitting position. 'How was the service?'

Richard walked over to the window. 'I didn't go,' he admitted. 'I meant to, but I stayed outside and watched the procession when they came out.'

'I don't blame you.' Graham swung his legs out with a groan. 'Funerals aren't my cup of tea either.' He grimaced as he pulled on his jacket. 'You should really finish packing. The car's going to be here soon. I'd help, but

I'm not feeling my usual athletic self. Maybe I could fold your socks or something?'

'I'm not coming,' said Richard.

Graham looked up in surprise. 'What do you mean?'

Richard sat down in the armchair. 'I'm not going back to London. Not yet, anyway. The room's paid for until next week. I thought I might stay here for a few days then travel around the place a bit, maybe see some of the sights.'

Graham prepared to argue but, seeing Richard's face, realised there was no point. 'You gonna be ok?'

Richard shrugged. 'I think I need some time to think. You don't mind, do you?'

'Don't be daft, course not. This way I get two seats to myself on the flight home.'

The windowpanes began to rattle, heralding the arrival of an enormous vehicle in the driveway outside. Richard went to investigate.

Graham winced and rubbed his chest. 'Is that our car, or have a posse of loggers arrived in a lorry?'

Richard smiled, suddenly feeling much better. 'It seems that the car hire company you called is very local indeed.'

Graham hobbled to the window. Down in the driveway a young woman in attractive sports leggings and a pink jacket leant casually against the hood of the largest, blackest SUV he'd ever seen.

Richard chuckled. 'Maybe your selfless exploits have a silver lining after all.'

Graham's eyes widened. 'It's her!' He waved down at Melanie. She waved back and smiled.

Graham's breath was fogging up the glass. He tore himself away. 'I must go.' He made a beeline for the exit, but hesitated in the doorway. 'You're sure you'll be all right?'

Richard shrugged. 'Sure. Don't forget your luggage.'

Graham lingered, one hand on the door handle.

'You know,' he said, 'I get the feeling this trip hasn't been all that straightforward for you, like there's been something on your mind the whole time. You know you could tell me if there's something you want to get off your chest, right?'

Richard looked at the picture of the old man on the wall for a moment or two. 'Maybe when we're back in London.'

The car's horn blasted a few times. Graham quivered at the reminder of who was waiting for him downstairs, but still looked concerned.

Richard stood and held his hands up in reassurance. 'I'll be fine, seriously. Now go, before she decides to leave you here with me.'

Graham grinned and spread his arms, bandages forgotten. They hugged through their bulky anoraks, slapping each other heartily on the back a few times. Richard pulled away and they shook hands.

'Here's to a job well done,' said Graham.

'A job well done,' agreed Richard. 'Pub celebrations when we get back?'

'Obviously.'

The horn sounded again. 'Here,' said Richard, 'I'll help you carry your stuff downstairs.'

Suzy the dog lay in the foyer with her head on one paw and gazed at the open door in half-curiosity as the two men loaded Graham's bags into the car. One got in and the other watched the car drive away. Richard stayed in the driveway for a while, breathing in the air and surveying the now-empty meadow across the road.* As he stepped over Suzy's body she weighed the decision of whether to beg for treats or not. His general demeanour did not appear promising and the only smells she could make out on him were soap, old wool, and disappointment.

With a yawn she settled back down onto the carpet for a nap.

*****

Consider Alistair Dawes: his exterior, one of patrician solemnity. He stands at the window overlooking the city with a preoccupied gaze. Occasionally he removes a piece of paper from his pocket and rereads it. His pale brow is furrowed, as though by some incomprehension, but in his eyes glows the light of predatory certainty.

Now observe the young man hurrying into the private lift downstairs. Luther Aberfinchley is not as we remember him. Hair askew, beads of sweat inching down the collar of his tailored shirt, his pallor is of a totally different variety to that of Dawes.

---

* Jerome the Goat, knowing an opportunity when he saw one, had escaped under the cover of mayhem and fled far into the wild, reindeer costume and all. He would eventually meet a wandering herd of ibex who, awed by his superior intellect, impressive set of felt antlers, and amusingly loud neck-jewellery, decided to make him their king. Under the wise rule of Jerome the First they would come to occupy the newly protected area surrounding the cave wherein were housed the precious paintings, thereby becoming a herd of special designation entitled to protection from hunting. Their wholesome presence would also contribute to ridding the area of the unnatural traces of the cave's former sentinels, for in their search for salty deliciousness squeezed from the rocks they managed to lick virtually all remaining traces of the black-lined wolves clean off the walls before someone from the council discovered and evicted them.

Luther is afraid.

The lift's ascent seemed interminable. Luther thought he could feel the very foundations of the building tremble around him. But it wasn't No. 31 Dratford Place trembling; it was only Luther. In fact, the pigeons outside had been remarking all morning that, for the first time in months, the building felt pleasantly stable.

Bing.

Luther exited the lift, breezed past Julian's desk, and reached for the heavy handle, preparing to charge through into his office. Instead, the door's parabola was abruptly arrested by the bolt and Luther's momentum carried his face straight into the wood with a meaty *thud.*

Julian kept his eyes resolutely on his computer screen, trying not to smile.

'My door's locked,' said Luther, massaging the side of his face.

'Is it?' replied Julian innocently, eyes still on his screen. 'Perhaps you need to pull the knob a little harder.'

Julian looked up to find his boss's face inches from his, resembling one of those gargoyles from the angrier side of the cathedral gable.

'Unlock that door at once,' snarled Luther, 'and then report to Personnel. I'm having you transferred somewhere nasty.'

'Such as where?' sneered Julian, 'your mother's house?'

Luther seethed. 'Open the door, you fucking faggot!'

'I'm afraid that's impossible, sir.' Dawes emerged from the side passage. 'I have the key.'

Luther held Julian's gaze for a moment. 'Very well.' He straightened, waiting for Dawes to unlock his office.

Dawes stayed where he was. 'I'm very sorry, sir.'

Before Luther could ask what he was sorry about, Dawes stepped aside. From behind him emerged the terrifying Mick, Head of Security.

'Grab 'im, lads,' growled Mick.

For a brief instant Luther was aware of two shadowy figures either side of him before the world was turned upside-down as he was lifted bodily off the floor.

'Excuse me,' said Julian over the yelps, 'it appears Mrs Europa Aberfinchley has evaded the front desk staff and is making her way upstairs in Lift No. 3.'

Dawes nodded. 'Best take young Master Aberfinchley down the other way, Mick. It'll only upset her to see him this way.'

Dawes handed the key to Alice, who was observing the proceedings with unholy smugness. 'Please unlock the door, Alice.' Then, as an afterthought, 'Best go head off Europa, Julian. Buy us a minute or two.'

The order came none too soon. Julian only just had time to hoof it down the corridor to Lift No. 3 and adopt a pose of casual nonchalance before

Europa burst onto the landing with the white heat of a cat escaping a pet carrier.

She extended a heavily manicured fingernail towards the affable secretary. 'You!'

Julian looked up from his phone. 'Excuse me, Madam. Were you addressing me?'

'Where's Alistair?'

Julian gestured gallantly to the comfortable chairs. 'If you would be so good as to wait, I'm sure Mr Dawes will be back shortly.'

From down the corridor came a squeal of distress. Europa's nostrils flared. Julian moved sideways but she was too fast and *whooshed* past before he could stop her.

'I'll deal with you later!' she hissed over her shoulder.

By now the commotion in front of the head office had attracted quite a crowd. They looked on with undisguised delight as Luther was pulled backwards kicking and screaming across the vestibule into the waiting arms of the lift beyond.

'Dawes!' he cried. But Dawes was implacable.

'I'm sorry, sir,' he said again.

Luther managed to hook his fingers onto the doorframe and clung there desperately, but was quickly dislodged. Even so Mick and his two goons barely had time to stuff him into the lift before Europa erupted into their midst. The doors slid shut with a gleeful *bing*.

'Alistair!' cried Europa. 'What is the meaning of this? And what's with the barrage of emails I received this morning? Where have Loo-Loo's shares gone?'

Much like the French at Trafalgar, Dawes turned to find a lethal presence bearing down on him. But the luck of Nelson was not with Europa; it was with him.

'Hello, Europa. I'm afraid things are undergoing a bit of a change at the moment.' The sound of Luther's hysterical weeping drifted up through the elevator shaft.

'Bit of a change, eh?' fumed Europa. 'It's a bloody junta! How did you get access to Loo-Loo's private investment platform?'

'I didn't,' replied Dawes innocently. 'I imagine young Luther must have had one of his waves of inspiration and embarked upon some new, innovative strategy. Apparently this involved selling a large percentage of his shares to,' Dawes consulted his smartphone, 'Mr Franz-Xavier von Guggenbühl of 11 Grimselstrasse, Rotzenwil.'

Dawes removed his spectacles. 'Doubtless whatever brilliant undertaking this presages will soon become apparent. Meanwhile, Luther has ceded his authority insofar as the company is concerned.'

Europa seethed, partly with anger and partly because she hadn't had her morning cocktail. 'What makes you think you'll get away with this?' she snarled.

Dawes gave her an even look. 'It's all in service to the company.'

Europa thrust her face into his. 'I'll flay you for this, Alistair. I don't care what you say or what sordid little scheme you're attempting to pull off. We own the majority stake. I'll bring this whole place down on top of you.'

She turned and addressed the assembly. 'Listen up, you gormless twits: I'm in charge now and my first decision as Acting Chief of Operations is to have this treacherous louse,' she waved at Dawes, 'removed from the premises.'

'I'm afraid that's a little premature, Mrs Aberfinchley,' said Leticia Crowley, emerging from the office.

'And whoooo,' growled Europa 'are you?'

'I'm afraid your boy's got himself rather tangled up,' continued Leticia, 'and unfortunately the net he's caught in is made of silk.' She leaned forward. 'In case it wasn't clear,' she whispered loudly, 'in this metaphor, I'm the silk.'

Europa's nostrils flared. Leticia reached out her hand and Alice placed a wad of paper in it.

'I'm terribly sorry to have to say this,' said Leticia, not sounding sorry at all, 'but evidence has been brought to my attention concerning the legitimacy of young Luther's claim to his stake in the company. This rather throws a spanner in the recent case of his late father's allocation of his shares—many of which, as Mr Dawes correctly states, have recently been sold off anyway by Luther himself. Obviously we'll have to wait for everything to be assessed, but until then I think it's best that Mr Aberfinchley devolve all responsibilities as chair to the next most important investor—after Mr von Guggenbühl, of course.'

Europa smirked. 'That would be Ahmid Sardharwalla,' she declared, 'and as Aberfinchley Inc.'s sole legal representative in attendance I must request you and the rest of your little clan of subservients vacate the premises immediately. Ahmid, meet me in Luther's office in five minutes.'

Ahmid quaked visibly.

'Wrong again, I'm afraid,' said Leticia. 'Taking into account recent developments, the next largest shareholder is no longer Mr Sardharwalla, but . . .' She pulled out her spectacles and peered in a scholarly manner at her papers. ' . . . Alistair Dawes.'

Europa was speechless. She stared first at Dawes, then at Leticia, then back at Dawes.

He shrugged. 'I did try to warn you,' he said.

Europa whirled on him once again. 'I'll fight you,' she hissed. 'This won't stand. And as for you,' she turned on Leticia, who smiled amicably, 'you'd better be ready for the most unpleasant court case of your life. I've got the best lawyers in the country and a First from Oxford!'

'Mine's from Cambridge,' replied Leticia smoothly. 'I fancy my chances.'

Europa stormed off down the corridor. The assembled staff, as well as the portraits on the wall, observed her departure with whole-hearted approval.

Leticia came to stand by Dawes. 'I've already spoken to our people,' she said. 'If the stuff you gave us is legitimate, I reckon we've got a hell of a shot.'

An exquisitely designed eyebrow rose in a shadow of concern. 'It is legitimate, isn't it?' whispered Leticia. 'You haven't been indulging in one of your little swaps, have you? Not with this?'

'Lettie, it's as real as you or I. I don't know how, but I'll swear to it.'

'Good enough for me.'

Alice appeared, holding what looked like the pelt of a dead animal.

'Ah, dear Alice,' said Leticia, 'always here when I need you. Thank you so much.' Dawes held up the coat and Leticia slid into expertly. 'Do let me know when you're tired of this lot,' she added, still addressing Alice. 'I'd happily recommend you to my old partners at the firm. Sadly they're a bit overstocked on PAs at the moment but something's sure to come up.'

'Actually,' said Alice, 'I do have a degree in Commercial Law if that's any help.'

'Really?' said Leticia delightedly.

'Really?' echoed Julian, less delightedly.

'Yes,' said Alice. 'I took this job after graduation because the money was good and I needed some work experience while paying off my student loans. But I'm ready to move on to something more stimulating.'

'In that case, go see Anselm Phist in the morning. Tell him I sent you.'

'Thank you so much, Lady Crowley.'

'Don't mention it. Now, which of these innumerable lifts is the one that will deliver me from this vortex of steel and wood panelling? Having met Mrs Aberfinchley in person I'd like to start on this case sooner rather than later.'

Dawes left Julian to show her out, then headed down the corridor to his office. Alice spared a moment to stick her tongue out at Julian before falling into step behind Dawes. Outside, senior staff broke out into a raucous rendition of "Yes! We Have No Bananas".

'Congratulations, Alice,' said Dawes as he sat down. 'You will be sorely missed.'

'Thank you. I suppose you'll be wanting those papers now?'

'In a moment, Alice. Leave me alone for a moment, please.'

She retreated, closing the door gently behind her.

Dawes ran a hand over his desk and eased into the welcoming leather of the chair. He closed his eyes, allowing its ergonomic curves to embrace him.

He removed the paper from his pocket and, though he now knew it by heart, perused once more the printed email in his hand. It read thus:

My dearest Alistair,

Circumstances being what they are, you will no doubt be surprised to receive this. Let me assure you, your astonishment is nothing compared to the pains I took to get it to you, so please give it nothing less than your customary assiduousness. And, when you're done, send a cleaner down to Desk 5 in IT; the keyboard on this computer is positively filthy.

Luther is a shit. I've always suspected this and I dare say you would have agreed had it not been for your unquestionable professionalism and loyalty. However it is only now that I realise quite how loathsome the little piece of refuse truly is. I shudder to think that such a turd could ever have issued from my (otherwise irreproachable) loins. But then, parenting has never been my family's greatest talent.

I have therefore taken the decision to disinherit him utterly. I've attached the necessary documents (Appendix A., witnessed by my notary and back-dated in customary fashion) and a new will (Appendix B., likewise) to exclude him from any position of responsibility within our company or belonging within my family. Your own commendable efforts should take care of the rest.

Furthermore I enclose a number of cheques to be conveyed to the inestimable ladies listed in Appendix C., a courtesy I was unable to carry out myself due to the sudden nature of my disappearance.

I am truly sorry to have put you to any inconvenience, my dearest friend, and for endangering what we built through my own short-sightedness. Please accept Appendix D. as my formal apology.

Yours affectionately,
Desmond, Lord Aberfinchley (deceased)

P.S: Sorry about the ornaments.

For a short time the office basked in a quiet peace, safe in the knowledge that it sailed once again under the captaincy of sanity.

There was a faint noise as the door opened. Dawes looked around to see Julian enter the room.

The secretary smiled. 'It would seem the rot has been cut out.'

Dawes sighed. 'Indeed it has, Julian. The healing may now commence.'

Julian approached and perched on the corner of the desk. 'I wish you'd told me it was today.' He produced a USB stick from his pocket. 'These are some recorded conversations between Luther and Alice we were planning to give to the police as part of her harassment case.'

Dawes reached over and picked it up. 'I couldn't tell you, Julian, or anyone. The important thing was for everything to happen at the proper time, without forewarning.' He placed the stick in his pocket. 'Still, these may still be useful for the upcoming hearings.'

'The company's still in trouble though, isn't it?'

'Yes. There is much to be done. But now there will be someone with a fully functioning brain running things around here.'

'Come off it,' said Julian, 'you've always been the one running things.'

Dawes' eye strayed down to Appendix D., which nestled in his lap. It explained how Lord Desmond Aberfinchley's legacy had been fraudulently misattributed to his son and how, except for those shares now safely in the hands of the unsuspecting Franz-Xavier von Güggenbühl—including those most likely to come under the scrutiny of UK law—all former holdings were now the rightful property of his friend and business partner Alistair Dawes.

The document shone with the brilliance of fresh paper. It was admirably set off by the aged ivory of the envelope beneath it, which contained a faded and venerable birth certificate on which the name *Lidney* was faintly legible.

For the first time since we've been acquainted with him, we witness Dawes smiling a smile of genuine pleasure. It suits him surprisingly well.

'I think I'd like to take a holiday,' said Dawes.

'What about the hearings? Won't you be needed here?'

'Possibly, but it will take Leticia some time to prepare the case. I think we should leave Ahmid in charge for a while. He'll like that.'

Julian grinned. 'I'll book your flights. Where to?'

Julian thought for a moment, thinking.

'Somewhere with mountains, I think.'

*****

Downstairs in the private lobby the lift doors opened with a discreet *whoosh*.

Allerby the doorman looked up from his book, but no one came out; the lift was empty. This struck him as odd, since the lift was key-activated and the few people who did have keys would hardly send empty lifts to spook him.

He sighed, put down his book, and crossed the lobby to investigate. He failed to note the tall man in the grey suit striding across the lobby, or the gentle hum of the maroon car that had just pulled up outside.

The Bentley's passenger door snapped shut. Its plush interior glowed with familiar warmth. The driver observed his passenger in the rear-view mirror.

'Evening, sir,' he said. 'All done for the day?'

The grey man smiled. 'Yes, all finished.'

For a moment he looked perplexed. 'You're new, aren't you? Where's Austin? I'd hoped to see him before I left.'

'I'm afraid Austin's shift ended early today, sir,' answered the driver. 'I'm his temporary replacement.'

The grey man looked out the window. 'I suppose that's to be expected.' His smile returned. 'Do you have any music up there?'

The driver waved an Ipod. 'Anything you like, sir. What takes your fancy?'

'Have you anything jaunty and fruit-related?'

'Certainly, sir.'

The grey man leaned back and closed his eyes. One re-opened a crack. 'What's your name, by the way?'

In the rear-view mirror a pair of very blue eyes gazed evenly back at him. 'You may call me Nubby, sir.'

The eye closed once again. 'Right-o, Nubby. Time to be on our way, I think.'

The driver reached down and put the Bentley smoothly into gear. With scarcely a change in pitch the car pulled expertly out of the driveway and sailed off into the night, strangely unaffected in its course by the evening traffic, the jolly echoes of banjos and saxophones ringing in its wake.

ALONE
CHAPTER THIRTY-FIVE

HE FIRST THING Richard noticed the day after Graham's departure was the silence. Not just the absence of snoring, which he'd been listening to for weeks, but in general. There wasn't a creak in the entire house.

The quiet persisted in the restaurant. All the other guests had disappeared. After the commotion of the past few days—the winter fête, the funeral, the press, the nocturnal attack courtesy of the undead—it was very eerie.

Frau Indergand came to serve Richard tea. When he asked his hostess where the other guests were, she informed him that they'd left following the disturbance on the night of the fête, in a tone that left him in no doubt about who was responsible.

Richard drank his tea quickly and left.

One can hardly blame Josephine Indergand for feeling resentful. Feral wraiths are seldom good for business and news of Richard's extraordinary find had yet to translate into fresh visitors to replace those who had fled. This would change. In the meantime, Richard's name was mud.

It was the same in the village. People crossed the street to avoid him. To the casual observer, Niderälpli appeared to have convened a meeting and decided that Richard was indelibly associated with the chaos of the winter fête and, therefore, no longer a man to be acknowledged by society.

The one exception was Silvio Indergand. Richard met him in the square shortly before noon and they shared a drink in the café. They were the only customers. The young man had exchanged his uniform for jeans and a fashionable black jacket with paramilitary epaulettes and a fur-lined hood.

' . . . So it is lucky,' said Silvio.

Richard started. He'd been staring absently at the fountain in the square outside. 'Sorry?'

'I am telling you, it is lucky we find you in the woods that night. Because of this we are finishing the exercise early and we are arriving in the village just in time.'

Richard wondered if there would have been quite so much commotion had the soldiers not started shooting everywhere. Maybe they might have recovered one of the wolves' bodies—if there were any. As it was, the chaos was so complete that by the time they'd harnessed the slobbering dogs there had been nothing left to look at.

'I wonder what they were,' mused Richard.

Silvio shrugged. 'Wolves? Wild dogs? It does not matter. It is good they are gone.'

'What'll you do, now your service is finished?'

Silvio shrugged again. 'Holiday, then university.' He sighed. 'I was supposed to spend the week with my girlfriend, but we decide it is not a good idea.'

Richard raised an eyebrow. 'Girlfriend?'

Silvio nodded. He didn't seem to mind the question. 'We argue, the night of, you know, the *woooh.*' He waved his arms about. 'She is not happy. I think we are not together anymore.'

Richard remembered the name in the book, taken from Silvio's private library and Melanie's reaction upon reading the inscription signed *Laura*. Something told him he knew what they'd quarrelled about. A pang of guilt shot through him when he remembered it was he who'd shown her the book. Then he remembered Graham's elation when he heard Melanie pull up outside the hotel. Any remorse Richard may have felt for his own part in Silvio being dumped was immediately cleansed.

'I'm sorry,' Richard lied.

Silvio shrugged. 'It has happened. Anyway, it was not working. She has too much . . . how you say . . .'

'Dog smell?' suggested Richard.

Silvio laughed. Then he clicked his fingers, remembering. 'Libido. This is the word, she like too much the sex. I am telling you, it is impossible.'

Richard hoped for Graham's sake that his injuries were, as was generally suspected, superficial.

He rose and made to pay the tab but Silvio waved him away. Richard thanked him and returned to the Gasthaus.

There's nothing like an imminent departure to highlight how messy your room has become over the course of your stay. In his search for missing socks Richard rediscovered items he'd forgotten he had, including many detailed reports and photographs. He perused these with not a little pride as he packed and soon forgot his moroseness. It was only when his suitcases stood bulging by the empty closet that gloom descended on him once more.

Whether it was the weather or the removal of everything that had become familiar over the previous weeks, a chill descended on his room. Richard could feel the cold through the carpet. He didn't know who to blame: the Indergands, for—presumably—turning off the radiators in the now-empty rooms below him, or Graham who, in leaving, had removed a dependable source of heat.

His thoughts wandered back to Ellie, despite herculean efforts to prevent them from doing so. Ellie was always a good person to talk to when Graham wasn't around.

The portrait of the old man on the wall gazed back at him knowingly.

Richard shook his head angrily.

That's enough of that.

He sat down to plan his itinerary, but his choices were uninspired. He could take the train and catch the connecting line to Sion, but the uncertainty of what would follow weighed on him. As afternoon became evening and the sky darkened, Richard found himself still in his hotel room, not knowing what to do.

Thinking it might be nice to watch something he opened his laptop, but quickly closed it again. He didn't need distraction, he realised; he needed something more.

Fat chance of that, he thought bitterly, but didn't open the computer again. Had he done so he might have come across a number of rather sensational articles regarding the arrest of a prominent London playboy-businessman and the accompanying video interviews with his chief of operations whose serious words concerning the future of the company were somewhat undermined by the fact that he was sipping glühwein on the balcony of a five-star hotel in Davos at the time.

Richard paced around the room for a while, absently running his hands over the woodcarvings. The floorboards creaked under his feet, making the room seem even emptier.

He gave up and lay down on the bed. But he didn't feel sleepy, just tired.

He got up again and went over to the window. His breath fogged up the panes. On a whim he opened it. The air was colder than he'd expected and it took his lungs a moment to get used to the chill. As he exhaled the warmth from his breath was stolen away and turned to a mist that floated away into the gloom.

He leaned on the sill and gazed out over the little village. He remembered how small and compact the collection of lights had appeared to him from the mountain trail, but from here there was no cohesion to them. The glowing points were scattered here and there, too many to be isolated from one another but too few to create the impression of true cohabitation. The lights seemed to shine in on themselves rather than outwards. What had seemed a tightly packed community from above now resembled a collection of private little lives; each one concerned only with its private histories and concerns. As evening fell, the spaces between the lights promised to become very dark indeed.

Richard's thoughts turned briefly to Frau Hürlimann and he felt sad.

It was early, but the village was quiet enough to give the impression that people were already in bed. Richard wondered what everyone else was doing and whether some of them felt as aimless as he did. He doubted it. The Swiss never seem at a loss for something to do. Even in boredom they somehow managed to look intensely occupied.

He wondered how many children had slept soundly that week. Having Meinrad Indergand tell bedtime stories about monsters was one thing; being chased through the mist by a pair of snarling yellow eyes and shot at by the military is quite another.

The sky evolved within the frame of the valley's encirclement. The clouds were still visible in the gathering darkness, moving quickly across the charcoal grey heavens. The wind Richard felt must be but a shadow of the icy draughts howling up above.

He'd just decided to go inside again when something caught his eye. There was someone on the path.

Richard squinted in the gloom. No one had walked past the hotel while he'd been on the balcony. The person wasn't moving in an especially determined way, like someone out for an evening stroll or who wasn't quite sure of which way to go. Could they be lost? Winter clothing obscured the face and silhouette.

Richard frowned. Who could that be? Bit late for a walk, especially in this chill.

He struggled to make the figure out against the shadowy mountainside. He leaned out of the window and saw them reach the fork in the path before turning towards the sanatorium.

His heart leapt.

The figure hesitated, then continued onwards; not along the walk to the old boarded-up building but up the narrow trail leading to the forest.

Richard peered in the gloom. Who was this person? Why head into the woods this late? Didn't they know about the attack? He thought of calling out but by now the person was out of earshot.

He flew back into his room and grabbed his coat with every intention of bringing this person back into the village. He looked for his scarf but couldn't find it and didn't dare take the time to look, in case he should lose the last of the evening light. He bounded down the flights of stairs, past the doorway to the dining room, the empty wheelchair by the fire, and through the front door.

He hesitated suddenly. The thread of his thoughts had snagged on something as he'd passed the front desk. He stood indecisively on the front step, the door half open.

He felt a bit stupid and laughed at himself. Then he stopped laughing, recalling the film from the drone and the wolves from the cave. His eyes had deceived him before.

Retracing his steps Richard circumvented the front desk and took the hunting rifle from under the counter. The weight of it in his hands was reassuring. He found the drawer with the live rounds, pocketed a handful and, with the rifle over his shoulder, reopened the front door.

Richard jogged up the path, reaching the fork within moments. Off to the side the pallor of the sanatorium glowed in the evening gloom. A sliver of gold pierced the clouds as the setting sun dipped below the horizon.

Richard decided to inspect the orchard in case whoever it was had changed their mind while he was inside the hotel. They could easily have decided to alter course; best to check there first just in case.

He realised he was running and forced himself to slow down. It's not her, he caught himself thinking, and realised he hoped it was. He crossed the length of the sanatorium promenade and scanned the small collection of trees, not realising he was holding his breath.

The orchard was empty. Richard searched amongst the leafless boughs, taking care not to trip over any headstones in the darkness. He paced up and down the grove several times before he was satisfied nobody was there.

Good, he thought; I've had enough shadowy nocturnal visitations for a lifetime.

Nonetheless, a voice inside him whispered, *you hoped it was her.*

Richard stopped to collect his thoughts. She'd been the obvious candidate. If it wasn't her he'd seen on the path, then whom?

The tree beside him looked familiar. It was the spot where they'd first met.

He began to lose interest in the mysterious figure. He resolved to return to the hotel and to remain in his room until morning came, along with the train that would take him away from this place.

He hitched the rifle onto his shoulder, glanced around the orchard one last time, then made his way back towards the derelict building. He paused at the corner of the promenade, his mind turning fitfully.

That might not have been a person on the path at all.

He was glad he'd brought the rifle.

You can't hurt a ghost.

. . . True, but they can't hurt you either.

The wolves could be hurt though, if not by men then by the dogs. But what had they been, if not ghosts?

Something else.

The thought of going into the woods at night was not appealing. The hotel lights beckoned from a short distance away and Richard shivered. Bedtime began to seem like a very good idea.

He was about to turn away when he caught sight of it again.

A dark shape was moving through the trees, only just visible at the edge of the wood. Richard watched as it disappeared into the dense forest, seemingly making for the waterfall. Once again his heart leapt, this time because he thought—no, he was certain—he'd spied the flash of a yellow ribbon in the darkness.

Richard ran down the steps, cut across the steep slope through the frost-stiffened grass, and skidded onto the path. The ground was icy but his daily hikes had made him sure-footed. He hurried into the wood after the shadowy figure. Who else could glide up the slope so effortlessly, and who would want to? She'd said she wished to visit the waters.

Richard's lengthened his stride and soon he was running full tilt through the trees. His heavy boots pounded the carpet of needles. Two months ago he would have been winded in moments but now his lungs were powerful, even in the cold, thin mountain air. His legs, hardened by weeks of climbing, carried him up, up, up until the ground evened out and he spotted the clearing and the frozen waterfall beyond.

He slowed to catch his breath. He realised immediately that the tall figure standing beside the pools of water couldn't be Ellie. Had he truly believed it would be? He bit his lip in bitterness and frustration. She was gone. He'd been a fool to get his hopes up.

His disappointment gave way to curiosity. He made out masculine features and overlong grey hair, but couldn't match them to any face he knew from the village. He advanced stealthily to see who it might be.

Richard was struck by the silence, which always seemed most intense where there had previously been noise. Now that the sound of his own footsteps had ceased there was only a faint wind to be heard, that and the thumping of his heart. At the foot of the frozen curtain of water the pools had wizened and shrunk almost to the point of disappearance. The water was still as a mirror, its surface frozen solid.

The darkening heavens were heavy with clouds. Snow must finally be on the way. Richard advanced without taking his eyes off the figure silhouetted against the sunset sky beyond. Whoever it was did not appear to notice him.

At last Richard stepped fully into the clearing. As he did, the frozen grass rustled under his boot.

The figure turned and Richard recognised him.

THE ICY POOL
CHAPTER THIRTY-SIX

ICHARD STARED IN astonishment. Fosco stared back.

It was no wonder that Richard hadn't recognised him. The beard was gone, as were the copious layers of clothing. He wasn't stooping anymore and Richard realised incredulously that the man must be over six feet tall. The easy way in which Fosco shifted his weight as he assessed the new arrival carried no memory of the gnome-like, arthritic old man Richard had known. In his gnarled hand he held his signature pipe, unlit, and his dark eyes were clear.

'Good evening,' said Fosco, in accented but flawless English. 'You seem surprised. You expected a monster with hair down to its knees and juju eyeballs, eh?'

This light-hearted address rankled Richard. He observed this new, changed Fosco with mounting resentment. How dare he speak with such familiarity? How dare he go for nocturnal walks in such temperatures? How dare he grow eight inches taller and forty years younger without permission?

Something—though for the life of him Richard couldn't tell what—was going on, and it was most definitely not acceptable.

Calm down, he thought. Remember the English rule: when in doubt, be aloof.

'Actually,' Richard retorted, 'I expected a ghost. Or a bear. Or possibly some kind of anthropomorphic man-bear psychopath. I wasn't sure.'

Not quite aloof, considering the quiver in his voice.

Fosco raised his eyebrows. 'That was surprisingly lucid of you, Mr Mathern.'

Richard blinked in confusion.

'I too feared such an encounter,' continued Fosco. 'Hence why I brought this.'

He turned fully, bringing his left arm out of concealment. It held a vicious-looking rifle identical to the one Richard had stolen from the hotel. It shone black against the moonlit clouds billowing across the open space in the distance.

Richard stiffened, regarding the weapon with a wary eye. Fosco remained where he was, smiled, and turned to look out over the valley.

Richard advanced cautiously, fingers tight on the strap of the gun over his shoulder, watching Fosco for signs of hostility. There were none, save for the general sense of lupine danger surrounding him.

Richard couldn't understand it; the man was utterly transformed. Gone was the hunched old geezer with his many woollen overcoats, replaced by a sinewy man in dark, well-fitting clothes. Fosco stood comfortably and reached for his tobacco, humming a strange tune under his breath. He allowed Richard to come within a few running paces from him, filling his pipe as he did so.

When Richard drew level with the largest of the pools Fosco's eyes snapped up. 'That's close enough.' There was enough of the familiar growl there to bring Richard to a halt.

Fosco finished filling his pipe in silence and struck a match. The smoke billowed around him, the breeze teasing it out in vaporous tendrils that flowed from him as he puffed on the pipe. The spectacles, Richard noted, were also gone and there was a disturbing glint in his eye.

The English dread of inelegant silences urged Richard back into conversation.

'So, er . . . you look well.'

Fosco regarded him over his glowing pipe as vapours curled about his ears.

'I was under the impression,' continued Richard, 'that you'd gone on holiday for health reasons. Am I to take it your cure has been successful?'

'I haven't travelled in a long time,' replied Fosco. 'I will be soon, though. It's about that time again.'

'Going anywhere nice?'

'Anywhere that's far enough.' Fosco's voice turned grim. 'Back in the day it was mostly pilgrimages or campaigns . . . Anything long enough for people to forget my face. Then I'd be back, for more hunting.'

For the first time, Richard felt like he was beginning to understand. 'You're one of them, aren't you? The people I've been seeing, the dead people.'

Fosco grunted into his pipe. 'I'm not dead. She's wanted me dead for a long time, but I've always been two steps ahead.'

Richard's brow furrowed. 'Who's "she"?'

'The same "she" you hoped to find when you came to this place.'

Richard was confused. He was also cold. The threat of bodily injury wafting off Fosco's new persona unnerved him. 'Why would "she" want you dead?'

Fosco exhaled a puff of smoke. 'Because she's a monster and she's always wanted me dead.'

'Well, she never mentioned anything about it to me.'

Fosco's eyes narrowed. 'You've *spoken* to her?' His voice rang with incredulity.

'Many times, down at the sanatorium.'

Fosco lip curled. He had very long teeth, uneven and sharp. 'I'm not talking about the consumptive girl. I'm talking about *her*—the Beast.'

Richard frowned, uncomprehending.

Fosco shook his head in exasperation. He leaned towards Richard and spoke clearly.

'The Bear.'

Fosco straightened and put his pipe back in his mouth. 'You've been tracking her for almost three months, haven't you? You've done a very poor job of it too, I must say. If I were half as inept as you and your idiot friend, she'd have had me a long time ago.'

He chuckled. Richard felt a new and intense dislike for the man.

'Then again,' said Fosco, reaching into his pocket, 'I should've realised. You didn't come here tonight looking for a bear, did you?'

He produced from his pocket a long yellow ribbon and held it up between his fingers. 'I found it in the grass next to the river,' said Fosco, his dark eyes on Richard. 'There was a box too, with a timepiece inside.'

Richard said nothing. His insides felt like they were being inappropriately stroked by a dozen tiny, icy hands.

Fosco crumpled the ribbon up and threw it to Richard. He caught it in his hands and held it nestled in his palms.

'Who is she?' asked Fosco.

'A woman,' murmured Richard.

Fosco's lip curled again. 'A dead one.'

Yes, Richard had to admit to himself: a dead woman. He'd run halfway up a mountain into the woods at dusk with a hunting rifle, looking for a dead person. Now he was standing on a wind-swept rock shelf beside a frozen sheet of ice, trying to work out how the grumpy village granddad had acquired the body of a much younger man and an unwarranted mastery of English.

From the bottom of Richard's soul echoed the desperate lament of his countrymen when faced with unexpected existential dread.

Bugger.

Fosco sensed Richard's distress. But he spoke without sympathy in that strange accent no one could place.

'I've seen the dead people—ghosts, I suppose we should call them. They've tried to speak to me a few times. I won't have anything to do with them. Spirits and the living shouldn't mix.' He gave Richard a knowing look. 'But I don't suppose you'd agree with that.'

Ellie's face floated in Richard's mind. He wound the yellow ribbon around his hand so he wouldn't lose it.

Fosco pulled on his pipe. As the smoke drifted away in the chilly air, Richard was struck by his evident contempt and his smugness at having so obviously deceived him. In what, though?

Something in Richard hardened and he met Fosco's sable stare. 'If you're not a ghost,' said Richard, 'then what the hell are you?'

The wind continued to blow, tugging at the hems of their jackets, getting colder with every gust.

Fosco paused, as though thinking how best to reply. Eventually, he exhaled a cloud of smoke, and told him.

*****

Mother Nature speaks to people. Rather, she speaks to some people, sometimes, in different ways.

She speaks to the village of Niderälpli, for instance. Every sunrise or cloud or flock of birds that appears at the edge of its little sheltered valley tells a story. She whispers to the weather prophet Kaspar and tells him of things to come. She converses with Jerome, Suzy, Berlioz, and the sled dogs in their kennel, reminding them how life works in their little animal worlds.

The living earth speaks to people, but not everyone listens. Many years before Niderälpli was dreamt of, she spoke to two legionnaires fleeing across the mountainside. The slave, so attentive to what the earth had to say despite his inability to understand people, wasn't listening when the air carried the sound of approaching enemies even as this same earth swallowed his feckless master.

The youngest of three brothers thought he knew the language of the hidden valley when he discovered its welcoming safety. But he stopped listening when he met a figure on the stone bridge and somehow it never spoke to him the same way again after that.

Elias, the young herder whose cow collapsed on the mountainside generations later, ignored the voices telling him to stay safe in the village away from the dark. He bought his own skin back with that of his dog, who saved him from a monster.

The mountaineers at Frederick Bellows' back weren't listening when they descended the cliff face just a little too fast, ignoring the trembling cracks and the black ice, until one of them slipped and pulled the others with him along the rocks and over the edge of the chasm to the long fall.

The engineers who brought the railway to the valley weren't listening as the ground groaned beneath their train, as the trees were blackened by smoke and sooty flowers grew from their iron gardens.

The sanatorium was built for those in whom nature spoke so strongly and so cruelly she couldn't be ignored. The orchard was full of those who'd heard too late, or whose own natures failed to respond with enough vigour.

The German pilots whose plane was ruined on the mountainside in the night didn't see the shadowy rocks in front of them as they flew too low. Marooned in the snow and hearing a cry from the darkness, their instincts failed them when they mistook a recognisable voice for a friendly one.

Richard wasn't listening the night he left the hotel in search of someone who was no longer there, and the thing he'd been seeking since he arrived finally found him.

And, before it all, Nature spoke to a Black-Haired Man, running alongside a hunting party in the primeval woods with a feral dog at his heel.

In Nature, as in Man, there's always a story for those who listen. Now, on the ledge by the frozen waterfall, Richard stood and listened to a story.

DAUGHTER OF THE MOON
CHAPTER THIRTY-SEVEN

Rhône River Valley, c. 3'900 B.C.

N A GROVE of broad-leafed lime trees, the clan gathered to witness the trial of Old Potter's daughter.

Potter was not the man's real name. The making of pots was his role in the small community by the river and the word comes closest to what they called him in their own language. Since the deaths of his child's mother and his own parents, Potter's actual name was a secret known only to him and—by virtue of a metaphysical process that the Elders never fully explained to him—the moon, Measurer of Time.

The valley's people believed it was the moon's responsibility to name every soul in the world. Each household kept a small statuette somewhere in a nook or alcove representing the moon's daughter. She watched over them, they believed, and made sure the lunar cycle continued. As long as the goddess's father danced across the heavens in his varying moods and manifestations, the sun was sure to follow in the morning, as summer follows winter.

On the night Potter was born the moon revealed his name to his mother in a dream. Thereafter it was his secret to keep. In his more contemplative moments, He-Who-Dances-With-Bumblebees found himself wishing that his mother hadn't eaten quite so much of a certain hallucinatory root on the night of his birth. The name Potter suited him better.

His daughter's name had been revealed to Potter's wife in a similar way. An impetuous woman with a quick tongue and a taste for culinary novelty, she experimented with the wrong kind of berry one day and expired in Potter's arms. Since then his daughter had been very dear to him—more so than was deemed appropriate, especially since she was of age to marry.

In addition to the usual lessons in weaving, sewing, tanning and a knowledge of plants, Potter had overstepped tradition and taught her to fish with a net and a three-pronged harpoon, even to hunt and track small game. These were not suitable skills for a girl to learn and even Potter's loneliness following his wife's death wouldn't normally have excused this. But he was a venerable and respected member of the clan family, having weathered over forty winters. His relationship with his daughter was therefore accepted as eccentric sentimentality on his part, her skills dismissed as youthful games to be corrected later by a suitably strict husband.

It was the subject of the girl's marriage that brought the clan together on that particular day. Since the children of one clan were considered to be brothers and sisters, they could not marry. Not all clans operated on this basis, but those that didn't had become notorious for their worrying tendency to spend their days sucking on rocks and bumping into things. Since Potter's daughter was of age, a young man had been brought from a neighbouring community to marry her and wean her from her over-indulgent father. Thus the clan would grow and thrive and the elders blessed the union in the name of various approving deities.

Potter was reluctant to let his daughter go. He'd had a good look at the young suitor and thought he saw behind the young man's features a hidden viciousness, betrayed by a concealed cunning in his dark eyes. He looked to Old Potter like the kind of boy who soiled the river upstream.

Potter's daughter, sharing her father's distaste, ignored the young black-haired hunter as he strutted past their hut, his wolf-like dog at his heels. But when the Chief Elder came to visit Potter in his humble dwelling and towered over him, all beard and sacred tattoos, the poor man couldn't refuse. Had his wife Nibbles-With-Surprising-Fierceness been there by his side, things might have been different. As it was Potter was alone and, begrudgingly, consented.

His daughter, meanwhile, had developed a magnificent loathing for the youth. For days after the hasty and awkward ceremony, she adamantly refused those rites of marital necessity that even in those early days of matrimony were understood to be crucial for family life. This, the elders agreed, would not do at all.

The brothers and sisters who lived by the river now gathered under the lime trees in front of the Great Hut, the largest of the dwellings that constituted the summer residence of the clan. A circle of earth had been beaten out, designating a consecrated place where the gods would sit and no injustice could occur. It was a beautiful autumn day.

The girl was summoned to be tried for her impious refusal to obey her spouse. She in turn told the messengers that they could eat dirt for all she cared. This was a futile display of bravery and she was summarily dragged out of her hut by her brothers and made to kneel in the circle.

326

As she knelt, she was bold enough to look up at the Chief Elder. He sat on a raised platform wrapped in furs and tendrils of beard, his face covered in a mesh of arcane lines and dots denoting his status.

One of her guards saw her look and slapped her, hard. She faced downwards, but could still see her judges through the curtain of her hair as it hung over her face.

Two men shared the platform with the Elder. On one side sat Tracker, lead hunter of the tribe. On the other was the Chief Elder's son, a haughty young man who observed the kneeling girl with disdain, a bearskin around his shoulders. He'd killed the bear himself.

The girl's black-haired husband had cultivated this young man's friendship since his arrival and the two had grown close. He now waited nearby, ready to speak his piece. His leering dog paced amongst the trees some distance away, its wolfish instincts sensing a fight.

Potter stood at the back of the circle, his eyes downcast.

The husband stepped forward to give his account of his new wife's disobedience. The court listened. She was wild, he said, and refused to give up hunting and fishing—pursuits unfit for a married woman. Moreover, when she did catch something, she never shared it with him. She wouldn't clean his fish nor cook his kills and she wouldn't tell him the name she'd been given at birth. Most importantly, she declined to share his bed.

He pointed out that he'd been invited to the clan expressly to marry the girl and had been promised a full life and an exalted place among their hunters. He demanded to know how they planned to keep this promise if his own wife—their sister—refused him.

Having said his piece, the black-haired youth retreated to one side of the clay circle.

Potter was then called to speak for his daughter. The only voice accepted by the court was that of a man and, as her next of kin, her defence fell to him.

Though his words were kind they carried little of the fiery conviction of her husband. He praised her loyalty, her strength, and her qualities of spirit. As a widower and a man of many years, the crowd's sympathy was with him. He could hardly say what he wished about the boy, however, as he'd agreed to the union in the first place.

The Elder sat for a while in silence. He leant over to Tracker and exchanged a word or two. The hunter's answer appeared to anger the Elder's son. The murmured consultation continued.

The girl watched secretly from where she knelt. The sun was shining but she sensed a coldness within the ground and knew that the summer had turned. Soon the mountainside would turn gold and red and the waters would slow. High up the great crowns of rock would freeze and the air would blow cold in the valley.

At last the lead hunter spoke. Tracker noted that, whether the auguries had been favourable or not, the signs for this marriage were bad. He asked the husband if he would choose a different spouse from amongst their sisters, one less headstrong and more suited to his needs.

The Black-Haired Man refused. He had a wife, he said, and wished her to be disciplined.

The girl wanted to scratch his dark eyes out, but waited to hear the Elder's decision. Her father lowered his gaze, hoping events wouldn't go the way he feared.

More consultation followed, and more arguing. When the Elder rose, there was graveness in the faces of the assembled men.

The marriage, he announced, would be upheld. If the girl would not go to her husband willingly, she would be made to do so. Should this fail to discipline her, she would be returned to her father as a pariah and the Black-Haired Man would be compensated for the inconvenience.

Such was the Gods' wish, intoned the Elder's son; satisfied his father had sided with him.

The girl let forth a burst of screams. One of her brothers kicked her in the stomach to silence her, lest she further shame herself. She gasped and fell to her knees, retching. It was feared she would soil the sacred ground but she merely gagged in the dirt. The man who'd delivered the blow stood over her, ready to pull her away from the clay circle. The rest of the clan looked on.

Her breath coming in gasps, the girl raised her head to face her judges. Her gaze came to rest on her father, who'd rushed forward only to find his courage wanting once he reached the circle's edge.

Potter was called upon to agree that the verdict was just, as the girl had been his property and the council wished to end all bad blood between him and her husband.

Her eyes begged her father for protection. Her lungs heaved as she knelt on the dirt floor. Potter hesitated.

He looked away. In a small voice he pronounced the verdict just and agreed to entrust his daughter to her new keeper.

The girl was dragged from the circle; the Elder declared that honour had been satisfied. The clan members stayed a while to renew the bonds between brothers and to swear that these would never be cut. The Black-Haired Man went smiling from one man to the next. At last he reached Old Potter and, with open arms, invited his embrace.

Potter's face showed obvious repugnance, but the clan's law had been upheld. It was time to renew the all-important connections that assured the group's solidarity. He accepted the embrace before excusing himself. In a loud voice the Black-Haired Man promised his next kill to the Elder in thanks. Old Potter went home to sit by himself with his head in his hands.

His daughter was dragged to the Black-Haired Man's dwelling and her guards bound her within so that she couldn't escape. They tied her mouth to stop her screams.

Her husband didn't hurry back. When he did return to his hut, he entered in a leisurely, self-satisfied way and didn't come out again for some time.

Some hours later, as the sun was descending behind the jagged crests of the mountains, he re-emerged, stripped to the waist, dragging the unconscious, naked body of the girl behind him. Her hands were still tightly bound and by these bonds he pulled her to her father's hut, where he left her.

The women waited until he was gone before approaching the prostrate form. At first they feared the girl might be dead. Her wrists and ankles were raw from her fetters and her bruised body lay unmoving in the dirt as they congregated around it.

Suddenly she drew a shuddering breath and vomited loudly onto the soil.

At this noise the curtain flap of the hut drew back. Her father emerged in the dusk and beheld his daughter shivering on the ground.

The sight of her aged him visibly. His eyes filled with pity—for her, for himself, for his dead wife, for his entire family line stretching back to beginning of days that had been shamed and humbled.

He stepped forward, picked up his daughter's body, and carried her into the hut.

The silver eye of the full moon hung in a cloudless sky illuminating the tiny settlement cradled by the mountains. The faintest of breezes blew over the river, laden with the smells of the forest beyond. The sleeping hunters wrapped themselves tightly in their furs. The women huddled by the embers of their hearths.

In the early hours before dawn an ear-wrenching scream sliced through them all. The hunters grabbed their knives and rushed out into the night.

One of the women had risen early to collect water. She'd come across a trail of dark liquid inching its way down the riverbank and followed it to where it issued from under the hut belonging to the Elder's son.

They found him in his bed. They also found him scattered across the meadow, but those bits took longer to find. His brothers searched for the girl in vain.

They went to Potter's hut next. He lay amongst his furs with a peaceful look on his face. Were it not for the bluish tint of his lips and the berry juice in his cup, he might have been sleeping.

Torches were lit. Bloodied footprints led into the forest.

The clan was questioned. One of the boys admitted he'd risen in the night to relieve himself and from the village perimeter had seen a wild-eyed young woman with dark blood shining on her hands and face, laughing as she loped into the night. The boy had assumed she must be a night-spirit and was so frightened that he ran back to his father's hut and lay there trembling until morning.

The brothers gathered under the supervision of the Elder and burned the girl's possessions. She was renamed Brother-Killer, a She-Snake, and sentenced to death. Tracker and others kept their opinions private. The Elder's son hadn't been universally popular amongst his brothers, even less so among his sisters. The victim was buried on a bed of deer antlers. Tradition dictated they place a feather in his mouth that he may fly in the underworld but his head was still missing, as was his bearskin robe.

Five men were chosen to retrieve the fratricide. The war party included Tracker and the girl's husband. They set off in single file at first light accompanied by his wolfish dog, their long legs and spears swinging in rhythm as they loped into the forest.

Several days passed before any of them were seen again. One man was discovered face down in the river some miles upstream, his head split by an axe. Another appeared in several instalments; first a grey leg seen in the mouth of a wolverine, then a dismembered torso tied to a tree high above the valley, and finally the wide-mouthed head mounted on a stake high on a ledge overlooking the floodplain.

Tracker's remains were never found. Neither was the girl's dark-eyed husband.

Only the youngest returned alive. After several days he emerged from the brush at dusk, his eyes sleepless and terrified, babbling in garbled words about horrors in the woods and shadows behind the rocks.

He was taken into the Great Hut and interrogated at length by the Elder. When he eventually re-emerged, his eyes burned like embers in the darkness and he wouldn't talk to anyone.

The Elder never revealed what the boy told him. But the following day, though the fishing was still good and there were several weeks left before the wild grain could be harvested, it was announced that the tribe would depart the floodplain. The Elder ordered his wheeled cart to be assembled and for the summer camp to be dismantled.

This news should have been met with objections from the members of the clan. But they took one look at the crouched, dribbling figure returned from the mountains, hunched over his feet with his hands crossed across his knees, rocking back and forth in silence, and said no more on the matter. The huts were disassembled.

There was little talking as they travelled. The river grew wider and deeper. They knew that soon the mountainous walls framing the floodplain would open up and the wide expanse of the Great Lake would stretch out before them. The Elder did not once come out of his cart, and the skin flaps covering it remained closed. At night four watchmen were posted instead of the usual two.

The next day they reached the river ford. Still the Elder remained in his cart, so it fell to one of the brothers to pay for their safe passage. Taking a carved stone axe head, valuable and unused, he placed it reverently in the shallows of the river. He crossed safely and the rest followed.

As the sun dipped in the sky they drew near the gap in the mountains and every heart was glad of it. The frontrunners hastened back to announce that the way was clear and that they'd seen no one. The clan breathed a collective sigh of relief. The cart caught up with the rest of the group and halted.

From behind the flap the Elder emerged. He looked north towards the opening in the mountains and his mood relaxed visibly. He turned towards his assembled sons and daughters with a benevolent smile and raised his tattooed arms to dispel all trace of disharmony in this, the first hour of the new season.

As he did, a sudden movement amongst the trees caught his eye.

The stone slammed into the Elder's face even as he turned to behold his attacker. It hurtled from the gathering darkness swifter than a falcon and smashed through flesh and bone, leaving a splintered ruin in its wake.

He fell to the ground and did not get up again.

The clan fled. They dropped their weapons and raced for the lake, not stopping until they cleared the forest and reached the mouth of the river.

It was many seasons before their descendants returned to the forested valley, by which time all trace of the old man's bones had disappeared. The river ebbed and flowed as it had before, game was plentiful and the fishing was good. But, in the twilight hours of the waning summer, the clansmen would return to the encampment and tell stories of a long-limbed huntress who walked the forest alone, her face daubed in blood, whose laughter foretold the death of those who heard it. She hunted with sling, they said, and favoured the stag and the chamois. No hound was fast enough to catch her. Sometimes she was beautiful, other times her hair was woven of fire and her eyes were ice, her breath cold as the wind in winter.

Children would dive under their furs in terror at the mention of her name and the hunters would gather more closely around the embers of their fire, a tiny pinprick of light in an ocean of darkness.

The women sat away from the flames and listened from the shadows. Had the men glanced over as storytellers described the huntress's many victims, they might have detected a smile or two, half hidden by the dancing shadows which flickered in the women's eyes and on the stone face of the Goddess in the alcove in the wall above them.

THE BEAST
CHAPTER THIRTY-EIGHT

OSCO'S PIPE HAD gone out some time ago. He fished around in his pocket for fresh tobacco.

It was now quite dark. The only light came from the moon lurking behind the heavy clouds. There was a flare as Fosco struck a match. A few puffs of smoke and then the tiny flame was snuffed out, leaving only the glow of the pipe.

'Then what happened?' Richard asked.

Fosco exhaled a cloud of smoke, which mingled with the steam of his breath. 'She caught up with me,' he said. 'I was alone in the mountains. I didn't recognise her for she was clothed as a monstrous bear, but I was ready and we fought.'

'And you survived,' said Richard. It seemed silly to ask how someone could transform into a bear. Hadn't he looked at Fosco for weeks and seen an old man?

Fosco gazed into the middle distance as he smoked, the embers reflected in his black eyes. 'My dog saved my life. I've always had an affinity with dogs, but he was my favourite. The monster nearly had me but he fought like a demon, like three demons, until finally she fled.'

Somewhere in the forest a fox barked, but otherwise everything was silent.

'My dog was a mess,' continued Fosco. 'Back broken, half blind, blood everywhere. I was injured myself but I climbed the mountain with him on my shoulders until I reached a stream, where I cleaned his wounds. I knew the beast would return, but I could go no further. Then I saw the cave.'

Richard started. Fosco gave him a sidelong look.

'The very cave you desecrated with your presence mere days ago. That was my refuge. I picked up my dog once more and together we hid in the cave mouth.'

Fosco moved his pipe to the other side of face.

'My dog died in the night. He'd saved my life, so I honoured him by drawing his likeness on the inner wall of the cave. I ate his body.'

Richard shivered, yet he felt himself being drawn in by the horror of it all. Fosco's voice was hoarse, as though he hadn't spoken this much in a long time. He cleared his throat and continued.

'I awoke before dawn with the feeling that I was being watched. I wheeled around to face the entrance of the cave, thinking the Beast must have found me. There instead sitting in the shadows was my dog.'

He said this in a very matter-of-fact voice, as though such apparitions were commonplace. Richard might have questioned this except that he'd met so many in the preceding weeks that to him, now, they were.

'He stayed with me until sunrise,' continued Fosco. 'His loyalty was such that he continued to watch over me from beyond the grave. I concluded that the water had something to do with it, as well as the ritual drawing on the wall. Since then I've made many such companions.'

'You say you're not dead,' said Richard, 'but you haven't told me what you are.'

'I forgot,' smiled Fosco. 'You're a naturalist. You people want to stick labels on everything.'

Richard didn't comment, waiting to hear more.

'One day I saw a man in the mountains. There weren't many people around then and I'd met no one since I left the lowlands. Every time I tried to flee the mountain I sensed her presence, though I didn't know her then for what she was. This man had weapons and supplies, so I killed him and took them.'

Fosco said this as calmly as if he'd bought an egg. Richard got that feeling you get when you realise that something apparently innocuous turns out to be lethal and there's nothing between you and it.

'I'd survived using traps and snares, but now I could hunt properly. I could hunt *her*.' Every time Fosco used the word it acquired a kind of grating quality, as though the mere sound of it was a disease. 'But,' he added 'I was starving. So I washed his body in the stream and ate him as well.'

Richard began to back away. Then he remembered the rifle over his shoulder and stopped. Fosco had a distant look in his eyes and paid him little attention.

'Immediately I felt reborn. At first I thought it merely the joy of hearty eating but as time went on I found that with every man I killed, the strength in my limbs was born anew. Years passed and the Beast lurked around the corner all that time. Still I didn't understand, but I fought her. When she got the better of me, I'd call on my hounds and she would flee. When she was far away tending her wounds, I hunted other men and added their portraits to the walls of my cave. I'd discovered a secret magic. I stole their lives, and their strength, their youth became mine.'

Richard slid the rifle slowly off his shoulder. Fosco didn't seem to notice and exhaled another cloud of smoke.

'Then,' he breathed, 'one day I met her in a wood. She'd been lying in wait for me in complete stillness like a panther, something no ordinary bear would ever do. Then I was certain; it was *her*.' Again, the sound of metal was in his voice. 'It was the girl, the She-Snake, the one we'd been hunting. She was still following me. She wanted revenge. I knew then she would never let me be.'

Richard wrapped one hand around the rifle and slid the other slowly towards the trigger.

'I decided to leave. One night I loosed my hounds, all of them. By then I had conjured many. They descended on her and, as they fought, I made my escape. I used all my skill to evade her and left the country. I travelled. I stole the lives of more men. I waited for her to die.'

Richard held his breath, waiting for Fosco to look away across the valley.

'Finally, out of curiosity, I came back.' Fosco sighed. 'That was a mistake. I'd grown cocky during my long absence. I'd forgotten what she was. She must have known I'd return, for she was waiting for me.'

He'll hear my heart pounding, thought Richard. He must hear it already. Still, neither man moved from where they stood: Fosco, smoking calmly on the ledge, Richard in the shadows by the pool.

'She nearly had me,' said Fosco. 'She came out of nowhere when I was off-guard and savaged me. Then, uncalled and un-hoped for, my friends appeared and saved me. I managed to drag myself to my cave. It was still there, my secret refuge, the walls heavy with the images of my allies, despite my long absence. I lay near death, but hunger for my own revenge kept me alive.'

Richard moved as slowly as the watch hand of a clock, levelling the rifle with Fosco's back.

'By and by, I discovered that other men had come to the mountains. They built houses, felled trees. Good, I thought; more lives for me, fewer hiding places for her. I revealed myself to them, made friends, even worked with them sometimes. Their numbers hid me from her. Eventually I moved out of the cave and into their community. I concealed my true nature, never staying long. I'd come and go, but always I knew that the shadows in the cave were watching over me. Occasionally someone would wander too close and they would be attacked. The village even hired me once to hunt my own dogs.' He chuckled. 'I used the money to buy bear traps. They didn't work.'

A horrible thought struck Richard as he remembered the unnumbered, ownerless items in Fosco's antique shop. How many people had they belonged to?

His hand slipped.

Fosco moved so fast that Richard hardly had time to blink before he was on the ground and his rifle was in Fosco's hand, unfired.

Fosco sneered. 'Nice try.' He threw aside the captured firearm. It clattered onto the rocks out of reach.

Richard gasped for breath. Fosco's kick had knocked the wind out of him.

Fosco sighed. 'I can see in your eyes you're revolted. But know this: she's as much a killer as I am. Remember your night in the shepherd's hut? That was her, trying to get in. She mistook you for me. She never once hesitated to annihilate others in her hunt for me. Besides, she drew first blood, all those years ago, and did so in the darkness like a coward. I had to scour the meadows for fragments of my friend's body. Remember that, in case you feel tempted to cast me as the villain in this sad little story.'

Richard looked up and spoke with a confidence he didn't feel. 'The only villain here is you. You've murdered people, you've stolen their lives . . . But what have you done with all that time? You sneered at Graham and me for failing, but we came here with a job to do and we did our damnedest. What have you accomplished?' Richard met the black stare with an even gaze. 'You're a liar and a rapist. *You* drew first blood. If this story has a happy ending, you'll pay for it and the world will be better for it.'

Almost faster than Richard could see Fosco wheeled on him and slammed a bony fist across his face, sending him falling over backwards a second time.

'Who are you to speak to me of villainy?' snarled the older man. 'Who are you to speak of this place as its defender? You don't belong here, neither you nor the rest. I am the only legitimate inhabitant of these parts, the only true son of these stones. There was no one here before me. This land is mine!'

Richard could taste blood in his mouth.

'Mine,' Fosco repeated. 'I've dwelt here longer than any living man and when at last I've eradicated that creature I shall be free to live here forever.'

He stared across the moonlit valley and spread his arms wide, as if to embrace the snow-capped mountains. *'I am born of stone,'* he recited, *'and the Earth, my mother, shall embrace me in the end.* That's what they used to say.' He let his arms fall back down to his sides. 'Not me, she won't. I am destined for greater things.'

He was silent for an instant. Richard wiped the blood from his lip.

'Tell me,' said Fosco, as he gazed out across the darkened valley beneath them. 'Have you ever beheld something and known it was the last time you would do so?'

Richard thought of Ellie and it hurt. 'I don't know.'

'Of course not. Yet you must have, without realising it.'

Richard pulled himself onto his side. From the corner of his eye he spotted the rifle where it lay by the pool.

'I imagine you've visited this place many times since your arrival,' continued Fosco. 'Imagine, if you will, that you knew the time of your death and that it was here and now, by a frozen cascade overlooking a foreign valley.' He turned with a distant look. 'Would it be frightening? Or reassuring?'

Richard didn't answer.

Fosco smiled, half to himself. 'And what of her, I wonder? Do you think, when I finally corner her, that the knowledge of certain death will be blissful, after the agonizing terror of an unnaturally long life as a hunted creature?'

Richard looked at Fosco, suddenly realizing how desperately he wanted to get away from there. The man was clearly insane. Richard judged that the surest escape was to talk himself back to the village and summon up whatever officer of the law was nearest.

Propping himself up on his elbow Richard galvanised what remained of his courage and glared back up at the other man, silhouetted against the night sky. 'Well, what are you going to do now?' he said, 'kill me?'

Fosco nonchalantly moved his pipe to the other side of his face.

'Yes.' With that he casually started to load his rifle.

Oh, thought Richard.

Fosco removed his pipe and tapped out the ash onto the rock. Then he put the pipe away and swung his rifle up to his shoulder.

Richard watched the gun barrel coming up. He prepared to leap into evasive action, but he realised he had no idea what to do next.

In the forest there was a sound. The gun froze.

It came a second time. Fosco turned his head to listen.

'It's *her*,' he hissed.

Richard heard nothing.

'Here,' said Fosco abruptly, 'take this.' He picked up Richard's discarded rifle and threw it over. 'Two have more chance than one. And don't bother trying it on me,' he growled. 'It won't work.'

Richard suspected this was a lie, but didn't dare move.

Fosco sneered. 'Impotent to the end, eh? So be it. I will face her alone, like the first time.'

Richard perceived a faint noise in the woods, getting louder.

Fosco threw aside his jacket. In the darkness Richard saw the glint of metal at his belt. Fosco unhooked the hatchet and swung it expertly.

'The old stories say that the only weapon worthy of a warrior is one made by his own hand,' he said. He knelt and placed it on the rocks next to him within easy reach. 'However,' he added, lifting the rifle to his shoulder, 'I've never been much for stories.'

He chambered the cartridge. As promised, the bolt went *ker-shpling.*

'At least I know the answer to my own question,' Fosco muttered, speaking more to his rifle than to Richard. 'Perhaps it isn't so strange that a man looks forward to a fight after running for so long.'

The noise in the darkness below them grew louder and mingled with the furious pounding of Richard's heart.

Fosco's dark eyes shone and his breath quickened with anticipation.

'Do you know what I most look forward to in death?'

From amongst the trees Richard now perceived a low thumping, like the steady grinding of earth under the pounding of heavy feet, and the hoarse, ragged breathing of a large animal. Even a man who has never heard the noise before knows he must escape to safety in some high inaccessible place, but Richard was rooted to the spot.

'What?' he whispered.

The pounding of great paws grew closer. He could feel it in the ground. Fosco closed his eyes and sighed. His voice was filled not with fear but relief.

'I'll never have to buy another pair of shoes.'

The next moment the pine branches at the edge of the clearing exploded outwards and the bear—huge, glaring, with limbs like great black trees—burst out of the darkness. Fosco's eyes snapped open. His dark gaze drank in the moonlight shining on the creature's glistening flanks.

The bear stood there for an instant, chest heaving, gazing on its prey. Then, with a deafening roar, it threw itself towards the two men.

In that instant Richard found his courage. Lunging forward he swept his gun up off the rocks. As his hand closed around the rifle he realised he didn't know which of the two he was going to shoot. His first thought was to aim for Fosco, but as the monstrous bear barrelled up the hill towards him he instinctively turned to face it.

Time slowed as Richard raised the weapon to his shoulder, pointing the barrel at the oncoming beast. He tugged at the bolt, the metal cold under his trembling fingers. The blood pounded furiously in his head and heart. As the red-eyed shadow crested the last rocky shelf and towered over him he exhaled and squeezed the trigger.

There was a ferocious crack and a blinding flash of light in the dark. The rifle slammed into Richard's shoulder and he gasped at the shock. A second later there was another flash as Fosco discharged his own weapon. The noise made Richard's ears ring.

Either they had both missed or the beast didn't feel their bullets, for it roared and kept coming. Richard flung himself out of its path.

There was a second shot from the hunter. The bear didn't even slow down.

Richard stumbled in the dark and fell crashing into the shallow pool, the brittle ice shattering under his weight. Fosco cried out in a language that neither Richard nor anyone on earth except the bear could recognise. Flinging aside his rifle and taking up the hatchet, he swung it about his head and threw himself towards the oncoming beast.

Freezing water seeped through Richard's clothes and seared into his flesh like knives. Disorientated by his fall he thrashed about and knocked his head on a rock. The world spun before his eyes. He would have cried out had the shock of the freezing water not also paralysed his lungs. Gasping, he pulled himself backwards out of the water. But before he could think of the cut on his head, his attention was seized by the terrible collision of animal and man.

The bear's enormous weight barrelled straight into Fosco and, carrying him backwards, crushed him against the rocks. The wounded man roared. He swung his axe even as his bones snapped beneath the great bear's paws, embedding it repeatedly deep within the beast's furry hide.

The bear bellowed in fury and delight. Its clawed and gouged at the hunter's body, ignoring the terrible gashes that the axe was opening in its face and neck. The two fighters whirled around the rocky shelf crashing through the icy water. Several times Richard thought they would crush him as he hid behind the rocks.

Eventually the axe fell clanging to the ground. The limp and broken arm swung no more. Even then the bear tore and trampled the lifeless body until it became an unrecognisable stain on the mountainside. The water in the pool turned dark under the moonlit.

At last the beast took the corpse in its jaws and shook it like a rag doll before flinging it over the cliff into the darkness of the pine forest below.

The bear collapsed with a groan and crumpled onto its side. Great clouds of steam rose from its lips and the hot mess in which it lay.

The disturbed water seeped through the gory mess that soiled the pool, already beginning to freeze once more. It trickled down Richard's hair and out of his sodden clothes. The scent of snow was heavy. Black clouds rolled through the heavens high above.

The bear raised its gore-stained head and, with its bloodshot eyes, gazed at Richard.

There was a sudden flash of pain from the cut in his scalp and Richard's head swam. He blinked several times, wondering if he'd fainted.

His eyes snapped back to where the bear's had been. For a moment he didn't believe them.

Before him, where the animal had lain, there knelt a girl, long-limbed and slender, no older than fifteen. Her body was covered in hideous scars that partially hid what looked like ancient markings on her skin. From her horribly fresh and gaping wounds rivulets of blood trailed down her body, mixing with that of the dead man as it collected in the pool.

Richard stared at her disfigured face. She looked back with sad eyes, the mist from her breath mixing with his.

As Richard watched, the girl began to move. At first he though she was gesturing towards him, though whether in threat or supplication he couldn't tell. She stroked the earth around her with slow circular movements and raised her fingers towards her bleeding face in a clawing motion, while making strange half-audible sounds in her throat. Richard realized she was collecting the blood from the ground and painting it onto herself, all the while ululating softly. These gestures expanded into a slow dance, as she undulated her upper body and continued to paint herself with her victim's blood.

Richard gazed in horrified fascination. He found himself torn between his wish to flee from the scene and the impulse to rush to her, to cradle her broken body, to find someone who could treat her awful, gaping wounds. But something told him that, like the strange apparitions he'd met on his adventures on the mountain, she was beyond his capacity to harm or help. The girl, who had seemed so young, now appeared as ancient as the mountain itself. As she swayed, her thin, muscular shoulders shuddered with such a violent release of grief, suffering, and loss, that Richard dared not approach.

She struggled to her feet and turned away from him to face the open space over the valley. Her limbs trembled in the cold and her moonlit skin was white from blood loss but she never ceased her soft chanting or her strange dance.

Richard shivered. If he didn't find warmth and dry clothes soon he was in grave danger of freezing to death. But he couldn't tear himself away from the sight of the girl. As the cold crept through his body, he beheld a tiny white star descending from the sky. It floated down onto the surface of the pool, hung there for an instant, and then disappeared.

He looked up at the great emptiness surrounding the mountain as a great white flurry began to descend.

Richard had never seen such snowflakes. They swirled down in billowing clouds that covered everything, first snuffing out the bloodstained rocks and then the pink snow on top of them. They dusted the emaciated body of the girl as she danced. They began to collect in the sodden folds of Richard's clothes, which were already stiff and icy where the water had begun to freeze.

Richard began to despair. He closed his eyes.

I must stop this madness while I still can. I'll go back to London, I'll go back to my life, I'll forget all about this place.

His body refused to move. He fought with himself as the cold numbed his limbs.

I'll go back to London. I'll leave this place, I'll forget all about her.

There was an almost imperceptible shift in the air, as if the rocks themselves had gently exhaled.

On the broken surface of the pool tiny ripples began to form. The coarse grasses at Richard's back quivered slightly. He now felt inhumanly cold, as though the iciness inside the mountain was rising up through his legs. The air stirred about him, swirling around his ankles and rising through his sodden clothes, his skin, his bones. The pumping warmth of the blood seeping from under his hair turned to ice the instant it bubbled forth. The breeze wove around and through him, making him want to scream in agony. Richard knew he must get off this mountain or freeze to death.

He forced his stiffened limbs to obey him and struggled to his feet.

The girl stood with her back to him, still singing in her strange language. Her face was raised towards the heavens, where far in the distance, over the jagged snow-capped horizon, the dark clouds were parting. A great rift opened up in the sky and moonlight poured out of it, illuminating the mountains.

For a moment there was a great stillness. Even the wind paused, as though in expectation.

Then Richard beheld the Great Hunt.

Out of the rift they came, first one by one, then by the score and the hundreds: a great host of beasts, birds, and riders. They issued forth from the sky in a long black column that billowed out of the heavens and, turning, galloped straight for the white mountain. They were cloaked in the falling snow, which heaved and billowed around them as they rode through the air. The rumble of hoof beats was like encroaching thunder; exhilarating, terrifying, and horrifyingly familiar.

The wind picked up again and buffeted Richard as he gazed open-mouthed at the cavalcade. It drew closer, moving impossibly fast. In a heartbeat the host had crossed the wide expanse of night and the sky above him exploded with the beating of black wings and pounding hoofs as they thundered over him. There were armoured riders on dark horses, pale women whose hair streamed out behind them as they rode, great bulls with steaming breath, leering wolves and fearsome prehistoric cats, twelve-tined stags with flaring nostrils, soot-faced nightmares and many-horned monsters. All around them flew a cloud of dark birds, and the sound of

340

their charge was so tremendous Richard could feel it shuddering in his bones.

Upon reaching the great horn of ice the column heaved. Bearing off to the side they circled the mountain's crown, saluting it as they passed. As they did the snow rose in great swells about them, and from the glacier's crevasses, woods, and caves there poured forth the souls of its victims.

First came the spectres of bearded and dark-eyed men: shepherds and hunters in crudely stitched clothing, accompanied by raven-haired women with sorrowful faces and naked, feral children. Then followed a throng of warriors with tall shields and proud glares, laughing as they joined their brothers in the Hunt. Behind them came a host of Roman legionaries, many the victims of the proud men in front. All were welcomed.

After them came score upon score of souls, all bearing some mark of premature death: blood-smattered soldiers; travellers having succumbed to their hijackers; pilgrims buried by avalanches or frozen in the high passes. A group of grey-robed priests appeared alongside two of the bandits who'd attacked them, all laughing and singing as they processed amiable into the air together. Behind followed a sombre man with a long beard guiding a stooped figure, its face a mangled ruin. There was a handsome youth on a white horse with a pistol at his side, followed by a woman and her entourage still in the carriage that had slipped off the road and dragged them over the edge of the precipice. A line of climbers appeared in goggles and white scarves, linked by the rope that had failed to save them. Then from the cemetery by the orchard came the men, women, and children carried away by the sickness in their lungs and bones, who had choked to death on their own blood or wasted away as their rotten limbs ceased to function.

Finally the girl herself stepped up off the rocks and into the air to join the great host of souls. She wasn't trembling anymore. With each step her stride grew stronger and bolder until she was running swiftly up into the night and was lost from view.

The cold gripped Richard completely now. He shivered so violently he thought his bones would break, but he couldn't tear his eyes away from the spectacle in the sky.

'Well, this is unusual,' said a voice behind him.

Richard turned his frost-rimmed eyes to the little desk that had definitely not been there before and the tall, angular man sitting behind it. It stood perched incongruously on a nearby rock and, incredibly, appeared entirely untouched by the driving snow around it. The iron brazier to one side gave off no heat whatsoever that Richard could feel.

'I knew things would be different this time,' continued Nubby, writing in his great tome, 'but this is certainly more melodramatic than I expected. You must have read some very strange things in that book of yours. The good news is, we've still got your notes from last time so there's very little to add.'

Nubby looked up, the brazier's flames reflected in his blue eyes. 'Don't mind me,' he said, 'I'm here in a secretarial capacity. It's them you should be concerning yourself with.'

He gestured and Richard followed his pointing finger. As he watched, out of the host in the sky rode two figures.

The first was clad in black armour and a white cloak and rode a formidable charcoal stallion with pale eyes. In his left hand he hefted a fearsome spear with an ebony shaft and a tip sharp as an icicle, while with his right he beckoned to the multitude above, which surged forth at his command to cast their shadow over the valley.

As Richard beheld Berchtold, the terrible Bringer of Winter, he felt the fear that all living things feel when they are faced with Death, against whom they are utterly powerless. The very sight of him caused Richard to tremble. His face was a mask of fury and the surrounding creatures obeyed him with a swiftness born of terror, like a flock of starlings before a hawk. Indeed so frightened of this apparition was Richard that he would have fainted with cold and fear had his attention not been captured by the appearance of the second rider.

She was a maiden, fair and white. She moved with the effortless grace of a flurry of snow and her long curls flowed about her as she rode beside Berchtold on a grey horse. Like her brother she was clad in a cloak of snowy white, but instead of a spear she carried a staff of pine and her only armour was a crown of silver upon her head.

Together they rode out and away from the column, stopping in the air over the vale. The host surged forth at Berchtold's command and his fair sister Perchta looked on, observing each creature as it passed.

Richard stood at the edge of the precipice, witnessing the ghostly spectacle in the sky above. He was still trembling but was now past noticing. He could think of nothing except the great cavalcade of death and the white woman on the rearing grey steed.

She dismounted and came to face her mount, stroking its nose to calm it. From its nostrils clouds of steam billowed about her. She paused, as though a thought had occurred to her. Then, without warning, she turned and looked straight at Richard.

Richard had never seen anything as blue as the White Lady's eyes. Next to them sapphires would have seemed as dull as lead. Looking into them was like staring into the glow of a distant star, wise and more ancient than the Earth.

Then she smiled. And it was like his mother smiling. Her smile made him feel that all would be well, that there was nothing to fear. He smiled back, like a child, because he couldn't help it.

This made the White Lady smile all the more. She raised a snow-white hand and, reaching behind her, gently brought forth a young woman.

It was Ellie.

Not as Richard knew her, though. Her face was no longer pale but flush with the fire of life. She stood straight and strong as her dress flew out behind her, whipping and snapping about in the icy wind. Her hair was loose and her smile was warm.

He tried to say her name out loud but he was too cold. Instead he thought it.

Ellie.

Nubby sighed and nodded to himself.

Reaching forward he seized a handful of pages in his implacable hand. In one great rending motion he tore them from the book and flung them onto the brazier, where they were consumed in a burst of flame.

In that moment Richard forgot everything else and felt only pure joy. He gazed up at Ellie and saw every vision of happiness he'd ever imagined and dreamt of and prayed for. The white lady released Ellie's hand and she ran towards him with all the swiftness of a girl in love.

Richard stepped forward, his arms open. There was a rush of wind and the force of her embrace smashed the breath from his chest forever.

REMEMBRANCES
CHAPTER THIRTY-NINE

ASPAR AWOKE TO the sound of nature's voice. The creaking wooden beams whispered *winter has arrived; we are covered in snow.* The bluish light behind the panelled glass of his window said *there is snow on the ground and the sun is not fully up yet.* The ache in the small of his back said *you should really think about investing in a new mattress.*

He swung his legs onto the wooden floor of his room and shook the sleep from his greying temples. He could smell more snow on the way and decided to make his rounds before it came. He dressed, pausing only to move his tiny bonsai tree from the mantelpiece to the windowsill to give it more light. He tied up his stiff boots, took his hat and stick from behind the door, and emerged into the quiet town in the half-light of dawn.

The village was unrecognisable. Everything was blanketed in snow including the roads, which had yet to be cleared. Kaspar didn't mind; he was sure-footed. With his steady pace he navigated the deserted streets and headed for the woods.

As Kaspar passed the Gasthaus Meierhof he noted the ruined carcass of the red car in the driveway, condemned by Pfister as unsalvageable. The Englishmen must have abandoned it when they left. Perhaps he would call Eckhardt, the mechanic from the valley; he could use the spare parts.

The path wound its way up away from the village, higher and higher into the glistening white landscape. By the time Kaspar found the fork in the trail he was caked in snow up to his knees. He strode up the path with leisurely assurance, noting the colour of the tree trunks, the direction of the clouds, the music of the wind and the rustle of the leafless branches beneath the unseen finger of the breeze. The path led him past the windswept skeletons of wild raspberry canes and beneath brooding firs. He heard the creak of trees buried under the fresh snow. Most would eventually settle, others would crack and break. Within a few days the noise would cease altogether, not to sound again until the spring thaw.

Enough of the forest, thought Kaspar; time for a quick trip to the foot of the falls, then home for a plate of sausages. He set out with a whistle and the comfortable gait of a much younger man, making for the rocky shelf where the pools of water collected. He breathed in great lungfuls of cold air, tasting it like a connoisseur.

Kaspar didn't know it but in the coming spring, when all the snow was melting away, a group of hikers would cut through the forest to where the river flowed from the base of the rocks towards the village. In the wake of the disappearing ice they would spot the curve of a yellowed skull. This in turn would lead researchers to the discovery of the neck, limbs, and entire mummified body of a prehistoric man, half frozen in the ice. Of particular interest would be the notched copper axe found near the corpse's grasping hand and the medicinal tattoos still visible on the leathery skin of the left arm, back, lower legs, and ribs. Though time had largely worn away the facial features and the bones were cracked in innumerable places— presumably from the shifting ice—experts were to gaze in fascination at the remarkable state of preservation of the body, still half-frozen in the melt water. They assumed he'd been washed out of some frozen grave high on the glacier and estimated that the man had been dead for at least five thousand years. The stream gently rocked the body as it came loose from its icy sarcophagus, trickling over and around the head from which there still hung several strands of long, black hair.

Today, however, the ice wasn't going anywhere. Kaspar tightened his woollen scarf against the chill. The forest was dark and mysterious under its canopy of snow, but he didn't mind. Darkness was only a problem if you didn't know where to put your feet and Kaspar could've walked this path in the dead of night without concern. Pausing only to check the moss that hung on the tree trunks, he made his way amongst the pines and emerged on the rock shelf scarcely short of breath. He admired the cascade of ice hanging from the cliff face like a giant, frozen finger into the rock pools, which had frozen solid and lay about the place like dark mirrors, dusted with snow that the wind had not yet blown away.

Kaspar approached the falls, breathing its heady fragrance. Exhaling contentedly, he made his way around the mirror's edge to gaze out over the valley. Most of it was shrouded in mist, but occasionally the clouds parted to reveal the dark flanks and bone-white glaciers of the surrounding peaks.

Something caught Kaspar's eye and he ceased humming.

He retraced his steps, following the glint of metal. Lying half submerged under the frozen surface of the nearest pool was a hunting rifle. Had it not lain partially underwater he would have missed it entirely, for the rest lay obscured under the snow.

Carefully, so as not to slip, Kaspar bent down and peered at it through the ice. He recognised it as Meinrad Indergand's—he'd seen him use it on the range more than once, though not recently.

He cast an eye about the rocky shelf. The snow was pristine and untouched, save for Kaspar's own footprints.

As his thoughts turned to the car still parked in front of the hotel and the young Englishman's preoccupied air the previous days, Kaspar was overcome with a creeping sense of dread.

He walked the length of the rocky outcrop, eyeing the snow for oddly shaped snowdrifts, places where it may have been displaced, anything that might hint at the presence of something lying underneath. To his relief, he didn't find any. Someone, perhaps indulging in some play at marksmanship, must have lost the rifle and been unable to retrieve it. No doubt they'd had one drink too many. Meinrad Indergand might be on his way there at this very moment to recover it.

Kaspar decided to have one last look around, if only to see if anything else had been misplaced. He glanced down the cliff almost as an afterthought.

For the second time, something caught his eye.

He leaned over a bit further and stood there for a second. Then, moving swiftly and without a word, he removed his pack from his wiry back and set it down a short distance from the edge. He unstrapped his short steel ice pick and, prudently, made his way down the rocky crag beneath the waterfall.

Slowly the old man descended, carefully hooking and unhooking his pick, steadying his thin frame against the rock face. He was fastidious in his movements, taking extra care with every step not to slip, not to lose his balance, not to think about what he would find at the bottom.

First one booted foot, then the other, landed neatly in the snow next to the frozen trickle of water. He turned and knew instantly he was too late.

Kaspar looked down at the body that had belonged to Richard Mathern, now stretched out on the rocks in front of him. It lay half above the surface of the ice and half below, as though emerging into the world from some hidden place beneath. His eyes were closed and the old man was surprised to see on his face not the horrible grimace of death or the grotesque open mouth ripped apart by the scream of a falling man, but an expression of deep serenity. On his lips was the faintest trace of a smile, like a man remembering a loved one.

Kaspar's vision clouded and the old man turned aside. As his gaze moved away it fell upon a clenched fist lying over the silent heart.

Kneeling, Kaspar took the stiff, youthful hand in his gnarled one and turned it gently over. In its fingers it clasped a long, soft ribbon of purest yellow.

EPILOGUE

OSCO RAISED A hand to shield his eyes.

He looked around, disorientated and confused. In the blinding whiteness he couldn't tell if he was still on the mountain, amongst the clouds, or somewhere else entirely.

The wind whipped past. Fosco shivered in the cold. Glancing around he could see figures in the mist, all remote and unrecognisable. They seemed to be watching him.

He turned and beheld one figure nearer than the rest. Fosco observed the lone silhouette with apprehension.

Eventually, with nowhere else to go, he approached. He couldn't make out what he was walking on, but he struggled as though through deep snow.

The figure was soon revealed to be a man of indeterminate age, sitting by himself. As Fosco drew level the man raised his head and called to him.

'Will you help me? I halted to rest for just a moment but now I'm afraid I can't get up.'

Fosco looked warily at the stranger. The man was shod in tattered shoes, reduced to rags. By his feet stood a small lantern, a simple taper encased in an iron frame.

The man gazed back at Fosco with very blue eyes. 'Please,' he said, in a deep, sympathetic voice. 'It won't take a moment, then you can be on your way.'

In the surrounding whiteness the distant figures looked on in silence, waiting.

Fosco hesitated.

Then he shrugged and, because he'd never listened to the stories, stretched out his hand.

And as he did, the man smiled.

THE END

ACKNOWLEDGEMENTS

This book would never have been completed without the help of certain key people, whose tireless editorial and personal input helped make this story into something worth reading. They know who they are. For your encouragement, support, and dedication, I thank you.

THANK YOU FOR READING.

If you enjoyed this story, please consider supporting the author and independent publishing by leaving a review and recommending it to others. Search for *The Winter Wilds* online.

Printed in Great Britain
by Amazon